Acclaim for

THE IMMORTAL ABYSS

"Katherine Briggs delivers a scorching sequel in *The Immortal Abyss.* Her brilliantly architected story world will capture readers with its fiery giftings, wondrous creatures, and political intrigue. With its high-stakes adventure and heart-stopping plot twists, this book doesn't quit. Fantasy fans, your newest obsession is right here!"

–**MEGAN SCHAULIS**, author of *Protector*

"In *The Immortal Abyss,* Briggs weaves themes of courage and sacrifice in the face of betrayal and utter loss into epic fantasy filled with compelling characters, an ever-deepening magic system, and vibrant cultures. For anyone who has wished life would be easier, *The Immortal Abyss* offers a tale of grace, healing, and redemption. This beautiful story will remain in my heart for a very long time."

–**CATHY MCCRUMB**, author of the
CHILDREN OF THE CONSORTIUM series

"*The Immortal Abyss* is a spectacular follow-up to its predecessor, providing the other side to the story that I didn't even know I needed. Briggs brings us once more into the rich fantasy world she has crafted and teaches the reader about the power of faith, truth, and light. With compelling characters and nail-biting conflict, each chapter left me waiting more. Fans of *The Eternity Gate* won't want to miss this adventurous and touching conclusion."

–**ASHLEY BUSTAMANTE**, author of THE COLOR THEORY series

"Briggs captivates with her artful storytelling in *The Immortal Abyss*. This tale of destiny, betrayal, courage, and hope is not to be missed."

–**Lindsay A. Franklin**, Carol Award-winning author of *The Story Peddler*

"A heroic tale of danger, dragons, betrayal and an impossible quest to overcome evil and heal humanity. *The Immortal Abyss* does not disappoint. Briggs crafts a stunning allegory of man's fight against darkness and the power of friendship when conquering doubt in the face of fear."

–**Sandra Fernandez Rhoads**, award-winning author of *Mortal Sight* and *Realms of Light*

"The Threshold Duology is epic fantasy as comforting as a slow-cooked stew. A hearty base of complex worldbuilding, awesome characters, unique and spicy magic, political struggles, and strong themes of good versus evil. It's difficult to express how much I enjoyed this read. Highly recommended for any fan of fantasy, adventure, or great storytelling in general!"

–**Jamie Foley**, award-winning author of The Katrosi Revolution series

"Dragons, fire wielding, and prophecies abound, set against the tapestry of a richly imagined world with strong allegorical themes. Briggs weaves a compelling and transfixing tale with a fiercely spunky heroine you can't help but root for."

–**Gillian Bronte Adams**, award-winning author of The Fireborn Epic

THE IMMORTAL ABYSS

The Immortal Abyss

KATHERINE BRIGGS

ENCLAVE
Escape

The Immortal Abyss

Escape

Published by Enclave Publishing, an imprint of Oasis Family Media, LLC

Carol Stream, Illinois, USA.
www.enclavepublishing.com

ISBN: 979-8-88605-146-9 (printed hardcover)
ISBN: 979-8-88605-147-6 (printed softcover)
ISBN: 979-8-88605-149-0 (ebook)

Cover design by Emilie Haney, www.EAHCreative.com
Typesetting & map design by Jamie Foley, www.JamieFoley.com
Four Forms of Fire graphic design by Lyndsey Lewellen, www.llewellendesigns.com

Printed in the United States of America.

To Jessica,
and all who refuse to give up
or surrender what is good.

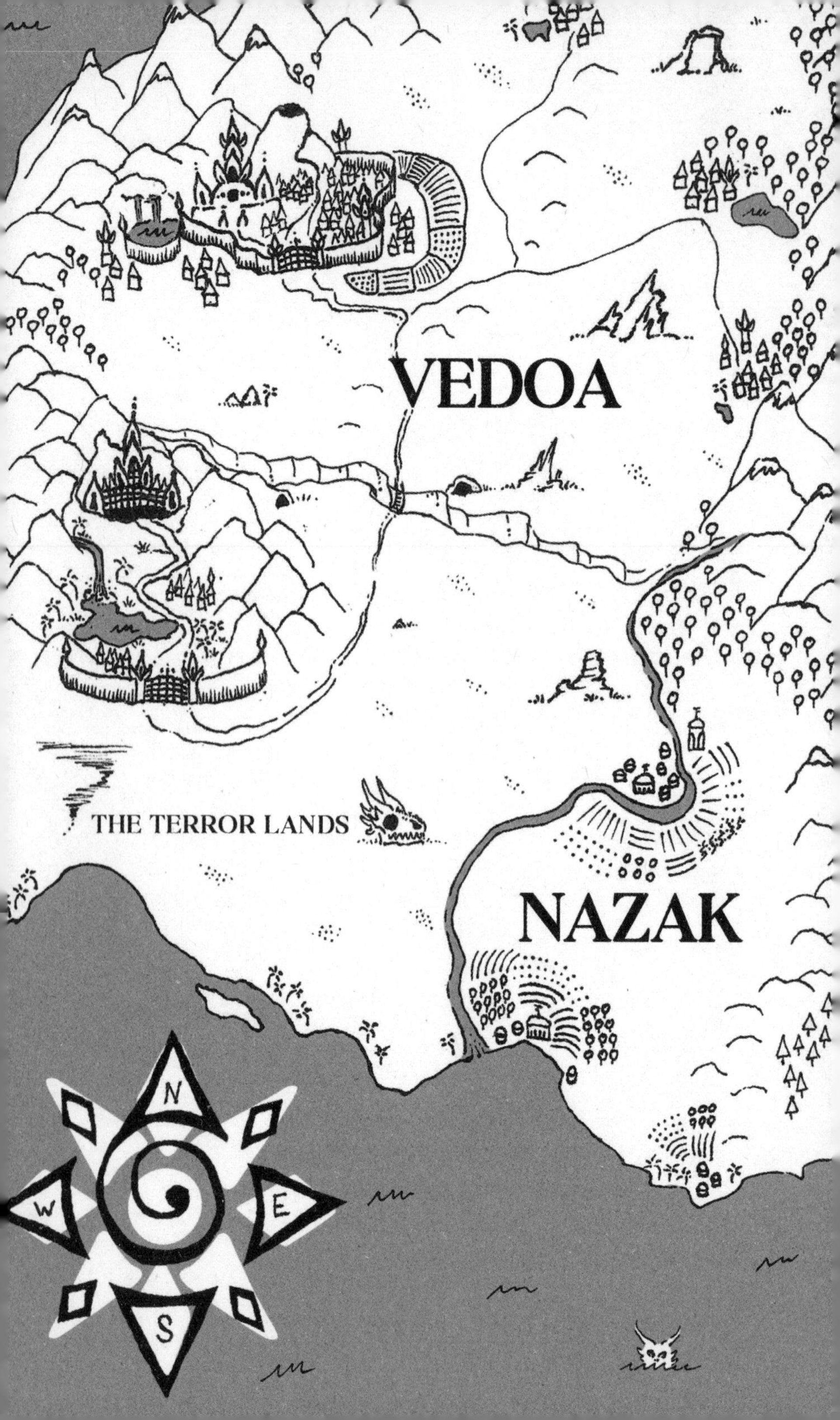
VEDOA
THE TERROR LANDS
NAZAK
N
W
E
S

AI'BIRO
LAIJON
HANDPRINT OF GOD
PIRTHYIA

The Four Forms of Fire

Magnificence

- Source of fire
- Limits the wielder

Justice

- Takes and gives fire
- The rarest Form

Starpalm

Wisdom

- Shapes fire
- Creates vanishing messages

Temperance

- Controls fire
- Connects the Forms

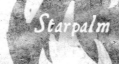

Tiers

Tier 1 - Limited Magnificence only

Tier 2 - All Forms present, with one focus

Tier 3 - All Forms present, with two or more reaching great power

ECHOES OF WAR

When the Eternity Gate opened, its twin doorway awakened. The Immortal Abyss–tucked within the nation of Vedoa's ancient volcanoes–breathed, and the winter rains dissipated into cruel, hot air. Drought, like disease, gripped portions of the charcoal desert.

Surely the divine starpalms, Vedoa's unseen frowning and grinning gods, punished the desert people for losing the war and the Eternity Gate. Even Vedoa's starpalm-given gift, the power to wield fire, could not save them from thirst. But fire offered protection against the monstrous Shadows flying across their closed borders.

Awaiting winter rain, the commoner, the noble, and the Rebellion remembered an old saying. None dared whisper the desperate hope, lest the dynasty overhear and silence them all. *A starpalm will walk the desert in human form. From an endless well, her fire will cleanse the monster's lair, kindle life within dead bones, and fill the depths of the world. She, the one born of legend, will slay her own soul to finish the age.*

Who else could be born of legend besides a daughter of the gods?

1

I'D BORROWED ELEVEN HOMES and outgrown ten guardians. All called me Tol, minus the delightful handful who'd preferred *You* or *The Girl*. By my fourth guardian, the desert had become my true parent and the stars burning across the night my counselors. Surrounded by charcoal-colored sand, I possessed experience and knowledge. But my desert stretched behind me now.

Like the unblinking eye of an immortal starpalm, the retreating sun hovered between the spires of a city piercing the iron sky. Towering, unscalable white stone walls gleamed beneath afternoon light and overshadowed a colorful sea of awnings and stalls. Despite the late rains and unrest building since the war, city dwellers held the seasonal Rain Market. The distant trade route, a dangerous path slicing through the desert, guided groups of travelers carrying coin for market.

I'd barely seen the trade route before. It didn't touch the remote villages I hailed from. And by the starpalms, Srolo Kapir's description of the city's enormity hadn't prepared me for the tight, squirming feeling in my stomach.

Why had I begged Srolo Kapir to let me be the messenger? Why had I declared that I was nineteen winters old, trained harder in fire than all my classmates—even though they'd progressed levels ahead of me—and had proven my undying loyalty to the Desert Rebellion? He was my guardian and supposed to stop me from doing foolish things. But after his long stare, preamble for "no," he'd shocked me by agreeing "yes." Not only that. He'd also said *Tol, you are ready.*

"*Ready,*" I whispered. That word meant everything to me, even if we both knew it wasn't completely true. Srolo Kapir said important sympathizers to the Rebellion lived inside this city. I would find them, and I would deliver the Rebellion's message.

Falling from among the stars and holding fire as strong and perfected as our blazing sun, a god was returning to Vedoa, like a page from ancient stories. This starpalm, reborn as a human, would overthrow the dynasty and its lifetime of tyranny with the loyal Rebellion rallying behind. The time was now.

By delivering this message, I would start a war. And by proving myself ready, I would earn my place in the battle.

I shouldered my haversack and pulled my traveling scarf, one meant for a man, tighter across my nose and mouth. May the city see a boy instead of me, thanks to my oversized robes, athletic build, and scarf hiding my long, midnight curls. I grasped my staff and planted the end into the dust. Adrenaline coursed through my veins, and fire surged with it to my fingertips. Srolo Kapir's warning whispered through my mind. *Tol, do not wield unless your life depends on it.*

"I promise," I murmured, as if he were here–wishing he was here before I plunged across the desert toward the trade route.

I reached the broad, dusty path and joined the other sojourners. It was a lighter crowd than normal, as Srolo Kapir had predicted, and mostly men, sweeping their robes behind them. The recent conflict and price for water would have prompted them to leave their families at home. Many led stinking beasts of burden and cast me cautious glances before ignoring me. Everyone feared uprisers–or was one. But what could I be besides a village youth, with my sun-bronzed skin, traveling to visit the festival, keeping a modest bag of coin to take something nice home to Mother?

The sun dropped a fingerlength by the time we reached the market, and I parted from the others to melt between the blessedly covered stalls. Jostling among humanity and goods, I kept my head low, pace slow, haversack close, and inhaled the scents of hot bread, souring juice, rich oils, and sweat. I held my breath, pushing through a group of hawkers murmuring to one another. I would've assumed city dwellers never bathed, except that I knew the Rain Market traditionally started at sundown. Curfews against the uprisings had forced the festival to begin at simmering midday. And if I didn't get inside before curfew, I'd be stuck spending the night out here among thieves, which was unthinkable, considering the message I carried. This risk was one of three reasons why Srolo Kapir almost forbade me to go.

I heard the loud conversation of soldiers before I saw them infesting the market ahead. Wearing scarlet armor and crimson Tier 2 tattoos inked across their foreheads–unlike the paint equally gifted civilians wore–they eyed colorful blankets spread with dried spices and spoke the capital tongue. It was a harsh babble in my ears, amplified by the hush their presence caused. Srolo Kapir had told me the capital was sending soldiers to every city and waypoint along the trade route. No one was permitted to speak of Vedoa's retreat from war with Laijon, a nightmare months old now, or the empress's "vanishing." But the people knew, unrest boiled, and soldiers invaded from the capital. Their weighty presence was the second reason Srolo Kapir almost denied me this task.

Capital soldiers made me ill, but I'd rather face them than the third threat Srolo Kapir warned me about. Since the war, Shadow monsters haunted the eastern desert. Eyewitnesses called them powerful winged phantoms that swirled like nightfall–a vile consequence of the dynasty's greed. A starpalm who could defeat the dynasty could also cleanse Vedoa of Shadows. And they hadn't invaded the desert interior. Yet. So, I'd focus on thieves and soldiers.

I moved closer to the wall. Seven local guards kept the nearest gate, so I circled the city, pressing between hagglers. The quality of wares deteriorated until the stench of hot livestock, fertilizer, and rotting fruit encouraged me to breathe through my mouth. The narrower south gate boasted two guards.

Give me an undermanned, seedy back door any day.

Though some time remained before sunset and curfew, a small stream of people formed a line to reenter the city. One husband and wife approached the gate, dragging their market wares behind. I translated their weary expressions as poor sales.

A guard left the gate in a flurry of agitated commands. These words I understood, as the locals spoke the common language, and the guard's gesture for money was obvious. Srolo Kapir had warned me about the entrance fee and given me double the required dacri, now nestled within my boot and unspent crossing the desert.

The husband produced three coins from his pocket. The soldier shouted, "Five dacri per person."

An unannounced hike in the toll. Some in line inhaled sharply. Or was I the one who gasped? The old writings of the starpalms demanded that we share our coin with the needy. But I was in need. Srolo Kapir had anticipated payment of two dacri and given me four.

The husband begged, pleading for his children. The guard lifted one hand in a single fiery flame. He wore no paint on his forehead. A Tier 1 wielder only.

I itched to fill my hands with fire and challenge him for his injustice. And to get myself inside the walls with everyone else.

The husband and wife retreated, allowing the next person to step up. Could the two of them make more sales in this poorer section of the market where travelers wouldn't go? Or would they sleep outside the walls until they did? Could I make camp with them? No, what I carried was too precious. I couldn't trust anyone but the allies, who were inside the wall.

I fantasized about burning the gate down. If I climbed the wall, they'd shoot me down before I could crest the top.

Someone grumbled behind me. A bushy-faced, pinch-eyed vendor threatened some deal concerning his bevy of bottles filled with snake oil.

I scurried deeper into the market to think. Trading goods was impossible unless I wanted to sell the homespun cloak off my back, but I had to get inside.

A gaggle of the wealthy passed the stalls ahead. Draped in shiny, slippery cloth, they paid entrance to the city with ease and even nodded to the soldiers.

I loathed them. Both the military and the rich sat in the pockets of the dynasty, an endless cycle of money, power, and oppression. But justice was coming, maybe sooner than expected, in large and small ways. The writings of the starpalms said something about leveling unequal scales . . . so if I lifted a couple dacri off the next nobleman I saw, that was righting one wrong among many, right? I wasn't resorting to common thievery. But no pickpocketing. I'd trained too hard to stoop to that.

A glimpse of a dark cloak, stitched with gold, caught my eye. The man wove through stalls, his face covered with a traveler's scarf. He wasn't much taller than me, and his stooped shoulders spoke of weariness or weakness. He headed toward the less populated market outskirts. Alone.

I followed.

Past clustered tables, fencing enclosed a herd of stocky desert horses–a conglomeration of bays, chestnuts, and grays. The animals huddled between poles supporting fabric offering shade and a small hut storing the animals' feed. A skinny horse trader sat in the building's shadow with his back to the market, playing himself in a game of dice. He remained absorbed as the man in the fine, dark cloak, slick as a specter, jumped the fence and disappeared inside the hut.

A strange move, but lucky for me. Unlike the trader's last dice toss.

I crept around the fence and away from the grumbling horse trader. Mares watched me, some huffing and a couple shaking their tangled manes. The stallions must be kept elsewhere, leaving the females and young. *Please, don't spook.* I hopped the fence onto their side. One mare snorted, but that was all. The trader didn't even look over his shoulder.

I stole to the hut, drew a breath, and gripped my staff at a point in front of me, left hand under, right hand on top. I reminded myself that the famous Srolo Kapir was my teacher and slipped past the door into cool shadows.

Grain bags filled corners. Where . . . ? I whirled–

A hand seized my arm.

2

I SWALLOWED A CRY AND TRIED to twist from the man's grasp. A bag of grain spilled across the close quarters. He wrapped one arm around my middle and covered my mouth. Really? As if I would scream and alert the horse trader, who would consider us both thieves. I paused to breathe, and he held me fast. By the starpalms, I'd underestimated his strength. My gaze trailed down to his cloak hem brushing against my boots. Cloth trimmed in gold, but dirty and tattered. He couldn't afford a second cloak? I lifted my staff and rammed the end into his gut.

The man gasped. His grip loosened, and I jerked free to face him, staff gripped at my side and stance strong.

Underneath his traveler's scarf, hunger haunted his sunken cheeks and sharp eyes. Hard times obscured his age, but he was likely ten or fifteen years older than me. My own scarf had slipped, allowing him to appraise my unpainted forehead before pulling his own cowl down. And that movement allowed me to see the scarlet stain he hid.

He was a Tier 2 wielder. Of course, I would accidently target a Tier 2.

He took a deep breath and, in a flash, seized my staff, then pushed me into the feedbags. I scrambled up and lunged for my staff. I managed to deflect his arm and strike his face, both of us slipping on scattered grain, before he twisted the weapon from my hand and shoved me backward against the splintering stall door.

We stilled, listening. Outside, animals snorted.

I caught my breath. No one disarmed me. Ever. Who was he? Bodyguard? Assassin? Why else would he hide his paint?

He touched his bleeding cheek and scowled. "You're a girl."

And you're a–I froze. I'd understood him perfectly. He spoke with the accent of the northern villages. My home for most of my life.

"You're trained well, but why aren't you carrying a knife?" His gaze rested on my haversack.

My heart quickened. Tier 2 wielders didn't go hungry. They served the dynasty and wanted for nothing–unless they'd escaped to the Rebellion. Why was he eyeing my haversack?

No. He couldn't know about the message I carried. But if he did, would he think me naïve enough to keep it in a bag?

He wiped bloody fingers down his robes.

Wild recklessness seized me. He had my staff. The security of the message was a life-or-death situation. I'd burn this hut down before he stole that.

I opened my left hand in fire. A tiny, unimpressive flicker that danced so close to wood, grain, and flesh.

His eyes narrowed. "Foolish girl." He dropped the staff and seized my hands, quenching my flames. I made a show of trying to wrench free, but he held fast and pulled my fire from my palms. Siphoning my fire to add to his. Draining me because he was Tier 2 and possessed all Forms of fire in varying modest amounts, with one stronger focus–uncommon Justice, in his case–which enabled him to take. I hadn't expected that, but it served my purpose.

His brow quirked when he realized that only my left hand yielded fire, but he didn't release my right. His Justice was weaker than Srolo Kapir's, making the draining uncomfortable. I refused to squirm, then gradually realized he was trying to be careful.

"You're like my kid sister," he said. Zero emotion.

Was she scrappy and loudmouthed too? Or left-handed? Well, I couldn't return the compliment. I had no family, and he would have reminded me of a thug, regardless.

"I won't take it all," he began, then frowned, because he finally noticed that my fire still flowed strong. He hesitated. Lowered his defense.

Poor Tier 2 had leapt into my snare.

"You can't hold my fire," I said, and unleashed my gifting into him.

He growled, doubled over, twisted. Hurting almost as much as it hurt me.

Don't cry out. I kicked him in the head, and he collapsed. Unmoving.

I held my breath as I watched him, then scrambled to search for his pulse. His chest rose and fell. I sighed relief. Thank the desert, I'd held back enough.

Tears pricked my eyes. I hated my weakness, and I despised worrying about this rogue Tier 2 who'd tried to steal the Rebellion's message. That message would open the door to Vedoa's future and mine. No one would take that from me.

I searched his cloak, heard coins clink, and removed the money pouch from his trousered leg, which was tied next to a wicked-looking dagger. I reached inside the pouch and removed one coin—not stealing but evening the scales. That would make the five dacri I needed. I stopped and stared.

I didn't hold a dacri. It was a military coin, bearing the executed empress's likeness.

Impossible.

I spilled the pouch empty. Five military coins and a handful of dacri.

I yanked his cowl back. He didn't wear smudged Tier 2 paint. He bore the scarlet tattoo of a royal soldier and, judging by the extra swirls, boasted a high rank. But he wasn't marching through the Rain Market in crimson armor. He was wearing a stolen nobleman's cloak and hiding in horse stables.

By the starpalms, he'd fought in Vedoa's war against Laijon, lost, and dared to return home. To cover unsufferable pride, the dynasty blamed their defeat on the surviving soldiers and placed a price on their heads. If caught, he'd be tortured and "vanish" like the unspeakable empress. The Rebellion fought against such atrocities.

He didn't know about the message. He was hiding. Separated from friends and family. Hungry. And I, part of the Rebellion, had just knocked out and stolen from one of the people we'd pledged to help, even though I personally could never trust a soldier.

I searched him again. He'd rid himself of his uniform and weapons, only keeping his permanent tattoo and the five incriminating coins. Why hadn't he melted or buried those?

Outside, the horses stamped and whinnied. The trade owner was singing to gather the animals.

Feed time. And I stood among bags of grain.

I slapped the soldier's cheeks. Nothing. Dragging him out of here would create a scene. I scooped the military coin into my pocket, added the soldier's dacri to Srolo Kapir's coin inside my boot, and spit into my hands to make a disgusting slurry with dirt and grain. This I smeared across his tattoo before pulling his cowl far across his forehead to hide the mark. Straining, I pulled him into the corner and covered his body with feed sacks, leaving him room to breathe.

If the starpalms really cared about humanity–those who wouldn't stoop to walk among us–he needed their protection now.

The door creaked open.

Staff in hand, I faced the horse trader. He gaped at me.

"Good evening?" I faked a grin and shoved past him, ignoring his cries and startled horses, before vaulting over the fence and disappearing into the market. I fought to slow my pace while meandering as quickly as I could toward the gate. Then I realized the market lay almost deserted.

Curfew was falling. The sun set as a handful of people remained in line to gain access into the city.

I neared the husband and wife, turned away from the gate before, who now huddled behind a small, random collection of household goods laid on a worn rug. Stooping to reach within my boot, I dropped the handful of dacri onto their mat as I passed. The wife's eyes widened before she scooped up the coins. No thanks given. None deserved.

I hurried to the gate, pausing once to collect the soldier's five military coins into my fist, before joining the line. My turn arrived.

One guard enjoyed a platter of market food. The second stepped forward, puffing his chest and looking down on me. Sweaty, smelly, and heartless. Being so close to him made my stomach churn.

He held out his hand. "Five dacri." Beyond him, the towering iron gate stood cracked.

Please blindly see what's expected.

I dumped the illicit coins into his meaty hand. He grunted and waved me through. I wove around him, past the gate, and strode from market and sunset to towering buildings, narrow alleys, and crowds hurrying through the darkness.

3

I'D RATHER CROSS THE DESERT for an eternity than this congested labyrinth. Either option was fit punishment for incapacitating the fugitive soldier. I couldn't believe I'd made such a mistake. What if the horse trader found him? What if he saw his tattoo?

He lay in the hands of the fickle starpalms now. Delivering this message was the best thing I could do for him, but first, I needed to find a blue house where the Rebellion sympathizers lived.

Walls, tall edifices, and sun-bleached fabric canopies hid what remained of the setting sun. Whenever a tendril of light pierced the darkness, I revaluated my direction before dodging past men, women, orphans, elders, and beggars, all of us heading in opposing directions. Twice, I circumnavigated lines twisting behind public wells, where soldiers demanded high thirst fees and took bribes without shame. Tension crackled. More uprisings occurred near wells than anywhere else. The longer the rains delayed, the higher water prices would soar.

Fingers reached inside my pocket. By the starpalms, city snatchers were plentiful. I leaned into the pickpocket, and then he disappeared empty-handed, while I'd gained an overripe mangi fruit from his robes. I tossed it to the next beggar I passed. Perhaps the pickpocket would be a beggar, too, if he didn't steal. Had I become a thief when I took the soldier's military coin?

A company of soldiers glutted the passage ahead. I ducked into a narrow, intersecting alley. If only I could elude my guilt as well.

The rooflines ahead dipped downhill. A dazzling, white building crowned the center of the city, the home of the governing clan, another one of the dynasty's lackeys. But near the city wall, a blue house stood between several other large homes.

Forgoing the front step and bolted gate, I scaled the privacy wall and landed in a garden. Somewhere nearby, goats bleated.

Srolo Kapir called Ami'beti and Bor'beti his old friends and secret supporters of the Rebellion. Unmarried brother and sister. Middle-aged. Goat herders. But those facts were only dried fruits and nuts offered before a meal.

A thick vine grew along the rough face of the house, its walls of sand, earth, and water formed and dried ages ago. I tucked my staff into my belt before climbing the thickest arms of the vine, parched from thirst but strong enough, and reaching a second-story window. After pulling the thin covering cloth away, I found myself in a vacant study boasting rugs and rare wood furniture.

Bad memories made my breathing tighten. I'd shown up at unfamiliar houses covered in dirt and sweat so many times, dreading meeting my next guardian. Knowing the arrangement would last two years at best.

But Srolo Kapir had been my guardian for four years. He hadn't sent me away. I was only delivering a message, and I'd moved to villages, outposts, hovels, and even a foreign land, but never a city.

Delicious smells wafted from deeper within the dwelling. Dinner hour.

I cracked the door open and stole down the hall. Instinct told me the two ornate doors on the left belonged to the master quarters. I snuck inside the first and faced a large bed and tall stone fire bowl. Flames crackled deep within the bowl to offer warmth during the cool night and to help the sleeper renew his or her gifting. Its faint glow illuminated masculine décor of animal skins and a collection of ancient, mounted swords. This room must belong to Bor'beti, who'd lost a hand defending our borders before purchasing a flock of goats and becoming one of Vedoa's finest clothmakers. The Rebellion was fortunate to have friends among the upper middle class, who usually owed their lot to the dynasty. I returned to the hall to approach the other door.

Srolo Kapir confided to me that Ami'beti had dedicated her youth as a priestess to the great temple in the capital. She'd served the starpalms closely until the dynasty demanded to be worshiped instead. She then fled the temple and its idolatry to work alongside her brother. Srolo Kapir said she shared the Rebellion's belief in the prophecy. Who was better qualified to recognize a starpalm reborn into human form than her?

I wanted this starpalm to be real more than anything. Most divinities didn't lift a finger to help humanity, but she would walk among us. If this goddess appeared, I would kneel and offer my fire and life to be one of her human Shields. To break the dynasty and restore Vedoa, if I proved myself worthy of her service.

Harming the soldier counted against me, so I would work harder to earn my place.

I entered the second room. Goodness, it was bare, but that fit a priestess. One chipped vase held dried flowers. The bed had its blanket tucked in tight. A stone bowl identical to Bor'beti's claimed the center of the room but stood cold. I needed to remedy that.

I lowered my haversack and staff to the floor, drank the last sip from my water skin, and reached inside my robes for the thick leather strap tied around my waist. I extracted the tiny lump of wax. Holding it again made my heartrate increase, and I pressed the message against my chest.

The 'betis, our noble and powerful allies, would hear my speech, see Srolo Kapir's message, and rally with us.

Heavy footsteps sounded down the hall.

Gripping the wax in my right hand, I quickly offered the stone bowl a single, modest flame with my left. So much for not wielding. Again.

The doorknob turned. A plump, gray-haired woman entered, garbed in fine, brightly dyed cloth. Muttering, she patted her no-nonsense updo before spying me and uttering a choked cry. "Bor!"

A stooped man peeked inside. Also wearing fine, colorful robes, and missing a forearm and hand.

Identities confirmed.

"Bor, an upriser!"

"Me? No." I dropped to my fists and knees and spoke into the polished wood floor. "Esteemed priestess, I come in the name of–"

"Get up, vagrant. How did you get past our watchman?" Ami'beti spoke in the common tongue, as Srolo Kapir assured me she would, despite her years in the capital.

I should have removed my traveler's scarf. This wasn't the glorious reception I'd hoped for. Imagining them leveling flames in my direction sent me scrambling upright. "I come in the name of Srolo Kapir."

Ami'beti paused. Bor'beti stared from the threshold, and a knife gleamed in his surviving hand.

I continued. "Srolo Kapir–"

"Kapir is dead." Ami'beti darted a quick glance toward her brother.

She said that to protect herself. Srolo Kapir was a known enemy of the dynasty and had faked his death decades ago.

"I have proof." I thrust my open palm and the lump of wax in front of me.

The 'betis stiffened. Attention snared.

Salvaging as much reverence as the moment deserved, I held my head high and dropped the wax into the lit fire bowl. We held our breaths as the wax melted. Then, a tendril of fire danced into the air. Thin and precise, an almost impossible display of Wisdom and Temperance, the tendril wove through the air in Srolo Kapir's unmistakable scrawl.

Pride swelled in my chest. Just a handful of Tier 3s existed, and only a Tier 3 could wield such a feat. Srolo Kapir had earned his Tier through perfect Temperance, and he'd given his fire to the Rebellion instead of the dynasty. He was my guardian, and he trained my fire.

The message completed, burning and hovering between us.

The one born of legend has come.
Prepare a room for my arrival.
~ *True Vedoa's servant, Kapir*

The thread of fire dissipated into smoke.

Ami'beti gasped. Bor'beti's cheeks flushed.

Now they believed–but wait. I stared at their bare foreheads. Neither wore paint. Could the 'betis, so vital to the Rebellion's cause, only be Tier 1s? Or lying? But why?

Bor'beti rubbed his eyes. "Was it forged?"

"You know it can't be." Ami'beti's portly frame shook as she shifted and leveled a glare at me. "But you are not the messenger."

"What?"

"Kapir trains royalty, nobility, the most highly gifted. He wouldn't send a *boy* to deliver our salvation."

"Quiet, Ami." Bor'beti growled and stepped forward with the knife. "Kapir is dead. You're not incriminating us, imposter. We want no part with the Rebellion."

I stepped back. "Srolo Kapir did send me. And I'm not a boy." I yanked my traveler's scarf from my head and neck, freeing my dirty curls and revealing my face. No red paint like a Tier 2 swirled across my forehead, just the emerald-green paint of a student training under the famous Srolo Kapir. A forbidden color since he'd broken his allegiance to the dynasty. The paint was likely smudged from travel. Why would an imposter endanger her life with such a detail?

One could hear a grain of sand fall.

Ami'beti's cheeks paled. "How old are you?"

"Older than I look. Nineteen winters."

"Kapir found you four years ago." A statement, and her mouth pinched as if she regretted speaking.

How did she know that? My stomach twisted. They were far removed from the Rebellion. If she knew that, did she know about my . . . problem? "You've heard about me?"

Apparently so. Both looked like they'd seen a ghost.

I forced a grim smile. "Srolo Kapir told me to wait with you until he comes. I'll pull my own weight. I'll stay out of the way." Stares. I swallowed. "I promise not to wield." Unless it's a life-or-death situation.

Ami'beti sputtered. "You're supposed to be a Tier 2."

Ouch. "I'm only a year late." Or so.

Bor'beti hissed. "She can't. Neither can he–"

She interrupted her brother. "When is Kapir coming?"

"Soon. He didn't tell me." Please don't kick me out.

Ami'beti's eyes hardened. "How can I stop Kapir's arrival? How can I send her into the streets and their nightly riots? She stays."

Bor'beti stirred. "Ami–"

"No one will know she's here." She leaned to whisper in his ear, making the man scowl, before turning back to me. "What do you call yourself, girl?"

"Tol."

"Come. I'll show you your room."

I blinked, snatched my staff and haversack, and followed.

Ami'beti ushered me to the end of the hall and up a narrow flight of stairs to a single door. She unlocked the room and gestured me inside.

I went into the cramped space and stared. One window covered in cloth, one plain bed, one worn rug. No stone bowl for fire, not that I would've wanted one. But the rough, earthen walls were covered in the carved copper images of starpalms. Every single known deity accounted for, so far as I could tell.

My skin crawled looking at them looking at me. Was this tower where Ami'beti maintained her priestly practice?

"A maid will bring a damp cloth for your bath."

A luxury. I nodded. "Thank you."

"You'll earn your keep until Kapir arrives."

I mentally added the respectful title *srolo*. Earning keep was important, and I was starving. "Yes, Priestess. And also–"

"Ami'beti is sufficient," she snapped.

Someone knocked, and Ami'beti swung the door wide. "Place it in the corner."

A baby-faced, broad-shouldered young man staggered in, straining to carry a heavy, lidded pot. I noted his deep tan, attesting to much time outdoors, and unpainted forehead. He was probably a Tier 1 like the vast majority of Vedoa. Like Ami'beti and Bor'beti. I could never look down on that, as some did. I had enough problems of my own. But how had the 'betis navigated a lifetime of intrigue as Tier 1s? Did that help camouflage their Rebellion loyalties?

He lowered the pot in the corner as instructed and cast me an inquisitive look.

Never seen a village girl before? I folded my arms.

"Out." Ami'beti waved the young man down the steps and watched until he disappeared. "That jar is your first task. I expect you to use it every morning and evening."

It clearly wasn't a chamber pot, so . . . "Priestess, I mean–Ami'beti?"

"Goodnight, Tol." She inclined her head and shut the door. Her footsteps plodded away.

My stomach gurgled. Until breakfast then, but at least she'd called me Tol. I stole to the pot and lifted the lid. It was filled with charcoal-colored sand.

By the starpalms, my reputation preceded me. She wanted me to drain my fire *twice a day*. Not even my most fearful guardians demanded so much. The sand would never cool! And it was probably harvested from the edge of the filthy trade route by that wide-eyed errand boy.

I stomped my foot. Loudly. Who cared if they heard? I'd rather sleep on the starpalm-forsaken, soldier-plagued streets than submit to this.

Against Srolo Kapir's wishes, I filled my left hand with flame, and shaped it into three tiny rings of perfect precision. A shape worthy of Tier 2 paint. Magnificence, one's source of fire, and Wisdom to shape it–but then my Temperance wobbled, and the rings shuddered.

I clenched my hands, extinguishing my fire, heart pounding. I didn't want to drain myself because she'd said so, but I hadn't trained since leaving Srolo Kapir, hadn't wielded in days, and my veins had started to pulse with built-up fire. Hissing through my teeth, I rolled up my sleeves and knelt by the jar. Counted to three. Plunged my left hand into the pot and began.

Shapeless, untamed fire poured from my fingertips and expired under the safe, heavy, smothering sand. Wisps of smoke burned my eyes.

Empty yourself.

I'm trying!

I groaned as the heat increased. If only I could expend myself by wielding instead, but it was too dangerous. I trained under Srolo Kapir, a Tier 3 famous for his Temperance, and still my own Temperance, the Form that held Wisdom, Justice, and Magnificence together, floundered. What was wrong with me?

Keep your eyes on the goal. Gulping deep breaths, I whispered the prophecy. "A starpalm will walk the desert in human form. From an endless well, her fire will cleanse the monster's lair, kindle life within dead bones, and fill the depths of the world. She, the one born of legend, will slay her own soul to finish the age."

I would master my Temperance. No more uncontrollable messes of fire. I would earn my Tier 2 paint. I would serve the Reborn Star as one of her Shields. Srolo Kapir's training wouldn't be wasted on me. And rain would fall in Vedoa again.

My shoulders hitched, and I ground my teeth. It felt like the skin of my hand peeled off my bones. Tears dripped down my chin.

Empty yourself!

I can't. My fire won't end.

I yanked my hand from the jar. No charred bones. Fingers and skin remained whole, like always.

My chest heaved. I scooted backward and leaned against the wall. Exhaustion gripped me, and I hated having so many images watching above me. I closed my eyes.

Through the partially opened window, the sounds of a riot deep inside the city rose to my ears. I willed myself to stay vigilant in this creepy tower, but weariness claimed me as uprisers and soldiers stirred trouble up not so far away, waiting for someone to claim Vedoa's throne. Everyone praying for falling rain.

4

A HANDFUL OF YEARS BEFORE

I was born, for reasons I'd failed to unearth, a Vedoan woman had fled to Laijon, our enemy country, to carve a new life for herself. Vedoa and Laijon were one nation centuries ago, and she could pass as Laijonese if she didn't speak. She married a Laijonese man, Daemu, one with sympathy for a homeless foreigner, and could have successfully disappeared if not for her loose ties with the Rebellion.

After her first time running away from her foreign home, the Rebellion paid her to return and hide me in Laijon. So my first guardian had swaddled me against her back and recrossed Vedoa's border into Laijon on foot.

I grew up in a home with my guardian, her husband, and their half-blooded twins, just a year older than me. By actions, my guardian taught me that twins were considered bad luck in our culture, and she grew cruel and neglectful toward all three of us, even her children. She demanded that I act like a servant, but Daemu had welcomed me as if I were his own, which still hurt to remember.

When we were older, Daemu taught his twins and me a Laijonese game using a wooden board and sixteen playing pieces. The boy, Roji, and I played, while his sister, Seyo, cheered for both of us or moaned when Roji captured my important pieces and plucked them off the board. Roji often celebrated too early. I'd do something silly, like gather his captured pieces and line them up on the edge of the board, declaring that the prisoners of war had changed sides and would now fight for me. Roji and Seyo laughed while insisting that my stunt didn't count, but I smiled and schemed before moving one of my pieces in an unconventional attack. Roji would sober and either win in a quick series of attacks or, if he was flustered, hand the game to me, which resulted in much sulking on his part.

Those happy days ended when I was nine, the night my restless guardian woke and led the two of us sneaking back into Vedoa. Having been ill in heart for years, she left her Laijonese husband and half-Laijonese children, only to die from sickness shortly after.

I felt like a game piece right now, moved by the whims of Ami'beti. Two days. Four drainings.

I trudged downstairs three times a day to eat with the 'betis. Tension was a constant side dish. Otherwise, they worked the property, and I stayed in my tower alone.

My excitement for the Reborn Star's arrival dimmed. She was supposed to show up on Ami'beti's doorstep any day, so Srolo Kapir believed. Where was she? When would she rescue me from this prison?

Doing nothing irritated me. Surely Srolo Kapir didn't mean for me to neglect my training this long. I decided practicing was different than defense and wouldn't break my promise.

Sitting on my knees, concentrating as hard as I could, I pooled fire into my hands. Just basic warm-ups and small, careful shapes. My control was stronger after draining–

My Temperance thinned. Shapes wobbled.

I closed my fist and quickly quenched my flames. All around me, hanging images boasted glowers and grins.

Magnificence was useless without Temperance. Why in the desert would the Reborn Star ever choose me as one of her Shields?

I vaulted to my feet and barreled through the door downstairs. Before breakfast was called. Who cared if the 'betis exploded at my display of free will? I rushed through the kitchen, passed a gawking maid, and burst outdoors into cool, early air.

Beyond the 'betis' droopy, thirsty garden, their stifling property wall, and the city wall in the distance, pink and gold touched the furthest reaches of the sky. If only I saw clouds. And my shimmering, ebony desert was so close and yet too far.

"Fine, Bor. Go and hurry back, before the crowds thicken."

I froze, hearing Ami'beti.

Her voice neared. "Take something to eat. The price for street food is atrocious."

I whirled to escape and plowed right into Ami'beti's generous frame.

"Tol!" She pushed me back and patted her tightly bound hair, flustered. "What are you doing? Where are you going?"

"Nothing. Nowhere. I just wanted"–*freedom*–"fresh air."

"Humph." Ami'beti eyed me. "You'll get more than that. Come."

She led me past the goat pen housing a herd of the silkiest, snow-white goats I'd ever seen. Goats that wouldn't survive one night in the desert, but whose coats made the 'betis rich. She ignored their bleating and stopped before a circle of stone covering a small cistern for rain collection. Of course, they had servants and fine meals, so why not their own cistern, while every northern village shared community water sources?

Ami'beti planted her hands on her hips and yelled. "Boy?"

The baby-faced, broad-shouldered young man hurried from the corner of the house. When not delivering a jar of sand to my tower, he ran errands for the 'betis or played night watchman, and not a very good one, since he'd missed my entry. In my mind, I named him Beck and Call.

He offered Ami'beti a bow, a far more practiced one than I expected, and shot me a glance.

"Open the cistern."

Beck and Call crouched to slide the heavy, stone cover away. Ami'beti looked over his shoulder into the reservoir, and her expression tightened.

Old rainwater pooled dangerously low.

Ami'beti handed me an empty pail. "Water's expensive. Spill a drop, you pay for it."

So, it began. *Move the fencing. Brush their coats–gently! This is*

Vedoa's finest breed, not slabs of meat. Oh, I'll just do it. Clean that up. You haven't fed them yet? I swear, she gave me twice as many tasks as Beck and Call. Was she testing me? I barely restrained my tongue from asking how she managed before my arrival. Ami'beti's thumb weighed more than the dunes. If Srolo Kapir didn't return soon, I was going to lose my mind–

A goat butted my calf. I shooed it away and turned to find Beck and Call staring at me.

I started, then offered a glare that made his gaze drop and his round cheeks redden. Enough. He was decent looking, but my interest in him was as strong as my dedication to the 'betis' livestock.

A flurry captured everyone's attention as a flock of migratory birds, flapping and chirping, landed among the trees and pen fencing, spooking the goats. Each was the warm color of seeded mangi fruit, with purple bellies and throats.

Ami'beti pursed her lips. "Now they show up. Late, like the winter rains."

"They've come *for* the winter rains," I commented. "Maybe it's a good sign."

Ami'beti hesitated. "You're right." Then she gestured. "Come, Tol."

I followed her into the house, leaving Beck and Call behind, on into the kitchen. Ami'beti directed me to begin chopping root vegetables for stew.

Emboldened that we'd agreed about something–and her trust in handing me a knife–I dared to speak again. "Where's Bor'beti?"

Ami'beti prepared a pot over the hearth, breathing heavily with the effort. "Weeks ago, a runner was sent to the capital to climb its mountains and track the incoming rain. His return has been sighted."

Hope leapt in my chest. Soon, the whole city would know when the rain was predicted to finally fall. Maybe I was right about the mangi birds. For once, I couldn't wait to see Bor'beti.

Questions burned in my mind. I chose carefully. "Do you think the Reborn Star is in the city?"

Ami'beti dropped a handful of spices into a mortar with a pestle. "Yes."

I blinked. "Really? Then she should arrive any moment. Even before Srolo Kapir."

Ami'beti ground the spices with renewed aggression, filling the air with pungent aroma. "We cannot guess or force the timing of a starpalm."

"How will you recognize her if she wears human form?"

"I've begun to wonder that myself." Ami'beti speared me with a look. "Do you think Bor'beti will return with good tidings for rain?"

She tested me. I stood taller. "No. The Immortal Abyss has stopped the rains because of the dynasty." I spat the word. "Innocent blood shed at their hands cries out from the earth. These cries awaken the Immortal Abyss and its punishments. Only the blood of the guilty will satisfy the Abyss."

Ami'beti nodded. "The Reborn Star will judge the dynasty. How will she call the rains?"

"She'll speak to her brother and sister starpalms, the gods of water, and demand rainfall."

"How? What if they don't listen?"

"She–ah–she's a starpalm."

Ami'beti's gaze narrowed, and she swept spice into the pot.

My toes curled inside my boots. I refused to lose this test. "She'll speak by–"

"What if the Reborn Star is delayed?"

"She–we–the drought would ravage Vedoa," I stammered. "The oases would dry. People would die. The Reborn Star can't be late."

"But if she is? The Desert Rebellion can't wait for her forever. They would need to seek justice unaided. If the Rebellion refuses to help when they're able to act, does this not also make them guilty of innocent blood?"

My stomach twisted. Could the Reborn Star be delayed?

Ami'beti brandished a spoon toward me. "What would you do?"

I took an involuntary step back and berated myself for it. “I would follow Srolo Kapir.”

“What if he were late? What if the Rebellion overcame the dynasty without him, and by a miracle, climbed deep into the belly of the western volcanoes and approached the Immortal Abyss? What would you do, Tol? How would you call the starpalms to stop the judgment, if you were the last rebel standing?”

What maddening interrogation. Was this what priestesses did for fun? I sorted through scrambled thoughts. “Starpalms, I–”

“Don’t utter foul language under my roof.”

My cheeks warmed.

Ami’beti heaved a sigh. “You’re young and inexperienced. Striving to prove your capabilities.” Her voice lowered, as if speaking to herself. “You’re not ready for what’s coming.”

“You ask questions that would stump the Rebellion’s elders!” I grumbled. “I am ready to join the fight. Srolo Kapir said so.” Because my Temperance would strengthen. It had to.

“I’ve known Kapir longer than you’ve been alive,” Ami’beti said. “He’s an incredible leader, but sometimes his optimism gets the better of him, such as his secret, heretical beliefs. How does he reconcile the Reborn Star to those?”

I didn’t answer. Srolo Kapir thought that all the starpalms, separated from their negative qualities, were pieces of a supreme starpalm, a singular, all-powerful being he called the One. I always changed the conversation when he brought it up. It made me uncomfortable, especially because my faith in most of the starpalms was almost nonexistent.

With a condescending laugh, Ami’beti returned to the pot. “What about the birds, Tol? If the Reborn Star is delayed, they will be the first to fall from thirst.”

I lifted my chin. “They would live because I will give them the last drops of my water before watching them die.” I strode from the kitchen toward my tower.

But not before relishing the surprise covering Ami’beti’s face.

Beck and Call poked his head inside the house to announce Bor'beti's return after dinner. He was late, close to breaking curfew, and I'd endured remaining with Ami'beti at the table as she stewed, plates untouched and cold.

Bor'beti filled the dining room doorway. He always jumped seeing me, as if I were a plague.

"Where have you been?" Ami'beti gestured to the food. "Sit."

Bor's features were twisted. "There's no rain coming from the sea."

Ami'beti paled but spoke calmly. "We expected this."

"I didn't," he countered.

"What kept you so late?"

Bor swallowed and looked at me.

Ami'beti noticed and pointed a finger toward the door. "I'll call you from your room when it's dinnertime," she said to me.

Dinnertime passed long ago. But I stood, exited the room, shut the door, and clomped down the hallway before tiptoeing back and pressing my ear against the doorpost. Ami'beti's murmurings were difficult to discern, but Bor'beti was not a skilled whisperer.

"It's a bad omen, Ami."

"Shush. Don't utter something so absurd."

"They've caught six."

"Are their identities certain?"

"They're all branded. They were in hiding."

My blood chilled. They were talking about fugitive soldiers. How had the city caught so many? I thought of the one I followed into the horse trader's hut.

"The clan leader is going to sacrifice them tomorrow. He thinks it will bring the clouds back."

Tense quiet reigned until Ami'beti spoke curtly. "Superstitious nonsense."

"What about Tol?"

My already pounding heart skipped.

Ami'beti shushed him, and both fell into mutterings I couldn't untangle. I slid down the wall to sit on my heels and think. If that ex-soldier were caught, it was my fault.

Past bedtime, after draining again, I paced my room and thought up a dozen possible courses of action concerning the soldiers, three of which were plausible. Finally, I made my choice.

I would sneak to the execution and free the prisoners, whether "my soldier" was among them or not. My mistake would be righted, and I would rob the city rulers of such a spectacle as executing cast-off humanity as penance to the cloudless sky.

Ami'beti called me unready. I'd prove her wrong.

I approached the window, pulled the covering cloth back, and stared.

First, a thirsty but sturdy vine climbed past my window to the roof. What a convenient, discreet exit from this house. Now I just needed a ride into the bowels of the city.

Second, a plump form moved purposefully through the dark. Ami'beti approached the water cistern and shoved the stone cover free. Lowering to her hands and knees, she dipped a pail into the lowest recesses, and placed the precious commodity under the clustering trees.

Jewel-toned birds, gray in the dark, swooped to perch on the bucket's rim.

Ami'beti struggled to her feet, shoved the cistern's cover back into place, and disappeared back into the house.

5

THE SUN BURNED ACROSS THE SKY toward the gleaming capstones of the city's wall. Ami'beti and Bor'beti hitched their stocky desert horse to their tiny, covered gig, and the carriage shifted and creaked as they climbed inside.

With a loop of rope biting into my middle, I clung to the mounting steps and undercarriage, my traveler's scarf wrapped tightly around my nose and mouth. Bor'beti clucked to the horse, tapping his foot anxiously, and we lurched forward. The four spoked wheels, useless for desert travel and thus confined to city cobblestones, squeaked annoyingly. I closed my eyes against a perpetual cloud of dust as we rumbled into the streets. The 'betis huddled above me in silence while I bumped against the carriage body with every uneven paving stone.

Attending the execution was necessary to maintain high standing with the city, but their forced compliance was nauseating.

As we neared the heart of the city, the crowd thickened. Bor'beti shouted for people to make way.

Close enough. I untied the rope and rolled out from under the carriage. Pulling my staff free from my belt, I slipped into the congested throng.

Towering edifices and sun-whitened awnings framed a public square glittering with afternoon sunlight. I stood on the balls of my feet and spied a knot of soldiers, some dressed in the colors of the city and some in the capital's scarlet, positioned around a small building with a single door. One guard opened the door and disappeared down into the earth. The dungeon.

"Move." A man dressed in servants' garb elbowed past me clutching a sloshing, opaque bottle and stack of empty tin cups.

Six tins. One bottle of cheap wine. He was headed in the direction of the dungeon.

I pressed close behind the servant, easy to do in this jostling crowd, and rammed the end of my staff into a certain spot in the back of his head. The servant stumbled, and I snatched the bottle and cups before he crumpled to the ground. Many gasped and grumbled at the nuisance of stepping over an unconscious body. I tucked the staff into my belt and headed toward the soldiers. Slowly and calmly–even though their armor and what they represented made my blood boil and my skin crawl.

One of the soldiers draped in scarlet spied me and spat something in the capital tongue.

My shoulders hitched. I didn't understand–

He yanked me through the others toward the door. I recoiled at his touch and their sweat-stained leathers, sheathed swords, and armor. I finally deducted that he'd said "You're late" and almost spilled everything when the capital soldier pushed me through the doorframe and down a flight of steps. I suppressed my instinct to flee and descended past flickering wall sconces to the bottom.

A gloomy hallway cut through the underground chamber. Murmuring ceased at my entrance, and the stink of unwashed bodies rolled over me. I set the bottle and tins aside and hurried down the corridor, ignoring men and women begging for drink, until reaching the final human cages.

Six men set apart, who carried themselves a bit too tall. A crippling aura of defeat pervaded my senses. I searched their haunted faces. Stranger, stranger, stranger–him.

The soldier from the horse trader's hut slouched against a corner. His eyes glittered with surprise, then anger. The northern dialect dripped from his tongue. "Had to ensure that the job was done, my fellow stable rat?"

"It's Tol." I grasped the cell bars. I was putting myself within his reach, but I didn't care. "What were you thinking returning to a city with military coin? By the–" Ami'beti's sour expression rose in my mind, and I swallowed the oath.

"Your accent is northern."

"Does that not lend a little trust? Listen, at least ten soldiers guard the door. Commoners pack the square. I can get you into the crowd. After that, you're on your own." I thrust my arms into his cell. "Give me your hands."

His mocking expression grew taut. "Don't toy with me. If I still possessed my fire, we wouldn't be talking. And I wouldn't have given you my fire for false promises of freedom."

They'd been drained. Permanently. They might as well have had their hands amputated. "I'll rekindle your gifting."

The words hung in the moldy air as he eyed me. "Who are you?"

"I already told you."

"Tol is just a name. Let me rephrase. *What* are you?"

"You don't have time for this."

"It's not difficult, Stable Rat. For example, my name is Samari, and I'm a soldier of the highest rank, punished for following my empress's orders into battle against Laijon. Your turn."

"Look, I never meant for this to happen. Please let me make it right. Give me–"

Samari lunged to grasp the bars. Now I could see bruising on his face from a beating. Where his military wielding tattoo was, an angry, blistering brand seared across his forehead. The brand of a traitor.

I refused to shrink back.

"Your Magnificence is impressive. You proved that through our . . . meeting. The starpalms dared bless you with Justice, too, if you offer to 'rekindle.' As if I would fall for that trick." He spat. "I have friends in unique places, and I don't intend to surrender to the grave today. But if I do, I will die an honest man. Slither back to the gilded serpent's hole where you came from, and throw my regards in the dynasty's face."

"Serpent's hole? What in the desert are you suggesting?"

"Justice is the rarest Form. Anyone who possesses it ends up in the military or the palace's employ, and you're not military. So why does the palace send you after me? There are easier ways to collect Tier 2s–like not hunting and executing us."

My blood simmered. "I would die your intended death before I would serve the dynasty." I whirled to face the other cell and its five captured soldiers. "Anyone else imaginative enough to believe I'm on your side?"

"She lies," Samari declared.

After a moment, a soldier with a long face and darting eyes nodded and reached for my hands.

I tensed at the feeling of his meaty fingers around mine, but reminded myself that he was a product of the dynasty's oppression. With extreme care, I eased my fire into him. Just enough to reawaken his gifting and give him enough flame to fight with. His eyes widened with surprise or maybe pain. I was thankful my Temperance was holding. Giving fire didn't hurt him as much as it hurt me, but I refused to let it show in my face.

Sweat gathering across my brow, I wrenched my hands free. The soldier rubbed his palms together and opened them in bright, healthy flames, which illuminated his shock.

The rest of the soldiers clustered closer and stretched their hands toward me, desperate.

I offered fire to the second soldier, third, fourth, and fifth, who resisted letting go. I tugged my hands free, gulping breaths, and turned to Samari. In different circumstances, his disbelief would have made me laugh. Instead, I bowed and spread my arms toward his awed comrades, each cautiously holding unshaped flames.

"Don't be a fool," I said. "Let me help you."

Samari studied me, then extended his hands.

I immediately seized them and poured fire back into him too. When he grimaced, I slackened my strength, though wishing very much to do the opposite.

"The palace would give a city's water ration to learn that someone like you had escaped their clutches. If you don't serve them–"

"I will *never* be the dynasty's lackey."

"Easy!" Samari's voice strained. "The soldier who drained me did so with greater gentleness. Who do you serve?"

I dropped his hands.

Samari uttered an oath and bent over a moment, before slowly straightening. He cupped his hands, and fire flickered in his palms. His narrow eyes lifted to mine, betraying his doubt.

I smirked, but then he spoke in the capital tongue too quickly for me to try to understand. His friends chuckled.

I stiffened. "Wield past the guards," I said. "When you reach the crowd, disappear."

"A thousand thanks, Stable Rat." Samari hurled a ball of fire at my face.

I threw a flaming shield in front of me, so hot it burned white, and Samari's fire absorbed into my flames with a whisper. I steadied my left hand, frantically shaping the fire flowing through my fingers with my right. It was one of Srolo Kapir's masterpieces, a smooth and swirling oval covering me from floor to head. I would thank the good srolo for forcing me to build such muscle memory and speed when he finally arrived. I could have wrung Samari's neck. "Starpalms, soldier. Is this how you repay a chance at freedom?"

His voice warbled behind my shield. "Consider it an enlightening test."

"You're unhinged." I extinguished my shield and glared at him.

He loomed against the bars, a peculiar look on his face. "Magnificence, Justice, *and* Wisdom to shape a shield? Three Forms in no small quantities? Your lack of paint is a blatant lie."

Imagine what it's like having those three without the fourth to hold them together. Thankfully, we'd never see each other again. It didn't matter what he insinuated or assumed about me.

"And your ability to give fire is . . ."

"Awe-inspiring? A thousand thanks, as you say, and good luck." I curtsied smartly and stole down the hall.

"Who are you?" Samari shouted after me.

I was an orphan rescued by the Desert Rebellion, and he didn't deserve to know even that. I raced past prisoners and dodged their desperate arms straining through the bars. I pounded up the stairs, wove around the guards, and vanished into the crowd. Squeezing forward, ignoring hands pushing against my intrusion, I reached a line of shops with overhanging cloth awnings sagging under the weight of some of the more daring spectators seeking a better view. I climbed the nearest awning and hunkered down next to a boisterous sibling group, my eyes on the dungeon.

Guards disappeared down the dim stairwell.

This was it. Samari and his comrades needed to wield their way out now. I glanced around.

In the center of the square, a stone platform oversaw a circular, walled amphitheater. Atop the platform, about a dozen finely robed men and women sat on cushions, surrounded by servants holding silk umbrellas. The city leaders. It took me a moment to locate Bor'beti, his face an unnatural shade of green, and Ami'beti, stoic as ever, seated in the back.

The dungeon guards returned with the six prisoners. Samari headed the pack, his wrists bound like the others, allowing himself to be pushed inside the amphitheater.

The spectators roared and shook their fists. The siblings scrambled for a better view and almost sent us tumbling off the awning.

I stared at Samari, trapped between the walls of the amphitheater. Why hadn't he wielded? I almost pounded the awning in frustration. They hadn't even tried! All around me, people chanted for an execution by fire trial. My stomach sickened.

Suddenly, the condemned soldiers lifted tied hands all simmering with fire. And Samari, if my squinting didn't betray me, actually smiled.

The crowd gasped. Because the six were supposed to be drained. The square erupted in shouting. Demands that the drainers be added to the execution.

I prepared to slide off the awning, but a strange feeling tickled the back of my neck. I glanced toward the platform, where the powerful shouted over the common, and made horrifying eye contact with Ami'beti.

Shock paralyzed me. Eyes of the starpalms. She couldn't possibly see–

Someone shrieked. "Dragon!"

Everyone looked up just as a large, winged shape arced over the rooftops and vanished.

I took in a sharp breath. Juvenile wild dragons–what remained of them–wouldn't stray this far north.

Fire flashed inside the amphitheater.

People screamed, and I jumped off the awning, hit the ground hard, and pressed against a locked storefront. People jostled past, and I looked up to confirm my horrifying suspicion.

The winged creature dipped across the setting sun, screeching like the undead. It wheeled toward the amphitheater and alighted on the abandoned noblemen's pedestal. Wearing human clothing, head held high and proud, it was a man, but not. The creature unfolded long, leathery wings.

My heart pounded. A Shadow. Here.

Run, Samari.

I darted down an alley and halted before a barricade of fleeing people. Cries reverberated against the stone walls. I and several others climbed windows to a second story roof and followed that until the building ended and we clambered down to the streets again. As people screamed, I looked over my shoulder.

The Shadow cut between buildings, in and out of sight, with a searing screech.

The crowd pressed me on. As soon as it thinned, I ran. Through alleys, around countless people, until I found myself in front of the 'betis' blue house.

A rush of wind, gravel, and dust rustled behind me, and I whirled.

The Shadow loomed in a pocket of gloom, as if it gathered the shadows of surrounding buildings around itself like a cloak, a head taller than most men. Its great wings remained outstretched as it stared, head cocked, a piece of lingering human expression there.

Warped creature doomed to the underworld, you're not taking me there with you.

I lifted hands filled with fire, and the Shadow blinked and staggered back. Did the light hurt its eyes?

As I waited for it to attack, I realized the creature wore clean, fine garments, untorn, and had a satchel strapped across its chest.

The Shadow snorted, and I jumped as it beat the air with its wings and took off into flight, soaring toward the outskirts of the city.

I slowly exhaled, unable to believe what I'd just encountered. Would it return? I extinguished my fire and watched the horizon.

Shadows were the product of wicked, ancient incantation, rediscovered only in the last years. The dynasty sold these secrets to Pirthyia, who created a vile Shadow army to battle Laijon. Now, rogue Shadows terrorized portions of Vedoa, a twisted representation of the dynasty's greed in recreating the monsters. I hated Shadows, and if we the Rebellion had our way, the flying monsters would be cast beyond the sandy edges of the world.

Willing my heart to calm as I started off again, I rounded the blue corner of the house and halted.

Beck and Call stood in front of the vine crawling up the wall to my window, ramrod straight, arms crossed, king of the lawn. Oblivious that a starpalm-cursed Shadow had landed just lengths away.

I hid my quivering, returned his glare, and stepped close enough to grasp the vine.

He didn't budge. "The 'betis asked you to stay inside."

"I will be inside if you move."

"The 'betis–"

"Will remain ignorant, unless you want to announce that you failed your post? Again?"

Surprise and hurt crossed his face.

I ignored a twinge of guilt and scrambled up the vine to climb through the window into my room. Surrounded by images, I pressed my hands against my ears.

Shadows. Srolo Kapir hadn't known they invaded so far inland. What if he was trying to enter the city right now? Or the Reborn

Star! But if the Reborn Star were already here, she would vanquish the monster.

Heated discourse rose from downstairs. The 'betis had returned, and for once, Bor'beti seemed to be winning an argument. One of them tramped up the stairs to my room. Ami'beti.

I hid my traveler's scarf, sprawled across the bed, and looked bored.

A fist pounded against the door. The knob turned, and Ami'beti poked her head inside and locked eyes with me. Like we'd accidently done just before that winged monster appeared.

But she couldn't have possibly seen me. I hoped. I faked a yawn. "Yes?"

"Tol, a Shadow breached the city walls."

I heaved myself upright. "Starpalms! Really?" Was that too dramatic?

Ami'beti's brow pinched, but this time she didn't scold my language. "Soldiers hunt it now. Until it is caught and killed, everyone is to remain inside. Bor and I will feed the goats."

After dinner, I attempted another training session before heaving a sigh and throwing myself atop the bed covering. Thank you, Shadow, for adding bars to my prison. At least I didn't have to drain after wielding today.

"Tol?" Ami'beti's muffled voice.

I almost jumped out of my skin. "Come in?"

She peeked inside. "Are you well?"

"Yes."

"I wondered if today's news disturbed you. I brewed tea to calm my nerves and had extra." She came in and extended a steaming mug.

Tea required water. What extravagance, and why the sudden concern? It was too much to imagine I'd started growing on her. However, crises did affect people. I unrolled myself and took the offered drink, the cup barely half full, white with a splash of goat's milk.

"Are you sure you're well?" she asked.

I sighed. Might as well throw her a bone to chew on. "With the Shadow, I'm worried about Srolo Kapir."

"Kapir's handled worse." Returning to normal, Ami'beti skewered me with a look that I didn't wish to interpret.

"Why hasn't the Reborn Star come?" I asked her.

Ami'beti pressed her lips together. "Nothing delays the starpalms. Goodnight, Tol." She shut the door and padded downstairs.

I swirled the hot tea, sipped the sour, herby brew, and lay down. So much for calming nerves. I couldn't slow my rampaging thoughts. After tossing and turning, I stood and swung my window open to punish myself with chilly, night air.

A mangi-colored bird landed on the windowsill.

I stilled. Watching.

The little bird tilted its head with a dull, listless gaze. Its feathers were puffed in response to the cold, but its movements lacked energy. It was thirsty. By the desert, I refused to watch the mangis become a sacrifice to the dynasty's oppression.

I reached into my haversack for my skin, refilled from the 'betis' cistern, and poured a thimbleful of water into my cupped palm.

The little mangita hopped to drink from my hand.

A sound startled me and the bird, and it flitted into the dark. I looked out the window.

Ami'beti stood at the base of my vine, a glinting hatchet over her shoulder.

I froze. Starpalms, she had seen me at the square. Beck and Call wouldn't have told her.

Ami'beti swung the hatchet and chopped down my escape.

I swallowed a scream and threw myself onto my cot. After several minutes, I lifted my head.

Try to trap me here. There's always another way.

But as I tried to think of one, heaviness spread over my mind, and even as I fought to stay awake, I drifted asleep.

6

SHADOWS CHASE ME. THEY SACRIFICED Samari for rain.

I'm trapped, Srolo Kapir. Come save me!

A giant of a man, young, his pale skin covered in foreign, swirling markings like tattoos, crouches and offers a helpful hand. Constellations and storms stir in his eyes.

Looping nightmares echoed in my mind. I couldn't stop the cycle. A terrible smell invaded my senses. My stomach turned over, but I couldn't sit up to vomit. A bitter taste filled my mouth before a thick liquid slipped down my throat and made me choke.

Wake up, Tol.

I forced my eyes open.

Moonlight poured through the window, and my hazy staff tip wavered in and out of focus, fingerlengths from my face. Ami'beti was huddled behind a charred, wooden shield. Her whisper sounded faraway. "Wake up, Tol. We're running out of time."

Starpalms, she meant to kill me. I opened my mouth and croaked. "Quench your fire. I beg you."

I looked down and saw fire filling my left hand. No. Three rings of concentric flaming circles, spinning on the verge of losing control. Without the shaping help of my right hand, which felt trapped under the quilt.

"Tol!"

I tried to move my right arm to catch my fire between my hands, but I couldn't command my own body. I closed my fist, and fire dripped onto the quilt.

Staff and shield clattered. Ami'beti darted forward and beat the flames out. I tried to assist, but I felt like I was clawing through an invisible sandpit.

"Please. Stop." Ami'beti pressed the sooty heels of her palms against wet cheeks and smeared ash across her skin. "Please."

Blistering, gray scars spread across the floor, where the pot of sand lay on its side, its contents spilled. The blanket lay crumpled in the corner, scorched and covered with soot from beating out fires. Angry blisters covered Ami'beti's hands. Even basic wielders could deflect some flames. She wasn't a Tier 1. She didn't possess any fire at all, and she wasn't trying to kill me. She was protecting me from myself.

Tears pricked my eyes. "I'm s-sorry. In my sleep," I stammered the words. "I–I haven't since I was a child–"

"It's the sleeping herbs. Oh, forgive me." Ami'beti lowered herself onto the edge of my singed bed, her face tear streaked. "The antidote took far longer than I thought."

I licked my parched lips and tasted that awful bitterness still lingering in my mouth. "You poisoned me."

Ami gave a weary sigh. "It's a sleeping cordial from a common desert plant. Standard medicinal training for those serving the temple. I wanted to give you less, or better nothing, but Bor watched–" She grasped my arm. "There is so much you need to know. But why should you believe me when I've doubted you until now?" Her voice shook. "Why did you give fire to the six soldiers?"

How had she guessed? I attempted an amused tone to cover my jittery nerves. "I'm flattered that you think so highly of me–"

"No one in this city is that strong. Only one of those soldiers possessed Justice. The others shouldn't have been able to take flames, but you enabled them to. By the desert, you've grown up surrounded by Tier 2s, even Kapir. What you've done isn't normal, Tol, and you have no idea." Ami'beti growled. "Of course, Kapir leaves it to me to teach you who you are."

"I know who I am."

"Then tell me." Ami'beti cast an anxious glance out the window. "Quickly."

This was silly, but the burns on her hands compelled me to comply. "Srolo Kapir became my guardian four years ago–"

She interrupted. "Before your guardians. What have they told you about your parents?"

I didn't want to talk about this. I tried to give the information blandly, as if I were teaching someone how to sweep sand off the floor. "That they joined the Rebellion, and I was born in a small northern village. Royal soldiers swept through the region, and there was conflict. They murdered my parents, and the Rebellion took me in."

"Bravo, Kapir." Irritation and pity crossed Ami'beti's face. "Your parents were part of the Rebellion, covertly. That part is true. But you were born to high nobility. They were cousins to the emperor who reigned at your birth, and they shared vital information with the Rebellion collected from the very throne room."

I blinked. Had she been drinking?

"You were born in the palace under a blood moon. The highest sign, a promise that your fire would be strong. The emperor feared your gift, so you had to be hidden. Srolo Kapir staged your death and carried you to refuge. Years later, when suspicions rose against him, he vanished from the capital's sight, so that he was also presumed dead."

Blood moons? Srolo Kapir rescuing me as a baby? "I'm a village girl," I insisted.

"Your Forms don't come from the villages. Justice to rekindle the soldiers? Wisdom to make and animate shapes–in your sleep, may I point out–and Magnificence to wield for hours? May the starpalms forgive my unbelief until I saw you wield, after giving you a sleeping cordial and keeping that nosy boy away so he wouldn't know. Tier 3s possess all four Forms, Tol, like Tier 2s, but with greater strength and one or perhaps even two Forms perfected. Every Tier 3 has a limit that keeps them under the authority of the starpalms. But three of your Forms display completion, as Kapir wrote me years ago."

Blood rushed in my ears. Srolo Kapir told her that? I didn't like the path of this conversation. "You haven't seen me train. I can't progress past my current level, even under Srolo Kapir's instruction. I'm stuck making tiny shapes while my classmates create whirlwinds and desert horses and advance past me."

"Yet Kapir continues training you," Ami'beti observed. "You grew up hidden in villages all the way to Laijon and back, correct?"

Involuntarily, I touched my ear. The one bearing the slave piercing, a disguise I wore growing up in Laijon, the hole long closed into a tiny, puckered scar.

"Your guardians have been accomplished Tier 2s until Kapir. Powerful flames feel normal to you." She sighed. "At last, after you've come of age, Kapir sent you to me."

"He only sent me to deliver his message." I sat taller and forced myself not to plead. "My Temperance is so weak, I basically don't have it, and that gets me into so much trouble that I know you've heard about. I only have three Forms, which is less than a real, ordinary Tier 3." The half lie smote me, along with calling Tier 3s ordinary. "All I want is to be good enough to serve as one of the Reborn Star's Shields. That's why I begged Srolo Kapir to let me deliver the message. That's why I'm here."

Tears pooled in Ami'beti's eyes, and faint amusement sparkled. "You, who lack Temperance, are paired with the greatest wielder of perfected Temperance in Vedoa's history."

I'd seen Srolo Kapir's unique ability. It was no wonder the dynasty wanted him dead after his loyalties changed, but his Temperance had barely helped mine.

"Kapir believes you will possess all four Forms perfected, so I, too, trust in this."

"He what? No. I just need enough Temperance to hold my fire together. Don't say that," I begged. "Please. It's impossible."

"I was a priestess, remember, and I assure you that starpalms laugh at impossibility. With that, I can die in peace." She clasped my hands. "Your life and Vedoa now depend on the truth." Her glistening eyes met mine. "Tol, we believe you are the Reborn Star and will become gifted with the power to overthrow the dynasty."

The world spun. I couldn't think. Couldn't speak. It. Wasn't. Possible. I tried to corral my thoughts. *Start with solid facts*, I told myself. Ami'beti drugged me. Woke me up in the middle of the–realization struck me, and I swallowed. "Bor'beti is going to betray me."

Ami'beti's lips trembled. "At this very moment, he exposes you to the clan leader. I couldn't persuade him from his fear."

Fear of my terrible reputation? No. Fear of harboring me, and of the dynasty hearing this wild tale. The clan leader ruled the city in the name of the dynasty, not the Reborn Star. Bor'beti was betraying me and the entire Rebellion.

Tears slipped down her round cheeks, and she cupped my face between her hands. "Many will seek to kill you, but they will need to go through me, Kapir, the Rebellion, and the starpalms first. Kapir has assigned a protector to you. Someone who will surprise the capital, mighty in fire, who will take you to Kapir."

I wanted to block my ears. "Where's Srolo Kapir?"

"I wish I knew. You're in more danger than he is." As we talked, Ami'beti wrapped my traveler's cloak around my shoulders and pressed my haversack, heavier than before, into my hands. "Find the boy. I told him a secret way out of the city, and he will deliver you to your protector."

Beck and Call was on our side? I jumped off the bed, slipped my staff into my belt, and grasped Ami'beti's arm. "You're in danger too. Come with me."

"I'm not fit for the desert anymore. I can delay the city's pursuit. You must move quickly. Go, Tol."

"I won't abandon you–" I began.

"No." Ami'beti wrenched her arm free and stepped back, head up. "Go. Confide in no one except your protector and Kapir. Don't waste the sacrifices others have made for you. Your guardians.

Srolo Kapir." Her expression hardened. "Your blessed parents, whom the emperor poisoned before they could name you."

A long, jagged spear sank into my soul. All my life, I'd believed capital soldiers killed my parents. Whether this new story was true or not, I refused to process it, and I had to protect Ami'beti. I snatched the quilt and tore it into strips. "Lie down. Please," I added.

"You must go!" Yet Ami'beti lowered herself to the charred floor, and submitted to being bound hand, foot, and mouth. May the charade protect her.

I left the room and raced down the stairs. Loud voices and stomping sounded below. Several pairs of feet. Bor'beti's voice rose like a whine, and a gruff, deep voice answered.

Back door.

I fled to the kitchen and crashed against Beck and Call. He caught me by the shoulders, his baby face pale, and whispered. "Thank the starpalms. I couldn't find Ami'beti, and I was about to storm your room to wake you. We need to reach the desert." He gestured, and I–trusting Ami'beti's word–followed.

We moved swiftly out the kitchen door into the garden. Moon and stars hung high, and darkness cloaked the ground as I ran after him. I'd prefer it if he had Tier 2 paint across his forehead. Hopefully he possessed a Tier 1's measure of Magnificence and could defend himself in a firefight if it came to that. When I turned south toward the back gate, Beck and Call pulled me past the cistern to the wall enclosing the 'betis' property, with the city's stone wall towering behind.

Something sharp pricked my scalp.

I reeled, startling Beck and Call, to find the mangi-colored bird perched within my hair. I gently cupped it in my hands and looked around. Lifeless bundles of mangi-colored feathers lay across the ground, under dry trees, and near the empty water pail. Perished from thirst. I tucked the surviving mangi inside my cloak, caught Beck and Call's observant gaze, and we climbed over the 'betis' fencing, heading toward the city wall.

Doubt claimed my thoughts by the time we reached the unscalable edifice. I followed Beck and Call's gaze up. A large, diamond-shaped incision, meant for allowing arrow shot, rose in the stones above us. Beck and Call jumped to grab the rim, pulled himself up, and squeezed his bulky frame into the space. He reached for me.

I ran, leapt, and grabbed hold of his forearms, bracing my feet against the wall. I hoped he had a better plan than jumping to the desert–and our deaths–from this height.

He tugged me into the incision. I also bent to fit, and he shuffled deeper inside and disappeared. A narrow aperture cut into the rough rock and mortar comprising the wall. A secret corridor. How did he–and ultimately Ami'beti–know about this?

Scraping, Beck and Call inched his way between the arms of stone. I pressed after him, turning my staff horizontal to maneuver it through. Breathing hot air, I waited twice as Beck and Call unwedged himself, and then our feet reached narrow, broken steps. Down we climbed, ducking under the ceiling. I stumbled and bumped into him, but he kept his footing. The stairwell coiled, and I finally straightened with the extra headroom. Beck and Call took in deep breaths.

Why was he helping me? "Who are you?" I sounded like Samari.

His shoulders hunched. "Uh, Tilur."

That was a lie if I ever heard one.

Faint light trickled from a sharp corner below. We reached another open shaft overlooking a sea of midnight-colored desert, darker than the night sky above, and a survivable drop.

Tilur–honestly, I preferred his former name–jumped first. I wrapped a protective arm around the bird and followed, stomach leaping, and tumbled upon moon-cooled sand before scrambling to my feet and looking up. By the clever cut in the rock, the shaft was invisible.

Tilur touched my shoulder. "They can see us." He jogged toward the distant rocks and dunes.

Forever we ran, fighting sand. But I felt no exhaustion, only adrenaline, and my frenzied thoughts sped.

Hidden truths were lies. My parents. Ami'beti. Four perfect

Forms. The Reborn Star. Why had Srolo Kapir kept this from me? Was it true?

Desperation spurred me, and I picked up my pace and passed him. His footfalls trailed me as I disappeared into the vastness of the desert, the one place that had always, counterintuitively, felt safe.

Was anything safe anymore?

7

THE BLUSH OF DAWN AND ITS promise of renewed heat touched the sky just as charcoal sand turned to rock under our feet. We circled a massive pile of stones jutting from the closest dune and crept into a shallow, natural cave. Peering into darkness, Tilur inspected one corner, and I the other, and found nothing. I slipped the haversack off my shoulder and let the bag ease to stone that could serve as a bed. Which of us would take it?

"We need a fire to ward off animals," I found myself saying.

"I'll make it." He ducked out of the cave with his pack.

Sand whispered as he built the most fastidious fire I'd ever seen. For a city boy, it wasn't half bad, if only I hadn't missed where he'd sourced the flames. Surely, he was Tier 1 and able to wield, right? He settled under a shady outcropping of rock, giving me the cave.

I entered the cool darkness, slipped my hand inside my robe, and pulled the mangi bird out. Its feathers remained ruffled, but its eyes seemed brighter. I offered it a few drops of water in my palm before placing the bird against my chest again. I stared at my haversack. Why was it so heavy? I emptied the bag, and my eyes widened. There was an extra filled waterskin, dried food, a bag bulging with dacri, a map, medicine, a vial, and an elegant, desert-gray robe, woven from the 'betis' goats and dipped in a stiffening substance. I recognized the fire-retardant coating that had covered all my guardians' garments. The robe of a wielder, and extremely expensive. I stuffed the garment back inside, uncorked a vial, and gagged. I'd never forget that bitter taste. Ami'beti had given me the sleeping cordial she'd slipped into my last cup of tea.

What had happened to her? Deep inside, I knew I wouldn't see Ami'beti again. She'd drugged me to satisfy Bor'beti, but she hadn't turned me over to the city. She'd saved me but wouldn't let me rescue her.

"I won't waste your sacrifice," I whispered, then I buried my face in my arm and cried.

I needed to slow down and think, but I was so tired. I couldn't be the–I refused to think about it. I needed Srolo Kapir.

Nightmares haunted me with the imagined faces of my parents, Srolo Kapir's kind gaze, a swooping Shadow, Ami'beti screaming, and flames. Lots of flames.

Through licking fire, the towering young man from my previous dream unrolled sleeves over his strange, marked skin, and watched me. He looked as curious about me as I was of him, and waited for something. For me?

I awoke breathing heavily. I never dreamed this much. What did it mean? And why did my imagination keep conjuring the odd, quiet stranger haunting my nightmares? Fire throbbed through my left hand, but thankfully I hadn't wielded in my sleep. I'd have to drain myself soon, but today we needed to put more rock and desert between us and the city. I hefted my haversack over my back, grabbed my staff, and stepped outside the cave.

Against a blazing, scarlet sunset, Tilur stamped the fire to ash. I blinked in surprise. He'd handled the rude adjustment to sleeping during the day well.

Tilur lifted his own satchel and smiled. "Good evening."

Way too chipper. I gave a short nod in acknowledgement and immediately started off between the pile of boulders. By dawn, we should reach an oasis and could refill our water skins, if it hadn't dried since the last rain.

Soon, we treaded desert again. A bright sprinkling of stars lit our path, and deafening silence enveloped us. No insect song, no birds, just my and Tilur's muffled, swishing footsteps. He walked behind me like a Shield, something I didn't need. I pulled my cloak closer against the nocturnal cold and ruminated.

We'd made decent distance into the desert. Now to find the mysterious protector Ami'beti had told me about. I comforted myself that this was *not* a new guardian, but how was I supposed to find someone . . . in the desert? Who was this protector? I imagined the usual Rebellion fare, a loner, outlaw Tier 2 wielder, enemy of the dynasty, reeking of travel and short of words from living alone forever. That summed up fifty percent of my guardians, and those were the ones who kept me the longest.

I didn't want this person, but he or she would take me to Srolo Kapir, who'd better have an explanation for turning my understanding of the Reborn Star upside down.

I paused in my thoughts. Ami'beti had said the protector would surprise the capital. So, not a desert hermit, someone new to the cause, and someone Srolo Kapir trusted. Who among the powerful would dare to defy the dynasty? She'd also said Tilur would deliver me to this person. Tilur knew who and where my protector was. What was I doing leading the way?

I spun around. "Are you part of the Rebellion?"

Tilur halted. His surprise was almost amusing. "Ah, yes."

"Prove it," I demanded. "Where are we going, and what are we doing?" Hopefully he didn't call my bluff. How much did he know about me? Definitely not the ridiculousness Ami'beti claimed. She'd said to confide in no one except the protector and Srolo Kapir.

"I'm helping you deliver a message to the Rebellion." Tilur walked by me and continued south. So, that was the story he'd been fed.

"Correct." I caught up. "I hear we're meeting a new member of the Rebellion. A surprising one. Who is it?"

Tilur flashed another annoying smile. "I'm sworn to silence."

"Who's going to hear us out here?"

"One can't be too careful."

I could make him tell me who this protector was if I wanted to, but I would pester him with verbal speculation instead. "There are two powerful lords ruling the two cities adjacent to the capital. Their wives are also incredibly strong wielders. Perhaps they've joined the Rebellion?"

"Wouldn't that be a stroke of good fortune? I've heard that, between them, they possess all four Forms to the highest strength."

I already knew that, and hearing *four Forms* made me think of Ami'beti, and my stomach twisted. Judging by his tone, it was someone else. "There's also the royal council inside the palace, but most of them owe their giftings to the executed empress–"

Tilur missed a step at my outspokenness. Good.

"–and her father, the old emperor." Who, according to Ami'beti, poisoned my noble-blooded parents. Not capital soldiers murdering village Rebellion members as I'd believed my whole life.

"You speak of blue fire," he said.

"Yes." Something I'd only heard of. One of our old emperors had requested it as his gift from the Immortal Abyss, and now his lineage could give the counterfeit, impossible-to-shape fire to whoever earned the dynasty's favor. Srolo Kapir said it didn't burn as hot, but still killed. "Every person on the council has inferior blue fire," I said.

"That's not true. Some refuse that vile offering."

Ah, he had opinions. "Who?"

"Well." Tilur straightened his cloak. "Older ones, since they're naturally Tier 2s, so I've heard. And Bohak of Taval."

"The capital's prized Tier 3."

"I heard he was invited at age six to move from Taval and train at the Royal Academy. Now he serves as the youngest council member."

"Taval is the strongest village in the north. Bohak's their shining star, boasting a full measure of Justice." *The rarest Form,* Samari had said. "I've heard that by brushing fingertips with him, he can drain your fire instantly."

Tilur's voice rose. "Really? Who says that?"

"All the girls–" *Among Srolo Kapir's students,* but I cut myself off before divulging that. "Girls I know talk about him constantly. They think he's the most powerful and handsome wielder in Vedoa, and any of them would likely surrender their fire just to meet him. Why do you care?"

"I'm a fan," he said simply.

Of course he was, along with everyone else. Again, I wanted to ask if he could wield, just to know my options if we encountered conflict, but it was too rude to do so.

"Judging by your expression, I gather you're not as enthusiastic about him as your friends?"

Those girls weren't friends. "Bohak serves the dynasty, and anything described as larger-than-life tends to eventually disappoint."

"I suppose you're right."

"But if we happened to cross paths with him and they found out, they'd lose their minds," I added and had to grin. Thankfully, Bohak of Taval and his capital loyalty resided far north of our path.

Tilur grinned with me, and I continued spouting potential identities for my protector. Tilur politely deflected every possibility until I fantasized about seizing my staff, sweeping his feet out from under him, and enjoying the brief satisfaction of seeing him swallow sand. Reason restrained me. Without him, I wouldn't reach my protector or Srolo Kapir.

Trudging between dunes and outcroppings of rock, we traveled all night. At last, between monstrous arms of stone, we came upon a patch of green and soon parted grass to refill our skins from the tiny finger of a subterranean spring. Two small trees guarded the pool from pollution by sandstorm. It wasn't listed on Ami'beti's map, which only showed large, established water sources supplying the trade route. Thankfully, four years of copying the Rebellion's maps of these secret water sources, at Srolo Kapir's insistence, were paying off. Our replenished water and supplies would last days–including morsels for the mangi–but I yearned for the comforting scurry of rabbit or the call of desert fowl.

We left the oasis and searched for a campsite. I bouldered up a rock face and stopped when I looked down and spied Tilur's queasy expression. City folk. I'd grown up scaling rocks to safety, but with a sigh, settled for another shady eave closer to him.

Tilur lowered his satchel lengths away, leaving me the overhang, and crouched to inspect the rocks.

I checked my own space for snakes, but I left him to the rest, and began clearing sand for a fire.

"Please, allow me." Tilur took over and began arranging a tidy brush pile.

I wanted to protest but refrained. Where would he get his fire from? His painstaking process soon bored me, and I decided to surrender and ask about his Tier later. Keeping my haversack slung over my shoulder and my staff in my belt, I climbed the rock face to the top to scan open desert toward the brightening horizon. Splashes of pink bloomed across the sky.

I stilled and sank into a crouch.

Against the sunrise stood a hazy dot. As the sky lightened, the shape disappeared.

It was likely a rock formation we'd passed, but my mind leapt into high alert. I wouldn't alarm Tilur. The strengthening wind would cover our tracks, and I'd wake up midday to check again.

I returned to my eave and curled under its shelter from the rising sun. The better part of me hoped Tilur had enough shade. If only my spinning thoughts would let me sleep.

A hawk screeched.

I jolted upright. Beyond my roof of rock, the sun touched its zenith. Midday. The bird of prey circled overhead and swooped from sight. As the mangi stirred inside my cloak, I whispered a soothing sound and peeked from my refuge.

Tilur's fire burned, but he and his pack were gone. Beyond the rocks, not five hundred lengths away, fuzzy with heat, a thick row of people made camp. Horses. Supplies. Blasted soldiers. The city had risked day travel to catch me.

I swiftly stood and took up the haversack. We had to run. Now. Where was Tilur?

I crept between natural corridors, sand silencing my steps. The hawk cried out overhead. Was it tracking me? I rounded a boulder and stared.

Tilur stood in the open and lifted a bent arm wrapped in the tail of his cloak. The hawk dipped toward him, extended its talons, and landed on his forearm to preen. A golden band circled one leg and sparkled with sunlight.

Reality slammed into me. He'd left the city signs. He didn't serve the Rebellion.

Tilur turned and saw me. Sending the hawk back into flight, he quickly closed the gap between us.

"Liar!" I spat.

"Tol, wait."

I vaulted over a boulder, dodging prickly bushes and slipping over sand, searching for a feasible incline up the hill of rock. Empty desert surrounded us for half a day's travel. I couldn't outrun horses.

Tilur gained. "Listen to me."

I jumped, grabbed a handhold of rock, and pulled myself over the top.

He skittered to a sandy stop below and shaded his eyes. "Tol, your protector's here."

"And snowflakes will fall in Vedoa. Wait–how in the desert do you know about the protector?"

There was a pause. "What are snowflakes?"

I filled my palm with fire and flung a wall of shoulder-high, unshaped flames along the rock edge.

Through the writhing blaze, Tilur fled.

Heart pounding, I raced around the peak of rock, wielding until the encircling wall of flames was complete.

The hawk soared over my fortress and screeched before bursting into a fireball. Swooping across the bright sun, it extinguished its feathers again.

A trained flamehawk. Of course, they had one of those. I climbed a pile of stones to create a second ringed wall, then a third. I surveyed the remaining space, enough room for hand-to-hand combat, and created one shape, a blazing dagger. I suspended it in the air and animated it to spin. Slowly. A makeshift hourglass to let me know when my Temperance ran out.

Hoofbeats thundered as a small army surrounded my clifftop. Three soldiers dismounted and formed flaming, defensive shields. All Tier 2s gifted in Wisdom. Shielding their bodies, they parted through the first wall of fire.

Power raged through my hand. Wielding with the left and shaping with the right, I threw spinning spirals of fire down the rocks. Careful to hit only their shields and scare them away.

The men squatted behind their shields before advancing again.

I flung volley after volley. My shapes held, thanks to my will to survive. I forced the three into retreat. But as they disappeared behind the first wall, seven more soldiers appeared.

I increased my attack, and they remained on the defensive. Why didn't they fight back? Then I noticed four soldiers sneaking up behind me through a gap in the first ring.

Gap. My heart skipped, and I beat them off, repaired the flaming barrier, then poured a river of fire to cover the face of rock in ankle-high flames.

The soldiers fled. One cried out, burned. His comrade covered him with his shield and pulled him to safety.

I gasped. How badly had I hurt him? My spinning dagger wobbled, and I forced my thoughts to focus. My Temperance continued to hold, the longest it ever had.

The army reconvened. At last, a powerful wielder emerged, wrapped in a scarlet, fire-resistant robe, covering him neck to ankle. Only his eyes and hands were exposed for battle. His cloak swirled at his feet in the smoke. He shaped and animated three shields to hover and protect him whether he stood, ran, or knelt.

Alone, he passed through the first flaming wall and waded through my lake of fire in thigh-high boots.

I swallowed. This was no normal Tier 2. It was perhaps the clan leader himself, if he could animate shapes. I hardened my heart. He would not take me–for the sake of the Rebellion. For Srolo Kapir. Shaking, I drew my arm back and hurled a river of fire toward him. Expecting him to cower behind his shields.

Instead, he reached both hands forward. Like a void, he absorbed my fire and straightened.

My heart caught. How did he do that? I attacked again.

He received my fire effortlessly, before lifting his three shields and climbing another level of rock to part the second wall.

"Retreat or die!" I shouted, not that he could hear me. I thrust my wielding hand in front of my feet and raised a final barricade around me. Fire hissed and licked close to my clothes and hair in a sweltering stronghold. The dagger, like a miracle, continued to spin beside me.

Through the veil of fire, the wielder's dark form neared as he unwrapped protective cloth from his face.

The dagger contorted in and out of shape, its turns increasing in speed. I sucked in a burning breath. If the fortress fell, the wielder's blood was on his own head. I seized the dagger and turned it the wrong way.

He stretched his palms and pulled a swath of fire from my fortress to extinguish between his hands. The stronghold writhed in the gush of fresh air before he stepped inside the created doorway.

We stared at one another. He at a ragged, desperate girl, and me at someone who should have been a stranger but wasn't. The dagger handle now sputtered in my hand like something living. His eyes lifted from the blade and widened.

Three things struck me too late. Tilur stood before me, but gold Tier 3 paint adorned his forehead. Srolo Kapir had sent a disguised demigod to protect me, and I was about to destroy us both.

My dagger burst into uncontrollable flames. I flung it away just as the fiery walls lost shape above us.

Tilur grabbed and dragged me into a crouch, knee to knee. He tossed a shield into a shining dome over our heads and lifted his palms to support it.

Flames roared and crashed all around us. Explosions rocked the cliff. Only his shield separated us from my own inferno.

He muttered to himself, begging Justice to withstand, his men to hurry. All in the northern tongue with a native's accent.

I pressed my face against my knees, despising his nearness, and hated myself for what I hadn't seen.

A new sound lashed around us. An assault of sand as fires hissed.

Tilur's relieved laugh burst forth.

Waves of sands slapped against his shield. Boots crunched, then the world stilled.

"Srolo, we're here." The words were muffled through the shield.

Tilur drew his shield into his hands, exposing us, and tried to help me to my feet. I jerked my hand free, almost tripped on his fancy cloak, and glanced at new piles of sand devouring the cliff. Smoke rolled between the feet of soldiers surrounding us, all unfamiliar faces. The horsemen of Taval dressed in blue like the sky. Panting from slinging sand, some bracing hands against their thighs, they flicked wary gazes in my direction before focusing on the young man standing next to me with respect and attention.

Bohak of Taval, a member of the royal council–posing as the 'betis' watchman–was my protector. And here we stood in the aftermath of my narrowly averted disaster.

I couldn't believe it, and I fisted my hands to face him. Knowing to expect fear, hatred, or even disappointment, like almost everyone else.

Instead, his familiar eyes crinkled with pleasure before he cupped his mouth and raised a northern rallying call. His men echoed the call, until the desert rang with victorious shouts. He clapped his hands–his Justice-blessed hands–and grinned. At me.

My traitorous heart jumped.

Bohak leaned forward and spoke in a low tone under the

continued celebration. "With all respect, Srolo Kapir's description of your gift didn't do you justice."

I caught the play on words, and my tongue refused to move. This transformation of the person I'd known for the past days shocked me. His confidence and chivalry were overwhelming, and yet he had displayed such attributes even at the 'betis'. How had I missed it? Why had he turned on the dynasty and joined the Rebellion?

Bohak spread his hands for silence. Then he faced me and slowly lowered to one knee, and his soldiers followed.

Surprise skipped down my spine to my toes.

Bohak pressed a fist over his heart and met my astonished gaze. "I, Bohak, heir to Taval, represent my father as his right arm. We swear allegiance to the Reborn Star, the promised starpalm of fire, savior of Vedoa."

The soldiers affirmed his declaration with another collective shout. I stared at Bohak. Absorbed his hope, zeal, and something like pure awe. It was too much. I couldn't accept it. I felt trapped, waiting for them to change their minds and laugh, all a jest. But they didn't, and I realized I was supposed to respond. What did a Tier 3 expect for his allegiance? What would a real starpalm do in this circumstance? Probably wield, but I didn't dare, instead awkwardly offering a shaky curtsy.

Sympathetic understanding crossed Bohak's face. It infuriated me until he stood, swept his palms underneath mine, and brought my fingertips to touch his inclined forehead. His rare, gold paint.

Do not *touch my hands.*

He released me before I could react, swept soot and sand from his knees, and shaded his eyes to scan the horizon. "Smoke will alert enemies to your presence. We need to move." He offered a dazzling smile. "At last, you'll travel the desert like a starpalm. Well-supplied with escort and too fast to catch."

8

KEEPING EASTERN STARS TO THE right corner of our vision, we rode hours under the gleaming moon until my body protested the privilege of riding horseback, despite the saddle of dyed skins. My encircling entourage was more suffocating than this endless desert. No protective rock formations or valleys. Rather, Vedoa's shining desert prince cantered beside me. Heir to Taval, strong guardian of the northern trade route, he offered me allegiance, believing me to be a starpalm. I choked back a rising hysterical laugh.

Bohak raised his hand, and the Tavalkian army slowed. He dismounted, and one of his officers led his horse away.

I slid off my borrowed gelding, then froze, seeing Bohak with one hand extended as if to help me down. He covered the gesture by grasping the gelding's reins and passing them to a second soldier. Awkward.

The mangi chirped inside my robes. I ensured the absence of the firehawk before scooping the bird out to perch on my shoulder.

Bohak faced his men and clapped. "Prepare camp." They jumped to obey, and he strode in his fancy boots into their midst.

I hesitated. He was Bohak of Taval, yes, but he was also Tilur. And Beck and Call, bearing Tier 3 paint and dressed in much finer robes than what he'd worn at the 'betis'. If only they'd known whom they'd hired. I raised my voice. "Wait."

He turned. "My lady?"

I blinked at the title, hated it, but pushed that aside. "This is open desert."

Bohak cocked his head. "We are Taval."

Deserts, of course they could camp in such a vulnerable position, being many, armed, supplied. Even the city in full might would be foolish to engage these famed warriors. "Ah, right."

He flashed a smile and vanished into the midst of camp making.

I realized I was gaping and frowned.

Soon, tents bloomed across the rolling expanse. I supposed I should have felt relieved to be surrounded by true desert people, but as I circled the caravan, its magnitude astounded me. So many horses linked bridle to bridle, all carrying packs. How long were we staying here? A new question struck me so hard, I nearly gasped.

Did Bohak know where Srolo Kapir was?

Before I could start after him, an officer approached and offered escort to my tent. We wound through camp, past more tents-in-progress, unloaded supply horses, and a pale medical tent.

My breath caught. The soldier I'd burned. How did he fare?

Then, a tent towered before us, its cloth woven with stripes of slate, rust, and cream. Two guards bearing Tier 2 paint pulled the tent flap open with a flourish.

By the deserts, this was too much, and I would tell Bohak so. I entered, pulled the opening shut, and felt my boots sink into carpet. My jaw dropped.

Opulence surrounded me like nothing I'd seen before. The thick rug covered swept sand. A low table hosted plates of nuts and dried fruit. Experience hinted that I should sweep the food into my haversack, just in case, but the traitor mangi swooped off my shoulder to peck at the meal. Mountains of quilts and pillows formed a bed and pooled at the foot of a trunk and leather changing screen.

I approached the trunk and lifted the lid to find slippery gowns, ointments, and perfume that would attract every kind of desert pest. Then I noticed the sealed jar. My brow rose. Did Bohak know about my mistakes and give me sand for draining too? Unbelievably frivolous. All I needed to do was peel the rug back and be done with it! Despite that, I pried the jar lid open, inhaled the precious scent of water, and quickly closed the lid, shocked by the extravagance. I'd almost have preferred to find sand for draining.

Just give me my waterskin and an overhanging rock. I didn't need all of this, and I didn't want to stand inside the powerful palm of Bohak of Taval, surrounded by an army waiting for me to wield divine flames and overthrow the dynasty. Offer the jar of water to those who had none.

Outside the tent, a Tavalkian cleared his throat. "My lady, Srolo Bohak invites you to dinner."

Perfect, because we needed to talk. "One moment." I stuffed my haversack under the quilts, not that anyone from Taval would find it worthy of stealing. I freshened my face and hands with drops of water from my water skin, tied my curls at the nape of my neck, and pressed through the flap into the growing night, where deep blue began to color the horizon.

The Tavalkian eyed me with curiosity before bowing and leading the way through this brazen, open-desert camp to a second large tent, pure ebony, like midnight. He parted the entrance fold. Drawing my shoulders back, I stepped inside.

More plush rugs carpeted charcoal sand. A central fire breathed smoke up a chimney hole in the tent roof, and a low table long enough to seat eight people–how had they transported this furniture?–stood flocked by vibrant cushions. Spread maps, laid edge to edge and corner to corner, covered half the table, and plates of fragrant, steaming food filled the rest.

Bohak stood beside the fire like a king, and dressed like one in shimmering silk trousers and robes colorful as a peacock. Barefoot and unarmed, he made me very aware of my staff tucked into my belt, while his true weapons spread open in greeting.

"Lady Tol, welcome." Bohak swept a bow and gestured to the table. "Please sit."

Starpalms, the formalities. Was this a private meal? I didn't want to dine alone with Bohak. Yet he knew the inner workings of the

Rebellion, while I'd been kept in the dark. He'd also seen me at my worst at the 'betis', but I refused to be intimidated. I'd had etiquette lessons from several guardians, should I ever need to interact with the upper echelon, and the first rule was to graciously accept hospitality, even from an enemy. I would represent Srolo Kapir well and secure answers. So, I offered a curtsy in return, slipped my shoes off, crossed the rug, and planted myself cross-legged atop the plainest cushion I could find. Then I saw the pair of guards standing at the farthest corners of the tent, for propriety's sake.

Bohak settled across from me and lifted his hands to bless Magnificence, Wisdom, Temperance, and Justice for the meal. I copied his posture and observed the passionate declamation, different from Srolo Kapir's prayers to the one starpalm. But Bohak's Tier 3 forehead symbol and its complex whorls of gold was just like Srolo Kapir's, when he wore paint.

Bohak completed his blessing and caught me staring.

Awkward again, but I refused to look away. His face pinked, reminding me of Beck and Call, before he reclined on his side, quite a city thing to do. Bohak swept invisible sand off his silken sleeve, the only indication that he might also feel nervous right now, and gestured to the food. "Please enjoy this humble meal. It's the best I can do away from home."

Cakes of dark grain that would melt in my mouth, roasted leg of fowl, and pale milk tea–the desert's taste of home–were not humble. My empty stomach betrayed me by gurgling. I gingerly scooped food onto a platter. He pushed meat onto charred flatbread and ate.

I mentally counted to ten. That was enough time for pleasantries. "Where is Srolo Kapir?"

Bohak grinned. "I was wondering when you'd ask."

What?

"The good srolo crosses the desert to meet us now, just as we are traveling toward him and our meeting place."

He was on his way. We knew where to find him. I took my first true deep breath in what felt like ages. "When will we get there? What meeting place?"

"We'll arrive in fourteen days. Lady Tol, is the food not to your liking? I can have something else made."

Bohak hadn't answered my second question, but there were only so many desert landmarks. "It's wonderful." I forced myself to eat.

Bohak offered me a cup of milk tea, filled to the brim, with little care for the drought. I took the warm, tangy drink and paused. Internal warnings flashed through my mind, as I remembered my last poisoned cup of tea. But Bohak had no reason to drug me. Then again, what in the desert was the dynasty's youngest councilman doing here, and why should I trust him? He matched Ami'beti's description of my protector above and beyond, however.

Bohak pushed his empty plate aside and interlaced his fingers, still propped up on one forearm. "While we travel, Srolo Kapir has asked me to continue your training."

Goat milk and green tea turned to ash in my mouth.

"It's imperative that you be ready for every circumstance, from the Terror Lands border to the palace. If that is agreeable to you," he added quickly.

"Train in what?"

"To start, Srolo Kapir listed the capital tongue. How much of this can you understand?" He sat up and opened his mouth in the noble language, its harsh words flowing smoothly over his northern lips.

I stared. By his inflection, he had asked a question . . . "Um, 'I' and 'you'?" I tried not to look as embarrassed as I felt.

He masked a look of concern. "There are many similarities with the northern tongue. Lots of useful cognates. Capital nobility uses it to keep conversations private from commoners. We'll practice, and you'll soon be brilliant with it."

"I'd rather face a Terror Lands dragon than speak to capital nobility."

Bohak laughed, and it sounded hollow. "Then happily for you, our second focus will be practicing in fire."

My inner being tightened. "That's not necessary."

"Srolo Kapir . . ." He stopped, and his tone grew formal. "I assure you that I received approval to become a Royal Academy instructor two years ago, the youngest teacher on record. I had the honor of training under Srolo Kapir in the Royal Academy as a child."

That wasn't possible. But then again, Bohak couldn't be more than a couple years older than me, and he was sent to the academy at a very young age, so flapping tongues said. He could have very well trained with Srolo Kapir before Kapir vanished into the desert to spearhead the Rebellion.

"With all humility, Lady Tol, I believe we'll both benefit from practicing together."

I lifted my chin. "I'm sure you're amazing, but only Srolo Kapir trains me."

Understanding dawned on Bohak's face. "He told me about your . . . challenge. Which I witnessed upon the clifftop."

I inadvertently curled my fists.

"I'm not afraid." He extended a hand across the table to me.

I held his gaze and searched for lies. Was he really working with Srolo Kapir? Or was this a trick? But all I saw was excitement and confidence that wavered with my hesitation.

A veil fell over his gaze. "I haven't earned your trust yet."

Had he read my mind? "You served the dynasty," I replied.

"Yes, as you mentioned before." He retracted his hand, and his broad chest expanded with a deep breath. "When word of Vedoa's defeat reached us, I watched messengers receive missives ordering that soldiers returning from war were to be killed. There would be no trials. These heralds rode the trade route to every city and village, including Taval." He looked past me, his face like stone. "I was a Tier 3, and I could do nothing to stop it."

My heartbeat quickened. Powerlessness was a feeling I knew intimately. Could I trust him? Given all the evidence and circumstance, I had to, a least a little. "When did you join the Rebellion?"

"Recently. The dynasty still doesn't know. They think I'm on holiday. But they will learn where my new loyalty lies soon, and they will hunt me as you are hunted. Then I can consider myself a proper member of the Rebellion." His lips quirked.

His new loyalty lay . . . with me. I pushed that pressure aside and grasped the thread that now connected us. "Then you need to know how to fight like the Rebellion."

"You'll train with me?"

"Yes." Maybe he'd have a helpful Temperance tip.

"Excellent! Let's start." He immediately stood and began performing a quick stretch series, a lazy person's warm-up.

Taken aback, I scrambled to my feet as well. "Here? Now? I'll–"

"Burn my tent down? Try it." He removed a flask from the pocket of his robes and dribbled three exact drops of oil into his palms before rubbing his hands together and offering the flask to me.

I shook my head.

"I promise not to brush fingertips and accidently drain your fire." He actually winked.

Heat flooded my cheeks.

"Besides, with your Justice, you might return the favor." He spun fire between his hands, a beautiful, delicate whirl of congruent spirals. And he grinned.

What had Srolo Kapir told him about my Justice? My stomach sank. Bohak wielded so much fire fearlessly. This was his world more than mine, and he was thrilled to show off.

"Lady Tol, when Temperance cannot keep up with your other Forms, are you able to feel it giving way?"

I locked my jaw. "No."

"What shapes have you practiced?"

"Shields. Staffs." And I'd like to throw a staff at him right now, except he'd incinerate it.

"All defensive weapons. We need to build your repertoire. Have you trained in side-by-side combat?"

"No."

"It's perfect for training Temperance, as your partner's life depends on you."

"I fight alone." He talked as if we played a game. *But I'm dangerous.*

"This isn't the girl who traveled the desert on her own to a city she'd never seen, snuck out from under Ami'beti's nose and mine to oppose an execution, and escaped capture through a city wall. Don't hold back. I promise I won't let you lose control." He captured my gaze, then formed a simple sword with a straight, double-edged blade, and tossed it at me.

I caught it.

"You'll need a shield. Use this." Bohak shaped his fire into a perfect, spinning sphere, and offered it to me.

I accepted the orb. Gripping it with all my strength and mental energy, I crafted a head-to-toe shield like Srolo Kapir had taught me. My thoughts strayed to Samari, laughing in his cell, when I'd used this shape last. What had happened to him?

"Flawless, Lady Tol. You make fire look smooth as glass. Will you hand both back to me?"

I did, and he scooped the fire into his palms, tossed it overhead, and swirled it into a semblance of an oasis, complete with crackling trees. So pristine, perfect, frivolous–and wonderful. Yet it was missing something, and I desperately wished to add a crag of rock to sleep under and climb for scouting.

He grinned, as if I hadn't seen anything yet, before capturing his fire in his hands and pressing his palms together, extinguishing flames. "Well done. That is the essence of side-by-side combat."

I had to laugh. "Right."

"It's true. Partners must maintain proximity to sense each other's needs and handle one another's fire. Let's try again." He tossed fresh fire into the air and grasped the rounded, ringed pommel of a fiery, ceremonial sword.

"I prefer . . ." I wielded a flaming staff.

Bohak eyed my creation. "I'd think you'd be embarrassed to carry a staff that small."

Cheeks burning, I grew its size carefully, until the staff reached realistic proportions.

"Good." He stepped closer to me, far closer than I was comfortable with, and then faced the opposite direction. "Always remain shoulder to shoulder or back to back." He leaned into me so that our shoulders brushed.

I stiffened.

"Throw your staff to me, and I'll throw my sword to you. Ready? Go." We did, each catching the other's fire. He looked over his shoulder. "It held its shape. Wonderful. Again."

The second try also went well. Hope, battered and bruised, dared to lift its head within my heart, but then my fiery staff wobbled in my hands. I straightened my arms and gasped.

Bohak whirled, swept the blaze between his palms, and extinguished it into smoke.

"I'm sorry–"

"See? No harm." Yet worry wrinkled his brow. "Can you extinguish this?" He tossed a small, untamed ball of fire.

I caught it and absorbed it between my palms.

Bohak regarded me. "When your Temperance wanes, you can't extinguish your own flames."

It wasn't a question, so I didn't answer. But the morsel of hope beating within my heart faded.

"Let's try again."

"After that?"

"Of course." He shaped another sword, this one with a single-edged curved blade, and took his position beside me.

We caught and threw staff after sword. Cautiously. Focused. I settled into the drill, even tolerating his shoulder bumping against mine as he began to speak.

"Justice, the ability to take and give fire. Wisdom, the power to shape fire and even, in a skillful hand, animate it to the wielder's will. Temperance, the key to controlling its sibling Forms and, in the case of a master like Srolo Kapir, even more. And lastly, Magnificence, the well from which our fire flows, some deep and some shallow. You and I are the only two wielders with Tier 3 Justice in the country. And yours will be stronger than mine soon," he added.

I didn't respond.

"You're also a Tier 3 in Wisdom, but less than a Tier 1 in Temperance–for now–which makes the magnitude of your other Forms quite difficult to manage, I imagine."

I flinched, almost missing the staff again.

"Do you grow weary from wielding so long, Lady Tol?"

"Not yet."

"I do." Hesitation crept into his voice. "I'm Tier 3 in Justice, Tier 2 in Temperance and Wisdom, but my Magnificence is Tier 1. Quite unlike yours."

He only had Tier 1 Magnificence? That meant he could only hold a small amount of fire. That would limit him from seizing fire he drained from someone else. Useful to know, but he was hedging about my own Magnificence, and I wouldn't fall for that. I shaped my staff into a sword and tossed it back.

Bohak caught it. "Ah ha! Wonderful. Your lines grow sharper as you relax and trust your Wisdom."

"I don't relax." I held my hands out for the sword, but it never came. I turned my head to him.

Sweat dripped down his forehead with the effort of wielding with limited Magnificence. He held my sword in one hand and his in the other. "See what you're capable of," he said, and handed my sword to me.

I grasped the pommel. The most delicate, flaming white-hot carvings ran up the fiery blade. Dragons, birds, and rivers. I didn't know that I could do that. My Temperance never held long enough to attempt such beautiful details. Then the sword exploded between my hands. I uttered a cry and tried to extinguish it, but the blaze sputtered out of control.

Tensing like a desert cat, Bohak grasped my flames and wrestled them into submission. "Steady." He folded its lashing tongues onto itself, breathing quickly, then closed his fists, extinguishing the coils of flame.

I tried to breathe and couldn't. One of the forgotten guards stirred.

Bohak glanced at the floor, now spotted with ash, and mopped his brow with a pocket handkerchief. "That was exciting."

"No, it wasn't. That was mortifying." My eyes stung. I would not cry. "I lost control."

"That's because you don't believe in who you are."

I raised my chin. "I know who I am."

"Really?" His eyes met mine. "A starpalm will walk the desert in human form."

The prophecy slithered over me.

"From an endless well, her fire will cleanse the monster's lair, kindle life within dead bones, and fill the depths of the world. She, the one born of legend, will slay her own soul to finish the age." He raised his brow. "I was getting the impression that being the Reborn Star was difficult to swallow."

I felt as though he'd struck a real staff into my chest. I knew who the Reborn Star was, but I didn't know how to be her. "You've witnessed why."

"Temperance will come."

Anger exploded from my frustrated lips. "I've heard that my whole life, but no one can tell me when or how." Abashed, I covered my mouth.

Compassion filled Bohak's gaze. "Srolo Kapir knows a way. When we reunite with him, he'll explain everything, to both of us."

Ami'beti had alluded to the same thing. I couldn't even comprehend it. If Srolo Kapir knew how to give me Temperance, why hadn't he done so sooner? Did the whole world toy with me? Would grasping the fourth Form turn me into a starpalm? I tried to silence my raging thoughts, before my mind exploded like my fire.

"Tomorrow, we'll train again, if you like." Teasing reentered his tone. "I may not be larger than life, but I hope I haven't completely disappointed you."

I wished I hadn't said that too. I avoided sighing. "Until tomorrow."

Bohak stretched out his hands. A customary parting farewell. Culture dictated that we grasp hands and mingle fire to bid one another goodbye. A perfect way to steal someone's fire forever, or accidently give too large a quantity.

I paled. I couldn't–

But Bohak only cupped the backs of my hands. "Once the desert sees your gifting, it will flock to you."

It felt like a dose of dread, rather than a compliment.

He retracted his hands. "If you have need of anything, I am only a call away."

"Thank you." I walked toward the tent flap full, exhausted, confused–then stopped and spun around. "Where are we meeting Srolo Kapir in fourteen days?"

"Ah, that. Let's discuss tomorrow. We've covered so much ground tonight."

"Where?" I persisted.

Bohak's gaze grew fearsome. "Bor'beti's betrayal–may the starpalms punish him severely–has resurrected both you and Srolo Kapir in the eyes of our enemies. I wish Srolo Kapir knew of this, but sending a message could disclose his position."

A chill ran through me.

"It doesn't change our course of action, only the timing. We will arrive before Srolo Kapir by a span of days. And once word reaches the capital, no place in Vedoa will be safe for you until your fire is perfected, except for one."

"The desert?" I whispered.

"No. My men and I are strong, but even we cannot take on the capital's long arm," Bohak went on. "And yet, the capital is the one place that can guarantee your safety. Srolo Kapir and I agreed that you must seek refuge within the palace. As a contender for the empty throne, by tradition, the council must give you protection until the winnowing battle, the day heirs fight for the crown. Srolo Kapir will arrive beforehand to ready you."

I inhaled. Exhaled. Numbness crept through my body. The suggestion was preposterous. I infused as much calm into my voice as I could. "I'm expected to take the throne?"

"A starpalm seems like the best candidate."

This was unbelievable. I wanted to pound my fists on the table, throw all his food and maps across the room, and demand reason. I hadn't trained in the Royal Academy. I could barely use the Temperance I possessed. He was much closer to being a starpalm than I was.

"But first we bring the council to justice and so satisfy the Abyss. The winter rains will be freed from their judgment, and the Rebellion will come to power. We can handle the throne later."

"What about you? This will expose your treason to the dynasty."

A faraway look came into his eyes. "A proper member of the Rebellion at last."

The suspicious part of me wondered if I were waltzing into an elaborate trap, but I discarded the thought. If he worked for the dynasty and wanted to end me, he could have done it by now. And if he spoke the truth, then he and Taval had thrown their whole lot in after me. He'd sacrificed everything. If something went wrong, there was no turning back for any of us. So if he and Srolo Kapir were ready to face the shame and danger of returning to the palace, it must be the safest place for us to go, whether I was the Reborn Star or not.

I had to play the game. Be the Reborn Star. Find Srolo Kapir.

9

AFTER EACH NIGHT OF TRAVEL, as the dawn sun climbed the sky, Bohak met me to train. I didn't mind training with him now, and I needed to be ready to meet Srolo Kapir. We practiced behind camp, away from his men's eyes, but after ten days, those not working still gathered to watch, including a soldier with a bandaged arm. The one I'd burned. Seeing him flooded me with relief—and intensified guilt.

I soon lost my self-consciousness and ignored their fascination.

Barefoot in soft, shifting sand, Bohak and I breathed deeply and performed warm-up exercises before wielding smaller and then larger shapes. His training style differed from Srolo Kapir's. We spent more time creating shapes with Wisdom and throwing and absorbing fire with Justice, Bohak's strengths. Like a miracle, he made my wielding look good.

"You must remain in physical contact with your partner, as if the two of you are one, even to the point of breathing one another's air," he kept repeating.

That sounded too intimate. I didn't want to stand arms and shoulders with him, even though our training was the business of life or death. His nearness made me feel too unlike myself.

"Here's one of the council's favorite maneuvers." Bohak spun a fiery shield in front of himself at a furious rate. "A strong wielder can hold this in one hand and brandish a weapon with the other. While the opponent is distracted, you can transform the shield into a second weapon. Like this." Bohak tossed the shield, and it morphed into a volley of arrows speeding across the desert.

I wanted to applaud but refrained.

"Try, Lady Tol."

I bit my lip and poured fire into my left palm and shaped a shield with my right.

"Your left-handedness is fascinating." Bohak's eyes flickered, and he stumbled over his words. "I mean, I've known others who–well, it's unique."

"Unique to wield with one hand?"

"I meant no offense."

I almost chuckled at his dismay. "I used to think the starpalms had punished me." Back when I blindly believed in them, before placing my last hope in the Reborn Star. "Then I decided to turn my right hand into a strength by shaping and deflecting attention, like that council trick." Holding my spinning shield in my left hand, I curved my right hand through the shape and flung a flock of fiery mangi birds that flapped after Bohak's long-extinguished arrows. I smiled to myself. I'd never attempted such large and complicated shapes, even with Srolo Kapir. Perhaps I was improving?

"Excellent." Bohak folded his arms. "Your left palm holds more fire than most wielders dream of. It reminds me of legends of ancient wielders who professed Tier 3 Magnificence, something unheard of for generations . . ."

I ignored his curious prying.

Too diplomatic to push, Bohak pulled a fresh cloth out of his pocket to dab his shining brow. "There are shapes particular to the dynasty. You should learn them."

"I'd rather eat sand than imitate the dynasty." Plus, we'd trained longer into daylight than usual, and he looked exhausted. "I want a break," I said and promptly sat down.

Bohak hesitated before sitting beside me, leaning back on his hands.

"Next time, we concentrate on combat," he said. "I am surprised Srolo Kapir hasn't focused more on that with you. Especially since he's the most powerful warrior in Vedoa, even at his advanced age. You must be prepared to attack from any distance, speed, and vantage. No more fiery staffs."

"Srolo Kapir taught me how to defend myself," I informed him.

"Indeed, but you also need to be able to end an attack." His eyes held a meaningful expression.

I remembered our battle atop the cliff, and my gaze faltered. I preferred defensive weapons. They didn't have to hurt anyone, and they were more stable than sharp, complex shapes. Yet I'd made more swords and arrows and daggers in the last few days than I had in years. My fire felt stronger and more controlled around Bohak, which struck me as odd. I'd never felt that with Srolo Kapir, and he was a master at Temperance. Srolo Kapir also valued personal responsibility, and he would never lend me an advantage.

Bohak's Justice was so strong, could he really give fire just by contact? The thought struck me. "Are you sharing Temperance with me?"

Bohak grimaced. "I hoped you wouldn't notice. Think of it as a tool until your Temperance comes."

That mysterious event only Srolo Kapir could explain. I swallowed frustration. "Then let me complete our partnership by sharing Magnificence with you."

He stilled. "Would you allow me to take some? I don't want to deplete you."

"Take as much as you want," I mumbled, then cringed at his intent look. *Please don't ask me about my Magnificence again.*

Instead, he shifted. "I wanted to be a royal Shield growing up, but the limits of my Forms dictated a different path."

His confession pierced my heart. Such a humble and shared desire. "I wanted to be a Shield too."

Bohak gave a wry smile. "It's ironic how fates turn, isn't it? But we trust the starpalms' gifts."

Speak for yourself.

"For example, along with attack, I can teach you to guard

yourself against fire stealing, even when mingling fire with another strong Justice wielder."

I stiffened. "I don't mingle fire."

"It's traditional. The council will expect this greeting, and have much more to fear from you than you from them. There will be witnesses, which makes the price of stealing too dear. In fact, I don't know of anyone strong enough to steal from you, so we can focus elsewhere for now . . ." His voice trailed.

He was strong enough. "Did the dynasty ever use you to drain enemies?"

Bohak didn't answer for a moment. "I refused. There's no dignity in it. I would only steal fire to save life." He hesitated. "Does that lend me trust?"

"Srolo Kapir trusts you, so I do too." He looked both surprised at my frankness and disappointed, as if he wanted a different answer. I moved on. "Who did you partner train with before, when you were in the capital?"

Bohak cleared his throat. "I've practiced with various partners."

He hedged. Why?

He quickly changed the subject. "Shall we practice the capital tongue?" He launched into titles, greetings, and common verbs.

After some time of this, I noticed clouds of sand rising from the horizon. I tapped his arm before pointing. Sandstorm.

We covered our noses and mouths and sought shelter between the arms of a nearby canyon. Soldiers hurried to construct my dwelling and began unrolling the carpets, arranging cushions, and lowering dividers to make my sleeping quarters. I didn't need all of that and tried to stop them but failed. After they left, I paced between platters of food and the refilled jar of water, and listened for the storm until its swirling winds hit, battering our tents like a raging battle.

My little mangi flitted around my head or huddled by its cups of seed and water, frightened. Poor little messenger of winter rains, so far from home.

After an endless night and day, filled with physical exercises and staring at my tent walls, rippling under gusts of sand, three soldiers entered, bowed, and parted to reveal Bohak, wrapped in scarves. He brushed his robes clean before uncovering his youthful face. "Lady Tol, may I meet with you?"

"Yes." I turned to set out yesterday's leftovers as a show of hospitality, but servants, also bundled against the storm, scurried in with covered platters of nuts, cut fruit, and pitchers of juice.

Soldiers took their stances around the room. Bohak lounged beside the table, straightened my errant cushions, and fidgeted with the dish arrangement. We were either becoming comfortable with each other or the storm made him restless too.

"The wind turns," I commented.

"Indeed. I think this will pass within a day." Bohak lifted a fruit and studied it. "Perhaps this storm will be a sign that strikes warning into the council's heart."

I held back a snort. Unlike us, the council stood sequestered within their lofty, stone towers. "We should train again."

"We will. But now is a perfect time to discuss entering the capital." He sighed. "I wish you spoke the capital tongue. I or Srolo Kapir, when he arrives, will need to speak on your behalf."

I hated the capital tongue, but imagining someone else speaking for me, and the council and their servants knowing I didn't understand their whispers, made me cringe. I would practice harder.

"Which gown are you planning to wear?"

"Pardon?" I said.

"May I?" Bohak rose, crossed to the trunk, and searched its shimmering contents. The mangi, perched atop the changing screen, flapped and twittered.

Was there no privacy? I supposed it was his trunk, and I kept my own belongings in the haversack, but my face heated.

"This is appropriate." Bohak lifted a silken waterfall of rich blue material and draped it over the screen. The mangi fluttered away.

"You expect me to face the capital in a rich woman's entangling skirt?"

"You can't wear travel trousers and a cloak," he informed me. "The first meeting is only diplomacy. The council will wear brocade, veils, jewelry. This blue will remind them of the drought they've brought upon themselves. Later you will wear red."

And how did he decide that? "Trousers. Sleeved tunic."

His mouth twitched. "It is unthinkable for me to appear better dressed than you."

By the starpalms, he was more capital than desert.

"One more thing." He reached into his tunic to produce a pouch, a small bowl, and a delicate paintbrush.

I stiffened as he began mixing paint. "I haven't passed my tests."

"You will. It's better for you to appear before the capital this way." Bohak tipped the powdered contents of the pouch into the bowl, rose, and stirred as he circled the table and sat facing me, knee-to-knee.

When had he added water to the bowl? Panic gripped me. This made everything feel far too real.

"Close your eyes and relax your brow."

I didn't appreciate the vulnerability, but I reluctantly obeyed, and a damp cloth brushed my forehead. Bohak's touch was gentle, and I felt him scoot closer. Why couldn't he teach me to do this myself?

The tip of the brush swirled across my skin. His breath tickled my face as he worked, stroke after stroke, until he sat back. "After it dries, the paint should last several days."

I opened my eyes.

Bohak studied his work with satisfaction before putting the bowl away. "Here's something I think you'll like." He extracted a fold of paper from his robes. Soldiers hurried to clear away the untouched food, and Bohak smoothed the map across the table. "This is the capital city."

My gaze devoured the detailed cartography. I would commit this to memory too.

"We will enter the capital loudly and publicly. This will act as a safeguard."

If I imagined that, I'd panic again, so I focused elsewhere. "Is there a palace map?"

Bohak quirked a brow. "How about a firsthand account? It's quite the labyrinth. A central stairway leads to the throne room and adjacent royal quarters."

Which led to the Immortal Abyss. Srolo Kapir taught me that. "Is it true the dynasty keeps an ancient monster below the dungeons? The Killer of Kings or something like that, for executions?"

Bohak cleared his throat. "Yes."

"What? Really? Was that how the empress died?"

"I don't know. I left the capital before she . . . passed. Let's return to where we'll be, the throne room. It's a large chamber, with a sunken arena used in ancient days to contain battles between heirs to the throne."

Was that where the Reborn Star was supposed to fight for Vedoa? "I'd rather go there." I jabbed my finger toward the southwest corner of the map, where the words *Terror Lands* sprawled over landscape decorated with hyperbolic cyclones, monsters–like the Killer of Kings–and ghosts.

Bohak allowed a small smile before sobering. "Two more things. First, I've heard rumors that the council keeps a valuable prisoner of war in the dungeon, a Laijonese soldier who was present during the battle that opened Laijon's Eternity Gate and routed the empress's forces. If he still lives and opportunity is given, I want to recapture him for the Rebellion."

That prisoner would be a wealth of information, especially if he'd seen the gate open. I hadn't seen someone from Laijon in years. I almost revealed that I spoke Laijonese, but didn't. That was a complicated tidbit to share with a fellow Vedoan.

"And the other thing?" I asked.

Bohak hesitated. "I haven't spoken to Srolo Kapir or the Rebellion about this yet, and it seems fitting to ask your counsel first."

He looked nervous. Or distressed. I leaned forward.

"Someone lives in the palace who is innocent of–indeed harmed by–the council's treachery. I would like to usher her under Taval and the Rebellion's protection before the battle begins."

"Of course, the Rebellion will support you in saving this individual, even if she was on the council." Like Bohak had been. "Who is it?"

"Princess Xanala."

"What princess?" I looked at him in bewilderment. "The empress is dead."

"This is the second child. The younger."

I blinked. "I've never heard of her."

"She would be an asset to the Rebellion. She has attained Tier 3 Wisdom, like you, and Tier 2 Temperance and"–he watched me–"Tier 3 Magnificence."

Apprehension took residence in my chest. Tier 3 Magnificence was almost unheard of, as Bohak had alluded to several times before. Such a great reserve of fire trained with Tier 3 Wisdom was an extremely powerful combination. How had I not heard of her? A wielder like that was not easily hidden, even under the shadows cast by her older sister the empress, and Princess Xanala would be the stronger sibling, no contest.

I spoke carefully. "How well do you know her?"

"We trained together at the academy." He rubbed the back of his neck. "She was my sparring partner."

So, that's who he had practiced with. He obviously felt close to her, someone who bore the literal blood of the dynasty. Why did that bother me?

"I know this might be difficult to accept," he said.

I pursed my lips, then spoke honest words, as painful as they were. "Srolo Kapir is a better judge than I am. If her hands are clean from the dynasty's misdeeds, then I'm sure the Rebellion has a place for her." A large place that she could fill with her bucketloads of fire.

"Thank you, Lady Tol." He reached to clasp my forearms.

I tensed. But he didn't touch my hands, and he looked so relieved, I grasped his forearms in return.

Bohak stood and bowed. "You will prevail."

I will prevail in my own way. The thought startled me, and I cast it aside and rose also. "May the Rebellion prevail."

He dipped his head before he and his men exited my tent and secured it against the continuing storm.

I went over to the trunk for a mirror to see Bohak's handiwork, avoiding the blue dress as if it were diseased. My heart caught, even though I'd expected the color.

Gold paint, not red, swirled across my brow. I hadn't earned it. I wanted to wipe my forehead clean. Accepting the council's forced protection couldn't be the only way. I wasn't the Reborn Star. Ami'beti and Bohak had to be mistaken. And now there was mysterious Princess Xanala. She sounded capable of challenging a starpalm's fire . . . and yet Bohak hadn't promised loyalty to her. Right?

I needed Srolo Kapir and answers. But he, like us, was headed toward the capital we aimed to overthrow.

I awoke uncomfortable. I was on my back, to preserve Bohak's paint, and the flames building inside my veins were reaching a level that was constantly uncomfortable since we'd stopped training, thanks to the sandstorm. I would need to drain soon. Suddenly, the stillness struck me.

I hurried to my feet and over to the tent flap to look out.

Dawn touched the horizon. Tossed sand coated everything. Rocky crags surrounding us stood solemn and ancient. Between their shoulders, I spied something far away, standing in front of the rising sun, draped with darkness. A grand spiraling tower.

Impossible.

I changed into my travel clothes and stole to the nearest rock base. Fitting fingers and the balls of my feet into crevices, I climbed the lowest cliff to its top and turned in a circle.

Infinite desert filled three-quarters of the vista, but northwest, there were swaths of green. Manmade rivers and oases surrounded by clusters of buildings that stretched on and on. Beyond lay a mighty stone wall, larger than the last one I'd escaped, and behind that, I discerned the castle and its primary tower. It was so close, I felt like I could touch it.

We weren't within days of reaching the capital. We'd arrived.

10

I DIDN'T WEAR THE BLUE GOWN under my traveler's robe, and I pulled the cloak's cowl over my gold Tier 3 paint, as Bohak did.

The heir of Taval ensured that our water supply was well guarded to avoid a scuffle when we reached the capital, before we mounted our horses and headed north across featureless desert. I leaned over my gelding's neck and urged a quickened gait until I lost myself in the sunrise of the second morning since the sandstorm passed. Within what felt like moments, we reached the well-trodden trade route, and desert sand faded into rural fields covered in dry, brown husks.

Homes looked looted. We circumnavigated pockets of impoverished travelers, those the Rebellion swore to help. There was more than enough water in our caravan. We could help them, but before I could shout to get Bohak's attention, the city wall rose before us, its gate open.

Bohak slowed to lead us through the gate. Horse hooves clipped against large, hewn stones paving the thoroughfare. The early heat promised that today would be a scorcher. People hurried to complete their bartering quickly and seemed less interested to watch us than those we'd encountered along the trade route. Until they noticed the quality of our horses.

More than one person exclaimed, "Watered steeds from Taval!"

Our path curved into a rowdy, crowded square. We made our way around the congestion. From my vantage atop the gelding, I saw about thirty soldiers barricading a cistern. People cried out for water and tried pushing their way to the front. Slinking thieves prowled the outskirts. But even they noticed our healthy animals and stared.

Bohak nodded to his officers, who called out in the common tongue, "Make way for Srolo Bohak of Taval!"

A murmur rippled through the crowd, and so many surrounded us our pace slowed to a crawl.

I kept close to Bohak, flinching as arms reached toward us. People wormed through our guards to grab tassels of the goat-hair blankets I sat upon and shout pleas to Bohak, one of the council, who had the ear of the dynasty. I saw the high, palace walls, but it didn't look like we would ever reach it. Fingerlength by fingerlength, we gained ground, until Bohak faced the army of scarlet-clad royal guards waiting to meet us.

My heart seized, but Bohak pulled his cowl from his forehead and demanded entry. The portcullis raised. I looked up to meet the hard, cold gazes of soldiers manning the ramparts above. Behind me, the palace soldiers shouted and forced our following throng back.

I caught up with Bohak and stared at the scene before me.

A garden of lush green trees and flowering bushes stretched across sprawling grounds. Bright sunlight radiated off the white stones of the fortress. Monstrous, carved statues of mighty sand serpents framed every corner of the palace. Iron claws, taller than a man, and terrifying maws threatened us from the corner bases, their back legs and tails coiled atop the roof to form its domes and towers. The highest tower I'd spied from camp rose as if to offer supplication to the sun.

Guards crawled the place like ants in their crimson Tier 2 paint, head coverings, and robes overlaid with silver breastplates. Each man was like a drop of blood smattering a battle site. If they themselves bled, how could anyone know? Behind the palace, I could see the even higher, brown square walls of the royal snowmelt reservoir, a national monument over a century old, and the snowcapped mountains beyond separating land from uncharted and undrinkable sea.

I thought of the people crying for water, and hatred for the dynasty built within me. I couldn't think about my true parents. I just needed to get through this and wait for Srolo Kapir. I would receive answers, and then we would act.

We dismounted, and soldiers opened the towering doors. Bohak strode to my side, blocking the view of the royal guards, and removed his traveling robe. I did the same and stood in the desert-gray, fire-retardant robe given by Ami'beti. Bohak looked confused seeing my attire, as if trying to remember packing it, and one of his officers reached to take my traveling robe and haversack. With difficulty, I surrendered both and warned him about the mangi bird nestled inside, which sent the man's eyebrows rising into his helmet.

Royal guards beckoned us forward in the capital tongue. We passed the nearest dragon-head carving, standing the height of three men, and left the blazing sun to enter the massive palace.

The palace was indeed a labyrinth. Tapestried stone corridors twisted or climbed stairs into many directions. Thick rugs silenced our bootsteps, and wall sconces spluttered with fire at every length. Finery glinted, glared, or whispered that we didn't belong here. I narrowed my gaze in return. Like an artifact, an ornate staircase of rare wood ascended to a second floor. It was a show of wealth, but the flammable material was also a failsafe if battle ever reached the palace. A good thing to remember for the Rebellion.

Bohak touched my elbow to prompt me to continue. We passed servants, untold luxury, endless hallways, and thickening ranks of soldiers. Bohak's men tightened around us until we halted at a tall door with golden knobs.

I glanced at Bohak. Enveloped in the shadows of the narrow hall, he clasped his hands behind his back in a semblance of ease, but his jaw was tight.

Samari's cool voice invaded my mind. *The palace would give a city's water ration to learn that someone like you had escaped their clutches. Justice is the rarest Form. Anyone who possesses it ends up in the military or the palace's employ.*

My stomach clenched. *Please let this not be a mistake.* And Bohak–

Palace guards reached for the gilded doorknobs, and light momentarily blinded us. I shielded my eyes.

Sunlight poured from large, arched windows. A defensive tactic, like cornering your enemy to face the sun. As if that weren't enough, tall metal torches cradled cupfuls of fire everywhere. Marble floors glittered with a rosy glow, stabbed with columns cast from ore, bristling with bare-chested Shields promising Tier 2 Magnificence, and there wasn't a scrap of tapestry or cloth. A stepped depression claimed the center of the chamber, the ceremonial arena Bohak told me about. Behind it, fire roared from two large stone bowls framing an empty throne. The throne itself was a wonder, cut from the heart of an extinguished volcano, and held the most precious color of stone, a glassy, transparent red with ribbons of iridescent gold reflecting inside. And the throne in its entirety sat within the unimaginably large skull of an extinct water dragon, its long teeth engulfing the ruler's seat. Smaller bowls of fire blazed within its empty eye sockets and wafted spiced, cloying incense.

Where was the rosy glow coming from? My eyes adjusted, and I realized the metal torches were made of glowing, crimson metal. Oractalm, I think it was called, an ancient export of Laijon's, and a material my childhood friend Seyo had wished more than once to see.

The royal council, all marked with Tier 2 paint, stood before the throne regarding us. Yellow-robed soothsayers waited in the shadowed corners with hands folded.

Bohak stood so close that we touched shoulders. I wished we were partner fighting instead. Every fiber of my being craved Srolo Kapir and the Rebellion's presence, even the battle we stirred. We all smelled it coming on the wind, yet Bohak and I were forced to beg their false pretense of protection. It dawned on me that the council counted six–Bohak had been replaced. They did not offer us a greeting but only stared at me and my gold paint.

My heart pounded. One councilman stood shorter than the rest, surely within the latter half of his third decade, perhaps older, judging by the gray in his trimmed beard. His scarred, tanned skin spoke of battles and much time outdoors, but in another country, where it was safe to do so. He and his short, belted tunic were clearly Pirthyian, which was of no small importance. How had a foreigner replaced Bohak? He carried himself as if he were a king, when he surely wasn't if he was here, and eyed me as if I'd risen from the underworld.

I looked aside and noticed the dog-like creature seated on its haunches beside him, wearing a gold collar around its thick neck.

The council's heads turned.

A delicate young woman appeared and stepped beside the throne. Long, dark hair, pulled from her face with coils of braids, showed under a sheer veil that did not obscure the gold paint adorning her brow. She wore white, with bands of rare ore decorating her arms. Her large, soulful eyes swept across our company and rested upon Bohak. She barely spared me a glance.

Princess Xanala. My outer self straightened as my inner self tightened.

Never taking her gaze off him, she lifted her palms in flickering fire. A display of welcome. Her council immediately followed, and I was amazed seeing so many blue flames. The Pirthyian had no flames to offer, but knelt on one knee.

Beside me, Bohak raised his own hands with fire. I didn't want to, but I followed suit, willing my flames to behave–I badly needed to drain–and extinguished them as soon as Bohak did.

Princess Xanala approached us. The Pirthyian stepped forward to gain her attention, but she shook her head and continued until she stood before Bohak and me.

I couldn't help but note that I was shorter, a fighting disadvantage. Her skin was so pale, she obviously never spent a moment under the sun. A scent wafted from her, mangi fruit and cinaspice.

Princess Xanala offered one hand to Bohak. He extended his opposite arm immediately, and together they cupped palms and filled each other's hands with fire. I'd seen the traditional greeting every time one guardian passed me on to another. It was a vulnerable position, but Bohak did possess superior Justice. And they'd trained together in the same class at the Royal Academy since childhood. They'd been sparring partners. They were both Tier 3s. Princess Xanala was the surviving daughter of the emperor, had perhaps attended her sister's execution, and stood whole as her country suffered from drought. Could she be trusted?

Bohak drew his hand back and inclined his head.

Tears glistened in her eyes as she looked up at him and murmured in the capital tongue. Warmth crept up Bohak's neck, and he answered something I didn't understand. I bit back irritation as Princess Xanala returned to the throne. Bohak cupped my elbow, and we followed her past the whispering council to an arched doorway hidden behind columns and bright with sunlight. We passed from the throne room onto a vast, uncovered balcony and into fresh, hot air. A short, iron railing overlooked a wall of nearby mountains. Between their heights and us, water shimmered in the huge rock reservoir below. Judging by the stain lines inside the stone rim, it was very low. An impressive, thin bridge reached from the balcony and disappeared into the mountains, just as Srolo Kapir had described to me years ago. The path to the volcanoes and the Immortal Abyss, if one could navigate the treacherous maze in between.

Princess Xanala turned to us. Her round eyes appraised me openly. Did she understand what our presence together meant? She could categorize me as a desert monster who'd bewitched her Tier 3 councilman. Then she offered me her hand.

I froze. Never. I wouldn't mingle fire with her.

She cocked her head and asked something in the capital language in a gentle tone.

I berated myself for not practicing more while we traveled.

Bohak intervened, the capital tongue pouring smoothly from his lips. But she shook her head at him and spoke again in the common tongue. "Welcome, Lady Tol. I've learned to speak your dialect for diplomatic purposes. But I've never traveled outside the capital. Isn't that humorous?"

I masked surprise at her openness and squelched impolite replies to her question. "Thank you, Princess Xanala."

"And you've never traveled to the capital, so we have much to learn from one another. Do you know the custom of mingling fire? I can teach you if you like. Bohak could as well." Xanala slid him a glance. "But from the rumors I've heard of a girl with Tier 3 capabilities emerging from the desert, perhaps I should refrain?"

Bohak cleared his throat. "Can we talk privately? The three of us?"

She inclined her head and linked arms with me as if we were friends. I would have yanked free, if not for Bohak's evident unease. She led us away from the door and council to the far side of the balcony overlooking the sprawling city. "Lady Tol, this balcony is where Vedoa's emperors and empresses greet the sun's return each dawn. But over here we have shade from the towers, and that's always been my favorite place to train with tutors."

Why was she speaking to me as if we'd met before? Had it been Bohak's favorite training spot too? Should I play along? I had a feeling she enjoyed imparting information.

"I love the mountains," she continued. "Sometimes they collect sea fog. I had no idea sea fog was so useful until befriending Bohak."

Dismay crossed his face.

What in the desert was going on?

The princess touched Bohak's arm. "You've been gone a long time. Much has happened since you left, and you don't return alone." She cast sad eyes upon me before looking up at Bohak again. "Are we still friends? Or has the Abyss stolen you from me too?"

Bohak spoke quietly. "Xanala, Laijon's triumph and the Abyss's judgment change everything."

Her pretty voice turned brittle, and her head dropped. "You think I don't know that?"

"Of course, you do. More than anyone. You also believe Vedoa has followed a wayward path, and now the starpalms call us to account. Lines are being drawn across the desert."

She pursed trembling lips. "You're abandoning me."

"Never. That's why I returned."

Bohak had slipped perfectly back into palace culture. The depth of their relationship was obvious, and her care for him appeared to go beyond friendship. I wanted to step between them, separating him from what she represented.

"Xanala." He lowered his voice to a whisper. "There is this side–our side that we know–and the other side growing in the desert. Powerful wielders add their fire to their cause. I believe they can right the wrongs we've hated since childhood."

"You're one of those powerful wielders." A single tear fell down her cheek.

"Xanala–"

"Is she everything rumors say she is?" Princess Xanala nodded toward me.

I stiffened.

"I believe so. Wholeheartedly." Fervor infused Bohak's voice, and he wiped her tear with his thumb. I felt like they were talking about me as if I wasn't here. "Srolo Kapir is alive."

Her eyes widened. "Impossible."

"He's coming now. Xanala, I can't remain here, hands bound, when I see Vedoa splintering and Taval suffering. You know I've longed to serve in greater ways than as another mouthpiece for the council."

"You do more than you think. The fog–"

"It's never enough. Especially with drought." He grasped her shoulders to look into her eyes. "Join the Rebellion with me. By my word, they will accept you. Help me restore glory to Vedoa."

I saw Bohak in a new, raw light. If I hadn't fully trusted him before, I did now. But the princess–

"Then it's true," she whispered. "You're a traitor."

Bohak grimaced. "To you and my country, no. To the council, yes."

"What of your family?"

"Safe." He expelled a tight breath. "Xanala . . ."

"The council will guess, but I will protect you. Never doubt that, Bohak. This is all overwhelming. I need time to think." She backed up and braced a hand against the palace wall.

I frowned.

Bohak's eyes widened. "Are you well?"

"Could you bring me a glass of water?" Her expression was unreadable.

Something unspoken passed between them, and Bohak swept a bow. "Of course." He turned and strode toward the throne room.

Starpalms, Bohak, don't leave me alone with her.

"Laugh with me, as if we're enjoying conversation, so they don't suspect what a muddle Bohak has created." Princess Xanala's sudden laugh tinkled like chimes.

I didn't join in.

"Lady Tol, I wish we could be friends. We share much in common, such as both being born in the palace. I suppose this is a confusing homecoming for you." She pooled fire into her right palm and began weaving threads of fire between her fingertips.

I tried not to stare. "How do you know where I was born?"

"I've heard about you for as long as I can remember. The emperor and empress did not forget threats to the throne." She pulled her fingertips apart to reveal a fiery spiderweb.

So, that was her Tier 3 Wisdom. I closed my own fists.

"But I don't see things as they did." Crafted out of a single flame, an animated spider crawled frame threads. "I think we could become allies."

My reckless side rose. "Are you joining the Rebellion, Princess Xanala?"

She laughed again. "Your desert frankness refreshes me. Forget the Rebellion for a moment. Can you imagine what we, two Tier 3 wielders, could accomplish together? And Bohak, too, if he hasn't completely lost his mind. Unless you really are the one Vedoa waits for, and Bohak hasn't fallen for a lie?"

My tongue tangled.

"Does the weight of pressure make your spine bend? Do you fear losing those who promised to support you? Do you constantly look over your shoulder fearing no one else will? Your eyes betray you. We have more in common than either of us realize, Lady Tol. I understand you." She lowered her voice. "Poor girl, you don't know if you believe their claims about you."

I made myself breathe. "You don't know me."

"And yet I can see your soul." She took a step closer to the railing. "I can assess your abilities, if you'll give me your trust. If you are a starpalm, I must also rally behind you. And after a few days, you may find that the palace feels more like home than the desert. That's far better than allowing Vedoa's two sides, as Bohak calls them, to determine that we will battle as enemies. We might be more than our spheres have determined for us."

"You speak riddles." Where was Bohak?

"How dedicated are you to the Rebellion?"

I drew a deep breath and held her gaze. "Unto death."

"I see." She gave a small smile, then flung her spiderweb toward my face.

I threw my hands up to catch the shape, but the web tangled around my fingers, forcing my palms together, and encircled my wrists like chains. Fire so hot, it burned white. I gasped with agony, unable to speak, and tried to twist my hands free from one another, but couldn't. Unable to wield.

Fear and surprise flashed across Xanala's face. "Wisdom triumphs," she whispered, and reached forward with both hands to shove me.

I staggered backwards. My knees buckled over the railing. I flailed with searing, bound hands, and plummeted over the balcony.

11

I TWISTED HELPLESSLY THROUGH blinding sunshine—and fell into arms.

Multiple men shouted curses. One sat me upright and wrapped a thick bicep around my waist. Gusts of wind buffeted us. Armor clinked. Sweat reeked. I opened my eyes to scarlet leather and silver scales, and then everything rocked and swayed.

I tensed. We rode a dragon.

A palace guard sat forward upon the serpent's nape, holding strips of leather to lead its iron muzzle. The long neck rose into an arrow-shaped head, decorated with bands of gold and jewels, and it bared curved teeth as it roared.

Pain registered again. I desperately twisted my wrists to break the fiery shackles, but couldn't. The knot was impossible. Princess Xanala's Wisdom and Magnificence were too strong.

The guard behind me tightened his arm. His comrade gave a warbling call, and the dragon dove.

My stomach lurched.

Undulating, the dragon curved around the palace. A turret and large, open mouth of stone protruded from the palace wall, too high to climb. Guards hurried to lift an iron gate, and our dragon tucked its head before rumbling to a landing inside the entrance. Men restrained the dragon's forearms in irons and dragged half a horse carcass in front of its jaws.

Still holding me tight, my captor climbed down footholds in the dragon's saddle and jumped to the ground. I landed awkwardly but shook it off, breathing in the putrid air belonging to what must be a serpent's stable. In the farthest reaches of the turret, massive iron stalls hid monstrous scuffling. I wrestled my shackles.

My soldier barked in the capital tongue and yanked me into a human-sized stone corridor. I fought. The brute cursed before swinging me over his shoulder and marching down the passage, his fellows clinking behind.

I tried to hold back a cry of pain. The corridor twisted and branched forever before ending in a gaping iron doorway, which opened to a chamber rimmed with flaming wall sconces. A stone chair dominated the center.

The soldier thrust me into the chair. A second guard enclosed my ankles with shackles, then clasped my neck with irons. I struggled as the chamber filled with guards. One frisked me for weapons. His skin glistened with a slurry of water, clay, and ground grain to deflect fire.

My wrists burned, and I tried again to break Xanala's fire. The flaming binding was so tight, I felt as though my veins would burst with my own restrained fire. Fury boiled my blood. Gritting my teeth, I glared back through the agonizing haze clouding my vision.

The Pirthyian stood in front of me wearing his short tunic, exposing muscular legs and fireless arms. He stared with startling hatred.

More scarlet guards entered the room and parted to present Princess Xanala, still in her white dress, her veil removed and hair mussed. She stopped, and her cold voice asked something in the capital tongue, ending with the name *Emeridus*.

The Pirthyian replied with sickening earnestness, his heavily accented words like blows to my ears.

Bohak. Where–physical agony seized me.

Princess Xanala clapped her hands and then gave a command.

With a rustle of saffron-colored robes, three soothsayers encircled me. The tallest and thinnest knelt. Tier 2 paint twisted across his forehead. He gripped my fingertips, avoiding my palms and Xanala's shackles, and dragged my fire from me.

I screamed. The soothsayer wrenched my gifting like a desert fox dragging a snake from its hole. Perspiration poured from his brow. He uttered a groan.

The second soothsayer took over, relieving the first, and the draining continued. And continued.

I couldn't sob. Couldn't speak. My vision blurred. The first and third soothsayers joined hands and touched the second's wrists, as if to contain my fire between the three of them.

Princess Xanala raised her voice. The third soothsayer begged something of the second. With a flurry of curses, he released me and pounded the floor with his fists.

Chest heaving, I tried to twist the fiery shackles off again. Her Magnificence was weakening, the pain lessening, but my strength was gone.

Princess Xanala stared until another of the soothsayers moaned. She snapped her gaze to him, and I struggled to piece known words together.

"How much . . . ?"

"No . . ." The soothsayer fell on his face pleading.

Xanala breathed a command, and soldiers forced the soothsayers from the chamber.

She looked at me. Her soulful eyes betrayed uncertainty. Fear. I took one small comfort from that. She had Wisdom and Magnificence, but not enough Justice to try to touch me herself. "Lady Tol."

I cringed hearing her speak my name in the common tongue.

"My soothsayers, all Tier 2s in Justice, could not finish draining you." She drew close and stooped to look me eye to eye. "Your Magnificence isn't Tier 3 after all."

I bared my teeth.

"That's why Bohak follows you like Emeridus's tracking dogs. I hardly blame him, but now he thinks you're dead, and he will return to his place. Curse the Rebellion for seducing him. And you. This cult of the Rebellion has formed your truths and lies since you were a baby, may they be exterminated like a rockwyrm's nest. My council wishes to end your life, but I will not punish you for the wrongs of others or waste what the starpalms have given you. If you knew what I did, you'd immediately turn against the Rebellion and undo them. Only you can decide how long that decision will take, from a locked guest room supplied with food and water."

"Never," I choked.

Emeridus spoke. Princess Xanala glanced at him, gave a response, and head held high, moved toward the door with half the scarlet-clad soldiers.

Emeridus bowed as she passed, then snapped something to the guards, who swiftly unlocked my iron shackles, leaving only Xanala's fiery torture around my wrists. Eyes blazing, Emeridus grabbed my upper arm and propelled me down a new corridor, opposite of the princess's direction, and her guards did not follow.

The hall twisted into darkness, but Emeridus was Pirthyian and couldn't fill his hands with illuminating flames. Only my glowing shackles provided light, and every moment took me farther from escape. The one time I struggled, he slapped me. We turned a corner to an iron door. He thrust me to the ground and pressed a boot against my back. Keys clanked, then Emeridus hauled me to my feet and pushed me through the open door. I toppled into the blind void and crashed into a wall of metal netting.

I weakly tried to run, but he seized my upper arm. Through clenched teeth, he whispered in Pirthyian and flung me forward. I landed on mesh, inside a cage, and its entire structure shook. The wire door slammed and clicked.

I gathered my last strength and pulled my hands apart, straining against blazing cords. Just a hair of space. Just enough. I siphoned Xanala's fire into my palms, unraveled her knot, and exhaled in relief as I stood free. I pivoted and without thinking blasted fire into sightlessness—but my drained Magnificence sputtered.

From a far corner of the adjacent room, Emeridus swore.

Trembling, I realized I could've killed him. Wire ceiling brushed my hair. I felt the metal mesh enclosing me. This was a wobbling cage suspended above I didn't know what, and the far end disappeared into gloom. Not a guest room. I wasn't sure if Xanala had lied to me or if the Pirthyian had disobeyed her orders.

The thought came unbidden. Did I hang over the lair of the Killer of Kings?

Emeridus tossed something into the air. A key clinked through the mesh and fell before I could catch it. And it didn't land . . . didn't land . . . didn't land . . . till it plinked far, far below.

Emeridus exited and shut the door.

12

I WAS IN A RICKETY MESH CAGE overhanging a fathomless pit.

I sank to my knees against the door, and the cage wobbled under me. Silence reigned, except for tiny sounds emanating from far away. My eyes refused to adjust. I wondered if I could melt my bars, once my gifting strengthened. Would I plunge to my death to whatever lay below?

I dropped my head into my hands. I'd known coming here would be a mistake. Hadn't I sensed the trap closing all around me? I reminded myself that I was part of the Rebellion, dedicated to rescuing Vedoa, and trained by one of the greatest wielders in our history, Srolo Kapir. My life and freedom could not end here! I almost called on the names of the starpalms, even the Reborn Star, but bit my tongue. If they didn't answer, I had nothing else to turn to. And they wouldn't answer. They never did. Numbness swept through me, but I breathed through my teeth and willed myself to stay strong. There had to be a way.

An otherly breath exhaled through my mind. I tensed, and then I heard my native tongue.

"I am with you."

My inner world tilted, and my heart began to pound.

Again, the voice, as if speaking outside time and space, blew like wind through my mind. *"You are mine."*

The power of the voice emboldened my courage, restored my fight. It couldn't be, yet my heart knew the truth. A starpalm spoke to me. I swallowed and dared to respond. *Please free me from this cage!*

It did not answer.

I moistened my lips. *Please–*

Someone murmured outside my thoughts, fairly close. A human voice.

I crouched and filled my hand with weakened fire. "Who are you?"

The cage bounced as a dim form shifted at its end. Long legs stretched toward me, and arms crossed over a hunched chest. A lanky young man grumbled to himself while eyeing me. "So, they want two of us dead, eh?"

I blinked. How in the desert had I not sensed his presence? Had he watched me this whole time? And I understood his language, but it wasn't any dialect belonging to Vedoa. He spoke Laijonese.

This was the prisoner of war Bohak told me about. The one who had seen the Eternity Gate open. It was the only reason he still lived.

His voice hardened. "Or maybe they sent you to kill me."

I extinguished my fire. A small pleasure curled inside me as words in his language rolled decently well off my tongue, despite the years gone by. "If they wanted someone as valuable as you dead, you'd have an audience."

"How comforting–" He spluttered. "You speak Laijonese?"

Something scrabbled atop the mesh above our heads.

He ducked, and so did I. I peered through blindness before filling my hand with flickering flame.

The movement halted. Through the mesh roof, intense, gleaming eyes stared. A wild mohawk crowned the creature's head. Large wings dripped from its spine. Claws gripped the lock to a secondary cage access on the opposite side of the one Emeridus had flung me through. It struggled to insert the key into the lock.

A Shadow. Like the one at Samari's execution. Howling and beating wings rose from the depths of the cavern.

I gasped and snuffed my fire.

"Keep wielding! They hate illumination." Laijon-boy filled his hands with light–his national gifting–and shone it in the Shadow's face.

The creature snarled and flung itself backward off the cage to flap in the air.

Laijon-boy crowed and punched his fist skyward. He'd snatched the key!

Three Shadows landed on the cage and clawed through the mesh. I'd almost prefer the mysterious Killer of Kings.

"Stay low." Laijon-boy nudged me down next to him, his gangly legs bent almost to his shoulders. The cage rocked. "We're secured to a ledge. Barely," he added.

I looked down at the plunging cavern below us. Increased squeals echoed. Claws swiped from above, ruffling my hair. One shouted in a garbled language I couldn't understand, a human turned monster.

Another Shadow answered, then another shrieked. A brawling mass tumbled across the top of the cage and fell off as more reached toward us, stirring the air, hissing and grunting. Piling on top of us until the cage creaked. Seven of them at least.

"Come on." I urged Laijon-boy to the door, helped reach up and feel for the lock, and he jammed the key inside the hole. But the lock wouldn't turn.

"*Qo'tah*." He swiped a hand down his face. "My life constantly hangs in the balance of a key!"

"Emeridus threw the key to the opposite opening," I said, pressing my back against the door to the tunnels, watching Shadows strain for us through the mesh.

The young man collapsed beside me and tossed weak light that sent the Shadows scattering. "I can scare one or two away for a while, until my light fades. This many . . ."

"Could tear the cage free." I finished. "I think I can melt our attachment to the ledge. Beat them to the task."

"No! If we fall, we die."

"I'll jump before becoming Shadow food."

"They don't eat–"

"Wait." I felt the door. "The cage is attached to the door. If they pull hard enough, and we move fast enough . . ." We stared at each other.

Laijon-boy nodded before taking a breath and hollering at the top of his lungs. I joined him.

Shadows screamed in return and congregated on the roof. Knitting their claws into the wire and tugging. The cage rattled and groaned, throwing the two of us off balance. Monsters shrieked as latecomers fought to join in. The far two corners of the cage ground free. The door to the tunnels snapped open.

"You first," Laijon-boy shouted, and propelled me toward the opening.

I wiggled my upper body through. Above, a Shadow got half of its torso inside the breaking cage and swiped for our legs.

Laijon-boy shoved me hard and shimmied after me. We gained our feet and hurtled into the lightless, stone corridors. Weariness from Xanala's draining nagged me, but behind, the cage groaned and Shadows screamed.

"Let's go." I grabbed his arm and turned him down a hall.

"Where?"

"Outside. Before they get through." I dove around the corner and followed the endless passage. It twisted and turned until pale light pooled ahead. Then the stench hit.

Laijon-boy huffed as he jogged. "Mysteries of the continent, I'm out of shape. Where are we?"

There weren't dragons in Laijon. Thankfully, I was a competent rider when not bound by flaming chains. "There's one way out," was all I said as we ran through a doorway into the massive, reeking chamber. The iron gate remained lifted above the exit.

He gaped as his eyes went from the huge irons lying along the floor, to the open portal breathing dawn's glow and fresh air, to the towering stables.

I touched his shoulder, and he startled. "The first one."

"What's in there?"

"Come on." I ran to the massive stall gate, and to his credit, he followed. Metal ladders welded into the wall gave access to the bars closing each stall. I climbed up and pushed at the bar until it swung down with a clang. "Hurry."

Laijon-boy clamored after me, eyes wide. I jumped onto the walkway built into the stall and edged across, feeling him close behind and hearing his gasp when he saw what lay below.

The dragon's scaled back rose and fell with breath. A coiled neck draped across the ground, but its eyes watched us. Still saddled, perhaps it was the one that had carried me to this awful place. The creature wasn't chained.

"See? It's muzzled," I said, and took a leap from the walkway onto its back. The dragon stirred, and I gestured for Laijon-boy to join me, before I dragged him down here.

Pale as death, he jumped and landed with a grunt behind me.

I held the muzzle reins loosely and gave a shrill cry, hoping Vedoa's dragon commands proved universal. The beast lifted its head and uncurled one clawed leg and then another to slowly stand, sending the two of us rocking. I started to slip down, but Laijon-boy pulled me upright. He wrapped his arms around my waist, and wriggled his feet on top of mine in the toe holds. "Pardon–"

"Thanks, and hold on," I interrupted as the serpent pushed the swinging stable door open and lumbered into the empty space facing the exit.

Guards rushed into the chamber and gawked.

I gripped the reins and cried out a second command. *Fly.*

The dragon rumbled in its throat and snaked toward the opening, stretching its wings. Guards yelled and tried to stop us, but who can halt a dragon? Bellowing, the serpent beat its wings and plunged from the turret into golden sunshine.

My heart lurched, and my eyes watered. With a powerful downward thrust, the dragon veered upward, and we soared around the palace walls.

"What is it doing?" my companion shouted in my ear.

"Don't worry," I called back. "I had a guardian who trained

dragons." What an ornery brute–the man, not his reptilian livestock. Always wearing his dragon whistle around his neck and demanding I muck the stalls. At least it had made dragons familiar to me. I pulled the reins, and the dragon curved toward the palace grounds.

"You're going the wrong way."

"My friend is here." I aimed the dragon closer to the ground.

Where are you, Bohak?

We blew past servants and soldiers who bellowed and notched bows and arrows, but their fire was too slow and useless against the dragon's scales. Then the attack stopped, and guards swiveled their attention to the swarm of escaping Shadows which–starpalms be praised–veered in the opposite direction, toward the mountains.

The dragon rose, evading the attacks, and cut around another tower and a large balcony with a bridge arching into the jagged rock peaks. From the balcony, a pretty young woman in a flowing, white dress, surrounded by the council, stared up at us. In the opposite direction, dust rose. Bohak and his men were fleeing the capital city, funneling through twisting streets, just ahead of an army of scarlet-clad soldiers. All under Xanala and the council's careful eye.

I made eye contact with Xanala–savoring her terror–and something shifted inside of me. I filled my palms with fire and raised them high.

"Stop! They'll roast us to crisps." Laijon-boy seized the reins and directed us toward the desert. The dragon bellowed again and turned sharply.

I almost lost my seat and extinguished my fire. Starpalms, what was I thinking? I took back the reins. "No. This way. We need to follow that army."

"What–"

"Just trust me."

We soared over city, eliciting screams and shouts from everyone who saw us. The dragon's shadow passed over Xanala's troops just before we swooped over the city wall and closed in on Taval and their horses. Charcoal desert stretched in waves before us, and crags twisted in the distance.

Laijon-boy pointed past my shoulder. "Your friend?"

"Yes." I led the dragon down.

Bohak, in his swirling scarlet cape, turned to take a last stand.

I bit my lip in frustration. He couldn't recognize me from this distance. He thought I was part of Xanala's forces. I urged the dragon lower. It didn't comply–dragons rarely did–so I opened my left hand to wield a replica of Bohak's firehawk and sent it zipping into the desert. I blinked in surprise at my wielding success, without borrowing Temperance, before passing Taval overhead. Bohak's victorious cry rose as he turned his men to chase after us. Xanala's army may be strong, but they didn't ride Taval's horses. Within moments, the palace soldiers melted into sunrise behind us, and desert stretched ahead.

Joy soared in my chest, and the dragon rose on its own accord.

The Laijonese prisoner groaned. "I'm getting sick."

"We're free! Stop complaining–"

I broke off as the dragon suddenly dove to skim the face of a monstrous dune.

My breath caught. It would throw us–I grabbed Laijon-boy's hand and hurled us off the flying serpent's back. We plummeted before crashing and rolling across desert swells. I covered my head as rushing wind showered sand into my face. The dragon pivoted around us, its wings brushing the ground, before flying back toward the capital. Desert quiet fell. Well-trained dragon, indeed.

Laijon-boy pushed himself out of the dark sand and spat. He rubbed grit from his eyes as he made a myriad of awkward faces and murmured fragmented sentences too quickly for me to decipher.

I rolled onto my back. We'd made it. Survived. Escaped Xanala. Put distance between her army and ours. And I'd nabbed the Laijonese soldier.

Laijon-boy drew a haggard breath. "Are you crazy?"

"I didn't tell it dive." I sat up and faced him. My jaw fell.

Hunger lined his angular features. Wild, dark curls framed

his face, suggesting an outgrown soldier's cut, and his skin—the portions that weren't bruised or scraped from chains—was almost as bronze as mine. He bore Laijon's characteristic height and elegance, but I recognized those downturned eyes. Though nearly ten years were lost between us, he wore the face of my childhood friend. "Roji?" I whispered.

He stiffened as if beholding a sudden vision. "Tol?"

I studied his haunted expression and glanced at his bruising again. Xanala did this to him. Starpalms, I would wield a flood of fire that would burn all the way to the capital. I would—

Roji's eyes widened. I became aware that I held fire in my hands, and closed my fists. "Sorry—"

But Roji took my hands. I started to tug my hands free but stopped. He didn't wield fire. I couldn't harm him.

Roji pulled me to my feet, continuing to study me in wonder. "Tol? Of all the people on the continent."

"Starpalms, Roji," I breathed. "You're the dynasty's prisoner of war?"

His lips thinned a moment before he wrapped his arms around me and hugged me tight.

13

ROJI WAS HERE. IN VEDOA. He was the Laijonese soldier imprisoned inside the palace. And he was smothering me, but I didn't care. A sliver of safety and joy, lost for years, was given back to me.

"Mysteries of the continents, Tol. Finding you is like fighting a sea tempest and reaching an island."

I would have chuckled at the Laijonese-specific word picture if I had the breath.

"I'm almost afraid you're a dream, or another awful mirage, and I'll wake up in that cage."

"No one will put you back in a cage." The hug was becoming awkward. I gently eased myself free.

"*Qo'tah*, Tol. I have so many questions, they're making my head spin. Why were you imprisoned? Why is there a gold smudge on your forehead? I feel like we could spend the rest of our lives catching up." His expression changed. "If only Seyo could see you."

Neither of us really wished her presence here, and the hollowness in his voice alarmed me. He trembled and looked ill. We needed to reach shade, Bohak, and water. More than that, we had to find Srolo Kapir. "Roji."

His gaze went to mine, as if I were a lifeline. To him I was.

"We need to reunite with my friend."

Roji's mouth twisted. "Won't they string me, a Laijonese, up to hang under the sun?"

He wasn't far from the truth, and I swallowed unease. "Not on my watch. Come on." I grabbed his hand and pulled him in Bohak's direction.

"Tol, you know I'm far from welcome here."

"They have water. There's nowhere else to go. I won't let them harm you."

He sighed. "Should I speak Vedoan?"

Truthfully, Roji and his sister were half Vedoan, but that only worsened his case. "Even Seyo, as skilled in language as she is, couldn't fool anyone into thinking she's native. You don't walk like you grew up on the desert. You sweat more, and your clothes are a dead giveaway . . . well, maybe not since they're ruined." I couldn't believe they'd never given him a change of clothes in months, but that was Vedoa's way toward Laijon. I'd get him clean, new garments immediately.

Roji's strides were long, but he breathed heavily and favored one leg.

I stopped. "You're injured."

"It's an old wound. A Pirthyian doctor healed me, but Vedoa's dungeons haven't helped."

He thought a Pirthyian had healed him? Was he suffering from heat distress?

He shot me a glance. "I won't go back to a dungeon, Tol. I'll fight to the death first."

"I promise to keep you safe. And you're valuable to my friends. They want to talk to you."

"Why?"

I rolled my eyes. "Be serious, Roji."

"Don't mock me. What do I have to share with a Vedoan? Descriptions of the color green or what rain feels like?"

The reminder of our drought made my stomach tighten. "We want an account of the war."

"Ask your soldiers," he said.

They weren't mine. As far as Vedoa's loss went, I felt divided, but I couldn't tell anyone that. "The dynasty is killing soldiers who return." Like Samari, almost.

"Of all the cruelty . . . incomprehensible waste. This goes beyond . . . does Vedoa have neither scruples nor honor?" He muttered something further under his breath.

I was starting to get annoyed with him–and my own country. "The dynasty doesn't tolerate defeat."

Roji halted. "Say that again."

"Say what?"

He grasped my shoulders so tight it hurt. "Say that Vedoa doesn't tolerate defeat."

"Let go–" But I stilled. He didn't know? How was that possible? I enunciated each word. "Laijon defeated Vedoa."

"I don't believe you. What of Pirthyia?"

"Routed and retreated." And so Princess Xanala inherited Emeridus.

"Impossible." He released me to thrust long fingers through his filthy hair until he looked properly mad. "How could we win?"

"Rumors say that the Eternity Gate opened, and it enabled Laijon to win the war." I swallowed hard. "You don't know that either?"

He gave a short head shake.

Implications of his ignorance bombarded me. Why had the council kept him? What purpose would Bohak find in him now if he hadn't seen the gate? "How do you not know any of this?"

"I was fighting above ground."

"Who was below ground? At the Eternity Gate?"

"I don't know!" he insisted. "We were battling a vicious knot of Pirthyians when something like wind swept through our battlefield. A heavenly messenger of the Father of Light appeared, and Pirthyia ran away. I thought the Messenger was helping me, but instead, he pushed me into a fleeing Vedoan camp." His eyes fell. "They took me."

I didn't understand half of the horrible situation he described. Why had the dynasty kept him alive? I couldn't picture what use Bohak would find in him now.

"So Laijon won," Roji repeated, as if afraid to believe it. "Seyo had the key to the Eternity Gate. If you're telling me the truth, then she–and my country–survives. I still have purpose."

I barely listened as I imagined dragging him into camp without good reason, like tossing one of the 'betis' goats into a nest of fledgling dragons. How many soldiers had Taval lost to the war? How hot did their hatred against Laijon burn? I needed to protect him.

"Tol, why did your country imprison you?"

His question brought me back to the present. "I . . ." How much should I tell him? That two of Vedoa's most powerful wielders thought I was a starpalm, or that I was supposed to battle the council and princess with divine fire I didn't possess? *Keep it simple.* "I'm going to overthrow the throne." I stopped, taken aback at my own boldness. Was it true? Yes, it was. Whatever it took.

Roji cocked his head and raised an eyebrow. An expression I remembered well from childhood, one he always used after catching Seyo and me involved in some shenanigan or another, usually spearheaded by me, although Seyo had her moments. "Tol, you haven't changed at all."

I opened my mouth at this, but thundering hoofbeats neared. Mirroring my now pounding heart. Plumes of sand and dust rose as Taval rode toward us.

"If only I wasn't unarmed." Roji took a step backward. "How much do you trust this friend?"

"Completely." Because I trusted Srolo Kapir. "But don't speak. Keep your head down."

The Tavalkians neared, their horses stamping and snorting as they slowed, flanks glistening with effort. Bohak, commanding and distressed, leapt off his ride and brushed his cape behind him.

I needed to talk with Bohak privately and convince him to offer Roji protection. We would reunite with Srolo Kapir, somehow. I would tell him that I met a starpalm . . . had I truly spoken with one? What else could it be? But I didn't have four Forms, so I didn't understand why a starpalm would reveal itself to me. An uncomfortable feeling wriggled in my stomach.

Bohak strode forward to meet me. But before I could speak, he knelt and grasped my forearms.

"What in the desert? Bohak–"

"Forgive me, Lady Tol."

Stand up, I wanted to beg. Instead, I looked awkwardly around at his watching men, and then to Roji, who was studying Bohak with a cold, calculating look, his hand fingering where his sword hilt used to lie. Of course, the hatred between our countries was mutual. He'd better calm down–

"I failed you." Bohak lowered his head.

I drew my attention back to him. My capture, even though the vile Xanala tricked us, undermined his protection and dishonored him. In some Vedoan echelons, exile would be demanded. Or worse, unless someone with greater authority covered his shame.

Memories flashed through my mind. I saw myself also sitting on my knees in sand years ago. A powerful Tier 2 wielder had traveled to assess Srolo Kapir's students, including me, and I had failed level advancement for the third time. Srolo Kapir needed no better reason to send me away. Others were dismissed after failing once. But my guardian had knelt before me, murmured something I couldn't forget, and helped me stand.

I dropped to my knees in front of Bohak, joining him in his humiliation, and he lifted his head in surprise. Drawing a breath, I whispered Srolo Kapir's words. "Battles are won by those who persevere. So, get up." Then I stood and brought him to his feet.

A moment passed between us before he bowed and released my arms. His gaze remained haunted.

I moistened dry lips and willed us to return to normal. "What's our plan?"

Bohak straightened. "Camp and a meeting."

Camp already? I looked up to arched rock formations blocking the sun's harsh midday heat.

Bohak hesitated before offering me his arm. I took it, then gestured for Roji to follow. His expression was strained. If he could have wielded fire, I feared that he would have burned the place down. At least Bohak, who walked through a mental fog, hadn't noticed him. Yet.

We passed through a natural split in the rock. I stepped across streams of sand and parting shadows, and Bohak released me to pass first through enclosing shoulders of rock. A sweeping valley view captured my gaze. Bohak's men settled their caravan into place and began to unpack, but only essentials. A near departure was imminent. We would likely rest for an hour or two before fleeing again, and only because the horses must rest.

Guards hurrying to set up Bohak's tent opened the flaps for our approach. We entered, with Roji still following, and it was strange seeing the space so bare and disorganized, with trunks littered here and there. Bohak raised his hand to send the men out before searching for a cushion, placing it near the table, and bidding me to sit. I did so, and he settled himself on the sand, his elbows on the tabletop.

I looked like a disaster, but he wasn't a prize, either. Bohak still wore his finery from the palace, as I wore the gray garment Ami'beti had given me, but his robes were travel-stained and torn, his face coated in sweat and sand from our flight. Roji had melted into the corner and alternated between watching me and the door. He would understand our conversation, so I might as well get it over with. "Bohak, I found–"

"I saw you fall off the balcony," he interrupted. "When she said you'd died, I suspected a trick and didn't believe her. I was going to gather the Rebellion and return." Bohak's jaw tensed. "Did she harm you?"

"I'm fine. We just need to put desert between her and us."

"Her army is strong."

"But do they have Tier 3 Justice? No." Thank goodness, because her Tier 2 soothsayers had done enough damage. "Starpalms–" Ami'beti's rebuke jumped to mind. After meeting a real starpalm, I probably shouldn't say that anymore. I bit my tongue. "We need to find Srolo Kapir. I can't do that alone. I need you."

He stilled. "Lady Tol–"

"*Please*, just call me Tol."

"But you're–"

"Are we not allies and friends?" I raised an eyebrow.

He studied me, and my stomach tightened. Why did he look at me that way?

But Bohak inclined his head. "Tol, I'm honored by your trust, and I am nothing if not at your command."

At my command, because I was supposed to be a starpalm. I repressed a sigh. At least he was starting to look alert again. I would take that for now. "Then let's figure out how to find Srolo Kapir. He still travels toward the palace." My eyes widened.

"He'll listen at the markets for news," Bohak assured me. "He'll hear of your escape before he enters the capital walls and will change course."

He was right. I breathed relief. "But now how will we find him?"

Suddenly, Bohak vaulted to his feet and pointed. "You! Who are you and what are you doing here?"

He'd finally spied Roji. "He's with me." I jumped to my feet also.

Roji had taken a defensive stance, having no idea who he was dealing with.

Bohak kept his hands open, but his face was darkening.

"Bohak, please meet Roji, the Laijonese prisoner of war," I said quickly and held my breath.

Bohak's expression twisted, and his eyes flashed. "Then thank the starpalms, you've survived this enemy too." He pulled one hand back and flung fire over my head.

I tried to snatch his flames out of the air but missed. Roji ducked. Flaming cords caught his ankles and one flailing wrist. With a cry, Roji lost his balance and crumpled to the ground.

"Stop!" I demanded as I stepped between them.

"He's dangerous," Bohak growled.

"He's under my protection." I snatched the fiery binding off Roji's limbs–Xanala's cords had been so much stronger and more complicated–and hurled the fire back.

Bohak caught the flames, eyes narrowed. "He's from Laijon."

I glared at him. "By the–desert–I expected more diplomacy from you."

"Have you forgotten what Laijon is? What they've done? You should thank the starpalms that he didn't attempt to murder you or trap you with a spell." Bohak scrutinized me as if looking for signs of incantation.

Roji huffed and began to speak.

"No." I held up my hand, silencing him. "If we're going to reunite with Srolo Kapir and take down the dynasty, we need to trust each other. And perhaps you should know that my first guardian took me to Laijon for safekeeping."

Bohak sputtered. "That's preposterous."

"I grew up among Laijonese. I speak their language." I really didn't intend to share this much, but there was no retreat now. "Every nation has good and bad people, and every person deserves respect. He helped me escape the palace." Plus, I grew up in Roji's home, but discernment stopped me from revealing that tidbit.

Bohak's gaze slid from me to Roji. "Does he speak Vedoan?"

Roji did speak, and his words dripped with sarcasm. Bohak's brow lifted, and so did mine. I'd forgotten that he and Seyo had learned the high tongue from what they could read in books, not the common language I knew. I understood little of what he said.

Roji repeated himself, then spoke in Laijonese. "Am I saying it wrong?"

Bohak cocked his head at me, still speaking the common tongue for my benefit. He seemed somewhat bemused. "He wants to know what gives me the right to shoot fire at him."

By the desert. What were we going to do about this language barrier?

Bohak went on. "I'm going to ask him about the Eternity Gate so we can release him into the desert–free as you wish–with my blessing." He switched to the high tongue.

Roji laughed and spat a response.

Bohak looked to me. "He didn't see it?"

Someone, help me! I switched to the Laijonese tongue. "Roji, we need to convince him that you're useful, or this will be beyond difficult."

"Why? He bowed to you. I thought he was your servant."

Bohak frowned. "You speak their language better than the high tongue."

"Tell Srolo Pompous"–Roji spread his hands–"that I flew a dragon. That's useful."

"You flew for two breaths. He probably owned dragons growing up."

Roji tsked. "Poor man. No wonder he's so irritable. Fine. Tell him I'm an encyclopedia about Shadows. How to defend yourself from attack, fight them, talk to those who retain some humanity–"

I turned to Bohak. "He knows a lot about Shadows."

Bohak passed a hand over his face. "What an abomination to discuss. We must show extreme caution . . ."

Roji tapped my shoulder, which thankfully Bohak didn't see. "What about an evil pool?"

"What pool?"

"Your empress had her guards drag me across a bridge into the mountains. We passed monstrous statues and mine shafts until climbing into a deep, dark hole with a pool at the bottom."

I froze. The path to the Immortal Abyss was shrouded in legend, said to be a maze of shifting trails filled with blinding darkness, falling rocks, and bursts of fire from the underworld. A ruler would invite an opponent to descend to its depths and fight in the invisible presence of the starpalms. Whoever failed would be offered as a sacrifice to the Abyss, and whoever prevailed would dip their hands in the pool to strengthen their fire and return to Vedoa stronger than before. This was the key to the dynasty's endless reign. The empress must have intended Roji as a cheap sacrifice, yet here he was, alive.

"There was a gold doorway under the water," Roji continued, voice not as firm as it had been. "And there's a golden aura surrounding the place. When the empress touched the aura, it killed her instantly, and a mighty breath blew through the cavern. We all ran away, but then they put me back in that cage."

Bohak looked ready to explode. "What is he saying?"

The unbelievable words tasted like something rotten on my tongue. "He says he saw the empress die trying to open the Immortal Abyss. With her death, the drought began."

14

BOHAK REGARDED ROJI. "THE EMPRESS tried to access the Abyss? Why should we believe him?"

I drove the implications of her fate from my mind. For now. "She was desperate, and why would he lie? This means Roji knows the way to the Abyss. Even Srolo Kapir hasn't seen the chamber. What's more useful than that?"

Bohak wavered. He was my protector, not my guardian or emperor, but I needed to convince him to keep Roji. If he did, his men would cooperate, and abandoning Roji to the desert was unthinkable.

A crazy idea popped into my mind. "I saved him from certain death, and he owes me a life debt."

Bohak huffed. "So, you want to keep him as a servant? To do what?"

"Ah . . . to guard my tent."

"I've given you guards."

"Such debts are sacred in Laijon." I plowed on. "He would give his life for me. That's not something to treat lightly."

Bohak's jaw tightened. "Many offer their lives to you."

I resisted squirming at the layers of meaning in his words. "He'll be a first line of defense." Except that wasn't necessary with my fire. "He needs a uniform, food, water, quarters, and a weapon."

Bohak's eyes remained locked on mine. "Will loyalty to you keep him from stabbing us in our sleep?"

He was buying the story. "Their god demands it." Didn't it? I remembered Seyo telling me rules of divine justice, mercy, and honor.

"One knife. I suppose someone who only holds light may ask for so much. But he cannot remain free at night. Between you and me, we could erect a fiery barricade."

I bit my lip. "Are you that afraid of him?"

Bohak stared me down, frustration etching his face. "Very well. Rope it is. For his knowledge of the Abyss and his life debt to you, he may stay."

My initial triumph quickly turned to indignation. *Bound by rope, really? I don't think so, King of the Desert,* I wanted to grumble. Roji remained tense behind me, but kept his mouth shut, thank the starpalms. I waved him into the corner. I'd explain everything to him later.

Bohak gestured that I sit again and resumed his place across the table to spread maps between us. "On to our largest problem. How far can we run from the council?"

I sat, turned a map to face me, and refocused.

Bohak drummed the table. "I thought her mind would be clearer. I thought she would trust me."

Who? Of course. Lovely, innocent Xanala proved her dynastic loyalties. I rolled my tight shoulders back and pointed at the map. "We need to reach Srolo Kapir."

"Your safety is first priority. Is there an unlucky village?"

"A what?"

"Or anywhere considered ill-fated?" Bohak asked. "Xanala holds to folk superstitions. Staying in an unlucky village could give us an advantage."

I'd rejected such beliefs when I saw Srolo Kapir defying them unharmed, but we were a rarity. I was relieved Bohak didn't hold to superstitions like most of Vedoa. "I can't think of one."

"Then a small village–"

"No," I said firmly. "I won't endanger them."

"And the price on your head would tempt the most loyal during a drought." His brow furrowed. "We can only trust the Rebellion, and they are scattered across Vedoa and won't gather until Srolo Kapir sends his word. Spies are everywhere."

Thank goodness, Roji wasn't understanding any of this. "So, we play cat and mouse in the desert and wait for Srolo Kapir."

"Our supplies won't last."

"How much water do we carry?"

He glanced at me. "Don't worry about that."

"Water is paramount." I eyed him. "How wealthy is Taval?"

"Very," Bohak replied. "I would flee to Nazak, but the council will close the border and separate you from the Rebellion. This shouldn't be happening. The Reborn Star should not flee like prey. But waiting for Srolo Kapir here is too dangerous."

"We need him," I insisted.

His expression faltered. "I don't know how else to protect you."

I massaged my brow. How long and far could we run? Srolo Kapir was ultimately more valuable than I was. What if we didn't find him? What if Xanala caught him? The title Reborn Star hung like a noose around my neck. Paralyzing me. Because of it, Srolo Kapir emerged from hiding–

But a starpalm had spoken to me, even though my Temperance was incomplete. The starpalms had never helped me before. Something had changed.

I whispered the Reborn Star's prophecy. "A starpalm will walk the desert in human form. From an endless well, her fire will cleanse the monster's lair, kindle life within dead bones, and fill the depths of the world. She, the one born of legend, will slay her own soul to finish the age." I spoke aloud. "Monsters live in the Terror Lands. It's the ultimate unlucky place."

Bohak steepled his hands. "We studied the Terror Lands at Academy. It is the door to the underworld. Cursed with storms and haunted by ghosts. I won't put you in such danger."

"See? It's supremely unlucky."

"No one returns from crossing the gorge."

"Even the Reborn Star?" I pressed on. "In the palace dungeon–"

"Xanala put you in the dungeon?"

"Yes," I said, refusing to sympathize with the dismay in his gaze. "And before I escaped, a starpalm spoke to me."

One could have heard a snake gliding across Bohak's rugs, he sat so still. "Describe this."

I had to think. "It was like . . . a quiet voice inside my head. It gave me courage. It said that I belonged to it." Shivers raced across my skin. I pulled my sleeves down to my wrists, like that marked stranger had done in my dreams. I'd almost forgotten about that, and returned my thoughts to the starpalm. Why was the encounter so hard to describe? It was vividly real, but sounded flat coming from my lips. "I asked for help, and we escaped," I finished lamely.

"Which starpalm?"

"It didn't name itself."

"But it spoke to you. It recognized you, even now." Bohak leaned across the table. "Lady Tol, this is incredible. A gift. My worry vanishes listening to you. If one starpalm rallies behind you, more will come."

"Bohak, the Reborn Star's prophecy says she will enter the Terror Lands." Well, it said she would defeat monsters, but we'd handle that later. "If a starpalm is on our side, who can stop us? We could claim the Terror Lands as a stronghold for the Rebellion. For Srolo Kapir's return."

Bohak nodded decisively. "May the council wring their hands and dread your ascent to glory."

Including Xanala.

"We must rest and prepare to leave at sundown." We both stood. A shadow crossed his face. "Convincing the men will be difficult. Let's train before sundown and let them see your fire again." His eyes rested on Roji. "Explaining him to the men will be almost impossible. He doesn't deserve your kindness."

"You didn't fight in the war, not with your position on the council. We need to let go of the past and face the bigger picture happening now," I snapped, ignoring that he may have wanted to join the battle. "Can you lay down your prejudice?"

Anger filled his gaze. I expected that–and another fight–but not the accompanying depth of pain. "I'm not my father's only son."

But he was heir. The implication hit me. He had other brothers who had fought in the war. Who hadn't returned, or couldn't.

Bohak dipped his head. "I don't want you to be misguided. Please exercise deep caution and know that I watch over you as well, as if your life were my own."

15

SWIRLING REDS AND ORANGES, offset by the burning orb of the sun, cast sharp, ebony shadows across the arched rock formations looming over us. By now, Xanala's army would have unfurled and drawn closer like a net, cutting us off from east and west. Resting was difficult, but imperative.

Before I slept, Tavalkian soldiers returned my haversack, including the little mangi, safe inside. One of the men had heard its chirping and kept it fed and watered, for which I thanked him profusely, embarrassing him. As soon as I awoke, I gathered my belongings, including the robe from Ami'beti, brushed clean from the palace, and rushed to Roji's nearby tiny tent to have him walk with me. The morning before, when Bohak had supplied rope to restrain Roji, I'd accepted the binding with a fake smile and instead stuffed it into my haversack. Few words passed between Roji and me now as we prepared to depart, Roji staying close and always glancing backward.

Packing camp commenced. Bohak and I passed one another, and he clasped my forearms with a penetrating look. We didn't speak, but I understood his question. Had I thought of a different path? No. Had he? No. Bohak inclined his head, and we parted ways to prepare our horses.

Soon, Taval was mounted. Whatever speech Bohak had given his men had worked, for none balked or bolted when we turned south, though tension gripped the atmosphere.

Only a sliver of glowing sun peeked over the western horizon when we reached the gorge. Cantering to the rim made me uneasy. A stone bridge once arched the divide. Now, its remains lay crumbled on the Vedoan side. A border that warned of no return.

On my left, Roji leaned over his horse for a better look. It was a miracle he hadn't been forced to run alongside us, and the men's expressions made it clear that they disliked seeing a Laijonese riding one of their horses, strong desert horses worth the water they drank, but efficiency won the day. They clearly despised him, but tolerated his service to me. He remained tense and tight-lipped, surrounded by Taval, but inclined his head toward a slope suitable for the horses' descent.

Bohak remained on my right. "Ancient stories whisper that, when the continent was new, a heavenly dragon lay down to sleep, carving this serpentine canyon dividing the Terror Lands from Vedoa. That when she awoke, she chose the Terror Lands for her dwelling, and all creatures possessing the land are her spawn."

"And mountain snowmelt used to flow across the land here, before the dynasty built the reservoir and channeled it to their tables and baths," I added.

"Anything could lie in the darkness beyond."

"Once we cross, we disappear." I dismounted and led my horse toward the natural downward trail. Bohak, Roji, and the Tavalkians followed.

We plunged into the gorge. At the bottom, a dry, stony riverbed, where Vedoa's lifeblood once roared, crunched underfoot. We searched the ravine for a path out. As horses labored single file up the opposing wall, I passed my horse to one of Bohak's officers, sought footholds in the rock, and climbed. Reminding myself of who I was, and who I needed to become. Someone called out below. Probably Bohak. My desert robes flapped as I grasped the lip of the gorge and hauled myself to stand and stared.

Under twilight, bleak salt pans, shining like silver, stretched into nothing. Ringing silence gripped the land, with no breath of life. I looked back. Our soldiers and skittering horses crested the edge.

The gorge collected darkness between us and Vedoa's far deserts, glistening like spilled ink beneath waning light.

Xanala's sword lay behind. There was no turning back.

Dust stirred as we crossed wasteland, our horses puffing and eyes darting, as if sensing our unease and unseen danger. Scales of salt crunched under their hooves. Time seemed to stand still yet stretch on forever.

Traveling scarves covered our eyes, noses, and mouths. I reached into my haversack to check on the mangi, farther from home than I was. Bohak kept us plodding toward the southern stars until even they disappeared under a canopy of haze, leaving us facing endless midnight.

Bohak spoke. "I will send the hawk ahead." He released the bird of prey, and after long moments, the hawk returned, and Bohak sent her out again.

I swiveled in my goatskin saddle. I'd never seen such a barren place. Even Taval wouldn't want to camp in the open here. We needed refuge. The desert always offered it, but would the Terror Lands? We'd lost the direction of the skies.

The hawk came back, squawking and ruffled.

In the hazy distance, tall forms contorted. "The dead rise!" someone cried.

My heart leapt just as Roji drew his horse closer to mine and extended a handful of light. But it illuminated nothing, and he closed his hand quickly to protect our adjusted eyesight.

Bohak cast him a quick glance, filled one hand with fire, and charged.

I snatched my reins to catch up, until the thin siphons of wind and sand whirled above and around us. My horse bucked. Bohak's animal screamed as a funnel swept through and dissipated to the ground.

"Are you all right?" I forced my horse to skirt other oncoming cyclones and closed the gap between us. "What are these?"

"I don't know. Harmless but forceful." Bohak surveyed the area. "I fear we could travel in circles."

"There has to be something." I spurred my horse on and plunged into nothingness.

"Lady Tol!" Bohak chased after me. As did Roji.

I scanned the darkness. A piece of the Reborn Star's prophecy couldn't possibly belong to this strange place. What if we became lost forever? What if we ran into a wall, a chasm, or ghouls as the legends whispered? It was my idea to come here. I was leading everyone into danger–

Dark shapes rose all around me. I slowed, my horse stamping. Twisting rock towers, arches, and cliffs devoured the landscape like the remains of a giant's lost city. But the smooth stones were carved by wind, not monster or man.

I calmed my horse and picked through the rocks, the animal stumbling once, and circumnavigated boulders. Rock balconies and buttresses soared upward around us and howled with wind. No sign of the living–or unliving. So many small, forbidding crevices.

"Tol!" Roji's voice called out behind me, and I turned as he looked up.

I followed his gaze. Hidden against gloomy skies, a wall of mountains, wind-lashed and jagged, brushed the heavens like midnight paint.

I turned my horse toward the sight, and soon the ground rose as we climbed the roots of the stone mountains. Gray rock splintered and scraped, and our horses slipped. We dismounted and led them around great boulders. Pale light warmed the borders of the sky and thinned the haze. Night was ending.

"Tol." Roji pointed. A crumbling rock doorway guarded a path winding into the mountains.

"Your Laijonese has the eye of a hawk," Bohak muttered as he stepped past me. He examined the passage opening. "Evidence of tools," he observed.

I touched the doorway. The shape was carved but not by wind.

"Anything could be on the other side," Bohak said.

"Or outside. We need shelter from the sun, wind, and dust," I replied.

Bohak held my gaze for a minute before inclining his head. "This time, I will go first." He held his horse's reins with one hand, filled his free hand with fire, and disappeared into darkness.

I did the same, keeping my fire smaller than I liked, but manageable, and felt Roji keeping close behind me, sensing his head turn back and forth to check the shadowing walls.

We entered into a labyrinth of curving, sheer canyons. Hoofbeats echoed against stone. Above, blade-like mountain peaks surrounded us. At every turn and fork, Bohak left two men like a proverbial trail of crumbs. After what felt like hours, our chosen passage widened, offering enough camping space for our entire army, with three corridors branching into different directions. I was taken aback at the relentless size of the place.

"Here?" Bohak asked.

I opened my mouth to answer, but a hand touched my shoulder. I turned my head slightly. No one was there. My heart paused. Was it the starpalm again?

Several of the men gasped as a bolt of emerald zipped through us and disappeared into the heart of the mountains, its chirping bouncing against stone.

The mangi in my haversack twittered. I shushed it and looked at Roji.

He gazed after the green bird. "We have those in Laijon."

"Songbirds don't survive in rock fortresses," I said and gave Bohak a questioning look.

He looked as flabbergasted as I felt before stationing two more men within the chamber with our horses and leading the rest of us into the corridor. Broken stone stairs, another sign of past human existence, climbed down as if toward the bowels of the earth.

Why would a bird fly down?

We stepped through another cut doorway, this one bearing faint remains of elaborate carvings, and entered a large, black chamber. Bohak held his fire high, but deep darkness acted like a living thing and filled the edges of the space.

I didn't like it. Judging by Roji's posture, he didn't either. Then something skittered. Two things. I filled my hands with fire, Roji wielded light, and the Tavalkians that remained followed until we stopped short.

Scaled, writhing creatures covered the walls. They lifted arrow-shaped heads and extended wings from every shelf and crevice. Nests of dog-sized desert dragons–more than I'd ever seen in my life. Rockwyrms with tight, strong scales impervious to blade and fire. Blind, eaters of small prey, fearful of daylight and people. Delicate tongues tasted the air for warmth, but if they sensed a larger threat or felt cornered–

"Extinguish your fire," I said, and snuffed my flames. Some hesitated, and hissing dragons took to the air.

"Get down!" I yanked Roji to his hands and knees. "There's an opening. Crawl."

He obeyed, and behind, Bohak shouted orders. Some ignorant Tavalkians continued to wield fire, drawing the small, flying serpents toward them. Swords swished and rang. Claws skittered against rock. Men screamed as dragons enveloped them.

I tried to yell instructions, but no one heard over the din. We just had to get out. Gritting my teeth, I pushed Roji to hurry him as panicked feet scuffled everywhere. Some joined us on the ground, and the chamber grew darker. Three dragons scamped over Roji's hands and across my back. He yelped and tossed the animals away. The chamber narrowed, and we scrambled into a blessedly empty corridor.

The battle waned as Tavalkians, bleeding and clothes torn, escaped into the passage. I rose to my knees to look for Bohak.

He was crawling out of the chamber, dragging a soldier with him. We all sat up, our backs against the rock wall, breathing heavily.

Bohak wiped his brow. "Is everyone present?"

His men gave the affirmative, but blood was splattered across the ground. Many bore long, deep gashes, and a few covered one or both eyes and moaned.

Rockwyrm claws were mildly poisonous. Wounds needed to be cleaned soon, but we couldn't go back for the rest of our group or horses until the swarm calmed. My focus drifted forward, and I gasped.

Through dried vines and branches veiling the corridor's end, a monstrous mouth rimmed with sword-like teeth gaped. Larger than the dragon remains kept at the palace. Watching. Waiting. No ordinary dragon. A wild legend alive.

All who were able bolted to their feet, blades and fire in hand. Roji crouched beside me, holding the meager knife Bohak had allotted to him.

I choked back an oath. The injured couldn't run. The dragon would only follow. Heart racing, I crept forward.

A strong hand pulled me backward, and Bohak pressed in front of me. His stance was taut as he hesitated.

We had to fight together or die. I forced another step, when it dawned on me that the creature didn't advance.

Bohak paused, noticing this too. He reached for the veil of vines and drew them aside.

I peered over his shoulder.

A larger-than-life dragon skull grinned just lengths away. Pale in the glowing dawn, picked clean, and bleached by many journeys of the sun. Young trees grew between its massive bones.

I looked around for a possible second creature in hiding–then realized what I was seeing.

Green. Everywhere. Like a castle rampart protecting us into an enclave, a valley poured into more mountains, filled with trees, bushes, flowers, and ivy climbing rock walls. Patches of snow crowned the highest peaks.

My mind couldn't comprehend it all–plants needed moisture. Then I heard the distant waterfall. The mountains kept an oasis. I covered my mouth.

Bohak raised a fist in the air. Uninjured Tavalkians melted into the gardens to scout. A flock of emerald-colored birds scattered across the valley at our intrusion.

The mangi chirped and wriggled outside my haversack. Before I could catch it, the fruit-colored bird took to flight and disappeared into the protected forest.

Tears stung my eyes. *Thrive,* I whispered in my thoughts. Bohak's victorious cry sounded from across the valley.

Roji appeared beside me and gaped in amazement. Because to him and the mangi, this place looked like home.

I drew a breath and ran down ancient stone steps into the valley, surrounding myself with leaves and branches heavy with fruit. I found a pile of stones and scrambled to the top. I saw a lake, filled by dual waterfalls pouring down the mountainsides, its surface blue and crystalline. A deep well that would easily care for us and our horses. Sounds of exultation echoed between the walls of mountains.

I squinted at the waterfall, and my heart caught. Carved stone steps. Manmade bowls of rock, meant to hold fire. An arched opening into the mountains, graced with statues so worn by time as to be almost unrecognizable.

This wasn't just an oasis. We'd discovered an ancient fortress.

16

BOHAK FILLED HIS HANDS WITH FIRE and molded an animated desert hare, nose twitching and back leg scratching a large ear. "Last one?"

Flaming rabbits wouldn't prepare me for Xanala. Sunlight had burned away dawn's haze long ago, trees no longer rustled with morning breezes, and scouts called out as they made rotations. After discovering this glorious oasis, we'd hunted for an hour before finding a secondary passage between us and the men and horses we'd left behind in the tunnels, a route without rockwyrms, which remained under constant guard.

My loose robes stuck to my skin. Readjusting to diurnal life was the worst. Bohak looked exhausted, and not just from our prolonged training, which I'd demanded early every morning since we'd made camp in this garden. We practiced with fire and speaking the capital tongue. We were preparing messages to send to Srolo Kapir and the Rebellion, and I needed to be ready when they came. The growing burn in my veins, signaling that I needed to drain, eased with so much wielding.

I'd progressed under his training, but it wasn't enough. He tried to take responsibility with annoying delicacy, but we both knew better. I glanced around for onlookers and chastised myself for the habit. There were always a couple, but fewer than before. It reminded me that I'd plateaued, and that wasn't going to be good enough.

My insides coiled tighter. I had to persevere, because Srolo Kapir and the Rebellion depended on me.

"Send something larger." I tossed a ball of fire across the glade.

Bohak caught the orb. "I think we've done enough. Weariness won't serve you."

"Please, Bohak."

He frowned but absorbed the boost of Magnificence and thrust his palm forward. A fiery Tavalkian foal, five times larger than anything he'd thrown yet, cantered toward me. Good.

I reached to slow it, projecting an invisible wall of Justice and Temperance, just as I had done with the hares. Resistance slammed into me. The foal didn't unfurl into a spinning orb that I could snatch and absorb. As if to demonstrate that a portion of its flame was mine, it reared onto its back legs and bucked.

By the desert. I hurled myself to the side, but the blazing animal veered to crash into me. I covered my face. Fire licked my robes. I dropped, rolled. Bohak shouted something, and flames pulled from me, until all were extinguished, and he knelt beside me gasping for breath.

Horror scrawled his face. "What have I done?"

"What I asked you to do!" What was wrong with me? I should be able to stop a full-grown flaming horse and–I dropped my forehead into my sooty hand.

"Here." Bohak dug in his satchel and produced the fancy wielding oil he always carried. "Open your hand."

"No."

But he gently captured my hand and poured a generous portion of oil into my palm. "Cover your skin."

The soothing coolness stayed me, and the herbal scent was calming. I massaged the oil into any exposed flesh. There were no true burns, just raw skin. Bohak had held back in his wielding, thankfully. I glanced around.

Congregated soldiers provided a respectful distance. But they'd seen their Reborn Star fail. Realizing how close we were to one another, I scooted back.

Bohak sat on his heels, his face grim. "You don't have to prove anything to me or Taval." He went on before I could object. "You need Srolo Kapir to come."

He meant that I needed the Temperance Srolo Kapir could unlock in me, this mysterious ceremony none of us understood. Temperance to defeat Xanala and bring the council to reckoning, so I could approach the Abyss, open it, and gain the life of a starpalm. The impossibility and pressure felt like barrels of water draped around my shoulders.

Bohak rose, brushed his palms against one another, and offered a hand.

Would he never take the hint? I stood on my own.

His expression fell. "What must I do to earn your trust, Tol?"

"I don't distrust you." I felt my cheeks warm as I struggled to express myself and couldn't. He thought I feared being drained. Far from it–

Bohak stood tall. "Tonight, we send messages to Srolo Kapir and the Rebellion."

Hope leapt inside me. "Your scouts don't need another day of reprieve?"

"I have another way." He turned and cut through the garden.

I followed. "What way?"

He glanced over his shoulder and flashed a grin. "Trust me."

Ancient volcanic peaks encircled us and provided landmarks for direction. We'd pitched our tents by the lake until a proper exploration of the carved mountain fortress could commence. The men's suspicions toward the place delayed our moving under its shelter, and Bohak thought it best to give them a couple more days to adjust. Thankfully, all had recovered from their rockwyrm wounds, except for the two who had lost an eye. No one brought up clearing the entry cavern of the tiny beasts. For now, they provided an extra layer of protection against unwanted intruders.

Everywhere, birds sang, and as we neared camp, the lapping of water and nickering of horses tickled my ears. There were other animals, too, good for hunting–a desert miracle. I sought elusive peace in that, until murmurings of soldiers arose.

Bohak and I shared a glance and quickened our pace. A cluster of officers hailed us.

"Esteemed Srolo and Lady Tol," one said, "A horse is reported missing."

"What of the herd?" Bohak asked.

"They're spooked, Srolo."

"What do the scouts say?"

"They haven't seen a thing, including signs of severe weather." The man cleared his throat. "There are rumors circulating."

"About?"

"They fear that spirits inhabit the fortress."

My eyes went to the carved stone structure. Of course, anyone who held to superstitions would believe it was haunted, along with the rest of the Terror Lands.

"A ghost didn't whisk a horse away," Bohak said shortly.

But a Shadow could. A jolt ran through me at the thought. Would Shadows travel here? But the scouts hadn't spotted anything.

The discussion shifted to management of supplies. I wanted to listen, but weariness was overtaking me. I excused myself, endured multiple bows and salutations, and wove through camp to my tent, situated in the center, as always. Guards pulled my tent flaps back, and I went inside.

Tavalkian-woven rugs stretched across lumpy grass, not swells of sand. The familiar table, bed, changing screen, trunk, and jar of water were in place. I still felt like a caged animal.

"Ah, hello."

I nearly jumped out of my skin.

Roji emerged from behind the changing screen and offered a wan smile.

"By the desert," I muttered. "How did you get past the guards?"

"They're less vigilant when you're gone."

"Your face. You're bleeding."

"Must have missed a spot." He wiped a hand across a thin crust of blood trailing down his neck and a blossoming bruise.

I pointed to the table. "Sit."

He flopped down on a cushion, and I dug through the trunk for something to serve as a rag. Brocade would have to do. I opened the jar to wet the cloth. "What happened?"

"Just clumsy, I guess. I can clean it myself."

"Apparently you can't." I sat to face him and met his gaze. His eyes were the same delicate shape and deep color as I remembered from childhood. A memory burst into my mind.

Nine-year-old Seyo leaned forward and whispered, "I found a way for us to be real sisters."

I cocked an eyebrow, enjoying the warmth of being wanted–I wished to be her true family just as much–and smothering the discomfort of knowing, because of my guardian, it was too much to hope for. "How?"

"You can marry Roji." Before I could guffaw, she rushed on. "He's always following you around. He and I both want you to be free . . ." She seemed unable to finish saying from Mother. *"What if . . . someday . . . we were truly sisters?"*

I blinked into the present and realized Roji was staring at me, but in an *are you well?* kind of way. I cleared my throat and dabbed his neck. We had a lot to talk about, such as his Shadow knowledge. Let the painful past remain buried.

Roji grimaced. "You're going to make me use ointment, aren't you?"

"Yes," I informed him. "And it'll sting like nothing you've ever experienced." I plucked straw from his overgrown hair. "You visited the horses."

"I wanted fresh air." He looked at me. "There was a ruckus about a missing animal."

I raised an eyebrow. "How did you hear that?"

"Half of Taval proudly served their esteemed Bohak in the capital and speak that tongue," he replied. "The rest must be fresh from Taval, and I can't fully understand their regional dialect, the one you speak. There's a division in the group over these differences, believe it or not. But the three who jumped me belong to the capital variety."

My eyes widened. “You fought three soldiers?”

“Impressed?” He winked before sobering. “No, I didn’t fight back. I couldn’t, if I valued my life. But Tavalkian boots are quite sturdy. I want a pair.” His attempt at humor fell flat, and he couldn’t completely mask his bitterness from me. “They’re also heavy, which gave me an edge in seizing liberation.”

That explained the bruise. He was Laijonese, and rules of defense didn’t apply to him. He’d taken what they’d given until he could run. Inferno blazed in my chest. “I’m telling Bohak. He said he ordered the soldiers to leave you alone.”

“It’s not worth it, Tol. Not yet.” He fingered a tear in his tunic. “Before that, while I mingled with the horses quite peacefully, I overheard other things. About you, actually. Extremely interesting conversations.” Roji cocked his head, eyes fixed on mine. “They don’t refer to you as Tol. They call you a reborn goddess.”

The words hung between us. I curled my hands in my lap.

“They say you’re like a shard of destiny, long awaited, to remake Vedoa. That Bohak, who they also liken to a god, even bows to you.” He searched my face. “What does that mean?”

“I . . . hoped you wouldn’t find out.” I exhaled slowly. I had to explain, as he’d never let it go. “Our fire manifests in four Forms. It’s normal to have just one, Magnificence, one’s well of fire. If you possess a taste of all the Forms and one is particularly strong, you become a Tier 2. About a quarter of Vedoa has attained this status. If you possess all Forms and one or two are of extremely high strength, you become a Tier 3. Only a handful of Tier 3s are known, and Bohak is one of them. His Justice is perfected. His Temperance and Wisdom are both at a Tier 2 level.” I chose against divulging his Tier 1 Magnificence.

Roji’s brow pinched with concentration. “So, you have all Forms.”

“No. I have three Forms at a high level.” Overwhelmingly high. “But the fourth Form, Temperance, the one that binds and channels the rest, I’m missing.” My hands trembled in my lap.

“What do they want from you?”

I glanced at his intrigued expression, then looked away. "For generations, the Abyss, said to be the source of our fire gifting, has been bound with chains and submerged in a pool. When its twin doorway, the Eternity Gate, opened, the chains locking the Abyss vanished. We believe that this was an act of the starpalms, and that one of them will be reborn to walk among humanity as a savior, called the Reborn Star. The Rebellion always planned to find and help the Reborn Star overthrow the dynasty, pass through the doorway into the Abyss, attain immortality, and rule new Vedoa forever." My voice dropped. "There are many worthy Tier 3s, such as Srolo Kapir, but they've chosen me."

"You weren't joking about taking over the throne." Roji shook his head. "Tol, that's a mountain of pressure. Do you believe it?"

I didn't, except for one thing. One thing I couldn't bear to tell anyone, even him. "I want to help my people. I want to protect the innocent and break their yoke of oppression."

"Me too. Yet you know my beliefs differ from yours."

He believed in Laijon's Father of Light. According to his faith, starpalms didn't exist, a doubt I'd mostly shared until one spoke to me.

"I don't want you to go near the Abyss. The atmosphere surrounding it is deadly." His expression tightened. "I saw it. The Rebellion probably thinks your gifting will allow you to pass through safely, but will it? So I hereby declare that I will do everything within my power to stop that from happening."

As if he could stop the Rebellion. But what if he was right about the Abyss? I pushed the thought aside. One thing at a time.

"I think something else can appease the Abyss," Roji added, "and I'm going to find out what that is. But as for taking over Vedoa, I'm joining you."

My head snapped up.

He nodded, fervor in his eyes as he leaned forward. "You have fire. Tons, based off your explanation. Enough for the palace to fear you so much that they threw you in a cage surrounded by Shadows. I joined the war against the same tyrants you're fighting.

We're practically allies, and the battle isn't over, but we can finish it." He let out a breath. "Finally, I know why the Messenger forced me here." With a flourish, he filled one hand with light. Golden and sparkling in his palm, pure and safe. So different from fire. Roji held his glowing cupped palm against his chest. "I, Roji, soldier of Laijon, swear loyalty to you, Tol of Vedoa, to guard your life, fight by your side, and serve you in any way I can, to bring freedom and peace to Vedoa and Laijon."

I sat stunned, tripping from one chasm of pressure and expectations into another. By the desert, I had too many protectors. And I wouldn't drag him into a conflict that could take his life. My chest tightened. "Roji . . ."

Light glimmered in his eyes. For the first time since we escaped the palace, he sat taller. Gaze sharp. Purpose decided. Precious hope rediscovered.

I swallowed. "I'm honored to fight alongside you." Now, we just needed to call the rest of the Rebellion.

Stars, sprinkled across a midnight sky, seemed to sing. Without the haze of the first night we arrived, they looked so close. It was breathtaking and promised success for what we were about to do.

After the cooking fires died down, Bohak and I climbed the steep trail to a lower mountain ridge and dismissed the scouts on duty. I drew my hooded cloak closer around me against the evening chill and looked his way. "How does one send messages without pigeons or messengers?"

Bohak smiled. "By the hands of the starpalms. Or powerful wielders." He reached into his robes and produced a small box. He opened it to reveal a shaped lump of wax, like what I'd delivered to the 'betis.

Bohak balanced the wax in the palm of his hand. "Years ago, the Rebellion leaders of every region gathered–an extremely dangerous enterprise–and wielded together to create a message that could span great distances and time to seek each other out, a call before battle to be used only once."

I stared at him. "It that possible?"

"With enough Tier 2s, Tier 3s, and Srolo Kapir's great Temperance, yes." His expression turned thoughtful. "Srolo Kapir entrusted it to me at the same time he chose me to protect you."

I swallowed. "Should we save it? Use birds and parchment instead?"

"No. This is the time." His voice quieted. "You should be the one to send it off."

I didn't want to. The weight of such responsibility was crippling. But I remembered Srolo Kapir and the danger he was in, squared my shoulders, and filled my left palm with fire. Just enough.

Bohak carefully dropped the wax into my hand. A moment passed.

Thin, quick ribbons of fire uncurled and shot from my hands. I gasped as they danced around us, tails flaming, then zipped into the desert. North to Vedoa, to their assigned makers, who formed them so long ago. To Srolo Kapir. I breathed amazement. When the last ribbon of fire leapt away, I extinguished my flames and brushed my palms free of hot, stinging wax. "How soon will the messages arrive?"

"I'm not sure–"

He broke off as one of the messages returned to circle us, then Bohak alone twice, and burst into a flurry of sparklers right in front of his face. Bohak blinked.

"Oh no." I tried to catch the fading wisps of fire. "It's broken. And we can't resend it."

"No." Bohak stared at the glow, a funny look on his face. "It was for me."

"But you weren't a part of the Rebellion years ago."

"My father was. Somehow, he foresaw that I would be . . ." He fell silent.

This meant a lot to him, though I didn't fully understand why. I stepped to the edge of the ridge, giving him space, and studied the northern horizon, the fiery messages long disappeared from view. "Please bring Srolo Kapir," I whispered.

Bohak joined me. "This is a moment the Rebellion will remember forever."

I hoped so. Then I caught him watching me, and I couldn't interpret his expression. "What?" I asked.

"I wanted to ask you . . ."

By the desert, was he going to question me about my Magnificence again?

A shout rose from below.

I pivoted. "What was that?"

Bohak's lips curved down. "Hopefully not a third missing horse."

"Third?"

"We're up to two." He looked downward at the camp. "Or they found something inside the fortress."

What? "They went inside it?"

"I offered a challenge that whichever division explored the fortress first would dine with us at dinner," he said with a wry smile. "You and I could've cleared the hole ourselves, but they needed to see their superstitious fellows unscathed. There are too many fears about ghosts. Once the Rebellion comes, we'll need the room–"

Panicked cries rang out, and firelight flashed against the mountains.

Bohak and I rushed to the head of the trail and came to a stop.

Glittering like onyx against a flood of stars, a serpentine shape twisted across the night sky, breathing plumes of smoke from its nostrils.

17

THE DRAGON, THINNER AND MORE snakelike than anything I'd seen before, beat gossamer wings, almost invisible. It continued to spew clouds of smoke.

"Go!" Bohak jogged down the path, one hand skimming the arms of the mountain. I did the same and jumped the last length to the valley bottom, just as a monstrous hiss ricocheted between our encircling towers of rock. Trapping us like a bowl of mice.

Tavalkians fell into formations and raised handfuls of fire high, many spinning their flames into spears. Others herded horses to safety.

But the dragon breathed fire itself, and its scales would be fireproof.

Bohak turned to me. "Protect yourself where the trees grow thickest."

I shook my head. "I won't hide."

"If we lose you, we lose everything." He grabbed my arm.

I resisted, but he dragged me toward the garden's edge and pushed me into a tangle of brush. Recovering my balance, I batted free from leaves and branches.

Bohak raced toward his men. The midnight dragon dipped overhead, undulating like a ribbon, and dove toward the army. Soldiers hurled flaming spears into its shining, scaly flank. But the beast turned and soared over the twisting shoulders of the mountains, stretching to a shocking length and blowing a stream of fire. Pockets of flames dotted the lush green. In the distance, horses screamed. The dragon spun at their sound, then plummeted again to roll upon his bed of flames, extinguishing them to a garden graveyard of ash, before swooping into the air again.

Men worked on a fiery net at Bohak's command. It wouldn't hold. We needed a way to get close enough to–

A hiss. "Tol."

Roji. I breathed relief. "Thank the starpalms you're–"

"No one else will listen to me." He hefted a large, earthen jar. "I have a plan."

We sprinted from the garden across a wall of smoke devouring a clearing. Lengths away, Bohak and his men were yelling. I didn't see the dragon. We plunged into another thicket and fought through thick brambles and bushes. My heart slammed against my ribs. The beast could belch fire across our path or at Taval at any moment. Then I heard splashing waterfalls. The lake. "Now what, Roji?"

"The dragon hears the horses and wants an easy meal. It's burning portions of the oasis, then rolling the fire out, trying to flush livestock into the open. If we can extinguish its fire, we can get close enough to slay it." He adjusted his grip on the sealed jar.

"And that?"

"As much oil as I could carry. We'll pour it across the lake, and then I'll need your fire."

Understanding dawned. "You're brilliant."

His sardonic tone held a sharp edge. "Hardly. It's a Vedoan trick I learned during a battle for the Eternity Gate. I'm surprised your Tavalkian prince didn't think of it first."

At the edge of the lake, Roji dropped the jar, lifted his foot, and snapped its neck with his boot. Thick cooking oil flowed into the grass. With a grunt, Roji heaved the jar upright, waded into the water, and poured oil across its surface.

I joined him in the lake and used my hands to encourage the oil to spread.

"*Qo'tah*, that better be enough. May this be the last dragon I ever see." He nodded to me.

My turn. I scooped the tail of my cloak over my shoulder, filled my palms with fire, and lowered my hands into the shimmering oil. Crackling and roaring, fire immediately consumed the slippery coating and raced across the surface. I splashed to the bank as flames devoured the lake, and oiled smoke thickened the air.

"We might live after all." Roji wrapped an arm around my shoulders. Just like the three of us used to do as children. His other hand went to his hip, to the hilt of a sword and not the measly dagger Bohak had allowed him to carry. "That's impressive fire."

I held my breath. The dragon was too dangerous for us to take on alone, even extinguished. "Let's get Bohak–"

Blazing flashes exploded off the lake. Roji and I dove as shapes bursting from my flames spun and cavorted through the air, hissing as they hit the bank, rock, or water. Shooting stars, desert hawks, arrows–

Roji gasped. "What in the continent is happening?"

"Deserts, my fire–"

"Can you stop it?"

I shushed him and pointed.

The midnight dragon dipped and circled over the lake. Flicking its tongue, it snapped at the shapes and roared. Rolling through the air, the monster plunged through my flames, but didn't land as expected. With a shattering splash, it crashed into the lake. Water, oil, and fire sprayed across the expanse, and the garden sizzled.

Roji and I batted fire from our clothes and stared.

Ringed with fire, the dragon swam across the burning lake surface, filling half of it and hissing.

"It's coming," I said, then heard thundering footsteps surround us.

Sweating, grim-faced Tavalkians filled the bank. Bohak, his robe now singed, stood beside me. "Unbelievably dangerous, but absolutely perfect, Lady Tol." He unsheathed a sword, waving to his men, and stalked the bank.

It was Roji's idea–but words died on my lips as the dragon neared, its glittering, ebony spine slicing water. Steam rose from its nostrils, its reptilian eyes focused on Bohak, who stood resolutely.

My heart caught. I took a step forward. Roji grabbed my hand to stop me just as a haunting shriek pierced the air.

The dragon thrashed, stirring the water and fire to foam. It struggled for the bank, but couldn't reach it, and suddenly disappeared under the surface.

All of us held our breath. Waiting. One moment. Five. The dragon didn't resurface, and fire lapped along the edges of the water's bank.

Roji and I exchanged glances. Was it really gone?

Then Bohak lifted his head and gave his rallying cry. All around us, Taval echoed the shout, a familiar sound to me now.

I exhaled slowly, even as regret for the loss of life twinged deep inside me. We'd taken down a fire-breathing dragon and lived. "What happened to it? Where did it come from?"

"Maybe it can't swim well," Roji mused. "It came from the fortress. I can't imagine how our friend Bohak is going to get his men to go back in there now." His voice turned brittle. "Unless he decides to send me in first."

"He won't, because I'm going to shout from the volcano peaks that you defeated a fire-breathing dragon."

"I think the lake did most of the work–" Roji glanced up the mountainside and choked.

I followed his gaze, and my blood chilled.

Men, camouflaged in desert-colored robes, covered the valley walls like ants.

I screamed. "Bohak!"

18

BOHAK WHIRLED.

Wild invaders roared and hurried down the mountains, lithe as animals. Royal guards in disguise? Or did our Nazakian neighbors dare to enter the Terror Lands?

Taval reassembled and marched from the lake back to the clearing. Hands filled with weapons and fire. Exhaustion melting in their fearsome focus.

I pulled my cloak hood over my head and gripped the staff from my belt. Roji grasped his filched sword hilt.

Bohak pointed toward me, and two officers jogged in my direction. Surely to whisk me to safety.

The Reborn Star wouldn't run. I turned and disappeared into a thicket to lose them.

"Tol!" Roji cried.

I snaked through the brush and then changed directions. Shouting rose ahead from those who battled for and against us. My fire would never be so valuable that I couldn't join the fight, and no one would stop me. I gripped the staff, one hand over and one under, and paused to study the clearing through a veil of brush.

Choking smoke hung in the air as both armies gathered.

Roji rustled behind me. He'd followed well and caught up fast. If anyone needed to avoid a fire fight, it was a light-wielding Laijonese. I turned to tell him so—respectfully—and froze.

Not Roji.

The man bristled with every weapon imaginable. Under that,

he wore loose, charcoal robes, earth-colored trousers, and a traveler's scarf that exposed hard, slitted eyes.

I dropped into a defensive lunge and thrust my staff forward. Then I spied Roji, the fury of a starpalm blazing in his eyes, sneaking up behind my assailant.

The man chuckled–which he would regret. But before I could attack, he unwrapped his traveler's scarf, revealing sun-deepened skin and a brand across his forehead.

My jaw dropped. "You're alive," I gasped, as I caught Roji's eye and pressed a hand downward to the ground.

Roji saw, hesitated, and melted back into the brush. Still watching.

Samari laughed. "I should say the same of you, seeking refuge in this cursed place. You're lucky we came as soon as we did." His face split into a generous smile. "How starpalm-meddled it is to meet you again, Stable Rat. And it would be poor taste to war against the Rebellion." He raised his voice in an ear-splitting, animal-like call and strode toward the battle.

I forced myself not to look back at Roji–may he cling to his senses and not announce his presence to fugitive Vedoan soldiers, if that's who we faced–and followed.

In the clearing, intruders in their desert-colored robes held up hands in peace. Taval, organized in divisions, watched with suspicion.

Then Bohak stormed in our direction, gold paint glimmering across his forehead like a beacon.

Samari muttered, "Old Taval's youngest son. Is he your foe or ally?"

"He's with us."

"So, the Rebellion cuts another sharp tooth."

Bohak halted before us. His gaze darted between me and Samari, as if he expected Samari to pull a knife on me and demand ransom, then stilled, assessing the ex-soldier's brand. I inclined my head. Bohak noticed, straightened, and spoke with authority in the capital tongue.

Samari replied.

I strained to understand. My capital tongue was improving, but not enough. By the desert, I would practice even harder from now on. I determined that they exchanged greetings, and Samari assured Bohak that he meant no harm. But I wasn't worried about Samari. What if Bohak called me the Reborn Star? Panic rose in my throat. No. Bohak wouldn't endanger me by exposing that identity unless it was necessary. *Don't let it be necessary!*

Samari smirked and switched to the common tongue. "Are we not all from the north and fighting a common war? Why do we speak the enemy's language?"

Bohak stiffened. "I–"

"But I accept Taval's northern generosity to evening meal." Grinning, Samari hailed his men.

Bohak, his face stormy, took my elbow and led me toward camp. "I did not offer a meal. This will cost half our remaining supplies."

I had to admire Samari's brazenness. "The garden will provide."

"How do you know this man?"

"We . . . he was one of the soldiers captured in the 'betis' city who escaped execution when the Shadow appeared." Although I had no idea how Samari had accomplished all of that.

Bohak's expression smoothed. "Really?"

I nodded. "I bet they're all branded."

"They call themselves the Exiles." Bohak looked at me. "Are they trustworthy, or will they rob us blind? There are too many military-trained Tier 2s."

I opened my mouth. Then it struck me. "Bohak, they're reinforcements."

"They're not part of the Rebellion. I would have been informed."

"But they could be. The dynasty has stolen everything but their breath. And, as you said, they're Tier 2s. Trained. Military. Ripe as winter mangi fruit to join us."

Bohak considered this, as trees parted to reveal our field of tents. "If they were willing, this could be the key to turning the conflict in our favor. Srolo Kapir said he hoped to recruit more soldiers to match the dynasty's strength."

Half of Vedoa would need to join us to accomplish that. "We need the Exiles."

"If they prove true. And we could inform Samari, since he seems to be their leader, who you are."

"Not yet." I fought to keep my voice even. "Let's test them first and see where their true loyalties lie." Bohak couldn't announce me as the Reborn Star. Not when Samari still referred to me as "Stable Rat," the girl who'd knocked him out through unorthodox means, stolen his coin, left him at the cruel mercy of a horse trader, then tried to make it up by freeing him from prison and almost failed due to a vile Shadow.

Samari knew better than to believe it.

The Exiles were a lean, tough crowd, and they insisted on having dinner in the tunnels, not the oasis. Taval called them "invaders," but the Exiles knew this place like the backs of their hands and walked the secondary tunnel access as if it were a path between market and home–leading me to wonder who the true trespassers were. These were the men Laijon had defeated and sent to their homeland in shame. These were the soldiers who'd lost everything at Laijon's so-called benign light-bearing hands.

Hemmed in by walls of wind-smoothed rock and lounging across woven rugs, the Exiles ate and drank our supplies with revelry.

I felt like I walked a canyon rim. We needed the Exiles. I grew more certain of this with every passing moment, but winning them over required a tactful tongue with such volatile and distrustful men. Especially while blazing Taval sat in stony silence under the sliver of hard night sky above. May Roji remain well hidden.

Samari downed his cup and heaved a sigh, drawing the attention of the men. "Legends say this oasis lies in the crater of Vedoa's oldest and greatest volcano. It's also said that Nazakian explorers were the first to brave the crater, and by their now squandered gifting, planted the garden that still flourishes today."

Nazak, the wild land to the east, was as untamable as the Exiles. Gifted with an ability to touch the earth and make things grow, other tales ran that, by using their talent for greedy purposes, they'd lost their gifting.

Bohak, sitting beside me in his finest silks and sticking out like a prince among thieves, looked unimpressed with the shared lore. I longed to nudge him. Did he want to earn their respect, or would his own suspicions ruin this?

Samari leaned back. "I hear you encountered your first firewyrm today. Thankfully, it was only a juvenile, according to your description."

I stiffened. Juvenile?

"This one came from the fortress between the waterfalls, yes? Perhaps it tended a nest. I would be glad to send my men to check, if Taval hasn't already done so. We've learned many ways to trap firewyrms. We spied a horde heading in your direction during our journey here. They're as common as sand rats, but good hunting and ample eating."

Bohak choked on his milk tea.

Samari grinned. "Their cooked flesh wants a strong hand with spices. The scales are decent for trade, too, and the teeth make fine spear points. If you're not keen on seeing another, I suggest lighting fires at every mountaintop."

Such thoughts made even my desert-tough stomach queasy. Good thing we'd lost the creature to the lake.

"The beast picked off three of our horses," Bohak responded.

"Fine Tavalkian horseflesh lost to a firewyrm? Impossible. Horses are too big. Firewyrms can only consume what they can carry off in flight. Humans are their preferred size." A troubled look crossed Samari's face. "There is much to discuss concerning this place."

Then where had the horses gone? Bohak opened his mouth to speak.

Samari forestalled him. "But other things first. Some of us have sympathetic friends and family across the border, in Vedoa and Nazak. They send us news. We hear that the drought spreads to foreign countries."

I hadn't known that, but it was a perfect opening to discuss the Rebellion–

"We also hear that the princess's Pirthyian warlord creates Shadows within the depths of the palace, and our latest tidbit was particularly interesting. A young woman, gifted in great fire and contesting ownership to the throne, dared to enter the palace and unleash this secret army of Shadows against their makers." He leveled his gaze in my direction.

My heartbeat quickened, but I refused to look away.

"Then, as we prepared to climb these mountains, we spied a volley of fiery sparks leaping from above and racing across the Terror Lands. The work of a master wielder, and likely several. Naturally, we knew this oasis was occupied and investigated to see if you were an enemy or not. So, which is it?" Samari now sat straight, and many of his men and Bohak's did the same, as passion infused his voice. "You spoke the truth when you told me you served the Rebellion. I admire the Rebellion's fervor, and I remember Srolo Kapir, your leader. He trained our best commanders in the capital, and offered respect to every man, regardless of Tier, before his untimely passing."

Everyone but the dynasty loved Srolo Kapir, and he trained me too. Surely the Exiles would join, and I couldn't stop myself from speaking. "Srolo Kapir is alive."

Samari's eyes widened. "I'd heard rumors."

Bohak leapt into the conversation. "I attest that she speaks the truth. Srolo Kapir has taken me into his confidence. On his behalf, I would like–"

"But Srolo Kapir is not here." Caution smoothed Samari's expression. "And I cannot imagine that he, Vedoa's finest warrior and tactician, would send you–just a portion of the Rebellion, as I know you are–into this wasteland, for it is cursed."

Insulted by Samari's continued rudeness, Bohak's face flushed.

I spoke to give Bohak time to collect himself. "How is this place cursed?"

"A starpalm of the underworld resides here."

Silence gripped the passage. All watched Samari, waiting for him to elaborate.

I attempted to keep my expression neutral. Was this intimidation? A joke? "Go on."

But Samari's voice was deathly serious. "First, it's a horse. Then a man. One by one, every living thing will disappear, devoured by this spirit. Every time we visit this vile place, and only once a year to gather medicinal herbs from the garden, we lose an animal. And the spirit already seeks you by taking not one, but multiple horses."

Curse Vedoa's superstitions, I thought, despite the goosebumps racing across my skin.

Samari leaned toward me and lowered his voice. "Do you think your fire will help you against such a being, Stable Rat?"

By the desert–

Bohak looked bewildered. "Stable Rat?"

Samari ignored him. "We leave tonight."

I startled. "What?"

"Before the starpalm claims one of my men, or worse. But out of my respect for Srolo Kapir–may he truly live–I invite you and Taval to join us."

No. We'd sent messages to the Rebellion. We couldn't surrender this perfect refuge due to superstition . . . except horses were disappearing, and true conviction filled the Exile leader's eyes.

Neck reddening, Bohak began to speak, but I touched his wrist to silence him, hoping no one saw.

Samari had called me *Stable Rat*. He obviously mocked our battle with the "juvenile" firewyrm and held wealthy Taval in derision. Srolo Kapir wasn't here to lend proof to our statements. We–I–needed to prove myself to the Exiles, or they'd never consider joining us. "Respectfully, we decline."

Bohak tensed. Indeed, he should be concerned about what I was about to do.

Samari scowled. "You don't know what you're facing."

"On the contrary, this is our purpose for coming. Srolo Kapir sent us to expel this spirit." The falsehood slipped too easily over my lips. "And when he arrives, we will have purified the oasis as one cleans a house, and the Rebellion will claim a stronghold in the Terror Lands."

19

FIRES ROARED FROM THE NATURAL canyon ramparts.

One rotation of scouts faced out to the Terror Lands to look for threats and the Rebellion, and a wary, second rotation looked inside the oasis for signs of an underworld spirit.

The Exiles remained in the outer tunnels to observe our hunt.

Bohak's horror at my declaration that we would capture this spirit exploded into a near shouting match between the two of us, concerning whether I would be allowed to participate in any hunting or if my life was "far too valuable," as he insisted. At last, he conceded that I could assist, but only from behind two divisions of his men.

Five days passed. Nothing–until the sixth night when another horse disappeared.

That evening, when camp fell quiet, I crept from my tent, dressed in my traveler's clothes. Nearby was a climbable tree. I shimmied up the trunk into the leafy canopy, straddling a thicker branch and bracing my feet against lower brush, until I could see the horses, bedded down by the bank of the lake. I would stay up and keep watch as if my life depended on it–just as I knew Bohak stayed up to support the scouts, which I admired–and waited for my lurker to join me.

"Tol?" Roji whispered.

I waved, hoping he would see, and branches groaned with his weight. Roji settled on a branch below me.

I absorbed the comfort of having a friend nearby. But what kind of friend was I to keep him like a prisoner here in an enemy country? Not for the first time, I digested the truth that he needed to return to Laijon.

"Do you wonder if someone miscounted? Or if this is all an Exile prank, even theft?" he asked.

"Samari did sound impressed with Tavalkian horseflesh, but no. The disappearances started before the Exiles arrived." I gazed past the barracks. "It always happens at night. I wonder if a fearful soldier is hoarding meat."

"What's your plan if it's something else?"

"What else could it be?"

I assumed Roji shrugged, because he gave no answer. Did he believe in otherworldly beings, like spirits? I supposed he did, since he talked about the Father of Light, Laijon's god, and heavenly Messengers.

Thinking of heavenly beings made me wonder if the starpalm would ever speak to me again. So many days had passed. I gave my head a shake–*focus on the task at hand, Tol.* If only Srolo Kapir were here. He would know how to handle an underworld starpalm.

One horse pushed to its hooves and wandered to the water's edge.

Roji and I both startled at the horse's movement, and the tree swayed. I scanned the surrounding rocks for signs of a dragon. Please, let it not be a Tavalkian or Exile poacher–

Roji craned his head from his perch. "The lake's rippling."

"So?"

Waves that danced across the surface undulated from the center to the bank. The horse lowered its neck to drink. A wave crested from the heart of lake. Slowly, it swelled toward the water's edge. The horse looked up.

The wave swallowed the animal without a sound, paused, then receded into the quieting lake. All fell still.

We stared. A cry rose from the scouts.

"By the starpalms–"

"*Qo'tah*, what was that?"

A childhood moment flashed across my mind. Roji, Seyo, and I were fishing, and I'd asked how fish breathed underwater. Roji had given me a shocked look, as if all children should know the answer, and said *Gills.*

My arms shook gripping the tree as I climbed down. Roji hurried to follow. I raced across the garden to find Bohak. Cutting around the last tents, I almost crashed into him and two of the watchmen. Far behind me, Roji skittered to a halt, half-hidden in darkness.

Bohak was pale. "Lake spirit. A watery hand reaching out–"

I shook my head. "The wave had a backbone and spines. That was no spirit."

The following dusk, Tavalkians with long, curved spears circled the lake, tied to ropes held by a comrade behind them. A horse was staked near the water's edge, and the air crackled with fear.

After hearing what had occurred, the Exiles covered the mountainsides again, coming as close to the oasis as their superstitions allowed. Samari rested his elbows on his knees, eyes sharp, hard.

I fixed my eyes on the volcano's rock bones hemming us into this false paradise. Pink and orange sky dimmed as the sun fell.

The horse nickered.

I gripped a borrowed spear and waited. Bohak had begged me to stay behind Taval's lines, and I would–for now. Roji insisted on remaining near me, spouting that neither Exiles nor Tavalkians would notice him when there was a monster on the loose. So, we sat in tense silence, neither of us mentioning how we'd waded into the lake only days ago. The moon rose, stars sparkled, and the horse rested. No waves.

We changed guards. Bohak suggested I sleep, but I refused until a new day dawned.

Men watched throughout the day to sunset. Again, nothing surfaced. We put our weapons away for the second time.

Bohak expressed frustration on his way to his quarters. "How long can it feast off our horses?"

"And a firewyrm," Roji muttered behind me.

The third afternoon, I began to hear complaints from our men. Fewer Exiles climbed the mountains to watch, but Samari was always present at sunset. Rumors circulated that he had ordered his men to break camp.

Seated behind a row of bushes out of sight, I curled my hands around the spear and refused to consider the worst, if Samari left. Roji sat behind me, deeper within the brush, still refusing to leave my side.

Bohak walked by. I ducked, but he saw me and stopped. "How many times must I beg you to stay back and rest?"

"I don't feel like arguing." I squinted at the lake and hoped he would keep walking, but he wouldn't. He would fight me like this every night we watched for this blazing beast. I shivered against the evening cold and hoped he didn't notice and add it to his argument.

"You are the most stubborn person I've met." There was a rustling of heavy fabric, and he placed his cloak around my shoulders.

Surprised, I remembered to whisper thanks as he marched to the next knot of lookouts. He didn't look back. Did this mean he would quit fighting me?

Roji huffed.

Focus, Tol.

I hunched over my knees and kept my spear across my lap. Deserts, I was exhausted. I closed my eyes.

"I'd rather face off with river serpents," Roji began to say, then sucked in a breath. "Tol."

I snapped my eyes open just as a collective gasp came from those on guard in front of us.

From the center of the lake, the rolling wave began. Heading quietly toward the staked horse.

No one moved. Bohak, arm outstretched and frozen in the air, looked like a statue.

The water swelled toward the sacrificial horse. The animal noticed, and shuffled backward until its lead ran out of length.

The wave curved into knifelike spines.

Someone flung the first spear. Bohak. The rod of metal and wood pinged off the spirit as if it wore armor. Bohak shouted, and his men converged upon it with spears. Someone cut the horse loose.

I dashed bankside, Roji at my heels.

The grove exploded with battle cries and clanging metal. With blinding spray, the spirit surged against the bank and swallowed three men.

My heart clenched, and I raced along the bank. Bohak shouted for me to go back, but I couldn't. The creature swam in circles, stirring water and unleashing waves upon us. Fire failed against the spirit's sleek hide. Soldiers pulled barbed spears attached to ropes back from the deep. The spirit rose high–dwarfing my memory of the firewyrm–and crashed down onto the lake. But not before I saw gaping scarlet flesh.

"Gills!" I shouted and flung my spear. It pinged off the spirit's armored side, but a second spear reached its mark. Roji's. The spirit reeled, and a deep, unearthly shriek shook the oasis. Roji lurched forward, yanked by the spear's rope he clung to, and I quickly grabbed him around the waist.

The curse prepared to dive, and several guards launched more roped spears into the spirit's gills. Others helped catch the tail of our rope.

Bohak flung his own spear aside and joined the rest of us. "Pull!"

We clustered in groups, shoulder to shoulder, pulling on ropes. A familiar voice grunted near me. Samari and his men.

The spirit thrashed. Ropes snapped, and men tumbled into the lake only to scramble back onto the bank and pull again. Length by length, we forced the heaving monster into the grass, ears ringing from its deafening cries. I couldn't believe what I saw. What looked like a wave morphed into the massive likeness of grass and bushes, as if disappearing in dry air, and yet I could see the serpentine outline of its form flailing, still halfway in the lake.

Someone grasped my arm. Bohak.

He gasped a breath. "We have to finish it off. The men can hold it still. You, my lady, for the glory of the Rebellion, or me?"

My blood chilled. I . . . didn't take life. "You."

Bohak swept a bow and strode toward the sea creature. Glittering long sword unsheathed, he pressed one booted foot against its neck.

I closed my eyes, opening them again when the harrowing shrieking ceased. The creature's monstrous body had stilled. Starting from its head, its armor changed color from mimicking its surroundings to a lifeless gray, its horrifying shape now plain for all to see. It was a cross between a dragon and a snake. Three times as large as the firewyrm, as long as seven men, with a spiked spine and blade-sharp fins instead of claws. Small gaps between scales allowed flexibility in its graceful, powerful movement.

For a moment, grief touched me. Dangerous, but so beautiful.

Taval raised a triumphant cry.

The Exiles joined in, and Samari called one of his own and knelt beside the head. Together, they stretched his maw wide, revealing an unhinging lower jaw and thick skin that stretched enough to swallow something its own size. Teeth boasted three points, none broken.

By the desert, this creature was young, but no one dared to voice that. Instead, everyone cheered, eyes on either the water dragon or Bohak.

Bohak planted his hands on his knees for a moment before straightening, then he strode toward me.

I pushed Roji away, who melted into a knot of trees before Bohak stopped in front of me, balancing the bloody blade across both palms. Then he knelt and offered me the sword.

I stiffened and inadvertently looked up.

Samari watched me, head cocked, eyes hard.

20

BURIALS COMMENCED FOR THE three lost soldiers. Emboldened by the spirit's demise, Tavalkian soldiers braved the stone fortress between the waterfalls and reported expansive chambers and no firewyrm nests.

Roji remained in his tiny tent. All day, he performed physical exercises, sat in silence for hours thinking, murmured prayers and memorized passages from Laijon's holy book, or stole into the garden for a solitary walk, at the risk of being jumped by Tavalkians, or worse, Exiles. Worry for him ate at me.

Bohak declared a celebratory feast that night between Taval and the Exiles, but I knew what that really meant. He planned to invite the Exiles to add their arms to the Rebellion.

I knew desert people. I was one, and Samari wouldn't respond to an extravagant, if generous, appeal. Only four things would convince him–fire, sand, coin, and the promise of justice–to make up what was lost at the dynasty's command. If I ever needed a starpalm's favor, it was now. Even if only for sneaking out from under Roji's sharp observation. Getting past Bohak, who was preoccupied by the feast, would be easier.

Shouldering through the thickest garden bushes, I breathed relief when I realized Roji didn't follow. Soon, crater walls rose overhead, and the exit passage through the mountains parted before me, and I halted.

As if he knew I was coming, Samari leaned against the rock walls. High above him, Exile scouts, blending into their rocky lookouts, shifted. I suppose I should have expected such vigilance from anyone who lived in the Terror Lands.

Samari inclined his head and turned to reenter the tunnels.

I followed.

The narrow stone trail wrapped us in silence, except for the crunch of gravel under our boots. High cliffs curved above, and between them, the sky ran like a river, soon to flow with the passage of glittering stars. Ahead, the sound of Exiles continuing to break camp echoed, but Samari took a fork littered with broken rock. He climbed over boulders, and I did too. If Bohak or Roji knew I was gallivanting after Samari without escort, they'd throw a fit. The path split again. I committed the way to memory and looked over my shoulder twice.

The trail ended. Samari scaled the slope of a large stone and disappeared over the top. I climbed after him, hauled myself over the edge, and stood.

Cliffs rose on our left and right. In front of us, past an arrow-shaped stone promontory, were the southern Terror Lands. Inky shadows ran long from intricate rock formations, towers, and arches, and there was a hint of something dark, perhaps even green, racing the horizon. Wind blew fiercely, and not even the most sharp-eared scout would overhear our negotiation.

"There's extensive scrubland with decent hunting, but drought touches even that," Samari remarked.

Swallowing shame, I reached inside my robes and tossed Ami'beti's clinking coin bag. "Debt paid with interest."

He caught the purse, weighed it in his hand, and laughed. "What use do I have for dacri in the Terror Lands?" Yet Samari secured the coins to his belt. "I have a gift for you as well, to prove that there is no lingering suspicion between us." He removed a disk wrapped in leather, and carefully unwrapped it to reveal a diamond-shaped scale, serrated on both sides, big as my head, and dark as night. He extended it to me balanced on the palm of his hand. "Test the edge. It is far sharper than even a firewyrm's scale."

I accepted the gift. "This is from the water dragon."

"I remember hearing stories in the capital that a rare water dragon scale is the sharpest material known to Vedoa. That one cannot break the tip. The Tavalkian heir gave us a portion–as you insisted, so my men report–and little did he guess that the largest scales, like this one, reside in the tail. Emperors of old mounted them on their ruling staffs. I thought it might be of use to you." He shot me a curious glance.

I remembered Bohak presenting the bloody sword to me and read into his insinuation. Rewrapping the scale, I set it at my feet and strove to calm my nerves. So much hinged on this meeting–

Samari lifted his gaze to the wide, fire-colored sky, turning the brand across his forehead gray in the waning light. "You escaped the palace. You killed the oasis's curse. This is what my people whisper. You spark hope for them. They long for a living legend. You won the loyalty of Taval. Even I admit that this is no small thing. I've seen a taste of your fire. If you wield in front of my people, they will follow you." The last words lingered like a question as he turned his gaze to me. "No one can rekindle a stolen flame, as you did for me and my men in the dungeon. Are you the starpalm we wait for?"

My tongue tied. I'd almost rather he'd called me Stable Rat again. We were figuratively walking the edge of molten lava, lack of water on one side and the dynasty on the other. "What am I? I am in the making, as we all are."

"Wisely answered. I assume passing through the Abyss and tasting immortality also factors into what you will ultimately become."

By the sincerity in his expression, he didn't mock, and deep within, I perceived raw desperation. He wanted to believe in me. And I wondered . . . was entering the Abyss how Srolo Kapir intended to complete my Forms? But what of its deadly air Roji described?

A shadow crossed his face. "Unrest grips Vedoa. The poor cry out. Scouts report that the princess forces those in debt to take the form of a Shadow in service to her."

I drew a sharp breath. "That's beyond evil. The Shadow form dooms them to the underworld."

Another strange look crossed Samari's face. "Scouts also report that your Rebellion travels into the Terror Lands even now, along with many desperate people seeking refuge. Everyone seeks you and your promise."

Pressure, heavy and cruel, pressed down further upon me. "We welcome their strength." I gathered my wits and my tongue. "The Rebellion welcomes you and the Exiles, too, Samari, with all the respect that the dynasty has denied you."

The statement hung between us. My nerves twisted. Had I said this well? Could they follow an almost-starpalm?

"I respect your strength." Samari's expression tightened. "But with sand under my tongue, I must also respect the power of the dynasty."

Not what I expected. "Your people crave freedom and their honor restored. Together, we can overthrow the throne. Consider the power of our combined strength."

Samari frowned. "One Tier 3 and a demi-starpalm are not enough."

"We have–"

He put up a hand. "You may be strong enough to fight the princess. You may be the Reborn Star. But you do not fight the princess alone. You fight the bulk of Vedoa and a growing Shadow army. Even if we, the Rebellion, you, and Taval join arms, it cannot be enough. Where does that leave my people? Destroyed."

The truth of his words did not escape me. Time for my last card. If he did not accept this, he was unworthy to join us. "We have Srolo Kapir."

"And what would you do if Srolo Kapir were lost?"

I startled. "He is leader of the Rebellion. Vedoa's fiercest warrior. My trainer. He cannot be lost."

"You don't answer my question." Samari reached into his robes and produced a thin, rolled parchment, dipped in wax as protection against the elements. "I hate bearing bad news, my lady, but my men captured the messenger bird yesterday."

My heart caught. From Srolo Kapir?

Samari extended the letter. I accepted the note and looked questioningly at the white feather caught in the twine.

"The bird was white, to ward away evil, and wore a protective amulet. We would have released it, but knew it would be shot upon its return across the Terror Lands border."

"Srolo Kapir isn't superstitious–" I began, then stopped as a thought gripped me. I ripped the twine free to unroll parchment and see the precise handwriting. The dynasty's seal bulged along the bottom.

Lady Tol,

I am disheartened that we parted on such disagreeable terms. It would have been far better had you remained in the palace under my care. I write to inform you that Srolo Kapir has joined me at the palace as my guest. He is greatly distressed for your safety, after you disappeared in the Terror Lands, and wishes to hold an assembly between the three of us. If you yet live, and we pray to the starpalms that you do, please return to the palace. Your presence alone is sought.

Sincerely,

Princess Xanala

With her gifting, she didn't need to send a physical letter, but this ensured that her vile words would spread and last as far as possible. My knees weakened. I should have guessed. I should have known. "Starpalms, she's captured him, and she lies," I said, voice shaking.

"I agree, but which part is the falsehood?" Samari's chest expanded with heavy breath. "I now fully trust that Srolo Kapir is alive. He is Tier 3. If Xanala has captured him, as we suspect, he will not be treated like the poor."

"You mean she won't warp him into a Shadow?" I restrained more caustic words as I pressed a fist against my chest. I would find and rescue Srolo Kapir. Xanala would pay dearly. I drew myself up. "We will fight for him. We will never give up. The real question is if you will fight with us? I freed you from the city dungeon. I gave you fire." I sounded like a raving lunatic, but I didn't care.

Samari's gaze sharpened. "With every piece of my being, I want to see the dynasty's blood poured upon the floors of the palace. But I will not endanger my people by following my pride into assured death, as Bohak of Taval does."

I glared at him. "He doesn't–"

"This news splinters the Rebellion, my lady, if any part of it is true. The capital will not surrender Srolo Kapir easily, and no one is beyond betrayal, for the right price." His voice soured. "What if he has turned against us, as the princess suggests? Either way, the Rebellion's cause is lost without him. And you have no plan. No, neither I nor the Exiles will join you."

Cowardly. Unthinkable. I wanted to speak but couldn't past rising rage.

Samari continued, "There is a reason no one returns alive from the Terror Lands. They either join us or die by hunger, thirst, or monster, but today I make an exception." He reached around his neck and removed a cord woven with what could only be rockwyrm teeth.

I took a step back. Would he dare insist we join the Exiles after he insulted and refused the Rebellion?

Samari sighed and laid the cord on the ground. "If you ever need to leave the Terror Lands or return, wear this, and my scouts will permit your passage. If you, the Rebellion, or the poor souls fleeing to you ever want refuge among us, all are welcome."

"What about the drought? Will you not act even to stop that?" I retorted.

Samari hesitated. "Indeed. How would you, as a starpalm, return the continent's rains?"

I fell silent. He twisted my question, and I didn't know the answer.

He inclined his head and then descended back into the tunnels. As I watched him leaving me alone with Xanala's letter and the raging wind, I realized something. The Exiles were becoming the so-believed ghosts of the Terror Lands.

21

I STALKED THE PROMONTORY, then sank to the ground, wrapped my arms around my knees, and sat with the rushing wind howling through my thoughts.

I had to come up with a solution to unravel this mess. And I wouldn't eat a bite of food or drink a drop of water or fall asleep until I devised a plan to rescue Srolo Kapir.

Rocks skittered below. "Lady Tol?"

I jerked upright. It was Bohak. *Go away!*

But he climbed the edge of the promontory and upon seeing me, heaved a sigh of relief. "Thank the starpalms, you're all right, as he promised." He sat cross-legged beside me, hands pressed against his knees.

Tears sprang to my eyes, and I blinked them away. I refused to cry. I had to fight.

"Samari's gone," he said.

I gasped. "Already?" Then I looked up. Night had fallen. Stars scattered the sky. Smoke from cooking fires arrested my senses.

"He told me everything." Bohak's voice was edged with disdain. "Good riddance to them if the Exiles won't join the Rebellion's noble cause. As for the letter . . ."

I clenched my jaw as he went on.

"You wouldn't believe the stunts she pulled while training at the Royal Academy. Princess Xanala wouldn't lie about Srolo Kapir's presence at the palace. There's always truth to her schemes. However, we both know he would never betray the Rebellion. She imprisons him to lure you into returning to the capital, for she would never dare to travel here."

If he mentioned their training at the Academy again, I would scream. "Why not lure you? You're the one she loves." I froze. Curse my wayward mouth.

Bohak cleared his throat. "Xanala is naïve. I've never reciprocated her feelings. Our ideals conflict."

Heat crept into my cheeks. "She wants to fight me."

"Yes, before your fourth Form is perfected."

She knew about my Temperance? Of course she did. If not for that weakness, she would never have been able to trap me. Heat surged through my insides again. "She wants me to come alone."

"Out of the question."

"Srolo Kapir is captured because of me. Everything banks on my Temperance. But to this day, no one can explain how in the desert I'm supposed to suddenly be able to possess and control it." I'd raised my voice, but I didn't care. Xanala's words, while her vile soothsayers tried to drain me, twisted through my thoughts. *"My council wishes to end your life, but I will not punish you for the wrongs of others or waste what the starpalms have given you. If you knew what I did, you'd turn against the Rebellion and undo them. Only you can decide how long that decision will take."* What could she mean?

"I wish I understood too." Bohak sighed, and his cheeks pinked, a rare glimpse of vulnerability. "Believe me, Lady Tol, that I would give you my Temperance, if only it were enough."

He'd basically offered to let me drain him and take. His Tier 2 Temperance wasn't enough to complete mine, which was true, but the offer was too much. I didn't know what to say. Was there anything he wouldn't sacrifice? I swallowed. "Thank you, Bohak. I'm honored, and I'll always remember that you considered that, though I would never rob you of something so precious."

He inclined his head. "It is an honor to serve you, Lady Tol. And we must keep courage. Xanala will not harm Srolo Kapir. Fire is sacred to her, and like crossing the gorge into the Terror Lands, she would never go that far."

His words comforted me a little, yet she turned people into Shadows. "I need to save Srolo Kapir."

"*We* need to save him."

"I'll take the palace by firestorm."

"As a starpalm should." Bohak blew out a breath. "Our path forward is simple. After the Rebellion arrives, we train to become a proper army, return to the capital, and fight for Srolo Kapir."

I stared at him. "Are you serious?"

"Victory is so close, Lady Tol. Can't you taste it? Look at what we've accomplished. Xanala knows she cannot withstand you. The palace will empty to pay you homage. We will claim the Abyss. You will pass through the doorway and join the starpalms. It will be like the glorious days of old. *Together*"–he stressed the word–"we will bring about Vedoa's recreation."

I stared, swept up in his beautiful words. Could I believe all of this? Yes. I had to. We would free Srolo Kapir. And he would help me find my Temperance . . .

But would even perfect Forms and immortality gained through the Abyss make me the Reborn Star? If the starpalm spoke to me again, my courage would be stronger.

A jolt of fire raced through my veins. I winced, but thankfully his eyes were so full of stars, he didn't notice. We hadn't trained in days, and my fire was building. I needed to drain myself soon.

Bohak stood and offered his hand.

I paused. If I trusted him, could I trust myself? Drawing a breath, I started to reach for his palm but grasped his forearm instead and pushed myself off the ground. He noticed, and the disappointment in his expression made me feel guilty. It wasn't him, it was me, I wanted to say. But Bohak gestured toward the descent to the trail, allowing me to go first. I scampered down the boulder, glad to escape the awkward moment.

He landed beside me. "Ready yourself," he warned me. "The cooks roast water dragon flesh tonight."

"Perhaps it will prove a delicacy."

"I hope not. I never want to face a water dragon again." He glanced at me. "You impress me, Tol."

I almost snorted. How in the desert could my fire impress him, of all wielders?

"Tricking the firewyrm into the lake was brilliant."

This was the moment. "That was Roji's idea."

"The Laijonese?" Bohak studied me. "You want something. What is it?"

We were spending far too much time together if he could read my thoughts like that. "I want Roji to receive equal protection and respect among the Tavalkians."

"He has it now."

I shot him a look.

Bohak's face was impassive. "We cannot change the experiences and hearts of these men in a day."

Including his, and the wounds he carried, yet this could be a start. "No, but our actions will dictate theirs."

After a moment, he inclined his head. "I will speak to my men, Lady Tol, but in return I request that the Laijonese draw a map to the Immortal Abyss. Please ask him." Bohak frowned. "He'll likely draw a better one if he thinks it's for you."

I bit my tongue. No kidding. I was the only one who didn't hold Roji in animosity.

"Back to our conversation. You were marvelous in thinking to spear the water dragon's gills."

I shrugged. In reality, that was thanks to living in Laijon too. "How long until the Rebellion arrives?"

"Not long at all. My men have spied them on the horizon. Just in time for dragon meat."

22

ONE DAY LATER, FACTIONS OF THE Rebellion arrived from the salt flats, those representing the closer, central villages. Following like a shadow, Vedoa's desperate poor also came. They were more bedraggled and heartbreaking than I could have expected, carrying fear, want, and illness like baggage. Many men, and many women and children. Few animals.

Bohak ordered me to stay within my tent and assigned a double guard. Given the strained circumstances, I complied. For now.

Bohak's men helped the people settle in assigned portions of the garden. In the blink of an eye, they doubled our needs, but would they increase our strength? For now, they stared in wonder at the garden, the lake, the monstrous dragon skeleton claiming the far corner of the oasis, and the curse's skull that Bohak had mounted above the entrance to the volcanic fortress.

That same day, five fights broke out between Rebellion newcomers and impoverished refugees over accusations of stolen supplies. Bohak intervened and created an emergency court to settle disputes. One of the first decisions made was to move Taval inside the fortress, to protect me. So much had happened, I'd almost forgotten my desire to explore the ancient place.

Despite lingering fears, we climbed the stone steps between the waterfalls to make camp inside the numerous chambers of the volcanic fortress. Across smooth rock floors, twisting lava tubes, and carved stairwells, tents bloomed. Bohak discovered a large chamber for himself in which to hold meetings and a nearby staircase leading to a single chamber overlooking the waterfalls through a chiseled, open window. This he gave to me, even installing a strip of fabric to act as my door, and had servants fill it with furnishings.

Roji saluted me with his folded tent braced over one shoulder and disappeared into nearby labyrinthine chambers, promising to return after a bit of exploring. He probably sought a secret place to camp in peace, even after Bohak spoke to his men concerning Roji's safety as promised. How far could one talk impact hardened hearts?

Surrounded by ancient stone walls and borrowed decor, I stood by my new window, the waterfall's crashing filling my ears and faint spray cooling my face. Below, I watched the newcomer camps separate and more squabbles erupt as the poor trespassed through the Rebellion camp for lake water.

I never imagined this would be so messy. How could we bind the people into an army in time? What would Srolo Kapir do? Thinking of him made me restless.

I vaulted to my feet, strode through the cloth covering my door, past surprised guards, and marched down the corridor until it branched into four directions.

One of the soldiers cleared his throat behind me. "Where to, my lady?"

Qo'tah! I needed to memorize this place. "I need to speak with Bohak."

The guard bowed and led me through various passages, our bootsteps clipping against stone, until we came to the gaping, carved doorway leading into Bohak's chambers.

The pile of quilts for his bed, central stone firepit, rug, and table stood where they always had within his tent. Tavalkian officers, congregating in a semicircle, looked up, but Bohak was bent over the table, studying a collection of maps before seeing me and straightening. "Lady Tol." He swept a bow. "Please come in. How may I serve you?"

I lifted my chin. "I have observed the refugees and Rebellion soldiers long enough."

"Ah, yes." Bohak quietly asked his officers to leave. Once they exited, he beckoned me to sit at the table, which I did. He sat again and lowered his voice. "What is your concern?"

"They're constantly clawing one another's throats."

"I know." He shook his head. "All of them are hoarding water. Our own guarded barrels are taken even with the lake open to all."

"They're afraid."

His face was grim. "We need them to be an army. Only half of the refugees can wield, but all want to fight. I'm dividing them into units and setting my men over them. By the desert, I hope the rest of the Rebellion arrives quickly. They ask about Srolo Kapir. I don't know how much longer I can keep them from the information we have, but they're not ready to know. Not yet. We need everyone unified first, or Srolo Kapir's capture could strain us to breaking." He paused. "They clamor for the Reborn Star."

I held my breath. Of course, they wanted to see me, the girl who had struck fear in the dynasty, loosed an army of Shadows, escaped the palace riding a dragon, and defeated the Terror Lands' curse. I couldn't hide from them forever, not from those who sought our shelter and desired to bolster our cause, with fire or without. The Reborn Star was protector and would unite true Vedoa. Who was I if I couldn't begin that? "Then I will stand before them."

Bohak raised a brow. "A demonstration?"

Anxiety coursed through me. Memories of failed evaluations for Tier 2 status drifted through my mind. "Yes."

Bohak rubbed his neck. "If Srolo Kapir were here . . ."

He doubted me. I doubted myself, but that didn't change the logical path forward. I made my spine straight as my staff. "Lend me Temperance."

"Of course." He shook his head again. "We've neglected training for so many days, Lady Tol."

"Tol." I remembered that neglect every time fire burned inside my veins, causing me pain. Tonight. I would drain tonight before it grew any more. I folded my hands in my lap.

Bohak forced a smile. "It pains me to call you by something less than you are."

"How is simply Tol less?"

"You deserve reverence. The Reborn Star requires honor." He gave a brief smile. "And I surrender. They need to see you. Just a short demonstration, impressive and powerful to inspire them to train harder. Perhaps you could wield a Tavalkian horse."

I didn't want their reverence. And had he forgotten my mishap with the foal? "An animated shape." I swallowed. A horse was large, yet so small. They needed more, like a firewyrm or Bohak himself. Considering that made me swallow a smirk. He would probably like that too much.

"Just one shape that demonstrates you are Tier 3, yet more. And I'll remain beside you."

In case I lost control.

Bohak spoke something in the capital tongue and stood.

I stared. "You want to practice now?"

He smiled. "Very good. Your understanding sharpens. And yes to practicing now. That way we can present you tonight after dinner."

My stomach twisted. I needed to drain first, or this would be a disaster, after so many days without wielding. He waited for my reply, and if I told him no, he'd ask why. I rose.

He filled his hands with fire. So did I. Without thinking, I offered a mental prayer to the silent, faraway starpalm. *Please give me control over my fire.*

"Let's start with a rabbit." He wielded a perfect example, a submissive animal that danced obediently from his fingertips and cavorted through the air.

My fire felt like a cauldron of evil potions. I could barely keep my flames inside my hands. Willing myself to succeed, I developed the shape of a rabbit, but a horrifically misshapen one.

Bohak cocked his head and an eyebrow. "That's unusual."

"You have no idea," I said through clenched teeth, then the shape wobbled and burst. I gasped as flames sparked against my face.

Bohak immediately gathered my fire, snatching it from the air and scooping it off the ground. "Extinguish your garments!"

Fire licked the hem of my robes. I bent to snuff it out, coughing on the tendrils of smoke, and rubbed my agonizing hands together.

"Are you burned?" Bohak took hold of my wrists and observed

my ashy palms. His brow creased. "What happened? That wasn't like you."

Oh, but it was. Tears burned my eyes. "My fire's stronger than usual."

"Come again?"

My voice faltered. "I haven't wielded in days."

Quizzical concern etched his face. "And that hurts you?"

I ground my teeth. "I just need to . . ." Perhaps Srolo Kapir had told him about this, as he'd told Ami'beti.

"Need to what?"

Apparently not. I forced myself to speak. "I just need to drain."

He blinked. "How?"

"Sand." Oh, just let the walls cave in already, this was so humiliating! My bane and my curse.

"I've never heard of such a thing, except perhaps as public punishment." His voice quieted. "Who made you do this?"

Everyone.

"Did Srolo Kapir make you do this?"

"No. He . . ." Bohak's gaze was full of compassion and anger on my behalf. It made me want to cry even more. I whispered, "He used his Justice to drain me."

Bohak stiffened. "That's unthinkable. The slightest mistake and he could take it all."

No. He couldn't. No one could. "It helps me control my fire."

"Helps you? I—I believe you." Bohak spoke slowly and released my wrist. "I possess Tier 3 Justice."

Oh no. Not now. Not ever.

"If I can help you in any way, I will. If you trust me to do as Srolo Kapir has done, I swear I will respect and lessen your gifting if it will give you control over your flames."

It would do both, but he wasn't Srolo Kapir.

"You hesitate. I understand." He considered me for a moment. "What if I told you my secret? That would make us even."

I huffed. "Nothing could make us even."

"Wipe your palms off and cup your hands."

"Are you mad?"

"Please, Tol." He glanced past me, checking that the door was clear.

What in the desert was he about to do? I took a breath and obeyed.

"Good. Keep your hands tight and hold them level." Bohak held his finger over my curved palms. For a moment, nothing happened, and then moisture gathered on his fingertips. Growing into droplets that tapped against my dry skin.

I gasped. "Water."

"Shh." He continued until I held a handful of water. "Drink."

I did, and it tasted fresh and clean. Wonder swirled within me. I stared at him in awe. "How can you do this?"

"My great-grandmother was Ai'Biroan." He cleared his throat. "I never met her, but I heard she was beautiful and that Taval revered her and her gift. Somehow, her gifting resurfaced in me."

Ai'Biro, one of the islands east of Laijon. This explained Bohak's deeper coloring. It could even explain Taval's wealth and strength, as she would have made his great-grandfather rich by supplying water. Had she come on her own? I'd heard that some foreigners were drawn to Vedoa's mystery and power. Or had she been captured in a raid along the spice trail? I wondered if her marriage had been happy. And if she had missed her ocean and islands.

I refocused. "Xanala mentioned something about you and fog."

"To wield any gifting, you need a source. During winter, when the mountains collect fog, I can fill jars with water. During times of drought–like now–the gifting is almost useless. I can wield here because the lake breathes into the air. Besides family, Princess Xanala was the only person I ever revealed this to. And now you."

He was double gifted. I'd never heard of such a thing.

He held his hands in front of him again, already dry from the hard air. "Please allow me to help you."

I exhaled slowly. Did I trust him? If not now, when? I held out my hands.

Carefully, he folded my palms against his. I wanted to wrench away. Memories of Xanala's soothsayers gripping my hands accosted me, along with darker recollections I pushed down as hard as I could.

I focused on the callouses thickening his skin, a testament that he had lived a northern village life at some point, and braced for pain.

"Ready?"

"Yes." I released my grip on my fire. Just a trickle. Enough for him to take, but not enough to hurt him.

My fire flowed into his hands, almost as if it wanted to. The transfer was so smooth, I gasped.

He stopped. "Did I hurt you?"

"No."

He continued, and I felt as though I'd just trekked the desert for hours carrying a haversack filled with rocks, and now passed the burden to someone else. "Your Justice is so strong, almost soothing. Even Srolo Kapir's wasn't . . ."

He hid a smile, working quietly and methodically.

I let my shoulders drop. "Do you want to keep the fire?"

"I wouldn't dream of it. It's dishonorable, and I can't retain this much. I'm simply releasing the elements into the atmosphere or, as elder Justice wielders used to say, returning the fire to the starpalms." Faint strain etched across his face.

"It's hurting you."

"I'm fine."

"It's enough." I extracted my hands and rubbed them together. Feeling instantly refreshed, but also guilty. "I'm sorry."

This time he didn't smile. "I understand why you don't mingle fire as a greeting. I have never taken so much fire from someone. I suspected but wasn't sure until now." His gaze pierced mine. "Your Magnificence is endless, isn't it?"

My mouth dried.

"Please, Tol. Explain it to me."

I struggled to speak. "It's–it's like there's a seed of fire deep inside of me. No matter how hard someone tries to drain me completely, to take it all, they can't. The seed always regrows."

"*. . . From an endless well.*" He recited the words slowly, reverently. "*Her fire will cleanse the monster's lair.* Tol, by slaying the water dragon, you've fulfilled two of the prophecies. And one in a way I never thought possible."

Many had slain the water dragon, not just me. My eyes pled with him. "Please don't tell anyone about my Magnificence. Ever."

"Of course." But his expression glowed with awe and triumph. "Until it is the right time to reveal it. We'll keep each other's secrets." He grinned. "We'll repaint your Tier 3 symbol. Tonight, you'll wield a Tavalkian horse. The people will trust that you're a Tier 3, but when we save Srolo Kapir, and you receive your Temperance, the continent will know that a starpalm walks among them."

Bohak said to wear red, that the people would expect it. I almost reminded him that the palace soldiers wore scarlet, but didn't. My quaking heart forced me into silence before I retreated to the privacy of my room to nurse my nerves.

Now I waited within the shadows of the fortress, pressing damp palms down my ruby skirts, and fought to peer through the knot of guards filling the fortress entrance and steps. Behind us, in the darkness of twisting chambers, I knew Roji watched.

Sunset had passed, and night overtook the gardens and what I could see of the lake. The Rebellion and refugees sat in the clearing in front of the steps, families making obvious clumps. Waiting for me to be revealed.

Bohak spoke to the crowd with an energy that made me forget he'd slept perhaps four hours the night before, holding constant meetings with his officers and the Rebellion leaders. He stood in the middle of the entryway, between large, carved stone bowls lit only with embers, kept banked to darken the night further and sharpen my display. His flowing robes whispered around his feet as he addressed the people, and his new breastplate of spirit scales reflected the absence of light. He said *Reborn Star* and bowed in my direction. The guards in front of me parted.

The hush was maddening as I crossed past Bohak to stand on his right side–close, to help as promised–and looked at the crowd.

They'd washed, drunk water, and eaten. The people looked more well on the outside than when I'd spied on them at their arrival, but fear, carried by a thread of hope, still haunted their eyes. And Bohak was only partially right. They didn't care about my dress color, focusing on the freshly painted Tier 3 symbol adorning my forehead.

I held my breath. Was I supposed to say something? I couldn't remember. It felt like putting on pageantry when we could be storming across the desert to save Srolo Kapir. My rational side reminded me that this display was for Srolo Kapir's rescue. Courage and unity for the people. I must deliver both.

I lifted my hands high. Without fire, and I really didn't know why. Perhaps as a tribute to the starpalms, who I hoped would speak to me again. Then I opened my hands with fire, preparing to wield a Tavalkian horse that would barely attest to Tier 3 status. Small courage. Possible unity.

What of a firewyrm that communicated power and danger? Bohak's eyes would fall out of his head.

No. Even a dragon wasn't enough. I needed to take a bigger risk and hesitated.

Bohak tensed, sensing my indecision. Armor clinked as guards shifted behind me, and the crowd below waited.

This was for them. Vedoa's wounded and lost. I could do nothing if I didn't give them my all. I drew a breath, felt the thin current of Temperance weaving between my Wisdom, Justice, and mighty Magnificence, and brushed my hands across the sky, painting into the starless night. A flaming waterfall, like those roaring from the mountains into the lake, poured from my hands. It splashed at my feet and burned across stone. Two rushing rivers, their searching tails like those of a dragon, surged toward the glowing stone bowls and filled them with inferno. I shaped a cloud and expanded it as much as I dared, making it writhe with storm. Let the people see my Magnificence, their hope. Some gasped. I smiled and split the cloud so one half hovered over one bowl, and the second thundered above the other. Then I made my hands dance and sprinkled tiny, flickering raindrops, the tiniest flecks of flame floating down into the bowls. Displaying my Wisdom.

People cheered, but I wouldn't stop, not when Temperance felt stronger than any experience I'd had of it in my life. I stretched my empty right hand toward Bohak. At first confused, Bohak's expression smoothed into understanding. He spun three concentric, revolving perfect rings of fire, and released them to float toward me. I reached to accept the gift and absorbed the shape into my hand with Justice. Before the crowd could react, I extended my free hand to them.

An older woman separated herself from the newcomers and hurried toward me. She bowed and presented her own offering, a single flame of fire, though a strong one for a Tier 1.

A thought invaded my mind, one so wonderful that I questioned if it was my own. Her Tier didn't define her. Fire or no fire, we needed each other.

I accepted her flame and flung my hands heavenward, and a flock of flaming mangi birds soared over the crowd, the symbol of the lost winter rains. I froze.

Bohak hadn't given me any fire until now. The first part of tonight's Temperance, which had felt so strong, was my own. My ears filled with resounding cheers, and I looked around in a daze.

The people were standing and calling out delighted exclamations. Loyalty to serve and to fight. *Reborn Star* shouted constantly.

Overwhelmed, I searched for something to anchor me. To Bohak.

Delight filling his eyes, he lifted his face in the Taval victory cry. Tavalkians responded like a thundering echo, and the newcomers cheered all the louder, then their chant changed to two names, mine and Bohak's.

Bohak offered me an apologetic look. Somehow, I laughed, and leaned closer to shout, "Together, yes?"

His eyes crinkled with a smile. He looked ready to speak but didn't. Instead, he took my fingers in his and, as if I were empress of Vedoa, raised the back of my hand to his lips. Below and behind us, guards and newcomers doubled their ovation.

Warmth flooded me. We were united, and we would unify the rest—and yet his gesture was something more. A far, new expectation settled upon my shoulders, balancing upon everything else. I refused to put it into words or accept it. As if another invisible hand touched my shoulder, I looked backward.

Filed among Tavalkian guards, Roji stood frozen in the middle of clapping, any smile wiped from his face.

Beside me, Bohak lifted one hand to the crowd, while continuing to hold mine with his other.

None of this meant anything, I told myself.

Reborn Star. Reborn Star. Reborn Star!

My fire wobbled. They didn't notice, but Bohak did, eyes darting. I quickly freed my hand from his and reached toward my flames. Drawing them to return. And they did, like a miracle, and I closed my hands, extinguishing it all, filling the oasis with darkness.

The crowd gasped before roaring anew as I startled. I'd never been able to contain my own flames once my Temperance was spent. Had a starpalm assisted me?

Fires flickered between wielders' hands, lending illumination again as they raised their palms and continued to cheer.

No. I didn't deserve this. I shut my eyes to block everything out. We celebrated today, but what about tomorrow? Tomorrow, I saw war. I saw blood spilled before palace walls. I saw victory, but I also saw great loss. I saw those who had dedicated their lives to following me—the well-equipped and those who were not, giving the best they could—losing those lives. All while Srolo Kapir suffered at Xanala's hands, waiting for an untrained army to save him.

Panic clawed up my throat. I couldn't breathe—

Several people screamed.

I opened my eyes and suppressed a cry.

Above the crowd and smoke rising from our flames, something shifted among the rocks crowning the crater's rim. It expanded bat-like wings and swooped over the mountains, disappearing into the night. A Shadow.

23

A SHADOW INVADED THE TERROR Lands. Did it serve Xanala?

Soldiers unsheathed swords, and palms burst with flames.

Bohak had taken my arm and now led me to my quarters, brushing past Roji. His breastplate of water-dragon scales undulated with color as we passed by wall torches up the stairs to my room. Bohak wielded a spinning star and animated it to hover in my open window as a deterrent, promising that, if I fed the shape, it would last until morning. Then I found myself alone in my room, staring at the revolving star, hearing the murmurs of guards protecting my stairwell.

When I finally slept, nightmares of Xanala accosted me. Commanding armies of Shadows. Slaying Srolo Kapir. Reaching into a golden doorway.

I thrashed awake, burning tears in my eyes. Quiet gripped the oasis. How long until dawn? The star continued to hiss in my window.

I longed to run to the desert, but the desert was so far. Stomach tightening, I rose from my bed, swept the travel cloak around my shoulders, and stole out the cloth-covered doorway to the stairwell.

The two Tavalkian guards on duty straightened.

I lifted my head and passed them, veering toward Bohak's chambers. Then I realized I remained barefoot.

One guard moved to follow me, but the other didn't. Both watched me go in silence.

As soon as the path split, I turned in the opposite direction of Bohak. Spiraling deeper and deeper into the heart of the volcanic fortress, beyond eyes and ears.

If the crater holding the oasis was created from an ancient volcanic eruption, the peaks surrounding us were like child volcanoes, born through its violence. In the center of this peak, this fortress, Tavalkians whispered that they'd found an empty magma chamber, a "pit of the underworld."

The stone corridor widened into a round chamber and a large, dark hole. I crept to the edge of the monstrous chasm devouring the rock floor. A jagged pit gaped. The emptied magma chamber appeared bottomless, but it couldn't hold the inner pressure I carried.

I sat and dangled my feet over the rim. If Bohak saw me, he'd be horrified and drag me to safety. I huffed. My life was no longer my own, but when had it ever belonged to me?

You are mine the starpalm had said.

But what did that mean? And why did the starpalm remain silent? Had it abandoned me?

Telling myself it didn't matter, I formed a messy ball of fire in my hands, as opposite of Bohak's glassy shapes as was possible, and flung it into the chasm. The fire fell and puddled into glowing embers at the bottom. Ah, the pit held a secret: a broken stairwell built into the side of the rock wall.

I eased over the rim and found the first step with my toes. Heart racing, I let go of the cavern's edge. Clinging to the wall, I eased down the stairs. My one foot felt nothing but air. I flung more fire and saw that the stairs ended in a stark ledge. My heart sank.

I couldn't continue, my path cut off. Tears of frustration sprung to my eyes.

Srolo Kapir suffered at Xanala's hands. Bohak and I waited for the rest of the Rebellion, training those present, including refugees. Discord erupted between factions. Cursed Shadows encroached on the Terror Lands. I didn't know how long my wielding demonstration would keep the people together, or if we could even fight as a whole successfully.

Xanala demanded that I come alone. Our plan felt weak, as Samari had said. Who were we against the dynasty without Srolo Kapir? What if we failed? Srolo Kapir would join my train of failures with my parents, whoever they really were, my guardians, Ami'beti–

I wiped my tears and gritted my teeth. I'd wielded well earlier that evening, and I could do it again. I would succeed for Srolo Kapir.

I stood on the ledge and filled my hands with flames. Relentless Magnificence, Justice to take, Wisdom to shape–there, I felt the strand of Temperance. I formed teeth and bone, the head of a firewyrm. Reaching and straining, I wielded its body and tail. Scales, spines, limbs. I animated the creature to soar in a circle over my head. I'd forgotten wings. I wrought delicate ones, but they didn't come out right. They looked like–

My Temperance slipped.

The firewyrm's body folded into one of a man. Arms and legs. Terrible, batlike wings. A screaming mouth. A flaming Shadow.

I held my breath, and the shape burst. Embers of fire rained down, and I covered my head and pressed against the wall. Unable to extinguish my own loss of self-control, as I had done so recently for the first time, and without Bohak to help. I swatted fire from my clothes, trembling as the threat passed. Ash covered me, and the floor of the pit below glowed.

I wept. It felt like my soul was cut open and scooped out. Everyone, including Srolo Kapir, was depending on a faulty foundation. How could I be a starpalm, wallowing in my own ash?

Stillness touched my consciousness. I froze, even as tears dripped off my chin, and held my breath.

The presence of the starpalm grew.

My thoughts rushed. *Where did you go? Who are you?*

"I am one."

One. Just like Srolo Kapir believed.

Why did you choose me before my Forms were perfected? Did you choose me at all?

Silence.

Please stay. I need your help. I'm not who Vedoa needs me to be.

"Will you follow me?"

The question took me aback. But there was only one answer.

Where else can I go?

I felt the starpalm's joy. And with it, hope soared in my heart. I pushed hair from my face with the heels of my sooty hands.

Can I see you?

The starpalm strengthened around me. *"Will you follow me?"*

Tears slipped down my cheeks.

I need you. I'm not enough.

The presence strengthened around me and then lessened. Receding up the stairs.

I gripped the wall and climbed over the edge into the top of the chamber. I felt the starpalm hover. Could almost see it. Then it faded away.

I reached up. Stretching as high as I could.

Don't leave me.

And yet, though I could no longer feel the starpalm, somehow a piece of it remained. Like an otherworldly friend.

"Tol?"

I startled.

A lanky form stood in the darkness. Roji.

"*Qo'tah.* What happened?" He drew near, staring.

The ash. I rubbed my forearm across my face.

"That made it worse. Here." Roji gently brushed soot from my face. "Are you well?"

My mind was still swirling. I focused myself. "I was practicing and made a mistake."

"What in the continent were you wielding?"

"Something impossible."

"Without Bohak of Taval?" He snorted.

Was Roji jealous of Bohak? Or did he just dislike him, being Laijonese? "What are you doing here?"

Roji shrugged. "There's a wealth of peace and quiet in these passages."

"Please tell me they're treating you better."

He shrugged again. "No one has picked a fight lately. Some of the high-and-mighty capital dwellers even respond to me in the high tongue, now that they realize I've been enjoying their gossip all this time." He studied the chasm. "How are you doing really?"

Terrible. Better now that the starpalm had spoken again, but questions still stirred. "I'm fine."

Roji shook his head. "You don't fool me. The hope placed in you must be unbearable, but you'll know what to do. You love your country. That's why they stand behind you."

If I loved my country, why did I keep hurting my friends?

He continued. "I can attest that, with your courage, you've got to be at least three-quarters light-wielder at heart, which gives you a fine edge. Which is part of why I gladly follow you."

I saw him glance my way out of the corner of my eye.

He wanted to help me smile, but my stomach tightened. Lives had been lost for my sake, with more to come. I couldn't lose him too.

Roji had to live. I wouldn't lose anyone else.

Unaware that he was the object of my inner turmoil, Roji tried again. "And the Father of Light will protect you."

"That's a Laijonese god. I'm Vedoan."

Roji's voice grew serious. "If there's a god–or starpalm, as you call it–powerful enough to create a path through this mess, to have a plan for it all, then that god is strong enough to rule everything alone."

That was interesting. I pondered. Could Laijon's god and the starpalm who spoke to me be the same? Would a divine being so powerful protect my friends?

"Follow me," the starpalm had said. If the starpalm was with me, then who could stand against us? And finally, I knew what I needed to do.

24

FLAMING CRIMSON FILLED THE SKY.

I hung my desert-colored traveling robes and scarf from the changing screen. My haversack, repacked and heavy, rested against the wall, one item lighter.

When I moved aside the cloth covering from my doorway, Roji stood with another Tavalkian as my bodyguard tonight, having been added to the regular rotation. Surely, the starpalm smiled on me again. I inclined my head toward both and descended the stairwell. They fell into positions behind. The carved entrance loomed ahead, congested with soldiers as was now usual. I went through the open doorway into the garden and savored the chirping and singing night sounds. The air hung thick with delicious dinner smells.

Bohak hailed me, and I felt as though I traversed a dream. Tavalkians and newcomers cheered at my appearance. I smiled, an act upon an act, and took my place at the head of the rugs and cushions making our grand table. As always, scouts manned the peaks above.

Drinks were poured and bowls filled with stew. Bohak lifted his hands to bless the starpalms as constellations twinkled above lush treetops. Everyone commenced eating.

Tavalkian soldiers circled with additional drinks. I stood and accepted cups for Bohak, his officers, the nearby Rebellion leaders, and even my Tavalkian bodyguard. But not Roji.

Bohak observed this with quiet surprise, but his eyes warmed as he murmured thanks and accepted the cup from my hand.

I sat again and avoided Roji's suspicious gaze as the powerful drank. *Please, let the timing work.*

At last, Bohak and his inner circle finished their meal and rose to attend a meeting with the Rebellion leaders. After they left, my bodyguards followed me back to my room.

I passed into my chamber, pulse pounding. I removed my gown, donned my traveling clothes, slipped my staff into my belt, and pulled my haversack strap over my shoulder. What of the scale Samari had given me? No, I would only take my staff and fire.

Roji's voice reached my ear. "Get up, man. Mysteries of the continent." There was a pause. "Tol!"

I pressed through the cloth.

The Tavalkian had collapsed into an unconscious heap across the stairs. Roji stood on the step above him and looked up at me. "He just fell. I barely caught him–"

"Inside." I grabbed Roji's arm and pulled him through the doorway.

"*Qo'tah,* Tol. What's going on? Why are you wearing that?"

"I drugged him with a sleeping potion." Thank you for the now-empty bottle, Ami'beti.

Roji spluttered.

"I also drugged Bohak, his officers, and the Rebellion leaders." I tried to ignore his shocked expression. "We have to get a message to Laijon."

"What?"

"The drought reaches across the continent. We've lost our strongest warrior. If we're going to overthrow the dynasty, we need Laijon's help. You can accomplish that." I gave him a little push. "Get your things. Do you have other clothes?"

"You're serious." His eyes widened. "My belongings confiscated by palace guards?"

I tugged at him. "I'll get you something. Come on."

We slipped through the fortress. Thankfully, the usual crowd of soldiers still ate or handled dinner clean up. We neared Bohak's quarters, and I lifted my hand to halt Roji. "Stay here."

He didn't protest. Satisfied that he would obey, I lifted my chin and strode down the corridor lined with conscious Tavalkian guards, blessedly congregating away from Bohak's quarters to allow privacy for any discussion. They offered my garments curious looks. One moved forward to announce my presence, but I shook my head and stepped through the leather door covering.

The central stone fireplace filled with dancing sparks. All around Bohak's table, his officers and Rebellion leaders lay across cushions, unconscious.

Somehow, Bohak had made it to his bed, and lay curled up, dressed in his elegant robes.

I let out a relieved breath and turned my attention to my task at hand.

Roji needed supplies.

Without ceremony, I raided Bohak's chests. Finding plain traveling clothes belonging to Taval's Tier 3 heir was as tricky as I'd imagined. I settled on the simplest thing I could find, then hunted until coming across a satchel, water skin–filled by Bohak's miraculous gifting?–and confiscated the dried meat, fruit, and nuts from the table surrounded by sleeping men. That and a good quality Tavalkian sword was all I needed, but I glanced at Bohak's still form and hesitated. I should write him a letter . . . No, there wasn't time.

Go, my rational side urged.

Instead, I perched on the edge of Bohak's bed.

In sleep, the concerns lining his face softened. I saw his Ai'Biroan great-grandmother's blood more clearly than ever. Hair fell across one eye, and his Tier 3 paint glimmered beneath firelight. I remembered my symbol and used my sleeve to rub the paint off my forehead until my skin felt raw.

He'd sacrificed almost everything for the Reborn Star, but his life was too valuable to be lost for mine.

Tears pricked my eyes as I whispered. "I'm going after Srolo Kapir. If the starpalm blesses me, I'll return with him. If not, lead the Rebellion well."

Carefully, I brushed hair from his eyes then rose and fled his chamber as if a ghost chased me. Remembering to slow as I passed the guards, I found Roji waiting where I'd left him. I handed him my laden haversack and the sword, carrying Bohak's partially filled satchel myself, and led the way to the fortress entrance.

Guards noticed our exit. How could they not? But I held my head high and passed into the garden with Roji–technically, my bodyguard–in my wake. None stopped us.

Fighting through the thickest portions of garden, we reached the original access to the tunnels, guarded by the monstrous dragon skeleton. Scouts surely kept watch above us, but they looked outside, not inside the oasis.

Roji balked. "We can't go in there–"

"If we don't wield, and remain apart, the rockwyrms will feel our heat without thinking we're big enough to be a threat."

"How do you know that?"

I sighed. "Desert living. I've seen a lot of rockwyrm nests."

"But–"

"Come on." I walked around looming bones and entered the darkness of the cave. Everywhere, countless creatures rustled as they sensed us. True to Vedoa's desert, these small dragons merely watched as I walked into the roofless, barren tunnels and waited. If he made me go back for him–

Roji emerged from the hole, pale-faced and wide-eyed.

I spread my hands. "Trust me now?"

"Please, don't ever ask me to do that again." He brushed his clothes off and shivered.

We started off through splitting, curving tunnels. It was a miracle that we ever found the oasis in the first place. If we headed east, we'd reach the vale of rocks we'd traversed to arrive here. A perfect place to sneak past Bohak's scouts.

Bohak's spare sword hung at Roji's hip. "So, how are we getting to Laijon? North or cutting straight east?"

"I'm deciding. First, tell me how to get to the Immortal Abyss."

"*Qo'tah,* Tol. Why now? We have more urgent plans to make."

"Humor me."

"Stubborn as Taval's highbrow horses," he growled. "All right. At the top of the palace, there's an imposing throne room with a balcony. Heavily guarded by delightful palace soldiers. A thin bridge runs from the balcony into the mountains."

"And?"

"There's a gate. The princess had the key."

Deserts, how was I going to work around that?

"Past the gate are seven chained dragons. Something like a dragon keeper entered first and fed the beasts, which allowed us to pass. The passage is dark and narrow. It branches into countless passages, chambers, and holes, like the fortress we're walking away from. Direction of sounds is impossible to discern, and it's hot. Follow your thumb crease."

"My what?"

He reached for my hand, making me halt, and traced the line closest to my thumb on my palm with his finger. "At the end of that, you'd reach an expansive cavern. In the far back, there's a seemingly bottomless hole. Stairs are built into the hole, and at the bottom is an altar and a pool. The stolen doorway lies underwater, beneath the pool."

Was it another emptied magma chamber? Stolen door . . . I'd forgotten the Laijonese histories that said Vedoa stole the gate from Laijon when our countries divided. I motioned him to start walking again.

"But you wouldn't touch the Abyss or its aura, right?" Roji pressed. "Of course, you wouldn't, because I won't let you. So, back to Laijon. Which path has the fewest firewyrms, Exiles, and Shadows?"

I stiffened. "East is best."

We wound on and on, choosing the thicker passages with the sprinkling of stars above beckoning us on, until the rock walls widened, and we came upon the windy expanse of boulders, broken stones, and soaring arches. Wasteland. How had we led the horses through this?

"I can't believe we're leaving." Roji exhaled and drew himself up. "I will introduce you to Queen Kiboro. Laijon will join the Vedoan Rebellion. Together, may we finish what opening the Eternity Gate started."

I studied him. His Laijonese elegance and kind eyes were a painful but sweet reminder of the only true family and home I'd known until Srolo Kapir.

I reached around my neck and tugged Samari's cord of dragon teeth free. "This guarantees safe passage through the Terror Lands. Take it."

Roji eyed the gift. "Why me?"

"Because you're going to Laijon, and I'm staying here."

Roji stiffened. "Come again? I'm not leaving you."

I won't let you die because of me. You only wield light! I fisted my hands and spoke carefully. "The Rebellion needs me here. You're a trained soldier, and Laijonese, our best hope for an alliance."

Indecision crossed his face. And hurt. "We can go to Laijon and then return."

He was tearing my heart to shreds. "There isn't time, and I can't keep protecting you. It hurts my position with everyone else. This is the best way you can help. Are you dedicated to this cause or not?" As soon as the words flew from my mouth, I knew they were both right and so very wrong.

He clamped his mouth shut. Damage done.

"We need this," I said, trying to salvage the chasm I'd created.

He stared at me for a long, unbearable moment. I thought he would fight me. His expression didn't soften, but he nodded. "I swore my loyalty to you, Tol. If this is how I can best serve you, so be it."

I tried to think of something else to say.

"One thing, before we part. Something I should've asked days ago, especially now that I know how much trouble my presence has caused you," he said, his voice clipped. "Our mother. Does she still live?"

I felt like I'd been slapped. My first guardian, the woman who'd hidden me in Laijon as a baby and walked me back out years later when she couldn't stand her foreign life, husband, and bad-luck twins any longer, was not what I wanted to discuss. And yet, since we'd reunited, I knew he would ask, and somehow, he sensed that she was gone. She had been so ill when she left. My parents were taken from me. What was it like to grow up knowing one of yours had chosen to walk away? "No. She passed after returning to Vedoa. I'm . . . sorry."

He offered a curt bow and strode into the night, long legs crossing over shattered rock. Alone. Barely armed.

I couldn't believe we'd just had that conversation, and now he was leaving. Everything felt so wrong. We couldn't part like this, but I was keeping him as safe as I knew how. Traveling the Terror Lands alone was better than what was coming.

I waited as long as I could, before I was sure he'd put enough distance between himself and our scouts, then I headed in the opposite direction. Not toward the oasis, but past it.

As soon as rocks turned to salt flats, I ran as fast as I could under the sliver of moon, until my breaths heaved and my body forced me to halt. Then I ran again, Bohak's satchel slapping against my back. Adrenaline coursed through exhaustion.

I couldn't live this half-life anymore, when my friends stood on the brink of defeat and Xanala imprisoned Srolo Kapir. A starpalm spoke to me and asked me to follow. *Let me die or become the Reborn Star.* And if I died, let it not be as a victim to Xanala's schemes, but by my own fire. Never hers.

25

WARMTH AND LIGHT TRICKLED across my face through damaged lattice roofing. I heard people talking and animals braying outside the abandoned stable. I sat up from a bed of dirt and straw and rubbed my neck. The satchel of dwindling supplies made a terrible pillow. A family of three, who'd also paid one dacri coin for the privilege of sleeping here, had already left.

Brushing off my filthy traveler's robes, I shouldered the satchel and peeked into the busy street to glimpse the capital city illuminated by day.

Thick congestion reminded me of a rockwyrm nest. It was worse than when Bohak had led me through like a parade. All of Vedoa flocked to the capital and the palace's reservoir of water as the rest of the country's oases dried up.

There would be more Shadows now too. But as long as I walked by light, I wouldn't run into any night-loving monsters.

And as long as I avoided guarded public cisterns, the thickest and most dangerous parts of the city, I'd make good time.

I pressed through the crowd, my hood falling across my brow. Through seedy districts, vile stenches, and sun-bleached awnings covering alleyways, the palace walls winked in and out of my vision.

Word on the street said that the palace held a festival—dared to do so during a drought—which I hoped would serve to my advantage. When I reached the high wall, noble carriages fought to pour through the open gates under the sharp eyes of scarlet-robed palace soldiers. I fell into line and pretended to lead a packhorse laden with gifts for the council, joining the upper class selling their heartless souls for favor and water, and got through the gate and into the lush gardens. The dynasty's gardens couldn't hold a candle flame to the refuge within the Terror Lands, but they would help me sneak behind the palace to the mountains, which rose like gods between Vedoa and the vast, empty seas. The sun dipped toward the horizon, casting rust-colored light and long shadows across the grounds.

Bohak, perhaps even Srolo Kapir, had envisioned a grand, traditional battle by fire in the palace amphitheater. But things never turned out the way we wished, and surprise was my greatest weapon. That, and encountering Xanala before her army could catch up.

I reached the back of the palace and sheer mountain faces. To the south, the monstrous, cut-stone reservoir, unscalable, sat between the palace and the city. To the north, high up the palace walls, the throne room balcony bulged, and a thin stone bridge arched from the palace into the mountaintops. That was where I needed to go.

Shrieks resounded overhead. I hid behind a clump of fruitless trees and watched several Shadows wing across the dusky sky and disappear over the city.

I tensed. I knew the monsters would be here, but they were so close. Too close. And coming off the mountains I needed to climb. How many were there?

The answer wouldn't stop me.

I crept through the falling darkness to hide among the crags and roots of the mountain, then looked up. It was a challenging climb that would take half the night. I wrapped the satchel tight around me, strapped my staff across my back, sought foothold and handhold, and began to climb.

I ascended into mountain peaks, reaching into thin breaks, gripping with my toes, pushing with my legs. Pausing for breath, moving slowly to avoid detection. My arms burned. I'd lived in a furnished tent for too long.

At last, as the moon arced over the world, the delicate bridge appeared just two lengths above me.

I pulled myself atop a sizable cleft and sat, trembling from exertion. I nibbled and sipped on the dregs of my rations, rested for a couple fingerlengths of the moon's passing, then crouched to remove my traveling clothes from over the beautiful, desert-gray robe that Ami'beti had given me. Woven from her goats' hair and stiff with fire-retardant coating, the same robe I'd worn the last time I came here. I left the satchel behind, repositioned my staff, and climbed again until I got to a place where I could jump, grab the bridge, and swing myself on top. I crouched and looked around.

Behind lay the unsuspecting palace. Ahead, rough tunnels shaped by ancient lava flows snaked into the mountains, leading to the Abyss.

I passed into this deeper darkness, officially safe from sight, and walked until the path ended in a deep, carved hole and metal gate. Just as Roji described.

Xanala had the key, but there were other ways.

I pushed the gate, and it cracked open. I pushed it in again and saw that a chain held the gate closed, which Roji hadn't mentioned, but the length was generous. Thank the starpalms, I was smaller boned than average. Holding my breath, I squeezed through the opening, turning my head, and found myself inside the tunnel.

Mystery and silence, so different from the quiet of the desert, reigned ahead.

My footsteps whispered against stone. Gloom consumed me, and a breath of stale air carried a reek that made my nose water. It was cloyingly fragrant, metallic, damp, and then I smelled excrement. Chains clinked.

I filled my hand with a flicker of flame.

A towering barred wall rose on my left. My breath caught. Seven pairs of shimmering blue eyes watched high above me through bars. The imprisoned dragons swayed their heads and stomped their chained feet.

I ran.

One dragon roared. The second blew a stream of fire.

I threw myself down and rolled. Heat raked over me. I covered my head, felt the gasp of cave air again, then scrambled forward, ahead of the second blast. I disappeared into darkness so thick, I needed to stretch both hands to skim the narrowing walls hemming me in. The dragons snorted behind.

I gulped breaths, feeling like my heart would burst. Anger flickered in my chest. Despicable dynasty, trapping such prized animals in perpetual darkness and training them to such cruelty. When the Rebellion prevailed, everything would change. I swore it would be so.

I felt my way forward. The passage turned, narrowed, descended, climbed, but never split. Once, I needed to turn my shoulders to pass and imagined the past emperors and empresses who had tread this same path. After what felt like forever, light glimmered in the distance. A second opening.

I stepped through to an endless chamber, pockmarked as far as I could see through the darkness by deep, spiraling wounds dug out of the earth. Centuries worth of mining for precious stones. But where was the light? I looked up. A sliver of the night sky shone above, speared by the heads of ancient volcanoes.

I traced my finger across my thumb line and looked in the blind distance and stilled.

Hulking, human shapes materialized in the darkness, but they remained motionless. I realized they were statues carved in the melded likenesses of starpalms and Vedoa's past rulers, frozen into stone. Beyond them, according to Roji's directions, the pit holding the Immortal Abyss would lie, but as much as I wanted to see it, I would wait here. For her.

My mind wandered to Roji. Where was he now? Was he safe?

Suddenly, I sensed a strength outside myself. I took in a quick breath, then reached for it, feeling the otherness hovering near me.

The faithful starpalm didn't speak, but it was there. If I asked, would it protect Roji instead of me?

Handfuls of fire burst to life among the towering statues.

I jumped back, startled, then filled my hands with flames. And froze.

An army of bare-chested Shields, skin slick with flame-retardant salve, stepped out from darkness. All bearing Tier 2 paint, their flames red and orange, none wielding the lesser blue fire, tainted gift of the emperor.

Xanala appeared among them, but kept a great space between us.

Chills crept across my skin. The lack of scouts, the missing dragon keeper, and dragons fed with fresh, reeking carcasses. All a trap. I bit back an oath and scrutinized Xanala's whispering, silken gown, not meant for fighting. She wore the empress's crown on her head. By the desert, she'd officially stolen Vedoa's throne.

Xanala studied me in return. From her rigid hands to the tension in her posture, I saw the war between confidence in her power and fear of me taking place within her. I smelled burning incense. Murmuring soothsayers paced the outskirts of the pock-marked chamber, likely warding away whatever vile spirits they assumed clung to me from my journey into the Terror Lands. If they only knew what I'd really battled, and the deity I came with. I stood taller. My hands ceased trembling.

At last, Xanala spoke in the common tongue. "You came alone. I didn't think you would. Is Bohak well?"

I avoided rolling my eyes. "He mourns the people you've transformed into Shadows."

"How little you both understand because you refuse to listen," she said. "Our conflict here is what keeps Vedoa from water. Even the strong hand of the palace cannot stop the uprisings and guerilla activity claiming the villages. The people flee to me for water and for strength. They beg me for a Shadow's stronger form and serve me willingly."

I glared. "Silver tongue."

Xanala stiffened. "I'm sorry for you, Tol, drowned in lies and dragging others with you, like Bohak, who was content to serve the good of the people here until the Rebellion began spinning falsehoods."

"Enough. I'm here for Srolo Kapir."

From among her Shields, the Pirthyian Emeridus stepped forward, one of his foreign, wild dogs darting around his feet. Unadulterated loss and hatred took me aback. He spat something in the high tongue, his accent harsh.

The princess remained focused on me. "Since Laijon, he's suspicious of anything having to do with prophecy, such as you. Ignore him." She spread out her arms. "Isn't it exhausting being so strong and alone? Having few to trust? We're not so different, you and I." Her eyes glistened. "I want so much for us to be friends. Imagine how strong we could be together. Tol, please cease fighting me."

A snake in silks. Where was she going with this?

"You see my crown and think I've seized the throne. Little do you understand that I had to, to keep Vedoa from crumbling under this terrible age while you retreated to the Terror Lands. You think I've kidnapped Srolo Kapir to trap you. Nonsense. But the truth is a mist in the back of your mind. How can you know it when you've been steeped in lies your entire life? It would have been easier if we could have trusted one another first, but I see that the Rebellion's efforts have been in place too long. So, I will tell you the truth, though it will hurt you." Without taking her eyes off me, she addressed her soldiers in the capital tongue.

The guards parted in the middle. Beyond them, surrounded by four monstrous statues, a man past his sixtieth winter sat in an ornate chair. White hair bound behind his neck. Spine straight. Unbelievably powerful hands free.

My heart rammed against my chest. Srolo Kapir. He'd been here the whole time. He wore rich palace robes, but he looked like he'd aged ten winters.

He squinted, saw me, and his Temperance-gifted hands gripped the arms of the chair. His eyes blazed, communicating something I didn't understand. Fury. Joy. Sorrow.

Emeridus, with his dog, moved a little closer to the chair but remained near Xanala's Shields and their handfuls of illuminating firelight. Srolo Kapir stiffened and shot me a look. But he did not stand or speak.

What had they done to him? Twenty steps lay between me and Srolo Kapir, and ten before I could reach Xanala. Heart pounding, I stepped forward. Srolo Kapir's eyes widened, and he shook his head.

"I brought Srolo Kapir here to tell you the truth," Xanala said, voice calm. "The Rebellion mocks the dynasty and calls us liars. So, if I speak to Srolo Kapir, he must respond truthfully to protect the Rebellion's honor, correct?"

I stared. What deception did she weave?

She inclined her head and faced Srolo Kapir. "Good Srolo, allow me to tell a story. It is well-known that the dynasty's strength comes from their fire, by which enemies were conquered and the throne was maintained. This is why every emperor and empress of old guarded the Immortal Abyss, to make sacrifices and dip their hands in the pool to strengthen their fire. Nineteen winters ago, the emperor and empress had a second child, and their cousins—high nobility—also gave birth. Both were girls born on the coveted blood moon, which promised a great gifting for each. But one was deemed to have the potential for four complete Forms, something unheard of, and the other only two."

I clenched my jaw. *Don't tell me about my noble born parents, poisoned by the emperor for my gifting.*

Srolo Kapir's eyes were boring into mine. Like when we trained and I would falter. He'd always said *Trust.*

Xanala continued. "The noble couple secretly served the Rebellion."

I knew this.

"But they wanted the royal child, with the greater gifting, to contend for the throne."

That wasn't right. My guard went up.

"In the dead of night, the nobles snuck into the royal nursery and exchanged the newborns. Of course, it was a foolish plan, and the emperor himself found out immediately. He poisoned the high nobility and sought to recover his child, but failed. Members of the Rebellion had kidnapped the baby to the farthest corners of Vedoan desert. How did the emperor cover this scandal and horrific loss? He sent trusted soldiers in secret to follow his blood child, but kept the nobleman's baby, the one who would still become Tier 3, as his own. And then you, Srolo Kapir, when you disappeared a handful of years later, suffered grave suspicion." She fell silent.

Her words struck my ears like knives. I refused to believe and stood tense.

"Tol, where could your gifting come from, if not from Vedoa's most deeply gifted bloodline?" Xanala's eyes turned sad. "Srolo Kapir, do I lie?"

I sought Srolo Kapir's gaze. His eyes glistened, and he looked down, as his grip on the armrests tightened.

My blood chilled.

Xanala gestured toward me. "It's horrific when those you call family use or refuse to accept you, isn't it, Tol? We understand one another, and we know that when one is lonely, one will listen to anyone who speaks with kindness. Elders, guards, servants–don't servants tell the truest stories, having little reason to share one tale over another? I learned many things from them."

Numbness took hold of me.

"Do you see that I am you, and you are me, Tol? Had the tiniest detail changed, we would have both become what we see and fear? Except you have no need to fear me, but I cannot convince you of this." Hurt filled her expression. "You have the Forms and royal blood, but I hold Vedoa's trust and loyalty in my palm. Will you continue to fight with the Rebellion, who has manipulated you from birth?"

Movement caught my eye. Srolo Kapir fiercely shaking his head. Emeridus stepped toward him, hand raised.

By the desert, Srolo Kapir could stop him with a single flame. Why didn't he?

"Can you continue to serve the Rebellion and find them good when they lie?"

"You lie." But as I spoke, pieces fit into place. Xanala diminishing her reputation. My excessive amount of fire. The Rebellion–even Taval–risking everything for me. Who else could overthrow the dynasty but itself?

"They hold your faith tightly, Tol. But trust or its absence cuts deeper than fire, even a burning sword. Here, one of you will reject the other, and I give you the opportunity to choose first. You may go to Srolo Kapir, but once you do, I swear he will reject you. Or you may deny the Rebellion and join me, for the unification of power for Vedoa. Choose, and may your path determine what you truly are." Her voice turned hard. "But know this. Even if you choose unwisely, you will eventually come to me, repentant, and it will be I who will save you from what you've made yourself to be."

What in the blazing desert did that mean? My chest tightened. "And then what? You and I open the Abyss together?"

"We are stronger together, Tol."

No, we weren't. She may expose a horrific truth–one I wouldn't accept–but where was the hidden lie?

Why had Srolo Kapir lied to me?

Past her Shields, Srolo Kapir gripped the chair, his body shaking. Emeridus remained nearby, looking ready to strike him.

I headed toward him.

Keeping her distance, Xanala moved with me, skimming her file of soldiers. "Don't be reckless. Take time to think."

You don't know me, do you, princess? I moved faster and kindled flames between my hands. The guards in front of me also held fire, but none moved to attack, only watched, uncertain. Because they knew, with my Justice, that I could snatch their fire out of the air and claim it as my own. I stalked through them, Srolo Kapir only lengths away now. Shaking his head violently.

I was going to rescue him as he had rescued me. I'd fight Xanala and prevail. Once Srolo Kapir was free, no one could stop our fire. We would overthrow the dynasty. We would claim the Abyss. Here and now.

Xanala came to a stop a length away. “How much fire can cover distortion? Wouldn’t the Rebellion discard you if you failed to be what they think you are?”

My fire was endless. A starpalm spoke to me. I sprinted through the last guards while shaping a sword. Pristine lines. Temperance strong.

“You’re a fool, Tol.” Xanala shouted. “Emeridus!”

The Pirthyian lunged and threw something across my path.

A cloud of silver smoke plumed before me. I skittered back, but the haze encircled me.

Srolo Kapir spoke for the first time, as if having nothing left to lose. “Don’t touch it!”

I lifted my sword, but the smoke enveloped me like a hazy cocoon. Humming around me with unnatural energy.

I whirled. No way out. What was this? I peered through the mist and saw Emeridus backhand Srolo Kapir. The older man slumped in the chair. Then fire flashed. The Pirthyian leapt backward, and Srolo Kapir, hands filled with inferno, rose from his seat. He moved quickly, reaching for me, as if to draw the haze to himself.

Whatever this was, I couldn’t let him touch it. My fire was strong enough. I formed a shield, and its edges sizzled against the mist. Remembering when Bohak pressed through my own refuge of fire atop that desert cliff what seemed like ages ago, I sliced through the haze and attempted to pass through. Fresh air brushed my face. The mist coiled around my ankles and elbows.

The world warped. My feet were swept from under me, and I slammed against the floor. Incantation in an ancient tongue whispered around me. My shield sizzled again, then expired above, joining the mist. I tried to wield, but mist gripped my hands and crawled over me, consuming me like a wave. Shouts garbled in my ears. I fought to stand, but my limbs were slow, as if I sank in quicksand. I couldn’t see anything. My staff clattered to the ground.

Something like a twisting hand seized the back of my head. Fire and ice. It reached into my mind and pulled.

I fought and screamed. *Help me!*

Strength flooded me. The starpalm returned. I pushed up to my feet. Whatever had entered my mind writhed but didn't let go. I bent over my knees, slamming fiery palms against the ground. Flames licked its surface. A strange power I'd never known coursed through my body with an inner raging that stole my breath. It was as if a spell tore my muscles from my bones.

I groaned and folded under the unnatural weight of my back. The spell climbed up my body and encircled my neck. I reached up with both arms, reached with my mind, grasping for the starpalm. For anything.

A floating globe formed above me, as the gloom engulfed my face.

"Will you follow me?"

I stretched my right hand high and snatched the globe to my chest. It popped into a spray of light, and the spell surrounding me turned brittle. Pain exploded through my body. I tumbled to the ground, and agonizing heaviness gripped me. I dragged myself onto my elbows.

As if from far away, a woman yelled, and boots filled my vision.

I crawled, biting back screams of pain. Conflicting thoughts that weren't my own raged through my mind. Fight. Flee. Destroy. Deep strength propelled me forward. I felt broken, but indestructible.

Fire roared all around.

I clawed the earth beneath me, rose unsteadily to my feet, and turned to see an old man. His enemies were shooting weapons of fire at him from multiple directions, but the old man did not fight back with his own fire. Instead, he held his arms outstretched, and the attacks against him transformed into a writhing, blazing mass, pivoted, and swept through the chamber after their original wielders.

After performing this feat three times, the attacks ceased, and the old man approached me. Tears streamed down his horrified expression. That frightened me. He said something, but I couldn't understand. A voice inside me snarled that he saw me as an abomination and meant to kill me. Then he gripped my hands.

I shrieked and pulled away. He took my hands again, his now bleeding, and he released fire into my palms.

Fool. I gripped his hands back and dragged his fire from him, making it my own. Magnificence meeting Magnificence. Justice joining Justice. Wisdom greeting itself. And boundless Temperance consuming mine. It hurt. I pushed the man away.

The woman's shrill scream rose.

A foreigner neared with dagger and lantern.

The light hurt my eyes. I stumbled backward and crouched.

More enemies, recovered from the previous battle, flung fire. At me.

Like a whirlwind, the old man intervened, deflecting blow after blow with his arm and batting fire from his clothes.

Help him! A faint voice inside me shouted.

Why? He couldn't wield anymore and wouldn't survive.

The foreigner tossed the dagger through flames into his target's chest. The old man staggered to his knees and fell, and the fiery attacks against him halted.

Part of me knew this was wrong, but not why. The deeper part of me screamed. I clawed forward and slammed the foreign champion onto his back. All around me, flames roared and yelling filled my ears.

A length away, the old man watched me. His eyes were wide, fearful. I abandoned the groaning champion to kneel beside the dying elder. I couldn't stop myself. That deeper part of me wept, and I touched his face. Long claws grazed his forehead. My claws.

The old man's eyes dimmed. Lifeless, no longer of use to me.

I struggled to stand, almost falling backward from my clumsy weight. A wooden stick snapped under my feet. I reached behind me and gripped long, heavy wings. Shock and exultation raced through me.

A young woman hissed and wielded balls of fire.

I flung the volleys away and charged. She gasped and waved a vial in front of her. What did I want with that? I shoved her across the floor and rose into the air, wings beating. Terrible pain pulsed through my back and shoulders, but I was stronger than that. Stronger than her. Stronger than death.

Men reeking of terror gathered below with hands filled with fire. But my flames would conquer.

That small part of me begged that I do not wield. If I began, I wouldn't be able to stop, and violence would make this spell controlling me permanent.

An inhuman shriek escaped my lips. I swirled and summited hot air up the ancient volcano's cone. Toward the night sky. Their fire chased me, but I was faster.

I burst through smoke into open sky. Agony registered in my consciousness where these unfamiliar wings beat from my back. I winged away from the volcano. Instinct drove me toward the gloomiest corners of the sky, and the receding, broken line of jagged mountaintops skimmed beneath me. The rims of the heavens bore the first gasp of dawn. Light hurt. I needed shelter.

A ghost of a memory tickled at the back of my mind. I'd lost something, but I didn't know what it was.

I soared between clustered buildings. People, rich, poor, even dangerous military, screamed. I spun around a street corner and leapt over a half-filled cart. Ahead, a group of men, dressed in thick leathers and salvaged pieces of armor, filled the alley. They tossed a volley of flames. I evaded their fire and veered to the right, hugging the building. Materializing from the roof, three more men tossed a metal net.

Heavy mesh captured my wings. I fought it as I plummeted from the sky, crashing among the mob. Strong bodies wrestled and pinned me to the ground. They struggled to pull my clawed arms behind me.

One grunted with effort. His eye was missing in a long scar down his face, and he asked a word I remembered. "Fire?"

Another shook his head. "It would be wielding."

I had fire, and heaved myself forward a fingerlength, causing their swarm to yelp. Straining, they tied my palms against each other behind my back, preventing my ability to fight with flame. I twisted and shrieked.

A large man loomed, his armor more complete than the others. The leading bounty hunter, fat from ill trade. He slapped a club against one clean hand, missing three fingers.

I snarled.

He returned the look, lifted the club, and struck me over the head.

26

IN THE DEAD OF NIGHT, BENEATH fierce wind howling through a thin alleyway, the bounty hunters sold me to a finely dressed man, who threw constant glances over his shoulder and spoke with a hurried voice. Their bartering passed through the airless burlap covering my head and the many cords binding my limbs and wings. Words disentangled in my mind. Two thousand dacri coins, more than the price of one mule prepared to carry and travel. The rich buyer protested that I didn't wield, but he paid an extra fifty for transport and chains.

My cart rumbled down broken and uneven streets, and rotten smells permeated my suffocating prison. I gritted my teeth around filthy rope. With every jarring bounce of the cart, I felt like someone kicked me. The binding was strong, and I ceased struggling.

We slowed. Someone gripped my middle, their touch like a strike, and rusted iron shackles clamped around my ankles. I shrieked around rope. Someone cut the binding from my hands, and bootsteps scrambled back. I ripped the burlap off my head, tore the rope from my mouth and limbs, and glimpsed towering, close buildings constricting open sky. I crouched atop the rickety cart and expanded my wings.

Trapped wind swirled around a cramped, high-walled courtyard and ruffled the bounty hunters' and buyer's cloaks. Some smirked. The buyer didn't. All gripped weapons or held flames and crowded the walls away from me. All Tier 1 wielders. The greater fire pulsing in my veins told me I had no fear of that, but their brightness burned my eyes. I lunged forward. The shackles binding my ankles snapped me back. Fire roared in my veins. I stretched my hands and hesitated at the remembered, repeated voice inside of me. *Don't wield.* I screamed and drew back to curl over myself, making the cart rattle and teeter.

The buyer pointed. "She's disappearing."

Club hanging from his meaty hand, the lead bounty hunter spat. "It's their way to vanish in and out of the dark. The chains will hold. Don't speak any secrets. Some of them still understand and talk back, especially the newly made."

The buyer wiped perspiration from his furrowed brow. "Food and water?"

"They're strong and can survive on a dog's portion."

"I paid two thousand. Enough for one with fire. The city has become infested with Shadows. Surely you can find one with fire."

The bounty hunters exchanged glances. "And our cart?"

None, the buyer least of all, looked willing to retrieve my decrepit throne. He shut his mouth, and all cautiously shook hands before the bounty hunters melted into the alley, leaving the buyer to scrutinize me.

I didn't fear him, and now knew I must hide my fire from him, since he wanted it. I waited. Motionless and staring.

The buyer turned toward the one occupied storefront claiming the courtyard, its dingy door secured with more chains. He unlocked these, stepped inside, and locked up again, abandoning me to the raging wind.

I gripped the chain around my ankles and twisted and pulled. Its tail was welded to a ring driven deep into the cobblestone ground. The pain of metal raking against my skin fired my fury. I stepped to the edge of the cart. It tipped, and I jumped to the rough ground, my clawed feet and shredded shoes scraping against dirt and stone. Even the garment I wore, a stiff, shiny, torn gray material, annoyed my skin. I strained to read the worn sign crowning the buyer's dismal establishment: Water Pots for Sale. He sold vessels for water during drought, and had two thousand dacri left over to purchase me? The sign belonged to an underground market liar.

Sounds assaulted me. I heard mice searching among stones and could smell refuse streets away.

Shadows shrieked. Bodies like arrows, a formation of three flew overhead.

I pressed myself close to the ground near the cart and remembered the buyer saying we infested the city.

Someone shuffled down the alley.

I peeked over the cart and spied a hunched form slinking close to the wall, like a rat. Invading my territory.

The man saw me. I watched in return. He shook his head, swore, and edged back the way he had come. A thief.

So, the buyer wanted me to be his store's guard dog.

Patterned brands laced my leathery skin. I could become darkness, almost unseen. A river of fire swirled inside me. I was glorious, breathlessly powerful, but subdued by chains and a ruthless, clawing otherness filling my mind.

Don't wield! Don't kill! the inner part of me repeated, like a fly buzzing in my ear. *Remember!*

I upended the cart like a wall, shoved it between myself and the street, and curled up on the dirty ground, watching the storefront for the one who held the key to my chains, as night grew cold.

Memories shouted from the recesses of my mind.

Your Magnificence is endless, isn't it?

You will possess four Forms.

You've got to be at least three-quarters light-wielder at heart. . . I gladly follow you.

A deeper human memory, always shut away, wormed its way to remembrance. My tenth guardian, a Tier 2 in Wisdom and a fearful man, made me kneel, bound my ankles and hands, and drained me–and not for my benefit. Greedy, he'd tried to take my fire for himself. Only Tier 1 in Justice, his draining felt like driving knives through my forearms and fingertips, and my fire quickly overwhelmed him. He wrenched his hands from me and locked me in a small, windowless room. I stayed there, hungry, thirsty, wronged, livid. When the lock finally turned, I seized the man's hands and snatched his gifting from him in one breath. All of it. Making him permanently fireless, because I would never rekindle him. My tenth guardian collapsed to his knees, screamed, and banished me to the farthest corners of the house out of sight.

I was free and kept his Temperance, but it was also Tier 1, and not enough. I rationalized that what I did was still justified after what he'd done to me.

Less than a day later, an enemy town raided his small village. My fireless guardian, who had been the only defending Tier 2 wielder, could not protect his community. I should have risen as protector, but my lack of control would have destroyed us first, and the village and its inhabitants were burned in the skirmish.

I alone survived, hiding in the windowless room, siphoning flames encroaching under the door until the raiders left. My hands and throat were raw. Soot covered me.

For a day, I remained in the charred ruins. Willing myself to die for my hand in the destruction and my inability to save.

From the eastern desert, a stooped, older gentleman approached. He wore no paint, but even from the distance, I sensed that his fire was great and that he came for me, like someone always did. As he neared, taking in the surrounding horror and me with a pensive glance, he did the most shocking thing–he smiled, if with sadness. "Hello, Tol. My name is Kapir."

He knew my name. "Are you my next guardian?"

"No, Tol. I am your last guardian."

I groaned and reached for something solid. To escape this torture of remembering.

Instead, the young man with the swirling symbols covering his skin encroached in my mind. His galaxy-filled eyes were mesmerizing, and his form was clearer than in my earlier dreams. He beckoned me to come, even though he saw me as a Shadow. I refused. Behind him, a second man captured my attention. The blood of all nations bore representation in his features, and he was neither old nor young. I felt power flow from him to the marked stranger and to me. And it made me afraid.

"Tol." The voice swept through my tangled consciousness, and my

inner rabble quieted. The spell's mist shrouding my consciousness retreated.

I recognized the voice and trembled.

"I see you."

Anger surged in my chest.

Leave me. See what I am. A Shadow!

Tears dripped down my chin.

You didn't stop this. Srolo Kapir died. I'm a twisted daughter of the dynasty. Are you weak among the starpalms?

Immense greatness swelled. It pressed me on all sides, holding me up, pushing me down. In one hand it held my life, in the other my death. I fought to breathe.

"Are your starpalms traveling? Sleeping? Do they hear you? Can they answer? Everything you see and do not see is mine. The gates are mine. Laijon and Vedoa are mine."

I buried my head in my arms.

I'm tainted. I let Srolo Kapir die.

"It is a greater love that one lays down his life for another. Will you follow me?"

I ground my teeth.

How can a Shadow follow you?

"You are Tol. You are mine. Follow me." The presence eased away.

Don't leave me!

I crawled onto my hands and knees, wings skimming the ground beside me. I fought to keep my human thoughts, but mist filled my mind. I waited in dread for the scrabbling Shadow's rage to consume me, but it didn't. There was only a lack of feeling, heightened awareness to every sound in this filthy street, every clink of the chains gripping me. I curled onto dirty stone, midnight above, and hid my face once more.

Warmth heated the stones I slept on.

Footstep . . . footstep . . . fearful footstep . . . pain lanced my shoulder.

"Someone reached my door and rattled my chains while you slept!"

I lifted my arm to break the second strike of the whip. Its cord wrapped around my forearm in biting pain. I hissed and wrenched the whip from his hands.

The buyer gasped and stumbled backward, pressing himself against his storefront. Away from me and into bright morning sunlight that pierced through my eyelids like blades. I retreated back into the shelter of my wooden cart and pulled the whip against my chest.

The buyer tossed a bowl of foul-smelling liquid and half a chicken carcass just beyond my reach, the drink spilling across stone. "Oh, the dacri I wasted on you." He swore. "Stay vigilant. And quit your constant shouting racket."

Each word fell heavily on my sensitive ears. I worked my jaw, and awful-sounding, rusted words issued from between my teeth. "You . . . shout."

Horror crossed his face. He hadn't expected me to respond. Inhaling a quick breath, he sidestepped around me, careful to keep his distance, and disappeared down the street.

I hid under my cart until sunset, when comforting darkness fell again. The buyer had not returned.

A Shadow squabbled close by. Far too close. With a whoosh of wings, its monstrous form landed lengths away within the gloomy courtyard.

It was male, far larger than me and wearing clean garments with a bag strapped tightly across its chest. I waited for it to attack, but it circled my limited perimeter, forcing me to turn to face it, my chains scraping against the ground. It cocked its head and rasped, yet spoke easily, "I know who you are."

I gripped the whip tighter and responded, my own voice scraping. "Leave."

"Your name is Tol. Do you remember?"

I shrieked and lunged. The Shadow fled, soaring down the street and rounding a corner.

Something scratched against stone behind.

A thief shimmied down the side of a shorter building rimming the square and picked at the storefront. He was too far from the range of my whip. With a glance my way, he discarded the lock and crept inside.

The buyer would kill me—or at least try to.

I struggled with the chains imprisoning my ankles, with its ring attached to the earth.

Soon the thief reemerged, his robes full. His gaze hardened upon me, and his hand filled with fire.

Pain struck me from above, and a rock tumbled to my feet. I hid under my cart and looked up.

The thief's two watchmen, cloaked and perched atop a nearby building, pummeled me with rocks. Their missiles battered and cracked the cart. I dropped the whip. My chains were too short to fight them.

A flaming knife *thunked* into the wood of the crate by my head.

The original thief slinked toward me, a second fiery blade in hand and malicious look on his face. A rogue Tier 2 with a thirst to kill Shadows.

Beating my wings, I stirred air and dust. Rocks fell harder. Another flaming blade hissed through air, and I caught and extinguished it between my claws.

The thief yelled and sent a volley of blazing weapons at me.

Tol, do not wield . . . unless your life depends on it.

I caught his shapes, twisted them into a hundred arrowheads, and shot them back. The thief dove to the side, crying out as one arrow singed his flailing arm. He stared at me.

I stretched both hands forward, summoned fire, and jumped as if to fly, but chains held me to the ground. Perfect, strong flames burst into my left hand, but my right filled with blinding light. I shrieked against the pain of seeing light, and then my body changed. Light cascaded across my skin, and everywhere it touched, I felt as though my flesh was being peeled away. I crashed to the ground, fire and light pooling between my hands. Thoughts twisted, and I tried to make sense of what was happening.

Run. The inner voice grew louder and clearer. A human cry burst from my lips, and I saw my fingers. Not claws. I touched my face. Tol.

I was Tol. I was human, and I held light like Laijon's in my giftless palm. My thinner, human ankles slipped free from the shackles.

The men above me hushed, and no rocks fell.

Go.

I gathered myself and ran down the street. My right hand continued to bear light, and I tucked it inside my robes, looking for somewhere to hide, chanting truth to myself.

I am Tol. I am human. Srolo Kapir gave me his fire and made me the Reborn Star. I possess the impossible four Forms in my left hand. Xanala and her red-clad army cannot find me. I now hold light with my right hand. How?

Shadows screamed in the distance. I dodged down another street, but their cries strengthened. Could they see my light? I closed my hand, as I did to extinguish my fire, and the light ceased.

I stumbled. Terrible strength once again infused my limbs, and claws stretched from my fingers, and wings unfolded from my arched back.

No! I groaned as mist consumed my mind again, my retransformation complete. Sounds from living creatures filled the streets from secret places. I ducked down an alley, my wings brushing stone, and wound as deep as I could into the underbelly of the capital, to the loneliest courtyards where torturous slivers of daylight couldn't touch me.

A memory chafed. Something beyond instinct insisted on my repeating it to myself over and over, as if the thoughts were precious drops of water. That if I forgot them, I would lose everything.

My name is Tol. Red is bad.

Hide your fire, or red will find you.

You are mine.

27

AT DAWN, A CART LOADED WITH a single barrel and escorted by ten men wearing red, struggled down alleyway steps and trundled over rock and cobble through my newest claimed territory.

I scuttled into the shadows of my vantage point, an empty second-floor terrace with broken windows, thoughts conflicting.

Red is bad. Red hoards water.

There were more of *us* in the streets than them. Proving my thoughts, thieves–human and Shadow–emerged from the alleyways and attacked.

The red soldiers fought and fled. Thieves overturned the barrel and–fools!–the barrel thundered to the ground and cracked, gushing its contents. Frenzied melee ensued.

I crept closer, like many others, and waited until the larger Shadows, swooping down and squeezing between the skinny walls of the alley, drank first, lowering their faces to the dirt. Then the human buffoons chased them away with weapons and handfuls of fire and then cupped the water to drink.

At last, I showed myself, startling many, and claimed my own portion. I remembered to drink from my clawed hands, not like a dog, but my claws scraped my face. I drank mud. Humans shouted at me. I ignored them but not the swords thrust in my face. I swiped another mouthful before scattering, jumping from their reach to soar over buildings. The sun rose, paining me, and that's why Red attempted to transport water with daylight. But they wouldn't try this route again, and so all of us would relocate. I flew over rooftops and then tucked myself into an empty alley, tasting the wetness that remained on my tongue.

Thoughts flitted through my mind. Hunger, weariness, thirst, and one that seemed more human. *You can't stay here.*

When the last Shadows left my territory after dusk, I trailed them through the quiet streets. When they stopped, I did too.

In front of them was an empty thoroughfare, spiked fencing and towering walls. From flight, I'd seen over the unclimbable wall, which was topped with spears, fires, and Red guards outfitted with weaponry. A pool of water lingered in the reservoir's depths, snowmelt channeled and collected from the nearby mountains and their rivers before the dry times.

I sank deeper into the gloom between the buildings, wrapping myself in veils of darkness as my brethren did, and watched. Why were they here?

Shadows zipped along the base of the curving wall out of sight, north of the guards and toward the mountains.

I followed until I heard squabbling, looked past the noise, and gaped.

Where city wall met reservoir water in a mighty stone corner, mountains rising behind, twenty Shadows congregated. Wings beating against stone and air, they pressed their faces or hands against the hydraulic wall, about a quarter of the way up, against the tiniest hole dribbling with water.

Drenched with midnight, Shadows cajoled, but never screeched, due to the knot of powerful wielder-Shadows guarding the drip. The subservient gave animal carcasses, stolen finery, sometimes clothes, for a drink. Or, if they had nothing, the gang would fight them until they fled.

I stared. What could I give them for water? I refused to part with my ragged garments. I knew it was dangerous to give any other piece of myself up, even torn shoes because they helped me remember. I wouldn't steal, but I couldn't recall why not. I wouldn't wield unless my life depended on it. I had light, though. Light was power, danger, and pain.

I leaned against my folded wings and the walls. Just out of their sight, but close enough to envy the feast. And plan.

Days later, I still needed to drink. In the recesses of my mind, something told me that my resilience so far was thanks to my warped form. The gang of Shadows continued to extort payment from their winged brethren, and their prices climbed daily. I still had nothing to offer but a fight. And fire.

Don't! I tried to remember why not, but I couldn't. I had an ocean of fire burning inside me. I mused and schemed as the sun rose. Once more, Shadows scattered to seek refuge in the sheltered streets. Still, the gang remained by the crack of water. They took turns scrambling up the wall to hold a grimy jar beneath the dribble. The one standing watch at the top of the wall flew down to escape the rising sun, and three of them crowded at the bottom.

When was the best time of day or night to approach–

Movement slinked near me. The Shadow with the rucksack tied across his chest and unpatched clothing appeared around a corner, saw me, and stopped.

I bristled. What did he want? I eyed the rucksack. What did he have?

The Shadow fiddled with his strap and came closer. Close enough to reach out and strike.

I tensed for his first move. A tiny tendril of fear wormed into my mind as I assessed his powerful bearing.

It whispered. "Do you remember me?"

Why did he ask me that?

"Can you remember your name?"

I remembered my name . . . but I didn't. I wasn't sure and scowled before my voice scraped. "Why should I tell you?"

"I can help you."

He spoke too easily. I lunged to swipe at his sack.

The Shadow quickly fluttered out of sight. Good.

Other Shadows congregated in the darkness, and I climbed the nearest rooftop to study the fray as the glowing moon rose with gentle-but-offensive light.

I needed water, but his question nagged.

What was my name?

The Shadow gang squawked, their bartering forgotten. They would give their treasure away with their noise. Would Red come to steal our drink?

I found another building with overlooking terraces and hopped from one to the next, until I could see.

Down a winding street, a being with two handfuls of brightness glowed, but it wasn't fire. It was greater than fire. Fear clawed at me.

The gang of Shadows snarled and drew darkness around themselves like robes.

The human's light bounced with each step and grew brighter as he neared, a tall figure cloaked with a cowl covering his head. A sword gleamed against his thigh. He paused at an alley intersection. His alert movements belied that he was young, and his blasted light illuminated everything.

The Shadows covered their faces with their claws, unwilling to retreat and give up their prize, even for this threat. They would fight the wandering human, I could smell it in their posture.

Why did that make my chest tighten?

Screeching, five Shadows burst from the gloom and surrounded the young man. He spun to face each one, holding his light close to his chest. He seemed to be assessing each Shadow's snarling face, but then he shook his head, backed against the towering wall, and released both hands with light. The Shadows howled and clawed the ground before leaping toward him, shrieking. The young man pummeled them back with handfuls of light, but his brightness was fading. Overwhelmed. His light was strong, but it couldn't last forever. A fool for invading a Shadow's lair, he would die.

The big Shadow with the rucksack returned and joined the battle, but fought his own kind, as if allied with the stranger.

This was the distraction I needed to get water. But something closer to my soul than my mind saw that the human's blood would be on my claws of I did nothing.

Choose your form!

I shrieked and charged toward the battle. Shadows stilled to stare. The young man did, too, before leveling a blinding but weakened flash of light toward a fresh assailant.

I crashed into the nearest Shadow, pushing off him to launch into the next. Light exploded around us, then abruptly stopped. Claws tore into my leathery skin, and rough hands grabbed my wings. I wrestled free, faced the rucksack Shadow, then turned toward the young man. His refined features and human eyes were knives to my heart. And I didn't know why.

His eyes widened and roamed over every aspect of my face. "Tol?"

I winced. My name . . .

"Look out!" He tossed a handful of light past me.

Claws sank into my side. I twisted from the Shadow's hold, tearing my flesh, then filled my hands with fire and slammed it to the ground in front of me, creating a barrier.

The five Shadows scrambled backward.

My chest heaved. The youth was behind me, safe for a heartbeat. Then I realized what I had created. Five fiery Shadows, the perfect likenesses of our attackers, crouched in front of me, animated, ready to fight. Obedient to me.

Red will find me.

"Witch," one of the Shadows spat with a garbled tongue. But neither it nor its comrades dared come closer.

I looked each one in the eye. I could finish them off, but I didn't, and my fiery creations continued to pant and wait.

One real Shadow looked aside and squawked. Under the high crack in the wall, the dirty jar of water, which had been balanced in a crevice and abandoned by its masters, tottered off the ledge and shattered.

Everyone's attention snapped to the dribble of water darkening the cobblestone. Instinct won, and the gang swiftly flew to the spill.

My options sped through my mind. Claim the water, or take the human who knew my name and go. I sensed him next to me, staring at my fire.

His knowledge was more valuable than water.

I reached toward the flames. The shadowy blazes lost their forms and returned to my palms. I pushed the youth into the nearest alley and kept the gang between us and water. Too bad he couldn't fly. It would be easier. Step by step, we melted into the streets.

He looked at me over his shoulder. Why did I recognize him, as if from a dream? His movements looked healthy. He didn't lack water.

I licked my dry lips and watched the rucksack Shadow scrabbling along the rooftops above. Like a stalker or a guard. Was the human his prisoner? I bristled.

The young man looked at me again. "Can you remember your name?"

I twisted my face and drove him closer to the alley wall, out of easy sight. "Where is your water?"

He almost missed a step. "I can give you water." His voice pitched higher. "Do you remember your name?"

Ire spurted inside me. He'd already said my name.

The young man drove his heels into the cobblestones and pivoted to face me.

I winced, expecting a spray of light. But he only stared, though I sensed uneasiness in his defensive stance. What a fearless fool. I stood tall, spreading my wings to bridge the alley. Did he want to fight me here? Enclosed by walls with a potential enemy watching above?

He drew a shaky breath. "You have to remember, or they said there's no hope left. I'm one of your oldest friends. If you can't remember your name or me . . ." His eyes glistened. "You have to!"

But I didn't have any friends, plus he was hiding water from me, and he reeked of weakness.

The young man swiped his cape cowl back from his head, releasing a thicket of midnight curls, and glared. "Who am I, Tol? Remember when we used to swim? Scare Seyo with our crazy mischief? Do you remember finding me in the princess's dungeon, and we escaped on the back of a dragon?" He spoke so fast it hurt my ears. "Please, Tol. You must remember."

He grabbed my hands. My claws tightened within his fingers, and he flinched but didn't pull away. Wouldn't look away. He gripped the flesh of my palms gently, his thumbs on top of mine. A human gesture. No one held my hands–

"Who am I, Tol?" He looked upward. "Don't let me be too late, Father of Light!"

Snatches of memory exploded. I wrenched my claws free and scuttled backward, as familiar faces flitted through my mind. Laughter. Terror. His name pierced like a knife.

"Roji," I whispered, the word difficult around my stiff tongue.

Roji. And he saw me like this. I cringed inside. A mindless, destroying, cursed monster. A Shadow who'd lost her humanity, who at any moment could turn on him. Emotions cold and hot trickled through my veins, and I swooped down the alley. Away from him.

He ran after me. "Tol!"

I careened around a curve in the walled street into something. Someone. The rucksack Shadow's massive arms pinned me against the alley wall.

"We can help you," he growled. "You can reclaim your mind."

Water wasn't worth this pain. I squealed.

Roji caught up. "Ysterdey, hold her."

Instinct gripped me, and I flung my free arm, my right, to wield. Light burst from my palm.

Transformation gripped me. I struggled and gasped, but they wouldn't let me go. I collapsed to my knees, dragging Roji down with me, and shook as my Shadow form melted away, until I saw my skinned knees through ratty clothes, matted hair falling over my shoulder, and my human hand fitting into his. And I remembered.

His eyes rounded, jaw slacked at my awful metamorphosis.

I snatched my hand free to hide my face, but Roji grasped my wielding wrist and held the orb of light aloft. His voice trembled. "Tol? That was incredible. How . . . ?"

I was weak. So weak. Tears burned my eyes. "Roji, you're supposed to be in Laijon."

"After chasing you across Vedoa–which I'm starting to feel a bit too comfortable and confident traversing at this point, I'll have you know–you tell me to leave again? *Qo'tah*, Tol. I stopped listening to you after we parted in the Terror Lands." His mouth firmed. "Thank the Father of Light, we found you in time."

"But I'm–"

Roji drew me toward him and held me against his chest. Gulping breaths, I pressed my face against his cloaked shoulder. He lowered his head, and his curly hair brushed my forehead.

"Roji, those Shadows could have . . ."

"I had them on the run."

My throat tightened. "Look at me. I'm–"

"You're the strongest person I know. You're a miracle, surviving after fifteen nights." His voice trembled.

I'd worn my warped body that long? I peeked over his shoulder. "You're working with a Shadow?"

"That's a delightful story," Roji said. "I'll tell you soon. Right now, your light is dimming, and we're exposed. It looks odd for a Shadow and two humans to converse. Especially us light-wielding variety. Congratulations on that shocking development, by the way. Can't wait to hear more about that, and I knew you had to be part light-wielder somehow."

We both knew that wasn't true. "I'm so tired."

"Is there Justice in light? Can you give her more?" The Shadow–Roji had called him Ysterdey–asked.

Roji's expression closed. "I would give anything to be able to do so."

I remembered that he considered his gifting weaker-than-average, and how much he regretted that. But in the darkness of the alleys and among Shadows, his light rivaled Vedoa's sun.

"Tol, hold onto your light as long as you can." Roji scooped me into his arms and jogged down the alley. I didn't resist, and as he ran, he spoke. "You need to repeat a single thought over and over, so when your light fails and you transform again, you trust us enough to follow."

Jostling with his strides, I dreaded becoming a Shadow again and the danger I would pose to them both. "I will."

"Good, good. What's your thought?"

"I trust Roji."

He smiled. "That'll more than do."

I nodded, even though he couldn't see it. *I trust Roji. I trust Roji.*

We crossed a new portion of the capital underbelly, past a maze of squares filled with abandoned and decrepit market stalls and torn, drooping awnings, until coming to an empty storefront, its door covered in chains, like my old buyer's place.

My light faded, and pain gripped me. I wrestled from Roji's hold and convulsed as my Shadow form emerged. He saw this–I clawed the cobblestones, trying to reorient myself to strange surroundings.

The young human man–Roji–gripped my claws. Repulsion rose inside me, but then I remembered the phrase, even as he said it aloud.

I trust Roji. I calmed.

Ysterdey yanked the chains away from the door and opened it. We entered and waded through a mess of crates, empty containers, trash, and remains of human and animal temporary housing. The rucksack Shadow and I folded our wings, and all three of us stooped through the store and its low, cracked ceiling. The Shadow approached a pile of rubble, pushed it aside, and opened a hidden door. We ascended a narrow, suffocating staircase to a room overlooking rooftops, complete with two broken windows, and two more Shadows, also wearing untorn clothing, waiting for us.

I tensed, but Roji stepped in front of me and waved a hand

toward the three Shadows. "Please allow me to introduce Ysterdey, Kean, and Watch, three of our beloved Samari's most trusted Exile spies."

Ysterdey lifted thick eyebrows, but I blinked. Roji's words meant nothing, and yet everything. My right hand itched to wield light, but fear of pain held me back.

"Srolos, welcome Vedoa's Reborn Star, redeemer of the Immortal Abyss. And . . ." He motioned to the far corner.

Two humans stepped forward from the darkness. One was a fearsome giant, his pale, exposed skin covered in desert-colored brandings, carrying a large shield across his back and leaning on a cane. My heart stopped, and I stared. It was the young man from my dreams. His looming presence made me bristle, and his roaming eyes were nut-brown, not filled with swirling galaxies.

The other was a tall young woman with long, curly hair. Her sad, familiar face tugged at me. She looked just like Roji. But I didn't remember who–

The young woman dropped her hand from the giant's shoulder, stepped forward, and took my claws. I froze, surprised.

"Human gestures will help you," she said, tears in her eyes, her voice strong as iron. "Hold on, Tol. Your light is stronger than your curse, my brave friend."

28

THE ROOM WAS CRAMPED. A sleeping pallet, a cracked heirloom water pitcher lying on its side, and a cold hearth spoke to the haste and scarcity belonging to whoever had vacated this place. One small barrel of water, almost dry. Like an hourglass counting down our stay here.

Seated on the bare stones of the abandoned high-story room we occupied, surrounded by stone-faced Shadows, the branded young man from my dreams, the best friend from my childhood, and Roji—his hand on my shoulder—encouraged me to hold light and transform. The agony and weakness of the moment terrified me, and when I tried, I found that my light had not recovered enough to do so. Unlike my fire, it was limited. So, I remained a Shadow, and they helped me recall myself. They talked of our growing up in Laijon, that the girl's name was Seyo. Like a deep murmur, I felt the misty presence inside my mind lift. I remembered other parts of my life, parts Roji didn't know about, like Ami'beti and Bor'beti. I felt too much, such as guilt that I still despised Shadows, even though I was one, which made me hate myself. I knew I'd lost my staff, and that I could still speak Laijonese, and that Vedoan Exiles, turned into Shadows, had formed an alliance with Roji, an enemy prisoner of war. Roji himself rejoiced at my observations twice every time my grasp on the high tongue, the language most of us understood, faltered, and I needed to repeat myself more fully in the common tongue or Laijonese.

I remembered my guardians. I saw Bohak, my protector, in

my mind, whom I'd drugged and abandoned in the Terror Lands. My stomach twisted. If I returned, and he saw me like this, what would he do?

Xanala's pretty face, contorted with hate, interrupted my thoughts. She had called me the true daughter of the emperor, younger sister to the executed empress, and promised to lure Bohak back into her grasp and destroy the Rebellion.

A second face came to mind. Srolo Kapir, who'd withheld the truth about my parentage, emptied his great gifting to give me his Temperance, and died freeing me from Xanala's grasp.

Others murmured around me, remembering more moments, but my heart shattered like glass. Human feelings pervaded my Shadow form, burning hotter than fire. Fire. Srolo Kapir should have slain me–an abomination doomed to the underworld–but he'd given me the fire of a starpalm. My fire was complete. I would never need to drain again, never lose control.

And my starpalm had given me an orb of light and then watched me become a Shadow. Why didn't he stop it? Was he so weak? He'd asked me to follow, even after my vile transformation.

The Reborn Star was not a Shadow. So who was I?

I pushed the uncomfortable thought aside and looked at the five faces watching me. "How did you find one another, and then find me?"

Roji shifted. "I disregarded your wishes and followed you from the Terror Lands, as you know."

Of course, he had. He was as reckless as . . . me.

"Before I crossed the Terror Lands gorge into Vedoa proper, Kean and Watch chased and caught me. And they probably would have finished me off if you hadn't given me Samari's necklace. Remember that?" He reached under his robe to pull the cord of dragon teeth into view. "Apparently, Samari sends spies on regular rotation to circle the Terror Lands, even the oasis, and bring information back from Vedoa. When I showed them this and explained that I was following you, they decided to join me and reunite with Ysterdey, whom Samari sent to keep an eye on the Reborn Star."

So, Samari was friends with Shadows. I wondered if the Shadow who attacked the day I visited Samari in the city dungeon so long ago had been a secret ally. It could even be one of the Shadows occupying the room right now. And Samari had sent a Shadow to trail me. Perhaps he held greater respect for the Reborn Star than he'd shown when he'd walked away.

Roji cleared his throat. "Ysterdey said you fell from the summit of the Abyss like a star from the sky after escaping Xanala's hand. He tried to speak to you but said you were stubborn. I told him that was typical." He gave a short laugh. "When you wouldn't listen, I decided to find you."

Because only a cord as strong as friendship could draw me out of my Shadow self. I'd almost cost Roji his life. "How did you know me?"

He smiled faintly. "By Ysterdey's description, then your choice to defend a human among Shadows. And your eyes."

My eyes? I supposed they remained human. I glanced at the three, trying to imagine human faces around their eyes.

"Tol."

I directed my attention to Seyo, still astounded that she was really here. Something seemingly so impossible, I almost wondered if I'd recovered my mind at all. If things were different, I knew I would have wanted to weep with her. Talk deeply of all the things lost and found in the years since we'd last seen each other. But my Shadow felt few emotions, remembering and talking were hard, and a large part of my concentration remained focused on the three other Shadows and Seyo's towering stranger.

"We've learned that it takes three nights for a Shadow transformation to claim a human mind unless the Shadow has companions to help him retain that part of himself," Seyo said. "Otherwise, the Shadow takes over."

Roji's gaze pierced mine, and he repeated what he'd said earlier.

"We found you after fifteen days. It's a miracle from the Father of Light that your mind remains whole."

Or the starpalm, and perhaps they were one and the same. In fact, I was growing certain that they were. I remembered Srolo Kapir choosing one starpalm out of the rest and calling it the One. The One was a more appropriate name for something so vast.

I folded my wings closer around myself, accidently brushing against Roji. Behind Seyo, the large, hulking stranger shifted, his heavy shield lying on the ground beside him. Human, yes, but I saw that great evil had touched him, as it touched me now. In my dreams he could see, but in real life he carried a cane to aide his blindness and always remained near Seyo. His posture spoke protectiveness over her, and I sensed much between them. Seeing him in real life, outside my dreams, filled me with foreboding. He listened, said nothing, and occasionally his brown eyes roamed from the floor across the room, like a Laijonese fisherman would cast a net in their sea. Even with my senses still dulled by my Shadow form, I feared his terrifying, marked face. Constantly, Seyo whispered Laijonese and sometimes Nazakian translation to him, and he would respond in his halting, plain speech. I learned his name was Geras.

I spoke another question. "Seyo, how did you come here?"

She hesitated before answering. "I saw you in a vision."

A chill ran up my arms. "What vision?"

"I was consumed by flames, and you passed through the fire to place your hands on my head and help me bear the burning. You promised that we'd see each other again."

Seyo burning didn't make sense, even in a vision, for reasons I wouldn't voice without her permission.

"We had to find you. Geras and I traveled the outskirts of Vedoa, beside the sea. Where the mountains begin, our Nazakian escort left us. When we crossed the mountains into Vedoa, these Shadows found us, with Roji."

That felt . . . divinely orchestrated. "Your vision. What form did I take?"

Seyo met my gaze. "Human."

Judging by the silent energy radiating off Seyo's form, she saw the potential significance in this too. Did she think I could regain my human form completely? How?

A recollection seared my mind. One from the awful moments following my initial transformation, as Srolo Kapir lay dying at Xanala's feet. I almost choked as the memory sharpened, a detail so tiny, but so important. When I'd cornered Xanala, and she became afraid, she'd waved a vial in front of me.

As if spurred by Seyo's words, Roji gripped my forearms. "You've reclaimed your human mind. Can you feel it? Your victory is just beginning, Tol."

No. My mind felt like it would burst. This desperate hope was too much. I lowered my head and spoke, my voice still sounding like gravel. "This is not victory."

"We'll keep remembering," Roji said. "I'll act like a sort of memory bank, just in case." His smile tightened. A small movement I almost missed. Were Shadow memories prone to slip-ups? Nausea stirred in my stomach.

"You're keeping secrets from me. I feel them." And I looked from Seyo to Roji to Geras and back to Seyo. "I need to rejoin the fight. Xanala seeks my fire. That must be her motive. With it, I think she thinks she can survive opening the Abyss. The longer we remain in stalemate, the more Vedoa will die. I need to return . . ." I couldn't return to Bohak like this.

How could I, as a Shadow, dare to approach the Abyss? And even as a human, if the Abyss accepted my fire, how would that bring back rain? I shook the thoughts from my head. There had to be a way. *The* Starpalm, the One, wouldn't bring me this far to abandon me. I would never give up or give in.

A tense silence fell as they exchanged glances.

I frowned. "What?"

Roji finally spoke. "We've debated your next step extensively. When I found you by the reservoir, you, ah, wielded quite the impressive display, which was a bit unfortunate, as much as I appreciate you turning the battle's tide."

I'd wielded five perfect replicas of the Shadow gang. "Xanala will hear," I whispered.

"She has heard," brawny Ysterdey grunted. "The false empress has set a dragnet of soldiers around the city walls to trap you. Nothing enters or exits freely."

"Fly over," Watch, the smaller, unruly Shadow, who often crawled on his winged elbows and clawed feet instead of standing, suggested.

"And have Xanala's Shadows chase us? No thanks." Roji shook his head.

I considered his lack of wings.

Kean, who could not speak and kept a quiver slung over his shoulder, signed something with deft claws, and Ysterdey spoke for him. "If we fly over the wall through the mountains, we can lose the traitor Shadows, follow the edge of the sea, and cut across the Terror Lands."

"But then there's the question of where to go," Roji pointed out. "I think Tol should return to Laijon and recover."

"I won't run away."

Ysterdey adjusted his position. "She doesn't have time."

Seyo paled. Roji shot Ysterdey a glance, and the Shadow fell silent, but his eyes blazed.

"What do you mean?" I said.

"He wants you to return to Samari," Roji answered. "I suppose that's a viable route back to Laijon."

"I'm not going to Laijon–or Samari, who rejected me already."

"Samari trusts Shadows." Ysterdey's gaze hardened. "Unlike others."

Roji sat frowning, as if also unwilling to supply *Bohak of Taval*.

What a cruel reversal. The Exiles were allies, and to them Bohak was nothing but a forced necessity to end our war, as Samari and the Exiles had been to us. And if Bohak saw me now, I couldn't imagine his horror. His shattered hope. My chest felt restricted.

I held four perfect Forms of fire and was both immensely powerful and seen as a weapon. But I was also a Shadow. Samari might accept me partway, but Bohak never could. Roji had battled Shadows to recover me, astounding me by doing something so dangerous. Xanala cloaked herself with her army and stood between us and the Abyss. I could defeat her, but her army? Not alone. And only a starpalm could open the Abyss and gain immortality, definitely not a Shadow.

My breathing quickened, and I saw the vial in Xanala's hand again. If we fought one-on-one, I would defeat her. I opened my left hand with the smallest flicker of fire. When I willed greater strength into my hand, the fire burst white as light. Knit with Temperance that could allow me to control my flame and with Magnificence that would last forever. Justice that could steal Xanala's fire, and Wisdom to make any shape I wanted. Losing myself in the flames, I molded them into a multitude of small shapes and remembered the replica Shadows I'd created in the alley. With no fear of losing control.

Ysterdey shoved Watch away. "Close your hand," he barked.

I lunged with a snarl before catching myself and seeing what was happening. Kean gestured signs to Watch, but Watch's eyes were transfixed on me.

Ysterdey's voice growled. "Shadows are drawn to power."

I didn't understand, and yet a deeper part of me did, and I extinguished my flames. Such displays could alter a weaker Shadow's mind, like Watch's, who'd settled back down, his gaze lucid again.

Seyo's eyes were wide, and Roji's narrowed. Two humans surrounded by four Shadows. And then there was unseeing Geras, who sat still, alert.

Roji exhaled. "First, we need to figure out how to sneak past Xanala's army." And he began bickering with Ysterdey again. A sight that would have been humorous without our present circumstances. They discussed the dwindling water supply. My thoughts strayed to Bohak. He could help us with his second gifting, but . . . would he?

Seyo leaned toward me, her eyes wide and earnest. "Tol, you need food and new clothing."

I glanced down at my rags and nodded, but my thoughts were elsewhere. Xanala had waved a vial and said *Even if you choose unwisely, you will eventually return to me, repentant, and I will save you from what you've made yourself to be.*

Xanala had expected me to side with her when she told me about my parentage, and then she expected Srolo Kapir to reject me as a Shadow. Both had backfired, but Xanala was no fool. She always left a back door for herself, and transforming me into a Shadow was an enormous gamble. She knew, if all failed, she would make me nearly invincible, but also unable to fulfill the prophecy.

The vial held an antidote to this curse. Xanala kept it to lure me back to her, to the Abyss, to her professed desire that we form her irrational alliance.

I would return to her, and I would seize that antidote from her treacherous fingers.

The group finally agreed that rejoining Samari was best. We prepared to leave at sunset, when failing light would both hurt and cover us. But as soon as we made it safely past the city walls into the Terror Lands, I would circle back to find Xanala, and even the Exile Shadows couldn't stop me.

Roji, Ysterdey, Kean, and I agreed to leave the water barrel and what was left within it on a street inhabited by children, and to put Watch on guard before making the delivery, so he wouldn't see the transfer of such wealth and become "confused," as Ysterdey put it. They also promised to procure three horses.

In the meantime, I changed into new clothes and allowed Seyo to discard the remains of Ami'beti's garment. Then I paced our small quarter to the broken pitcher and back again. I imagined the great sun touching the mountaintops, our belongings strapped to our bodies, flying over the wall, chased by Shadows in red leather armor.

Roji sat in the corner, leaning against the wall, his arms folded and eyes closed. I remained amazed that he could sleep among the four of us, and realized I'd never asked him more about being a Shadow encyclopedia, but he was proving that. Did he know why Shadows adopted new names? I assumed it was a way of assimilating into their form, a way to relate to one another, but I hadn't received a name. When the three Shadows whispered about me, they referred to me as the Reborn Star with great reverence, as if emboldened knowing one of their own was touched by a starpalm.

Seyo and Geras rested near him, their human states weaker than ours. Geras did not sleep, I could tell by the rhythm of his breath, but Seyo did, and her head had fallen to rest against Geras's shoulder.

She was my childhood best friend, but I felt the chasm between us. So much I didn't understand, and there wasn't time to ask. It seemed like Roji had known Geras before, and offered him great respect, but I'd caught him watching Seyo's and Geras's interactions more than once. I wanted to ask more, but there wouldn't be opportunity.

A squawk issued outside. That was Watch. With a swoop of wings and scratch of claws, Ysterdey filled the terrace doorway, sweat drenching his vest.

Seyo startled awake. Geras stood, and Roji rose to his feet, too, and rubbed his eyes.

Ysterdey quieted Watch, then signaled Kean, who hissed and swooped out the doorway. The monstrous Shadow pushed himself into the cramped room. "The false empress leaves the city with three-quarters of her army."

Roji blinked. "Why?"

"I don't know." Ysterdey grunted and looked at me. "Perhaps if you see for yourself, you will understand."

But trying to understand Xanala was impossible.

We shouldered our belongings–those of us who had any–strapped weapons to our legs and chests, and crowded the hot terrace. Already the sun fell, and the three promised horses nickered below. Tall and lithe, Roji saluted before scrambling over the balcony and shimmying down. After a moment, he whistled.

Seyo looked over the balcony, touched Geras's forehead in an odd gesture, and also climbed over the balcony. Geras, his shield strapped across his back again, followed her, feeling carefully with his hands before disappearing.

We Shadows leapt and soared through shaded streets and stone courtyards, low to avoid attracting attention, with Kean leading. I glanced back toward Ysterdey as rearguard. The humans cantered close behind. After another turn, the city gates stood before us. Gaping open.

We veered toward a rooftop and landed on the covered terrace, seeking its darkness. Over the wall, its ramparts emptied of guards, a sea of armor-clad humans carrying torches billowing with smoke devoured the southern desert. Soldiers marched into organized positions. As drums rang, I smelled livestock, and much of it.

Ysterdey's low tones reached my ear. "They head south, and I don't know why."

Kean sniffed the air and vaulted off the terrace. The rest of us waited, and after a moment, Roji dismounted to join Ysterdey, Watch, and me on the terrace. When twilight claimed the world, Kean returned with a flurry of signed words.

Ysterdey's expression hardened. "The princess and her bodyguard have reached the riverbed, Vedoa's border, and her army, including many Shadows, gathers to her like a line slicing the desert. They bring a calvary and dragons. Soothsayers prepare sacrifices and rites with sacred volcanic rock along the canyon's edge."

I could go to her now and seize the antidote before the rest of her army reached her. But they prepared sacrifices. I'd caught the stench of livestock. Her implied intent could not be. "Xanala's superstitions won't allow her to cross into the Terror Lands."

"Samari said the same, but some beliefs falter before desperation," Ysterdey responded.

My breath stilled. "She's going to attack Bohak."

"Bohak is bait." Roji's eyes, filled with flames, darted to me. "Tol, she's trying to flush you out."

Of course she was. I wanted to do the same to her. And she was giving me opportunity to meet her now, before she surrounded herself and the antidote with more warriors than I could overcome. But if I fought her, she could send part of her army, especially her wielding Shadows, ahead of us, and the sacrifice for such a position was unthinkable. The Rebellion at the oasis wouldn't be ready, and their fire wasn't strong enough.

I gritted my teeth. "I won't abandon Bohak." Not after he'd given up everything to champion me, even if he forsook me now. I tried to calm my shaking. "If we don't reach the oasis before Xanala's Shadows, we could lose Taval."

Ysterdey solemnly inclined his head. "I follow you."

My heart steadied. Kean nodded agreement, and observing him, Watch did the same, whether he meant to or not. I glanced at the others.

Roji, his expression firm, offered a curt nod, his rationality outweighing his dislike for Bohak.

Seyo, who looked as lost as she surely felt, also nodded. Trusting me. And Geras would follow her, perhaps anywhere, from what I could tell.

"We must outrace the dynasty's Shadow army." Ysterdey nodded toward Roji. "May your light shine brightly, Laijon."

Roji lifted his chin in acknowledgement. "For Tol and for the continent."

29

I JUMPED OFF THE BALCONY and soared over gloomy, dusty alleyways. The others followed by wing or horseback to the opened gates ahead. I zigzagged through abandoned outdoor marketplaces, and my vision filled with night-washed, charcoal desert. Guards gave a shout at our disturbance, but none followed.

Ysterdey remained close behind me, and we veered west, skirting the mountains barring us from the sea, to circumnavigate Xanala and her army. Roji, Seyo, and Geras kept up well. Snatches of beach showed between the thinning mountains before the deep cut in the desert, the riverbed, became visible in the dark ahead. Glistening salt flats that cracked under footsteps stretched into the Terror Lands. We slowed to allow those on horseback to cross the gorge, allowing me to feel the muscles of my back pull with every hovering stroke of my wings.

To the east, Vedoa's army curved along the riverbed like a snake of men, supplies, and flaming bonfires. Smoke rode the wind, and the world seemed to hold its breath. How long until they saw us?

Kean scouted ahead, belonging to this forbidden place just as the rest of us now did. Eventually, he would need to push farther to look for spinning storms–if we weren't sighted first.

Something streaked across the night sky.

Faster than I could blink, Kean let his bow and arrow twang, but the sure shot glanced off the Shadow's hide, who screeched and zipped back toward Vedoa. But not before we saw its imperial red garments.

Ysterdey shouted, "Don't chase!" Watch, who'd already leapt into action, returned, and Kean drove us faster across the salt flats.

The game was up. The race had begun.

Low, guttural cries rose behind us. Despite expecting them, my blood turned to ice.

In the distance, royal troops abandoned their sacrifices and crossed the gorge into the Terror Lands, most on horseback. Seeking to net us against the mountains.

Dressed in robes so white, she glowed in the darkness, Xanala crossed the riverbed on flighted dragon in a race for Taval. For me.

We flew faster. Watch swooped back and forth, and Ysterdey continued to keep rearguard. Below, our three horses and their riders pounded across wasteland.

Shapes marred the open expanse to our left. Enemy Shadows.

Kean slowed to notch an arrow.

"Don't look back," Ysterdey ordered.

I fixed my gaze ahead and felt the snarling hoard descend. Fire, light, and shrieking exploded around us.

Burns seared my skin. I dipped and evaded the barrage of fiery weapons, while keeping an eye on Kean, Watch, and Ysterdey. They returned fire just as strong. They were soldiers, and I was trained too.

I formed and tossed orbs of fire, but aim was impossible in flight. They outnumbered us, but none had what I possessed. I swerved between them and us, held my claws open, and caught their bombardment of fire. Their flight slowed, as did ours. I set my jaw, absorbing their attacking flame. If I stretched harder, I could I pull their fire from here.

"Go!" Ysterdey roared.

I looked up and saw a second contingent of enemy Shadows coming our way. I immediately turned and flew hard after him.

Kean led us low to the ground toward a forest of rock formations.

We twisted and dove through arches and columns, rising high and low. Below, Roji sprayed handfuls of light.

This couldn't last. How close could we make it to the oasis before their giftings ran out? Roji, Seyo, and Geras were falling behind.

Geras rode between Seyo and danger, holding his shield. He must not be gifted, but she was, possessing a unique defense in Vedoa.

We escaped the rock formations and came out ahead. Here, the horses could almost fly. I chanced a glance backward and saw that we put considerable distance between us and the armor-clad Shadows. But they gained.

Hold on, I wanted to tell them all. Because there was only one way out of this.

Skimming the salt flats, we tore across the face of night. My unhuman vision revealed swirling cyclones, and I saw the far ring of volcanic peaks, pushed to life from the earth and surrounded by sand, standing valiant and alone in the Terror Lands. Like stone teeth reaching toward the heavens, shrouded in vile lore. Bonfires flickered from all heights. As we drew closer, I noted humans with handfuls of fire, and one at the forefront who held a shield that flamed bright as the sun, though it taxed his Magnificence.

Bohak. He would attack us, thinking we were part of Xanala's forces.

The four Forms surged between my fingertips. I couldn't escape the inevitable. The others slowed behind me as they also realized our danger. I pivoted and surged toward the ground.

"Tol!" Roji yelled.

I brushed my feet against sand and lifted my hands full of fire. Bearing down, Xanala's Shadows filled their hands, too, focused on me and not the attack positioned among the towering rocks.

My heart hammered. I pressed my palms against the desert sand, and flames burst from my fingertips and rose in a wall. I pressed harder and stretched east and west. A handful of Xanala's Shadows screamed and zipped over my growing fire onto our side. They didn't attack, and I couldn't stop. My wall of fire rose as I dragged, pushed, and shaped, until the barrier stretched as far as I could see. A shimmering, roaring division between Taval and the Exiles and Xanala and her army. A display of fire that declared to the world that the false empress may control Vedoa, but the one who wielded Magnificence like the fabled starpalms, spoken to by the One, stood guard here.

I closed my fists and gasped to regain my breath. When I raised my head, I saw that my fire was shaped into bricks and parapets, a construction that mixed the style of every city I'd ever encountered, and tall enough to rival our volcanic fortress.

I could defeat Xanala here and now, if she dared march her army around this.

Behind me, Ysterdey, Kean, and Watch had also landed. Roji, Seyo, and Geras dismounted, Seyo hesitating before touching Geras's forehead again without speaking. Roji just stared, then turned his gaze to the top of the oasis where Bohak's soldiers still stood. No weapons were released against us. Taval knew I had returned.

Xanala's Shadows headed toward me, then stopped, some on two legs, but most on their winged elbows and feet. They cocked their heads and eyed me curiously. Kean stood guard, and Watch did the same.

Ysterdey appeared beside me, his huge frame menacing in firelight. "Your power calls to them. More will try to join you, to the false empress's chagrin."

"I know I should understand, but I don't."

"Be thankful that you don't understand." Weariness crossed his face. "They've lost their humanity. Their minds are unstable, and any retained speech is untrustworthy. Until a moment ago, they perceived the false empress as strongest, but your display has usurped her authority."

My stomach clenched. "Can they be healed?"

"I haven't seen it accomplished, but I keep hope. We will leave them here. They will wait until you give them a command, or until your wall falls."

Through my fire, I saw that Xanala's army had caught up and slowed, ghostly figures behind the flickering wall of flame. Somewhere on her person, she held the antidote. Despite my power, I couldn't fly over the wall and seize it from her. The antidote kept her safe from me, as did the barricade of people she positioned around her.

Roji stepped beside me, the breath of wind from my fire ruffling his hair. But he remained silent.

"How long will the wall hold?" Ysterdey asked.

I lifted my chin. "Until I take it down."

Ysterdey didn't speak for a moment. Considering. "How do we move forward?"

I drew a breath. "This fire will be a signal to the Exiles. You, Kean, and Watch should meet Samari and escort him here."

Ysterdey visibly relaxed. He wanted to avoid Taval as much as I did. "And you?"

"I–and Roji, Seyo, and Geras–will go to Bohak." There was no other choice.

"In what form?"

Unease coursed through me. "I'll wield light."

Ysterdey grunted. I couldn't tell if he approved or not, but he offered a bow that almost rivaled Bohak's. I wondered who he had been as a human. "Until we return with Samari." Then he swooped to Kean and Watch. After a brief exchange of signs, they flew into the southern night.

Above, on the mountain peaks, scouts with handfuls of fire watched.

I swallowed bile and faced the opening of the stone, wind-carved path cutting through the volcanoes. Roji, Seyo, and Geras followed me past the arched gate into the maze of open tunnels. Protection from blowing sand and curious firewyrms, where Samari had camped his men, enveloped us.

Roji broke the silence. "Tol, I can go for you."

It was a desperate idea. I wanted to smile, but I couldn't. His protection and loyalty meant too much. "This time, we go together."

We took the alternate route, the one devoid of rockwyrms. The mouth of the oasis greeted us, barred with metal rods, a new addition since my absence, and filled with blinding torchlight and the silhouettes of Taval's finest officers waiting for me.

Panic clawed at my throat. I hated this, but there was no other way. I wouldn't run, and I would tell Bohak everything–but not yet. I retreated behind a previous bend in the path and pooled light into my hand. Just enough to last as long as it could. Like a long slash through my body, that sounded like an endless shriek in my mind, my Shadow form vanished like a shed cloak, and I emerged human into the light of their torches with blinking, faithful Roji beside me, and Seyo and Geras behind.

The chain of officers parted. Bohak, striking, dressed in leather and the breastplate of water dragon scales, stood in the gap.

30

HIS FACE, LIT BY TORCHLIGHT, was handsomer than I remembered. His presence stronger, but wearier. He drank me in with his eyes and inclined his head. Unable to speak at first, because he'd seen my fire and knew. "Let her in."

His men swung the gate wide, and Bohak came through to meet me, extending his hands to grasp mine, but I could only offer my empty left. When our fingers touched, I failed to suppress a shudder. He was so human. And I wasn't anymore.

He saw my handful of light, which I tucked inside my robes too late, and quickly looked up at my face. "Tol?" Then he glanced over my shoulder at my Laijonese and non-Laijonese entourage and stilled. His men also froze, and animosity rippled through the air.

"Please have your men take their horses," I said. "They are my guests."

"Of course." Bohak tucked my hand into the crook of his leather-clad elbow, shot my friends another look, then led me into the oasis. I'd forgotten how long and purposeful his strides were. I glanced over my shoulder. Tavalkians were casting Geras concerned looks, and Roji marched in the lead, resolute. We passed the verdant garden and lake under the watchful, stunned gazes of endless ranks of soldiers, their eyes bright in the dark, their bodies far healthier than those left behind in Vedoa. There were more now. The Rebellion was answering our summons, sent so long ago, doubling the strength of our army. Many bore spears tipped with the shards of curse scales.

The volcanic fortress rose before us. We ascended the stone stairwell to the mouth of the volcano between the two cascading waterfalls. High above, knots of scouts snatched quick glimpses of us from the encircling mountain's heights before snapping their gazes to the wall of fire and Xanala's army beyond that.

Bohak paused to speak to the ranking officer on duty. "Keep the divisions ready and men upon the battlements," Bohak said. "Prepare my quarters with food and drink."

We passed under the roof of the mountains, and cool darkness swept across my skin. Our footsteps resounded against stone.

Stunned at my presence as before, Bohak held a thousand questions in his exhausted eyes. He darted a glance toward Roji, and said in a low voice, "I want to speak with you privately."

Perhaps that was better. "They need your order of protection," I told him. "A safe place to stay."

Bohak's brow creased. "Of course." He motioned at once to a nearby officer, who offered a bow.

I turned toward my friends. "This soldier will lead you to quarters where you can rest. I'll rejoin you soon."

Roji's gaze flickered. He opened his mouth to speak, but didn't. Seyo nodded. The Tavalkians remained focused on terrifying Geras, who stayed close to Seyo.

Old suspicion flooded Bohak's gaze, as if he were seeing Roji again for the first time. But I pulled on Bohak's arm, and we passed through the doorway into his chambers. In the familiar setting, soldiers placed food and drink upon the table before bowing and exiting. Leaving Bohak and me alone.

Where there wasn't refreshment, Bohak's table lay covered with parchments and maps, and the firepit roared, strengthening his fire and mine, but I didn't need it. My eyes went back to his table . . . he was never this messy. I prepared for an onslaught of questions.

Bohak's expression was unreadable as he faced me. "Have you come back to me from the dead?"

I swallowed. "You have no idea."

"I thought you were lost. You disappeared, and the scouts didn't see you. I led search parties." He ran fingers through his hair. "I worried that a firewyrm had attacked you. Or a Shadow."

I winced.

"Then my officers and I realized we'd fallen into an unnatural sleep, and I feared that perhaps a spirit did reside here."

I took a deep breath. "I drugged you. And raided your trunk."

"You *what?*"

I faltered. "I couldn't let Xanala kill you."

His eyes flared. "So, you returned to Vedoa alone? Will you ever cease mocking the heavens? Must you always test the universe, trying to best fate? Do you–" He broke off and calmed himself. "But now here you are. Returned to me like a gift from the starpalms." Hesitant, he took my left hand. Not my right, as if unable to bring himself to accept the light he saw.

I tensed but didn't pull back. I imagined Roji watching us, frustration written across his face. And imagined wings unfolding from my back, my hands morphing into claws, and Bohak beholding a Shadow. And then what would happen to us?

Only Bohak could choose.

"Starpalms, when I saw your fire, I didn't know what to think. It's more than a trio of Tier 3s could wield . . ." I sensed his mind churning as he pieced things together. "Your Temperance is complete. How?"

The moment I dreaded was coming. "I returned to the capital. I found Srolo Kapir, and he gave me his fire. All of it."

Bohak sat back, as stunned as I remained by the srolo's sacrifice, then spoke quickly. "Is he here?"

A numbing chill washed through me. "Srolo Kapir died protecting me from Xanala."

Bohak's expression pinched, and his voice hardened. "Srolo Kapir may not be with us, but his fire lives on with you. She will pay. Restitution will be made. Now it can be made in full."

My pulse surged with the pressure of his words. Xanala would face me, but she could never repay what she had done. And I didn't know if the guilt of the dynasty belonged to her or to me.

"I see the Forms in the wall blazing between us and Xanala. They're powerful. Perfect. The prophecy is fulfilled. It's flame without measure. None can overcome you, Lady Tol. Look at your wall keeping your enemies at bay! With your power, you could sweep your flames across their camp."

I tensed. "My battle is with Xanala. Not Vedoa."

"Of course. You must fight her as tradition dictates, and soon. To end this." He looked at me. "Samari will join us now, but we could send him away."

"No. We need him."

"Of course. I'm just still astounded by your strength. Xanala followed you even into the Terror Lands, something I never thought I'd see, and she was a fool to do it. Now she sees her defeat in you. I would like . . ." His gaze fell from my face to my hands. For a moment, I thought he would ask me to wield, to see the four Forms up close, but his gaze lit on my right hand and frowned. "You didn't disappear alone. The Laijonese prisoner of war vanished as well. You return with three of them, and now you wield their inferior light. Did the prisoner do this to you?"

Inferior light. "Roji? By the deserts, no. And Geras isn't Laijonese, and light *is* powerful, as much as fire."

Bohak's eyes narrowed. "How can you say that with the wall you've wielded? I fear their influence upon you."

"*Qo'tah–*" I pressed my lips together, realizing what I'd said.

Bohak's brow lifted, and his gaze dropped to the light in my hand again.

I felt the orb of light weaken. I would transform, but only on my timing. I forced myself to speak. "No, Bohak. Xanala's bewitchment is far more dangerous. She finally told me the truth." I drew a deep breath and couldn't keep the edge from my voice. "Apparently, I am the emperor's daughter. Srolo Kapir took me from my cradle and lied to me and to the Rebellion all these years. To overthrow the dynasty by the dynasty. Xanala doesn't possess a drop of royal blood."

His expression shifted from one of horror to one of awe. "It was deceptive but brilliant. That the blood of kings flows through your veins–this makes sense of everything. When the people find out the truth, they'll flock to the Rebellion."

"How can you say that? Everyone has lied to me."

He didn't seem to hear, he was so caught up in this revelation. But then he sobered. "What do you mean by Xanala's bewitchment?"

The words wouldn't come. But he needed to know. I couldn't live under this pretense and wasn't strong enough to keep up this disguise. I needed to know what he would do with the truth about me. I closed my right hand to extinguish my light, immediately gasping and doubling over.

"Starpalms, Tol." Bohak knelt beside me, supporting me.

I grimaced as the mist of the curse enveloped me. Helpless. What had I done? I tried to speak but pain robbed me of my voice. Starting at my feet, the spell crawled up my body to my hands. Bohak jumped back. Part of me wished he'd stayed beside me, and the rest of me seethed that I should never have returned. Sudden, familiar pain sent tears to my eyes. My skin hardened like leather, my emotions cooled, wings expanded from my back. Claws tangled and tore into the rug underfoot. It was done. I was a wretched Shadow dressed in Vedoan clothes, and I tried to peer at Bohak while covering my eyes against the near firelight.

He stared, aghast, his hand poised upon his sword hilt. Oh, a profession of loyalty and now the threat of destruction. How the tables turned.

Reject me. Gorge your hatred for my form. No. I brought my raging under control and spoke in my terrible Shadow's voice. "This is the price for four Forms and the blood of a corrupt dynasty flowing through my veins. Now, what do you say? Am I the Reborn Star?"

Hand still on his sword, Bohak stood as if carved from stone.

I waited for him to call his officers, even drive his sword toward my heart, as if he would succeed. That was what the Rebellion was supposed to do. *We Shadows* were part of the mess the Reborn Star was meant to eradicate.

Instead, he spoke, his voice agitated. "Why would she do this to you?"

A sensible question, at least. I tried to moisten my parched lips. "She wanted me to reject the Rebellion and join her. I refused. She wanted Srolo Kapir to serve her."

He straightened, and his voice firmed. "She wants your fire." He gave his head a shake. "Of course, that's what she would do. And she'll have an antidote to dangle in front of your eyes, especially now."

I startled that he guessed that and looked up, blinking in the light. "I saw the antidote."

Bohak barked a bitter laugh. Through the fire's blinding glare, his form looked blurry. "She hasn't changed one bit from our Academy days." He looked at me. "You're squinting. The brightness hurts you." One hand still fidgeting on his hilt, he reached toward the fire and drew the flames to himself until darkness covered the room. His voice wavered. "When you wield light, it frees your human self. Where did you get the light?"

Hope stirred. He believed me. "The One–the Starpalm gave it to me."

He considered this. "How strong is your light?"

"Small. Like a Tier 1 in fire."

"Which starpalm supports you?"

That felt like a trick question now, but I didn't dare share my true thoughts. Not yet.

"Perhaps–is it possible?" He ran his free hand through his hair again, avoiding my gaze. "There is one who would honor both your fire and the Shadow form, seeing it as a double portion of power. Could . . . could an underworld starpalm keep watch over you?"

Hope crashed into horror. "No. How could an underworld starpalm give light?" I challenged, hating my difficulty of speech.

"The starpalms are said to steal gifts from one another."

By the desert, he was desperate to make sense of my chaos. I hissed. "Do not suggest that I align with evil."

His eyes widened, but he inclined his head. "Of course not. I apologize." He drew a short breath. "Do the Laijonese know?"

"Yes." More than anyone else could ever understand.

"Can you take their light to strengthen your own?"

Roji had offered this very thing. I growled. "It's impossible."

Bohak held up placating hands. "Then you must command them to keep their mouths closed. We'll hide this from the Rebellion. When your light is strong enough, we'll make appearances together before them."

I opened my mouth to object. Samari would know the truth, thanks to Ysterdey, Kean, and Watch. And then I realized what he was saying and froze.

Bohak hadn't rejected me, even as a Shadow. My inner defenses crashed. Tendrils of sharp, human emotion pierced the numbness that pervaded this ghastly form.

He began to pace. "You're the Reborn Star. Taval stands behind you. The Rebellion stands behind you. Srolo Kapir gave his life for this. Soon, the Exiles will see your fire and fall into line, as they should have from the beginning. I promise you, by my own hands, I will seize the antidote from Xanala and see you, Lady Tol, restored."

31

I RETURNED TO MY ORIGINAL quarters atop the stairwell. Roji, Seyo, and Geras were to be given chambers near mine, also kept by a guard.

During the night, a sandstorm crashed over the mountainsides, and the Exiles, headed by Samari, barely beat the swirling tempest into the protective arms of the oasis.

Come morning, gray and brown filled the skies with perpetual twilight. The floating veil of sand engulfed everything. Fallen sand covered the ground, and our clothes, and invaded hair, mouths, and nostrils. Peeking through my window did no good. I couldn't see across to the opposite mountains enfolding us into this refuge, or to the tunnels where Samari and his exiles found protection from the elements, as Roji had told me when he regained his post as one of my bodyguards. Soldiers pulled tarps across the lake, raising it only to draw water for us or our horses. Plants were covered, and the horses brought indoors.

Dust coated Xanala's camp, and long strips of cloth now shielded their supplies, too. Their fires lay extinguished, but not mine. Through the storm, my wall continued to stand, though I felt it strain under the onslaught of sand.

I waited for the meeting between Samari, Bohak, and I to commence and moved restlessly about my room. I felt trapped in the small space. At night, before the storm, I could draw darkness to myself and flit through the fortress and garden unseen. Not so by day, when the sun burned, and I needed to conserve my light.

Bohak and I had agreed that, in public, I would appear in human form, but the half truth chafed inside me.

At last, a guard rapped on the stone doorframe of my chamber and called through the cloth covering that Bohak had summoned me.

I filled my hand with light and suffered transformation in the privacy of my own room, pressing my lips tight and willing myself into silence. Then I hid my glowing right hand in my robe, away from Vedoan sight, covered my mouth and nose with a veil, and stepped through my door covering to meet Roji.

He accepted my human appearance with a sad nod and escorted me through the busy fortress, now smelling of horseflesh, to Bohak's quarters. His stride was rigid, his face firm. I knew he wasn't angry with me, but the one we walked toward.

"How are they?" I asked quietly.

"Hidden and fed. Seyo says she needs to see you–" He fell silent as we reached Bohak's chamber.

"Keep to the corner, even if he dismisses his men," I instructed, and moved in front of him.

Bohak paced his thick rug before the firepit, hands behind his back and head down, until noticing me. He almost reached for my left hand, but hesitated and bowed instead. Why? Because I was the Reborn Star or because I was Shadow? "My men fetch Samari now," he said.

I swallowed my insecurity. "I doubt anyone can 'fetch' Samari."

Bohak offered a wry smile. "Perhaps not, except for you. And we will keep the meeting short." He glanced at my right hand, tucked out of sight.

Footsteps tramped toward us.

My heart pounded. I thought of Samari's and my last horrible meeting in the nearby rocky heights. And then I remembered that Bohak didn't know about Samari's friendship with Shadows, or that Samari knew about my transformation. "Bohak–"

Samari stepped into the doorway, leaving three human members of the Exiles to wait in the hall. I should have known he wouldn't come with Shadows, even though I suspected that Ysterdey ranked high among his officers. No, he would continue to keep his secret.

Samari's gaze roamed across Bohak's fine furnishings and the filled table, his lips twisting, then settled on me. He offered a knowing look before bowing deeply in my direction.

I stiffened. Samari had never bowed to me before. Bohak stood tall beside me, eyes calculating. Likely remembering how Samari rejected us less than a season ago. That memory pained me too. He may have never come now, if not for Ysterdey, Kean, and Watch–and if he didn't perceive that Xanala, if victorious, would go after him next. But we needed to leave the past behind us, to unite for our country. We couldn't remain divided.

I stepped forward and inclined my head. "Welcome, Srolo Samari and all Exiles." I extended my hands to mingle fire, almost naturally. The gesture still filled me with dread, even now. I glanced out of the corner of my eye, thinking Bohak would be impressed. Rather, he looked ready to step between us.

Samari studied my gesture. "Thank you for your welcome. I have seen your fire, and how it fights the sandstorm. I would be a pompous fool to accept such a greeting from you, like the star in your name, shining far above." And, to my amazement, he knelt before me on his hands and one knee. Like Bohak had once done.

My chest constricted. Reborn Star. Not like this. Not until I took the antidote from Xanala. Yet Samari, in a great show of humility, offered me his alliance. I found my voice. "Rise, and please hold council with us."

He rose. Bohak led me to the head of the laden table before seating himself on my right. Samari sat at the opposite end facing me. Roji remained silent in the corner.

A Tier 3 northern heir, a ranking Exiled soldier, and a Shadow Reborn Star. Everyone watched everyone else with wariness. Could we hold a reasonable council?

Samari traced a fingertip along the rim of a golden bowl laden with cut garden fruit. "My scouts report that the storm will pass in a day. That will give us a half day to prepare before the false empress strikes. Her army outnumbers Taval, the Rebellion, and we the Exiles three to one, with the Reborn Star's incredible display of fire in between. What are the Rebellion's plans to avoid full-scale combat?" Then he looked at Bohak.

"Tradition dictates that contenders for the throne fight one-on-one," Bohak replied.

Imagining fighting Xanala filled me with misgivings. She was full of too many tricks.

"Tradition also dictates that the battle occur in the amphitheater of the palace," Samari said. "And this is no ordinary battle. Xanala is not a fool."

Bohak nodded terse agreement. "I plan to write and hopefully sway her to her senses. Whatever grasp she has on the throne will never stand as long as a contender lives. And the people will not accept any person as ruler who does not best their opponent in the traditional manner." He looked toward me. "My lady, will you help me write the missive?"

He meant wielding a message by fire, such as what we sent to the Rebellion, and what Srolo Kapir had created for the 'betis. I nodded.

Samari raised his brow and turned his attention to me. "But what place does tradition have when her opponent is a Shadow?"

Bohak erupted. "How dare you suggest such a thing? The Reborn Star is human before your eyes–"

I touched Bohak's arm, before he made a fool of himself, and spoke quietly. "He knows." I met Samari's gaze and hesitated. Did I call out his scouts for what they were too? No, until the right time, I would protect them, even as Samari hid them. "Your men found me in the capital in my Shadow form, recognized me, and gave me water. They traveled with me back across the Terror Lands. I will, for my entire life, be indebted to that." Bohak's arm flexed under my hand. Likely surprised that I hadn't shared this with him and displeased that I suggested an obligation to the Exiles, but I would never take those words back.

My silence gave Samari the opportunity to speak again. "You

seek to arrange a one-on-one battle–which she'd be a fool to accept. If she agrees, you will surely triumph and gain the chance to open the Abyss and seize its gift of immortality, joining the starpalms, as they say. You would remake the government and rule Vedoa forever in the four Forms."

Tension gripped me like a fist. He didn't mention ending the drought, and he spoke of the starpalms with little reverence. I realized Samari did not believe in the starpalms, not really, and that I should have guessed that. Perhaps he trusted in the Abyss's promised immortality. He believed that Vedoa could only be remade by human means, by a new government.

Samari lowered his voice. "But will Vedoa accept a Shadow empress, even one who presents herself in human form?"

Bohak's voice deepened. "Vedoa will praise the starpalm who saves them."

"Your lust for glory blinds you, Taval."

"And you–" Bohak muttered something about not hiding in Nazak and drew a calming breath. "She will reclaim human form, because Princess Xanala possesses an antidote to this curse."

Samari's brow lifted. "Is such a thing possible?" He slid his gaze to me, and his mocking tone vanished. "My Reborn Star, if you can remake yourself, would you seek the same for others?"

Roji stirred in the corner. He'd picked up enough of the common tongue to understand the exchange.

I held my head high. "As Reborn Star, I will do everything I can to undo the curse of the Shadows for all."

"And if . . ." Samari's voice trailed, and his gaze darkened.

I knew what he wanted to ask, and found my voice. "If the antidote fails, I will not open the Abyss, but will choose a successor to take my place and pass into the heavenly realms." And I would die a Shadow. Imagining that possibility hurt me physically, and my traitorous voice wavered. "I can't live forever in this form."

Silence fell. I couldn't miss the horrified and perplexed expressions on their faces as they considered such bold words and what that could mean for them. A successor? We all knew who the obvious choice was, sitting beside me in fine robes.

Bohak, his expression shaken, leaned toward me and murmured. "We will not fail."

Samari rubbed his jaw. "There is no one who can hold your perfected Forms. If you do not pass through the Abyss, this gift will be lost to Vedoa."

What did he want from me? How could a Shadow pass through the aura and approach the Abyss? My throat tightened.

Bohak shook his head. "This is unthinkable. The antidote is only lengths away–"

Samari interrupted impatiently. "Yes, I hope and will even pray to the starpalms that you can claim it. But if she cannot break her curse, and she cannot surrender her gifting, what happens to her fire?"

"Taval will keep her safe," Bohak insisted. "She will be transformed and revered. I tolerate no other outcome."

"You do not understand the cost of her form." He hesitated. "My lady, are you prepared to hear this?"

I sat taller. "Hide nothing from me."

He nodded and continued. "I am a friend to Shadows. I am familiar with their deterioration. It is a slow process for some, and quicker for others, but it is sure." Samari looked at me. "One of my scouts is a Shadow named Watch."

Bohak's eyes widened at Samari's confession, and I tensed. I knew where he was going with this. I'd seen the signs.

"Watch crawls on all fours. He speaks in broken language. His time is running out until he will turn on those he knows, as the curse always dictates, and is killed in an act of self-defense by friends. And this is merciful, because the alternative is being drawn to a source of greater power, such as the false empress's. My fear is that the Reborn Star would, eventually, turn on all of us and follow someone who she sees as powerful."

Ire rose at his words, but could this happen, that in my Shadow form I could decline and be lured to mindlessly serve another?

Bohak's jaw tightened. "She holds light."

"And perhaps that will make a difference." Samari leaned toward me. "My Reborn Star, I encourage you to fight the battle now, and not delay. Seek the antidote. Keep Vedoa as your goal. And if you prevail, remember those less fortunate than you."

Both men stood as my thoughts swirled in turmoil. Terrified. Angry. Cold. I had to fight now.

Her fire will . . . kindle life within dead bones . . . I wanted to block my mind from the Reborn Star's prophecy, and the impossibility it implied. Then the light in my hand flickered.

Bohak noticed and quickly ended the meeting. Roji started toward me, but Bohak took my elbow to personally escort me to my room. I didn't miss Samari's sharp glance before we parted. Approaching my quarters, I did not return Bohak's bow before I passed through the cloth covering the doorway. Once there, my light died, and my Shadow form overtook me. I bent double and choked tears, breathing hard, until my wings pulled me to the floor, and my unhuman strength returned. Head pounding, tears dried. Feeling nothing.

Be the Reborn Star. Get the antidote. End the drought. Save the Shadows. Pass through the Immortal Abyss. Save my friends.

Magnificence, Justice, Wisdom, and Temperance weren't enough. Opening the Abyss wasn't enough.

Don't let me die a Shadow–and Vedoa fall with me.

32

IN MY RESTLESS AND TOSSED sleeping, my light slowly rebuilt inside me. I could feel it, even as I felt endless fire flowing through my veins. Ready to fight. Waiting for Bohak's letter to reach Xanala–one we had created together after I recovered from our meeting with Samari–demanding a one-on-one battle. And how would we deal with her refusal? Her army could march around the wall and attack us, but they hadn't. She knew I needed the antidote, and though she feared my fire, her numbers exceeded ours. Xanala also wanted something from me, something I would never give her.

"Seyo needs to see you." Roji's words returned to me. I remembered how far Seyo had traveled–to find me. It was a death wish. Now here she was at the border of enemy civil war.

Dice rattled outside my room. Tavalkian bodyguards today, no Roji.

I drew gloom to myself as if it were a cloak. Thanks to the sandstorm, light was dim at all hours. I crept to the covered door and peeked out.

My two guards sat with their backs to me, gambling.

Quietly, I slipped through the door covering and climbed the walls. Perhaps due to the draft from my movement, the guards looked around, but they couldn't see me, like an invisible bat above their heads. When they returned to their game, I slipped along the wall, perch to handhold, then swooped into the air to disappear into the bowels of the fortress.

Darting through corridors, my gloom covering me, I searched for my friends, but couldn't find them. Running out of passages, I entered the far, expansive chamber and its great chasm splitting the rock floor like a gaping mouth. Pit to the underworld, where the Abyss stood in another volcano, close and yet so far. The tail of a rope lay tied securely to a ledge, as if to carry food or people up and down from the depths. Surely, Bohak hadn't . . .

Expanding my wings, I dove down to the bottom of the crater, where the end of the rope dangled, and flew through corridors and passages, searching. The silence was deafening.

I soared through lonely caverns, and it wasn't long until I sensed the presence of life, and faint torchlight offended my senses. I crept closer to the light illuminating the rounded opening to yet another chamber and stopped short at the threshold.

In the far corner, Seyo sat leaning against the cave wall. Plates and a jar that surely held water attested to some level of care. Roji sat beside her, deep in conversation. He looked more serious than I'd ever seen him before.

The sight took me outside of myself. I couldn't believe they had been placed here, in a prison, and I would confront Bohak about this.

But while I wrestled with myself up in my chamber, Roji and Seyo had had days of isolation to catch up on a lifetime of perilous events. Did Roji tell her about their Vedoan mother? Geras sat on her other side, listening and occasionally nodding. He remained close to Seyo, always looking toward her, even when Roji spoke.

They'd already seen me as a Shadow, had even brought me back to my humanness. But allowing them to see me like this again filled me with shame. And I wanted to see them as a human, not a calculating Shadow. Dissolving into the gloom, I bit my lip and forced light into my hands. The gifting was weak, even though almost rebuilt. The transformation was more harrowing than usual. At last, human again, I stumbled into their torchlight.

Roji looked up, saw me, and scrambled to his feet.

"Tol?" Seyo touched Geras's shoulder, and both rose as well.

My legs shook, and I stumbled again. In a few strides Roji caught me before I fell to my knees.

"Sit down." His voice sounded far away.

"I'm so tired." I struggled to remain awake, and looked up to see Seyo's face of concern swimming in front of me. My back ached where my wings would soon grow from my Shadow form. The light in my hand flickered, and the world went dark as I fell.

Help me.

I awoke on my back touching cold stone. I forced myself to sit, claws scraping rock, and wings brushing the ground. My emotions ran cold, then I felt someone beside me. Every fight response redoubled, and I lumbered to my clawed feet to stare at Roji, who had frozen in an attempt to hand me a tin of water. My emotions cooled, and I dropped my gaze. I'd lost my human form so easily, like sand slipping between my fingers. That had never happened before.

"Everything's fine," he said, but his eyes betrayed his concern.

I noticed the other two with us. Seyo and her branded friend Geras standing beside her.

I felt my strength. My powerful Shadow form. Yet I wanted nothing more than to wrap darkness around myself.

Tears fell from Seyo's eyes, and they made me feel a sadness deeper than anything I'd felt as a Shadow. I touched my own face, wondering if I cried too. But I didn't. I couldn't. The Shadow was eating me from the inside out. My voice shook. "I'm deteriorating."

I shied backward, but Seyo wrapped her arms around my middle and hugged me. My wings brushed her arms. My skin was rough, and my claws–

"Walk with me," she said, her voice so delicate and familiar. She stepped toward a narrow passage cut into the rock.

Geras moved to follow, but Seyo touched his arm. Both he and

Roji stayed behind as Seyo and I passed into the adjoining chamber. A breath of cool, trapped air wafted over us.

"I hear you, the Tol I've always known, in the strength of your voice. Your light is stronger than you think, and it's not only to be held in one's hand. I knew a Shadow before. He never wielded light, and he never surrendered to the Shadow form."

"How . . ." Despairing my rasping voice, I pressed on. "How did he resist it?"

"He chose what was good, even unto death." New tears sparkled in her eyes. "You returned my brother to me from the dead. And we are reunited." There was so much packed in those words. Our last childhood days together. Our promise at nine and ten years old to remain side by side forever, even if my first guardian ran away from home again. Instead, the woman had grabbed my wrist in the dead of night and forced me to flee Laijon with her.

As if she were remembering the same things, Seyo said, "I've always felt the responsibility of finding you again. Instead, the Father of Light sent you my brother." She clasped fidgeting hands.

Did I make her nervous? Then I noticed the faint, crisscrossed scars covering her arms, the cruel handiwork of a fire wielder. I hadn't seen that before and halted. "Who burned you?" The vision she had shared back in the capital tugged at my memory.

She noticed my glance and pulled her sleeves down. "There is so much to say in too little time."

"Then let's begin. What are you really doing here, beyond finding me? Who is the giant you brought with you?"

Seyo smiled. "Geras saved my life, more than once, and was . . . blinded in the process, only able to discern darkness and light. When I began my journey to find you, he insisted on coming with me. I am his eyes, and he is my shield."

I thought he was more than that, judging by the way they interacted. "Roji knows him."

"Yes." I could tell there was much behind that statement, but she didn't elaborate. "Geras opened the Eternity Gate."

I stared at her. "He caused Vedoa's drought."

"No. He set an ancient wrong right."

"You were with him," I said. "You saw the gate open."

"Yes," Seyo acknowledged. "No matter how hard I try, I can't describe it, even after Roji asked me to retell the moment for the third time. Opening the gate cost Geras his sight. But not before he saw you too." Her eyes on me were steadfast. "Geras saw you in a separate vision, but he didn't know who you were. When he told me of it, I knew we had to find you. We've been seeking you since."

And I'd been waiting for them. The Geras of my nightmares literally stepped into my real life. But why? "Tell me his vision."

"It's better for him to show you."

"How can he show a vision?"

"You'll see. The gates also give gifts, and . . ." Her eyes glistened again.

"His vision makes you cry."

"Yes. Because I think the Father of Light has chosen you for a difficult purpose. The Eternity Gate's judgment has not only spread here to Vedoa. Drought races across the continent, even to Ai'Biro's islands. Armies march toward Vedoa to destroy it." She looked at me. "Roji told me Vedoa calls you the Reborn Star. Someone who possesses unlimited fire, able to open the Abyss and claim immortal life, with power to put your enemies under your feet and end the drought." She reached into her skirts, removed a cloth-wrapped bundle, and carefully unwrapped an archaic, leather-bound book. I shouldn't have been surprised to see her holding such a thing, with her love of history. Opening to one of its last delicate pages, she hesitated. "I found this manuscript long ago. It has been a source of vital fascination since, creating so many connections between everything that is happening."

"What connections?"

"The translation has been difficult, but it tells of the twin doorways, the Eternity Gate and the Immortal Abyss, written by a Laijonese princess during the war that split Laijon and Vedoa. It explains how . . ." She hesitated.

I knew Laijon's history and the accusations it threw at mine, and finished her sentence for her. "It explains how Vedoa, after it split from Laijon, took the Abyss and forced it to warp our gifting of light into fire."

She spoke softly, with cultural Laijonese face-saving, and also regret. "One cannot unmake the past."

"No, but we must guide the future." I studied the relic in her hands. "What do you want to show me?"

"This last page. I'm not confident I translated it correctly, and I hope that you can confirm my work."

Unease crept up my spine. Seyo spoke many languages. She was the history fanatic, not me, or even Roji. Why should I be able to decipher this?

Seyo opened to the passage she wanted and placed the book in my claws. The manuscript was frightfully old, and I wished I wasn't touching it. The delicate pages were stacked and bound, and a horrendous scrawl confronted me. And not in the Vedoan language. "This is," I began, then stopped. As if by magic, I sensed meaning in the words. I felt as though my mind twisted to grasp what was being said, a horrible feeling that made me want to wield fire and torch the book. I hissed.

"Can you read it?" Seyo said.

"Yes." The translation slithered through my brain. "We polluted our land with blood, and one will rise who will shed blood to make atonement." I grimaced. "What is this?"

"It must be an old foreign proverb. It's taken me great time to interpret. So much cross-referencing and longing for writings that don't exist. And once I thought I had a translation, I still doubted. I wanted to doubt. It is the language of the first Shadows."

And I, a Shadow, could read it. The walls inside my heart thickened. "Why do you care about what this Shadow says?"

"He saw the destruction of Laijon. From other passages written by the princess, he turned away from his destructive loyalties–like my Shadow friend–and so foresaw how the wrongs could be made right and wrote the path forward here." Seyo looked at me. "The Immortal Abyss was carried into Vedoa and turned into a giver of illicit gifts, but no longer. When the Eternity Gate opened, it unlocked and awakened the Abyss, and now it will consume all of us if we don't stop it." She hesitated. "Tol, even a starpalm's fire cannot undo its judgment. The drought will end when the wrongs committed against the Abyss are satisfied."

Like the blow of a hammer against tile, her words sent hairline cracks shooting through my understanding. I remembered the One who remained at my side when the Shadow curse consumed me, but he did not stop it. Haunting feelings of inadequacy, like all my failed attempts to wield Temperance, flooded me. But she was saying that my Shadow form didn't stop me. That even if I became only and fully human again, even if I passed through the Abyss, I wasn't strong enough to end the judgment. And then her deeper meaning became clear.

I lowered my voice to a growl. "The Rebellion seeks to send someone through the Abyss to become an immortal protector of Vedoa. You say the opposite. You think I should approach the Abyss and surrender the four Forms. Not only that, you suggest I take the punishment that belongs to the dynasty upon myself? I have not participated in their wrongs. What of Xanala? How can I defeat her and save Vedoa from her rule without the four Forms?"

Seyo remained silent a moment. "Not just anyone can open the gates, and not in their own way."

"How did Geras open the Eternity Gate?"

"I'm not sure. I've wondered if the blood of ancient kings flows through his veins."

Like the dynasty's blood flowed through mine? I scowled.

Seyo's eyes landed on me. "The gates break curses."

I stilled. "What curses?"

"The Eternity Gate broke Geras's curse when it took his sight."

She said this as if she expected me to understand. What curse had Geras possessed?

"My friend who became a Shadow, he died as a human when the Eternity Gate opened." A tear slipped down Seyo's cheek. "Perhaps opening the Abyss could save you too."

"And what of your 'curse'?" I spat.

Her gaze fell. "No. My . . . confusing gifting . . . was not taken from me when the Eternity Gate opened."

That made no sense. I turned away. Give up my fire. Die as a Shadow. Fear and offense both twisted around my heart. I would not pay for the sins of the dynasty when I had done nothing . . . almost nothing . . . wrong, even if I shared royal blood. I would not waste the lives lost on my behalf by giving up my fire, Vedoa's gift. It only confirmed my previous thoughts. Seyo must not stay here any longer, nor Geras. No one else would lose their life for me.

"Come back with me. Geras can show you his vision . . ."

I ignored her, ran upward, and flew from the chamber. Past an astonished Roji and Geras, through the volcanic rock corridors, wrapping myself in darkness again. Flying from the mouth of the magma chamber, I headed into the loneliest portions of the fortress.

I extended my claws and skittered to a stop in an empty passage. Alone. Far from all of them. Something weighed heavy within the pockets of my robes. I felt the lump, discovered that I still had Seyo's book, and shrieked, my cry reverberating and echoing all around me. Let Taval, Exiles, and Laijonese fear their Reborn Star. I slumped over, my wings folding around my body, dragging me down, exhausting me. Maybe I could stretch my elbows and brace myself a bit, ease some of the weight.

No. That's what Watch had started to do.

I growled, extended my wings, and darted into deeper darkness.

33

SAMARI'S MEN SIGHTED XANALA'S returned missive first, but Taval caught the glinting, fiery orb from the oasis ramparts.

Within my chamber, the bed still made and food untouched because I rarely partook of either, I filled my hand with light and fought free of my Shadow form to stand in my human body, gasping for breath and trembling. This time, the transformation held. Hopefully the mishap with Roji, Seyo, and Geras had been a fluke.

I changed into presentable robes and passed my bodyguard, including Roji on rotation again, toward Bohak's quarters. Roji raised his brow before following, reminding me that I hadn't spoken to him since fleeing Seyo and the magma chamber. I assumed Seyo had kept our conversation to herself, and that Roji didn't know the unthinkable plan she had proposed.

I acknowledged him with a nod, to silence any ill feelings from my Tavalkian guards, and fixed my gaze ahead. My thoughts wandered in many directions, and I almost longed for the cool, narrow thinking of my Shadow self as I neared this meeting.

Had Xanala accepted our proposal? Accepted it but turned to trickery? If she came to the oasis to fight one-on-one, was I ready? My fight training my whole life had been defensive, except for my sessions with Bohak.

May the One help me do what I needed to do. Although I hadn't heard his voice in a long time, he wouldn't leave me now, would he?

I turned the corner toward Bohak's apartments and faced

Samari, a handful of Exiles, and Ysterdey approaching us from the opposite direction. The Shadow and Roji shared a quick and silent greeting. So Ysterdey was here, inside the fortress. Samari meant to lay all his cards on the table during this meeting.

Samari spoke to me without preamble. "How far do you trust Taval?"

I stood tall. "With my life."

"Let's hope your trust is well placed, because I fear it's about to be tested. A cornered dragon is above no trick." He spoke of Xanala, and with a dark look, spun toward Bohak's quarters.

I followed, the others behind me.

Bohak's officers saw us and stood at attention before opening the door wide.

Samari allowed me to pass first, and I could feel his restlessness as I stepped across Bohak's ornate rug.

The flickering fire hurt my eyes. I stilled. But I was in my human form. Had I felt that sensitivity as a human before? Was this another sign of deterioration?

Bohak, surrounded by his chief officers, offered a nod toward Samari. One of the first genuine gestures I think Bohak had given the Exiles, but his gaze hardened seeing Ysterdey, and his entourage murmured to one another. Thanks to that focus, Roji passed into our midst without notice.

I blinked in the too bright firelight again–stuffing down panic–and watched Bohak. Daring him to make peace with Samari bringing a Shadow with him.

Bohak's gaze softened upon seeing me, though he refused to glance at Ysterdey again. "Lady Tol, gentlemen, welcome." He gestured to the corner.

Two of his highest-ranking officers, Tier 2s with strong abilities in Temperance, stood across from one another, their palms outstretched to balance the blazing orb between their hands, holding Xanala's message intact. It strained toward Bohak, so she must have animated it to unfurl upon reaching him. Beads of sweat gathered on soldiers' brows from the effort of restraining the orb.

Knowing I could contain her missive in one palm sent adrenaline coursing through me.

Samari folded his arms. "She writes you personally, Taval. Will you read the message privately too?"

"Look around and answer your own question." Bohak turned to me. "Are you ready?"

"I am," I said.

Bohak signaled to his two officers. They closed their hands, releasing the orb, and it spun across the room to hover in front of Bohak. Waiting for the intended recipient to initiate unsealing it, though it was not encased in wax.

My insides coiled. Xanala's Wisdom, Temperance, and Magnificence were so great and skilled.

Samari huffed.

Bohak's neck reddened at the attention Xanala had purposely bestowed upon him, and he hesitated before pooling Magnificence into his palm and catching the note. Thin, perfect fire, like the brush of a quill, swirled from between his fingers into elegant lettering before our eyes.

Dear Bohak,

A wall of fire stands between us. How has it come to this? How has one girl forced us apart? Can you remember what life used to be like before? When I consider the past, I weep.

You've seen Tol as a Shadow. Don't listen to a word she says. She had her choice–I never dreamed she would choose so poorly–and I offer the antidote to her Shadow form as I promised her. All I ask for in return are the branded giant and Laijonese woman with him. Emeridus of Pirthyia recognizes both from battles in Laijon, and I see it as a fitting exchange. If this arrangement is agreeable to you, please bring both persons alone. I will not trust the antidote with anyone besides you. Once the exchange is complete,

I will agree to the battle as requested, though I hope your heart softens first, Bohak, to avoid unnecessary loss.

No matter what, your return will always be welcome. No matter how often the council warns me against your betrayal, I miss you.

Yours always,

Xanala

Bohak tensed and brushed the message away. His men stirred as Samari raised a brow. Ysterdey gave nothing away, and I didn't want to see whatever expression Roji was making. I ignored the officer's and Exiles' puzzled looks as they assessed my human form. One murmured that Xanala was turning mad. Good.

This was interesting, considering in her last message she'd only wished for my presence–

Like an afterthought, another tendril of fiery script raced before us. I barely caught the meaning of the veiled threat before it dissipated.

Without you, Taval runs out of water and seeks asylum in the capital. They beg that you do not forget them.

Bohak turned rigid and fisted his powerful hands. "Lies," he gritted. Yet he always said Xanala never promised what she couldn't fulfil. "I've taken too long to return. Taval is forced to go to her, and with their connection to me–"

"Everyone is running out of water." Samari grimaced. "The best thing we can do for your village is engage in battle. Why does she want the Laijonese?"

Bohak shook his head. "I have no idea. Perhaps revenge."

I did. Seyo had told me why, although Seyo and Geras's experience with the Eternity Gate would gain Xanala nothing. I looked to Roji.

He stood in the corner, lips pressed together. His eyes darted from Samari to Bohak, those with the power to decide much about his and his friends' futures.

"But we could send them," Bohak added. "If she does promise fighting one-on-one."

"You would trust her to keep that promise?" I said, aghast.

"Not completely. But–I can't . . ."

Roji looked ready to explode.

"No," I said. "Why would we give Xanala anything she wants, especially people?"

"With all respect, my Reborn Star"–Samari's voice was smooth–"if she agrees to deliver the antidote and fight you instead of all of us, and if it saves from bloodshed, isn't it worth sending the two?"

This came from a soldier whose own country had turned against him, who called Shadows his friends, yet still held Laijonese as lesser. I turned to Bohak for support.

He avoided my gaze. "Lady Tol, we must serve the greater good."

Not like this. But desperation gripped the room, and a small voice whispered that challenging this decision now would accomplish nothing. So, I did not reply, holding my tongue like suppressing fire, as Samari and Bohak bickered over the exchange.

Roji watched me in return, almost quivering with energy, but when I lifted my chin, he stilled.

There was no way under Vedoa's sun that Xanala would touch my friends. The four of us needed to meet immediately, but I knew only two would agree to my plan. Roji would stay–as he always had. And this time, I would respect and support him.

Thank the One, the sandstorm had dissipated.

That evening, Bohak hosted another feast for Taval, the Rebellion, and the Exiles. A gesture of hope and determination, when I knew he felt sick at heart over Taval's plight. What mercy would the capital show them, as Bohak's people?

I remained in my room. My light was drained, and there wasn't enough for me to make a public appearance, and this suited me well. I asked Bohak to create a bonfire, one of natural flames, across the oasis exit as a symbol of strength, so I could watch the proceedings from my window. Bohak bowed, more than happy to do so, then hesitated before sharing that the two Laijonese prisoners would be sent to Xanala tomorrow. Without him.

If he didn't trust Xanala enough to go himself, why did he think we'd gain anything from delivering half of her demands? I refused to hide my displeasure, but again, as much as it chafed me, I did not argue.

Uncomfortable with my silence, Bohak bowed again and returned to the proceedings, leaving me alone.

The festival dinner rang with merriment below. I disdained this last moment of joy before the battle, and someday, if I had any power at all, Vedoa would learn to see Laijon differently.

My own feelings for the dynasty and for Shadows came uncomfortably to mind. Justice was one thing, and hatred another.

I wrapped myself in darkness and flew through the chambers of the fortress. No soldiers blocked my path, as almost everyone gathered in the oasis. Swerving through passages, I skittered to a halt upon the stone floor, and perceived Seyo, Roji, and Geras waiting for me in a narrow, lightless tunnel, the meeting place I'd asked Roji to bring them to.

Seyo bowed. "Tol, thank you."

I wished their escape was less risky. I wished she and I had spoken again after I'd left her in the magma chamber. The inner part of me wept that we parted, and like this, perhaps forever. I forced human words past my Shadow lips. "I'm sorry."

She wrapped me in a hug, speaking more through that than by words. I thought she might tear up and tell me goodbye. Instead, she straightened and said, "I want you to see Geras's vision." And she touched his arm. Geras nodded and reached toward me. Just like my dreams.

For Seyo I would do it. I stepped forward, so he brushed the rough skin of my shoulder. For the first time, I noticed that he wore an oractalm bracelet around his wrist. Geras moved his hand to my chin, searching, then pressed his fingertips gently against my forehead.

Images exploded into my mind. Transfixed, I no longer saw Geras or the rock fortress surrounding us, but an unfamiliar, darkened room. It was so real, I felt the chill pervading the air, and noticed my lack of wings. I was human again, just like they'd promised. Breathless, I turned and faced a door, shining like gold, lying fallen on the ground. I stood before it. With human hands, I pulled the door open, unable to make myself look within, and lifted my left palm swirling with fire. To cast my flames into the doorway and surrender my gifting.

Stumbling back, away from Geras's hand, I took in the real world, the fortress, my Shadow claws, breathing hard. The Eternity Gate had not only stolen Geras's physical vision but had given him this ability to share inner sight. I didn't know what to do with this. I didn't want to consider it any more than Seyo's words.

Geras gazed in my general direction and spoke in his careful way in practiced Laijonese. "May light guide your path, Tol."

Seyo grasped Geras's hand, determined, and repeated the familiar words before saying, "Now." She glanced at me one last time, eyes bright with tears, then looked forward, touched Geras's forehead to relay the image to him, and they began to run. No farewells.

"Hide," I hissed to Roji, who paused, casting a long, pained look at his sister, before retreating into the fortress.

I swooped back through the corridors to my room, to my window, and waited.

Seyo and Geras crept through the outskirts of the oasis garden toward the bonfire. I held my breath, as the sharp-eyed scouts above saw them and cried out.

Go! I wanted to shout.

Seyo and Geras hurried through the brush. Hand in hand, Seyo guiding the way, Geras protecting her from behind with his shield across his back, discerning patches of light from darkness. Soldiers swarmed toward them, but the pair was too far ahead when they emerged from the garden and raced across open ground. Wielders filled their hands with fire to attack.

My chest tightened. I could not intervene without giving them away.

Seyo and Geras dodged fiery weapons. Geras suffered a hit and stumbled, pulling Seyo to slow with him, but quickly regained his balance. They ran three lengths from the bonfire. Two. One. With a jump, both leapt into the fire and disappeared.

The Rebellion shouted in an uproar.

I drew back into the darkness of my room. They would call it suicide, but Roji and I knew differently. They lived because Seyo's illicit, half-blooded gifting was not taken when the Eternity Gate opened. She maintained her ability, one that could earn her the rare title fire-walker here in Vedoa. Clasping Geras's ungifted hand afforded him the same protection to walk through flames, to the concealed exit on the other side, through which they would make it back across the Terror Lands to their allies in Nazak and on to Laijon. To deliver my word of peace to their queen, if I should triumph over Xanala and claim Vedoa's throne.

And Roji, who chose to stay behind, had better be hidden deep within the fortress as promised.

I would keep this first secret from Bohak–besides abandoning him to seek Srolo Kapir before–and I felt the weight keenly. Uncertainty about tomorrow enveloped me. Bohak, Samari, and I no longer possessed what Xanala wanted, thanks to me. Somehow, I had to convince her to fight without her proposed bargain. I gasped for breath, pressure weighing on me like the surrounding mountains.

"Will you follow me?"

I paused at the One's remembered question. Hadn't I already promised that I would follow? I was willing to fight her.

But Seyo, who had seen the Eternity Gate open, had spoken of more.

34

A TAVALKIAN OFFICER SUMMONED me to meet Bohak. How I'd dreaded this.

I filled my hand with light and traded my armor and spines for my frail, human appearance. How I hated it, how I hated trading forms. Immediately my light-filled palm trembled with its weight, making me want to curse my growing weakness before I exited my room. My guard and I passed through the volcanic chambers to Bohak's door. Guards pulled the leather covering back.

I blinked at the disarray. Platters of untouched food lay in the corner. The rug was rumpled from pacing, no guards or officers stood on duty, the fire burned low, and the usually organized and sorted table bore scattered papers and maps. At the head of the table, Bohak sat with his head in his hands, hair mussed.

I wanted to assure him that everything would turn out right. That Xanala would be defeated. Vedoa would be saved. To offer him the hope that had always been given to me. Instead, tears pricked my eyes. How could I offer him encouragement I didn't possess? I crossed the room and stirred the fire's dying embers, squinting against the hurtful illumination.

Bohak looked up and stood. "Tol."

I acknowledged his greeting, then said, "Please sit."

He did, and I lowered myself beside him. *Qo'tah*, I wished I wore my stronger Shadow form, so I felt less. The treacherous thought caused my heartrate to accelerate.

Bohak rubbed his face. "Samari's scouts have shared that the nations gather and march toward our borders. I can only imagine that they do so in response to the drought."

So, it was as Seyo had said. Nerves coiled inside me.

"Samari and I agree that we must first finish the imminent battle camped before us, which will determine all that is left to come." His words sounded naïve to my ears, but he went on. "I can't believe what happened. The exchange for the Laijonese and the antidote was sure, Xanala agreed to fight, and then the Laijonese did the unthinkable."

"Nothing with Xanala is sure," I said.

He ignored my comment. "What do we have left to barter with?"

"Me." I willed my heart to slow and failed. "If she won't surrender the antidote, I will fight her in my human form, not as a Shadow. I will go to her camp alone, and I will keep my right hand filled with light behind my back. I swear to do so."

"Impossible. I forbid you to put yourself in such a vulnerable position."

I fought to keep my voice even. "I won't let her hurt anyone else."

"What of you?" he countered passionately. "Are you not most valuable? If you think I won't–" He leaned over and took my empty, powerful left hand between his palms, like a desperate reflex.

Habit kicked in, and I stiffened.

"Even if you weren't the Reborn Star–" He noted my expression and released my hand, as if it burned him. "Forgive me, Lady Tol. I forgot myself."

No. In fact, I wished he hadn't let go.

Bohak stood and ran fingers through his already wild hair. "You will not surrender yourself to Xanala in such a manner. I will go to her as she asked in exchange for the antidote."

"No." Now I was on my feet. "No. She'll–" I couldn't get the horrible words past my lips. Imprison, coerce, torture him.

"We need the antidote." Bohak's eyes met mine. "Even if it costs my life."

"That is letting her win."

"My life is worth your glory."

"By the desert, Bohak!" I exclaimed. "You must live, for Vedoa's sake. I will defeat Xanala, and if I gain the antidote . . ." I found myself at a loss of words again.

"If you gain the antidote, you will pass through the Abyss and join the starpalms."

"And if I don't?" I took a breath. "If I don't, I swear allegiance to you, Bohak of Taval. If I cannot care for Vedoa, if my curse keeps me bound, then you must take my place."

Bohak choked. "I could never rule in your place. No one can. Who else can hold all four Forms? You'll be healed. We must, by the starpalms, succeed. You are destined to sit on Vedoa's throne. And I will stand beside you. Together, we–" He cut off abruptly.

Together, we will what? There were only three ways this would turn out. I would become a starpalm–which I couldn't believe anymore–remain a Shadow, or Seyo's ominous words and Geras's vision would be proved true. I looked down.

Bohak threw up a frustrated hand. "If only the Laijonese hadn't given themselves to the flames."

If only I could tell him the truth. "If I pass through the Abyss, how will I stop the drought?"

"As a starpalm, you will have command over many things."

"Are the starpalms so powerful?" Why did I say that now? When he didn't answer, I lifted my head.

He was studying me. "Do you doubt?"

Yes. More than he could imagine. If the One was the same as the Father of Lights, and he reigned over both the Eternity Gate and the Immortal Abyss . . . then he had caused or allowed the drought in the first place.

Bohak gestured for me to sit again. "You–we–are under incredible strain. It is natural to doubt." His voice softened, and he sat also.

Had he ever doubted? I couldn't imagine it, and bit my lip. "What if the Abyss is not a doorway to walk through, but a debt to be paid?"

His brow furrowed. "How could one pay such a debt?"

I took a shaky breath. "By opening the Abyss and offering it myself and my fire."

He sat back, and I wanted to cringe.

"Does your light waver?" he asked.

"What?"

"I'm asking if your light is running out."

"No," I said quickly.

"You're squinting. Does the firelight hurt you?"

My stomach sank. "Perhaps . . ."

"I'll extinguish it for you." Bohak stretched his hands toward the flames and drew tendrils to himself with masterful ease, until the room darkened. Just like the first time I'd shown him my Shadow form. "Tol, when did the light start hurting you while human?"

I squirmed. We went from talking about giving up my fire to this? How obvious was my regression? I blinked back tears. "Days ago."

"I see," he said quietly. Agitation colored his voice. "And it's touching your mind, because otherwise you would not consider throwing your fire away."

I stiffened. "Bohak–"

"Why else would you, standing on the cusp of victory, consider discarding your starpalm-given power and Srolo Kapir's sacrifice, as if it were nothing, along with the trust of the Rebellion?"

Srolo Kapir's sacrifice. His words struck me like a fist. By the desert, for a second, I despised him, the Rebellion, this path we were forced to walk, even Srolo Kapir. "You know that this is everything to me, my very life, and I would only surrender my fire if it was best for Vedoa. We've been through too much to quarrel like this. We can reach an understanding." My voice wavered. "You're my strongest support."

"Fine," he said crisply. "Let's reach an understanding."

I lifted my chin, determined to be the Reborn Star, whatever that meant anymore. "The Rebellion wants me to pass through the Abyss's protective aura, which requires perfection–"

"Once you have the antidote, your perfection will be secure."

"I'm not finished. I am to pass through the doorway and gain immortality. But then what? How does this save Vedoa? How does this end the drought and war between us and the rest of the continent?"

"Vedoa, united under you, can withstand war. And whatever imbalance exists between our world and the starpalms will be righted. Rain must return."

"But how? How will I accomplish this?" My breathing came too quickly. Now, in earnest, light wobbled in my hand, but Bohak didn't notice or speak. "How can I heal Shadows?"

"That was never expected of you."

"But I'll be a starpalm. Shouldn't that be within my power? I will end the war because–" I bit my lip. Should I tell him? Yes. No more secrets. "Because Seyo and Geras still live. Their jumping into the flames was an illusion, and I have sent them to make peace between me and Laijon."

Bohak stared at me in disbelief. "They live?" Then he blinked. "Peace with Laijon?"

"For the good of Vedoa."

Bohak's face grew grim. "If this is a joke, it's cruel and not worthy of you."

My heart sank. Why couldn't he see that Vedoa needed this?

"Tol," he whispered, his eyes haunted, "am I losing you?"

I reached to touch his hand. He didn't pull back. "No. May that day never come." I swallowed. "Tell me how to do all of this. Help me to understand."

"You know everything. The power of a starpalm . . ." He studied the messy table before looking up at me again. "After you defeat Xanala, do you truly intend to give up your fire?"

"Only if the Abyss proves that doing so is necessary."

Then he flung his hand toward the ceiling again, brushing mine aside. "I don't know why I ask. I can't stop you. I've never been able to stop you. But if the Abyss accepts you, you will pass through the doorway as we have always agreed?"

"Yes. Bohak, trust me. I'm not compromised. But if I cannot satisfy the Abyss–"

"Why wouldn't you be enough?"

I pressed down frustration. "Do you think I consider this lightly?"

"Of course not. Everything you do has been for Vedoa." But his eyes were guarded.

"And you have proven the same of yourself." I forced myself to speak calmly. "So, we are agreed, and we must move forward. What will we write Xanala?"

"We will write what you wish. That you will meet her as a human, holding light."

It seemed he was giving in too easily. "No objections?"

"Only one. That she will meet you here, not at her camp. Yes?"

"Yes."

Bohak bowed. "I will send the message tonight."

"I'll help you." But my light wobbled again, and I pressed my right hand to my chest.

Bohak's sharp gaze flickered, his protectiveness returning. "A message requires little Magnificence, and my Wisdom is enough for this task. You need to rest."

I began to protest, but he shook his head and gently cupped my elbow, his hand trembling, to escort me to my bodyguard waiting outside his chamber. Weariness accosted me, and I did not fight him, only cast a glance at him over my shoulder as I was led back toward my apartments.

His look of despair burned itself into my mind.

After sundown, Bohak's flaming message flew from our camp into Xanala's. Soldiers dashed into a frenzy of cleaning. Pushing supplies aside, making room in the oasis, even reinforcing earthen barricades in preparation for battle.

For Xanala would either agree to our demands or may advance upon the oasis by storm.

Wrapped in my Shadow form, I climbed among the sheerest rocks of our ring of mountains. My fiery wall still smoked and blazed between us and Xanala's camp. I stretched my hands toward my own fire, reaching. Begging.

My flames obeyed me. Starting at the top, my blazing wall disintegrated into a long, wide road of ash. Gasps of amazement rose from our scouts. The Shadows that had deserted to me squawked with confusion.

I retreated through my window into my room, to wait for Xanala to rouse her army and come. Fear seared through my being, but the part of me that was Shadow didn't feel it. Couldn't.

I had to end this.

35

SCOUTS UPON THE RAMPARTS heralded Xanala's approach and passage through the tunnel's mouth into the oasis. Soon, our trumpets also sounded with her arrival.

In my Shadow form, I watched from my high window between the oasis's gushing waterfalls as fiery light licked the edges of the tunnel mouth, the one the Exiles used. My eyesight sharpened as scarlet-clad soldiers marched into our midst and claimed the opposite half of the oasis. There were no more than twenty, as close as we could expect Xanala to come alone, and all Tier 2s. They marched toward us, chanting and carrying bowls of familiar, burning incense that offended my memories and my senses. Did they seek to cast evil from the oasis for superstitious Xanala? They disrespected us with their show. Fine beasts of burden followed, bearing empty water barrels. As if Xanala could defeat me and Taval, and then scoop precious water from the lake over our bodies.

Trumpets blared again. A storm-colored dragon paraded into the clearing. Strong as a tree, graceful as a bird, neck swaying, its unblinking eyes surveying us over glass-smooth reptilian armor. Seated upon the proud animal's back, Xanala wore arrogant white again, this time robes worthy of battle, and lifted her regal head high, searching for Bohak. And me. But only the Rebellion's leaders would greet her for now.

I gazed at the falling sun before casting light into my hand. The pain of transformation gripped me before I stood as a human, and the emotions that my Shadow side resisted crashed into me. Gasping,

I stumbled to brace myself against an ornate Tavalkian trunk. Breathing heavily, wondering if my heart would break from beating so hard. Curse my human weakness. With shaking fingers, I washed my face one-handed. No jewelry. I donned loose blue robes. The color of water, for Vedoa's hope, to remind the Rebellion of what I had wielded for them so recently but felt like ages ago. Back when I was whole. I swallowed the thought, put on my desert boots, stepped outside my room.

Two guards, Roji and a Tavalkian, stood on either side of the door. I met Roji's gaze and saw both his worry and his confidence in me. I felt the weight of his life added to my shoulders–yet I fought for him and my country. I would not rob him of his right to fight beside me. I lifted my chin, offering bravery that I both felt and lacked.

He straightened, inclining his head in return, and both of them escorted me through the fortress, past files of guards at attention. Through the arched door leading to the oasis, floating, stirred dust pricked my sensitive skin, and fading light shimmered everywhere in a blinding sensation. I perceived the rest of Taval, all who had sought refuge with us from Vedoa, and the Exiles spilling down the steps and across the garden in ranks. A double portion of scouts watched from the volcanic peaks above.

I fought to calm my heart and sought Bohak.

Between the two flaming stone basins, he claimed the head of the steps in his finest garments. Seeing me, he bowed, as everyone below did the same, and came toward me to offer his hand. I accepted his nearness, like a rope thrown to one who drowned, and leaned too far into him.

Bohak bent his head. "My lady, are you well?"

Compassion colored his voice. It almost broke me. "Are *we* well?"

He squeezed my hand, and his voice grew tight. "I am well when you are well." He surveyed my appearance. "You are beautiful, Lady Tol." His eyes widened. "I forgot your gold paint."

I touched my forehead. "She knows what I am."

He frowned but didn't say anything more. Placing my hand firmly on his arm and covering my fingers with his own, he turned us toward the garden.

I wished I were the Shadow, without nerves tingling down my

arms, my legs, my neck, my back. The feeling of fear was more than unsettling, and Bohak's agitation simmered beside me. I closed my eyes and concentrated on the fire flowing through my veins, strong and free. Limitless. Warped, as Seyo had said. I ignored that and drew a deep, night-cool breath through my lungs and glanced at Bohak as we walked through a corridor of soldiers. Sweat trickled down his neck.

Ahead, surrounded by her own escort, Xanala dismounted from her lowing dragon and awaited our approach. Young and perfectly human. Head held high. She, who'd caused Srolo Kapir's death, who'd subjugated Vedoa, who'd almost destroyed me.

Xanala's quick gaze swept over my human form to my arm upon Bohak's. Then she smiled.

Smiled.

I felt for the endless fire within me. Soon, this grass would lay charred.

Bohak kept his face neutral.

The elaborate ceremonies began. Like a dream. Bohak bowed low to the ground, and Xanala almost surprised me by inclining her head to him and then to me, though her eyes were hard. Our soldiers stood so far away, while Xanala's army stood closer to her. If she attempted to pull a trick, I stood by Bohak alone. If she dared try to attack him in a sleight of hand, she would regret it.

All the while, Xanala's eyes blazed as if on fire toward Bohak.

He noticed and shifted.

My light grew heavy in my hand. Was it weakening already? Panic bit at me.

"Lady Tol," Xanala said, speaking the common tongue.

I startled.

"My original offer still stands. Publicly, I declare that if you join me and turn away from the Rebellion and its lies, I will restore you in every way." Her eyes glittered. "And whoever follows you will be welcomed back, like lost sheep." She swept her hand toward Taval and the Exiles. "What is your final choice?"

By the desert, how did she sound so calm? It was as if she were a Shadow inside. But my fire surpassed hers at last, and she knew it. I didn't respond.

Xanala's gaze narrowed. "So be it." She raised her hand, and her men brazenly drew a circle in the dirt, an arena for our fight. Twenty of Taval's strongest wielders rimmed our half and raised shields of fire. As if they could keep my gifting contained, or hers. Royal soldiers also took their stances, but only five.

Those gathered bowed, demanding that the ceremony and battle start. Taval gave their rallying desert cry, and the Rebellion joined in. Palace soldiers stamped their feet and swore allegiance to the dynasty.

Xanala arched her brow and extended her hand. A demand to mingle fire, as tradition dictated. I felt a sliver of respect worm its way past my defenses. After all, she offered to do so with two Tier 3s in Justice.

Bohak stepped forward and cupped his palm with hers, and both pooled fire into their hands. The memory of watching them do this at the palace annoyed me. Before we fought, it would be my turn to mingle fire with her. I could snatch her fire without shame.

No. That was her way. A Shadow's path. I would not become like her.

Xanala gave Bohak a sharp look and snatched her hand away. He seemed taken aback by her abruptness.

Tingles of warning raced through me. What was she doing?

Bohak turned and offered his hand to mingle fire with me. Let the ceremonies end before we wasted more of my light. I didn't want to look away from Xanala, but when I met Bohak's gaze, my heart faltered. Tears sparkled in his eyes.

I pursed my lips, wishing I could speak. Willing him to believe that whatever trick Xanala planned, we could stop her together. Fighting as one for the Rebellion, for Srolo Kapir, for the Exiles, for Vedoa. I slipped my left hand into his and mentally willed bravery into Vedoa's strongest wielder of Justice, who'd left the palace to fight beside me. I poured a gentle, controlled measure of my fire into our joined hands, and dared to offer him Magnificence. Just in case, as we always did.

Bohak's eyes widened, then he seized my hand with both of his. Before I could blink or question why, like yanking a rope, he grasped my fire and pulled.

Wisdom, Judgment, Temperance, and Magnificence tore from my hands. I cried out, knees buckling. I tried to wrench away in vain.

Sweat poured down his face, his eyes shut tight, breathing heavily with effort. Then he flung me away.

I collapsed upon the grass, and my light extinguished. In front of the world, Shadow devoured my human form. Twisting, terrible transformation. I clawed the ground to stand and open my hand with fire. But I couldn't. My fire felt as weak as my humanity, like a gasp. Too depleted to fight.

Bohak doubled over and retched.

Royal guards shoved me to the ground, twisting my limbs and wings behind me. I looked around frantically for support, but the Rebellion and Taval were staring at me or Bohak, surprise and horror on their faces. The Exiles roared, weapons high, and attacked Xanala's soldiers. Like a nightmare, royal reinforcements, an army materializing out of the tunnels, poured into the oasis.

Then Bohak stood upright. "Let her go!" His shout was in the common tongue.

Xanala marched to him, tense as a coiled serpent, speaking in the high tongue. Understanding came much easier now, and I almost wished it didn't. "No. Now give it to me."

"I released her fire," Bohak said, continuing to speak in the common tongue. "I can't hold it."

Xanala slapped him and shrieked what could only be an insult. "And you took . . . all?"

Bohak slowly lifted his head, darkness in his eyes. His gaze flicked to mine and away so fast, I had to have imagined it. "You promised she could have the antidote. We agreed that she would take it and follow the Exiles to Nazak," his voice faltered. "With her body and mind restored, she can make a new life and never to return to Vedoa. The Rebellion and Taval are to be pardoned."

"Did you take . . . all . . . fire? Answer . . . first . . ."

Bohak switched to the high tongue. ". . . Something . . . a seed . . . can't reach. If . . . you or . . . we . . . die."

Xanala looked to strike again but didn't. "Then . . . fire will return. And we will try . . . again."

Anger clipped Bohak's words as he shouted something I didn't understand.

Now Xanala switched to the common tongue and watched me from the corner of her eye. "How by the starpalms can I trust a double traitor, Bohak of Taval?" She whirled, lifted her hands wide, and wove shimmering white-fire handcuffs. Toward me.

I roared, straining to expand my wings and fight those forcing me to stand, but then I felt the burn of the handcuffs upon me, my palms forced together, and a biting strike across my back sent me stumbling. They tied my legs, my wings, and mouth with chains. I was a Shadow. I was stronger. I writhed, but more soldiers joined in. Many wielding burning fire. Shadows landed nearby, dressed in scarlet. My own kind and my enemies, loyal to Xanala again.

Xanala raised her voice in the common tongue once more. "Taval and all traitors, thank your leader, the heir of Taval. If not for him, you would all be slain this day."

I wrestled with my chains until they tore my flesh.

Xanala gave a shout, and royal guards flooded in and ransacked the oasis. They piled our supplies and weaponry, and forced Taval and the Exiles to carry them toward the mouth of the oasis, before filling her barrels with lake water. Any who rebelled were slain by the sword at Emeridus's command, who had appeared among the rabble.

In dread, I twisted, looking for Roji, willing him to run.

Bit by bit, scarlet-robed guards emptied the oasis. By the time the moon reached its zenith, Xanala ordered us returned to her camp. Her thugs hauled me over their shoulders and carried me through the garden, past all those who had sworn loyalty to me, and through the tunnels to the desert.

The rest of Xanala's camp, sprawled across the Terror Lands, lay packed and ready to depart.

Xanala mounted her dragon and led our captured train toward night and Vedoa.

36

NIGHT FELL. DUST, THE TAIL OF the sandstorm, cloaked the stone capital.

An army of scarlet armor escorted us through towering walls, led by a silver dragon and the false Empress Xanala. Bohak stumbled beside her, just a misstep, but enduring the invisible, symbolic iron collar he'd accepted in exchange for emptying and surrendering me.

I felt for my fire deep inside. The "seed" of Magnificence remained, but it was too small to be of use until it could grow. Leaving me helpless.

I plodded on, weighed down with chains, surrounded by uneasy guards fearing me, even now. Xanala's fiery cords bound my hands fast, preventing me from wielding until my fire built enough to overcome it, burning even through my thick Shadow flesh. Weariness gripped me, but my Shadow body continued on. Unstoppable. Unbreakable. Onward toward whatever came next, unable to stop. Unable to fight. I was a wanderer again, living outside my own skin. Forced to follow to places I did not want to go. Returning "home."

Yet my inner being whispered, *Escape.*

If Xanala wished for a humiliating parade through the city, she failed. For few dared reveal their faces from the buildings and stores I staggered past. I was no hope for them to mourn, neither was Xanala a champion to cheer.

The white stone palace walls loomed before us. Her entourage flung the gates wide, a terrible homecoming. Xanala dismounted her dragon and proceeded to the palace, as servants hurried to lead her dragon to its stables.

The once lush palatial gardens had begun to look withered and dry under dawn's young light.

With random shouts, soldiers herded the Rebellion, Taval, and Exiles in the opposite direction by sword point and handfuls of fire. Where were they taking them? My captors held me back. I twisted to look for Samari, Roji–

The front doors to the palace opened, and a fresh army of red soldiers flooded onto the grounds. The Pirthyian Emeridus joined us, a whip over his shoulder, and his expression tightened seeing me.

Xanala swept up the stairs in her white robes. Seeing her, Emeridus tore his eyes from me, bowed deeply, and escorted her inside the palace. I caught a glimpse of Bohak's broad frame before he disappeared after them.

Growling in the high tongue, a soldier pushed me forward.

We tramped inside the palace, through the grand entry into cool corridors. Servants peeked at us as we passed. Terror covered their faces. Because of me? Or because of the dying royal gardens and she who controlled it all? Grains of sand, escaping indoors, shifted between marble and my clawed feet. Torchlight from wall sconces burned my eyes as we went up the wooden staircase.

The golden double doors of the throne room opened. We walked within the hallowed, round room, dominated by the fabled fighting arena, rimmed with windows that exposed the mountain range and the mighty stone aqueduct where gangs of Shadows squabbled–all veiled by lingering sandstorm.

Early morning sunlight, filtering through the windows, drenched me in agony. I flinched, and guards forced me forward. My claws scraped across fine tile, my chains dragging behind me. I overheard a council member mutter that our devilish kind were not allowed in this sacred space. Emeridus took the liberty of remaining near me, his long whip in hand.

I turned my gaze to the stolen throne.

Xanala sat, encircled by the gaping jaws of the ancient water dragon and stone basins left unlit to avoid strengthening me. Cold and calm as glass. Her council clustered around her, some displaying cautionary handfuls of blue fire. Through my squinting, I caught their nervous glances.

Bohak stood beside the throne, stiff as a statue. I could feel his striving to fit in, to grasp his bartered honor–what used to be. But bartered honor was no honor at all, and he knew it. When he finally looked at me, his handsome, boyish face paler further.

Emeridus raised his voice in the high tongue, but the meaning behind his thick accent was plain to me. "Behold, the promised Reborn Star of the northern desert."

The council devolved into a muddle of obscene calls and tittering laughter.

I did not cringe. I stared at Xanala. Willing her to begin this false trial. Daring her to face me, even now.

She ignored me as she spoke, her soft voice harsh to my sensitive hearing. "Make her bow."

Red haze consumed my vision, but Emeridus's whip curled around my torso. Hands forced me to my bound wrists, elbows, and knees.

Help me! I felt for the kindling of fire within me, but there was only an ember. Not enough. But I was more than fire. The Shadow inside me wailed to attack.

With a surge of strength, I lunged free of the soldiers' hands and ripped the whip from Emeridus's grasp with my teeth, as if he were my old buyer in the city. As if he were Xanala, and I was seizing her fire from her. Cries and exclamations rang. I rose to my full height and whirled toward Emeridus, chains whipping around me.

But tendrils of burning fire immediately wrapped around my limbs. Xanala stood at the foot of the throne, wielding fiery hooks that gripped my limbs and back. I collapsed again and shrieked.

Bohak raised his frantic voice. "Let her live!"

"A starpalm will walk the desert in human form. From an endless well, her fire will cleanse the monster's lair, kindle life within dead bones, and fill the depths of the world. She, the one born of legend, will slay her own soul to finish the age. You've failed, Tol, and it didn't have to

be this way." Xanala mocked in the common tongue, then released me from her fire and motioned to nearby guards. They ended my public humiliation by pushing me from the throne room and the wary-but-contemptuous glares of the council, Bohak's stricken expression, and the false empress's unfeeling eyes.

They put me in an inner cell so deep and isolated within the dungeons that I felt the walls would close in on me. Cramped even for a human prisoner. Smelling of dryness and rot. Surely, we had descended to a true corner of the underworld.

Emeridus, with the help of five Tier 2 wielders, including a Shadow, fitted me with new, very short irons, secured to the cell's bars. Firelight from their hands bounced across stone and stung my eyes. The palace Shadow averted his gaze too.

Emeridus locked the door and pocketed the key. He spoke in the high tongue with his rough accent, and I guessed at words I didn't understand, his intent clear. "The empress would do well to choose a swift execution." He spoke with bravado, but I sensed a tremor in his voice. The fear he still held for me and what I was supposed to be. "I should . . . her wings while we're here."

"No." Bohak's voice emerged from the corner, as far from the others as possible. Resistant to following these ruffians in their task from the moment Xanala ordered him to join my unceremonious escort. "You are under orders not to harm her."

Emeridus barked a laugh. "Shall I listen to you . . . desert snake? Empress Xanala also . . . orders for you . . . her."

Bohak stiffened in the dark. "There hasn't been time for her to—"

"Your orders are to . . . daily. Starting now. Begin."

"You wouldn't . . . me . . . in front of Xanala."

Emeridus laughed. "Begin."

A pause, and then Bohak sank into a crouch near the bars of my cell.

I pulled away, but the chains were too short. I glared, sick to my stomach being near him.

Bohak ignored me as he deftly unraveled Xanala's intricate cords binding my hands. Then he gripped my hands and pulled, though with weariness this time. There was so little fire to take, little pain left for me to feel, but the effort clearly cost him, by his gasping breaths.

I remembered when he'd offered to partially drain me, and eased my fire with great care as he discovered my Magnificence. I also recalled that he'd once promised to teach me how to defend myself against what he now did.

Emeridus spoke loudly. "The . . . sandstorm reveals . . . enemy armies crossing Vedoa's deserts. The empress has . . . all walls, and her soldiers are ready. Once we are finished with this . . . she will be ready too. How goes your task? About . . . as bad as last time?"

Bohak expelled a furious breath. He ceased draining me, bound my palms together with shackles, and pushed himself onto his feet.

I gritted my teeth and felt for my fire. So low. Barely a flicker of warmth.

"May the starpalms deal with you," Bohak whispered in his mother tongue, but he aimed this toward Emeridus as he shouldered past the man.

Out of nowhere, an aged, crippled Shadow crept into the room. Bohak recoiled, but Emeridus extended one arm toward me, as if expecting the creature. The Shadow shuffled to my cell, set a filled wooden trencher down with a clatter, and scraped the vessel under the break in the bars where I could lower my head and eat it like an animal. Then he scuttled away.

Emeridus's laughter bounced against stone as he and his thugs shut the atrium door and vanished with Bohak, taking their cursed torchlight with them.

Darkness settled around me. I pulled on my chains, but I couldn't break them. I needed to reach the Rebellion, the Exiles, even Taval. I needed to find Roji and know if he was dead or alive. I tried to fill my hand with light, but I couldn't with my palms bound. They even took the sliver of me that remained human.

The One did not speak to me.

I had failed.

I began to chant to myself with desperation. *Tol. My name is Tol.*

37

ANOTHER DAY PASSED, EXPOSING the turmoil and indecision created by my presence, as foreign armies neared the capital.

Again, Bohak entered my chamber first and set a flaming torch into the lone wall sconce.

"Go on," Emeridus barked.

Bohak's face contorted with revulsion before he knelt on the filthy stone floor, wordless, just a fingerlength from me. He gripped my claws in his powerful hands, hands that used to offer me loyalty. With my wrists chained to the bars, I couldn't pull away or scratch.

I wanted to scream and send him hurtling backward, away from my cell. If only I was free or had been granted a fair fight. But I would never receive one. Even with my fire drained, I would be delivered to Xanala's feet so she could try to pluck my seed of fire with her weak Justice, against Bohak's warnings. A cheap victory.

Xanala both honored and punished Bohak's faithless Justice by sending him to me. But when my life ended, so too did his usefulness to her. His life hung in the balance, and I hoped when he looked at me, he saw his vile choice.

Bohak drained the flickering ember of my remaining fire. Sweating. Ashen. But gently this time, like once before. I felt the increased tension in the air. Something was different.

Emeridus watched from the darkened corner, a short spear now in hand, a superior weapon in these dank, close quarters. Reminding me of the staff I used to carry, but without the teeth.

He looked ready to use it, on either me or Bohak. Although Xanala would not let him kill me, there was much he could accomplish before reaching that point. Even the kneeling double traitor's life was not as dear as mine. But Emeridus acted differently today. No more jabs. All seriousness.

"Take it all. Don't leave a drop," the Pirthyian growled.

My stomach twisted. This was my last draining.

When he could take nothing else, Bohak released me and rose on wobbling feet. Each draining, despite my lack of fire, seemed to take more and more from him. He stumbled after Emeridus with the torch and left me in darkness. I searched wildly to feel the untouchable hint of flame he could never extinguish, as my eyes adjusted again to the fathomless darkness.

I fought my chains until I was bruised and bleeding, twisting and pulling with all my strength. *Have you, the One of the twin gates, rejected me too?*

It didn't make sense. The One hadn't abandoned me when I'd become a Shadow. Where was he now? I rested my ghastly head against my arm, my wings curled beside me. How long until Xanala came?

The door scraped open.

Through the blindness, the old, bent Shadow who brought my meals returned. He groaned a little as he scraped a wooden trencher out from my cell, still filled with a vile substance supposed to be food, and replaced it with another. He kept himself pressed close to the wall, fearing me and my empty hands. As before, he did not wait for me to eat, but turned and shuffled to the door. I watched him. Could he still speak?

I moistened my thick tongue. "Is it night or day?"

The old Shadow stiffened and spoke in a rasping voice. "The moon rises high."

My heart thudded. He retained his language. What could I glean from him? "Since when does Her Majesty, the false empress, commission Shadows beyond the prime of life?"

The old Shadow scratched his chin in a very human gesture. "Anyone can trade their humanity for water."

I hesitated. "Who helped you keep your speech?"

He cocked his head, as if confused by my question. Perhaps he didn't realize that his ability to continue speaking was a gift. "I have a friend among the servants. Her sibling is a Shadow too. I had a sibling. That is one of a handful of things I can remember, thanks to her." His tired eyes fell upon me. "They call you the Reborn Star."

His simple statement touched the human part of me, and it hurt. "Are you here to torment me?"

"No. I remember the Reborn Star. And I remember who you were before. Even without the servant speaking to me, I could never forget you." The old Shadow shuffled forward, drawing his reeking mass closer. As his form materialized, I saw that he was taller and much thinner than I had realized. And one of his arms, from the elbow, was missing. Why was that familiar?

His eyes, now so near the cell's bars and mine, gleamed in the dark. His voice strengthened and rang memory bells in my mind. "You were the last to see Ami alive. Before they took her."

I choked back a gasp. "Bor'beti?"

"The girl who was to possess four Forms, the promised Reborn Star. Here." Bor grunted and stooped to all fours, his arched spine like spikes, his face near mine. "I sold the goats. I would have died for lack of water if I hadn't accepted the empress's offer."

I felt a trace of fear. I had ruined his life and was now chained to the wall at his mercy. Trapped. Almost fireless.

Bor'beti lowered his voice. "Some say you are powerful enough to save Shadows. I don't know if it is true, as you are here. I do know that because of you, Ami did not need to succumb to this worse fate." And then he reached through the bars and grasped my clawed hands in his.

I gasped and desperately tried to sink my claws into his sparse flesh. "Do not touch me."

But Bor'beti's rasp became a whimper. "Don't fight me, girl. Take it. All of it."

With shock, I realized he was pouring fire into my hands. So, he had been Tier 1, unlike his sister. My Justice, beaten down inside me, leapt to seek his fire and seize it. And I felt Bor'beti's gifting flow into mine and strengthen my Magnificence.

His limited store of fire ran out, and we released hands to sit back. Me with his fire simmering inside my veins, him breathing heavily and leaning on his side.

I stared at him. "You gave me everything."

"Good." Bor'beti nodded, his posture still bent and broken, but strength infusing his voice. "Ami died in honor. For her sake–for all of us–may this give you a chance, even if we lose in the end."

I blinked, reeling. Unable to believe the gift he had given me. I fought to find the right words. "I will remember you. I will fight for you. Bor'beti . . . go in peace. For me and Ami'beti."

When I said "peace," he murmured something I couldn't hear and shuffled back to the door. Within the doorframe, he stopped and looked back. Then he passed into the hallway, and I knew that, like Ami'beti, I would never see Bor'beti again.

I squeezed my eyes shut and felt the quiet fire simmering inside me, growing rapidly with his humble and costly gift. It was meager compared to Srolo Kapir's, and not enough to fight. But enough to kindle. A precious gift that only needed time before I faced Xanala, regained my humanness, and saved Vedoa.

38

I AWOKE TO HURRIED FOOTSTEPS tramping down the hall.

Emeridus entered first with his spear in hand. Bohak followed, gaze down. Then Xanala, in loose robes and light, fitted armor, graced my tiny atrium with her presence. Behind her, handpicked guards carried torches and filled the corridor beyond with light.

I forced my breathing to remain even. Fire pulsed in my veins, still weak, but growing. Almost enough.

Xanala skewered me with an assessing look. Raw, agitated emotion enveloped her.

I refused to break eye contact and willed her not to sense the gift I'd received.

"It's time," she said in the royal tongue. I grappled with the interpretation, filling the blanks where she spoke unfamiliar, terse words. "Laijon will soon reach our gates, with Nazak and Ai'Biro behind."

My thoughts skipped. The nations were already upon us.

"Then we must act quickly. It would be better to end her life here," Emeridus grumbled and nodded toward me.

Bohak stiffened, and Xanala held up a hand. She murmured under her breath. *Barbarian.*

Emeridus shifted his weight. "Her fire has had time to grow."

Bohak's expression became one of dread.

I held my breath. I could not lose Bor'beti's gift–

Xanala hesitated, looking between the two of them, derision in her gaze as she beheld Bohak.

Emeridus tapped the end of his spear on the floor. "The Tavalkian should drain her–"

Xanala stopped him. "Bohak's Justice is unparalleled." Her gaze flicked to me and back. "And his last draining is enough. Free her, but keep her bound. Hurry."

A knot of royal Shields approached my cage, dressed foot to head in fire-resistant cloth and armor, with one hand on their swords and one free to wield. They unlocked the door and stood.

"Get her," Xanala ordered.

But the soldiers did not move. It was Bohak, trembling, who came inside the cramped cage to unlock my shackles, as a couple of the bodyguards bickered with one another over who would stand in front of me.

"I . . ." Bohak's hands were shaking, his voice almost inaudible. "I regret everything." He looked away.

I wanted to spit in his face. Guards gripped my arms and bound my wrists with rope, letting me keep my hands in front of me, but my palms did not touch. Free to wield what they didn't know I possessed.

Emeridus scowled. "You're only binding her in ropes?"

"She's drained," Bohak snapped, then his hand brushed my claws. He startled and made eye contact with me.

I held my breath. Had he felt my fire?

Emeridus's voice pitched in frustration as he saw that no one listened to him. "Am I not an expert on the making of Shadows? She won't remain bound for long. She should be drained again."

Bohak turned toward him and growled. "If only you were gifted enough to try."

Emeridus's chest swelled, and he took a step forward.

Xanala clapped her hands. "Enough! Bring her out."

Bohak vacated the cell. Surely . . . he'd felt nothing. Soldiers tested my binding before leading me out.

Xanala swept from the atrium, Bohak and Emeridus following. Guards shoved me in front of them into the hall and the blinding light of filled wall sconces. Walking in their midst, I reached deep within to feel my growing fire. To wait for the perfect moment.

39

STONE CORRIDORS TWISTED IN countless directions, a precaution against escapees. For none who came down here to the dungeons likely ever came out alive. Except for me.

Over the heads of the Tier 2 Shields, I could see Emeridus and Bohak following Xanala. Between them and us, an older soldier led the way, perhaps one of the few who knew the paths in and out of this lonely labyrinth. But I remembered these corridors from my last ill-fated visit, and twisted my bound wrists, feeling rope cut into my skin. Rope that would soon burn.

Bohak drew near to Xanala and whispered urgently in the high tongue, his gaze darting to Emeridus. Xanala responded in a sharp mutter.

They didn't understand a Shadow's keen ear, and I untangled their words as best I could until their plan became clear. They were taking me back to the throne room, and Xanala would fight me in the amphitheater. The Tier 3 princess against a drained and bound Shadow—so they thought—an imbalanced fight on many accounts. I should have guessed, as it was the only way to secure the throne in the eyes of the people. Though they didn't say it, I knew Xanala would seize my hands and try to take the last of my fire from me, which would be useless. Even Bohak with all his Justice couldn't take it. And I wouldn't willingly surrender my gift for any offer or threat. But Bohak's intensified murmur gave me pause. Speaking as smoothly and confidently as ever, as if he still held any sway in this place, he tried to convince Xanala to release me into the Terror Lands as an Exile. Thereby creating a stronger impression in the people's mind than taking my life, especially before war.

I didn't want this act of charity from him. Or his belated guilt.

Emeridus ignored their conversation and cast frequent glances over his shoulder at me.

Every time I glared back, he startled. And when he fixed his gaze ahead, I walked a little faster, forcing the Shields around me to quicken their pace.

We turned a corner and approached a steep stairwell to either the second or third floor. This portion looked different. Xanala lengthened her strides. Bohak pestered her with hurried questions that she ignored. Something had shifted.

This wasn't the way to the throne room. The plan was changing.

I exhaled and tried to feel the gifting of the guards around me. Were any of them strong enough? No. If I had one chance at gaining the upper hand, it had to be Xanala, her fire, and then to seize the antidote.

A lone doorway to descending stairs met us. As soon as Bohak saw it, he slowed and uttered a protest. Shields also slowed, darting eyes at one another. When Xanala continued on, Emeridus followed with his head erect, unsurprised. Then Shields filed down into the passage before and behind me, cutting me off further from Xanala, but giving me ample space.

The stairs led to a lightless, widening atrium, smooth floor, walls, and ceiling. A tense hush gripped everyone. Some Shields wielded fire into their hands to see.

Bohak tried to catch Xanala's attention again, but she walked more quickly, tension evident in the carriage of her graceful shoulders. All followed, and I noticed an upcoming long, thin crack in the stones at our feet. It spread horizontally across the flooring and met parallel cracks climbing lengthwise down the chamber. A rectangle big enough for six people and no more. With a jolt, I guessed where we were, which was confirmed when I saw the links of iron hanging on the right against the wall.

This was where the Killer of Kings was kept. A monster lay below this floor, under the rectangular slab we neared.

Xanala wouldn't risk fighting me in the throne room. She would drag me over a monster's pit and wave the antidote in my face. My humanity for my fire. And then she would throw me to my death.

I stumbled to my knees with a muted shriek.

Xanala jerked in surprise. My guards didn't move to help but only watched me. Still afraid. Still suspicious. But Emeridus pushed through their ranks and grabbed me by the back of my neck. "Walk," he hissed.

When I didn't obey, he tried to haul me to my feet. My ruined clothing scraped and tore as I regained my footing, wings throbbing against their restraints. I stumbled and fell again. Tucking my hands under my body and snapping the ropes binding me.

Xanala waved to her Shields. "Drag her."

Emeridus raised a booted foot. "I'll break your wings," he spat.

There was a sudden movement, and Bohak pushed Emeridus away, facing him with hands outstretched with fire. "You go too far, Xanala. You need the people's trust," he warned. "This move will only weaken your reign. Reconsider."

Hatred filled Emeridus's eyes, but he didn't dare come closer to Bohak's Tier 3 fire.

Xanala's cold voice traveled across stone, and her hands filled with flames. "If she gives me her fire, I'll give her the antidote as requested, and we shall battle one another in the throne room, weapons only, no flame."

"No, you won't." Bohak's tone was crisp. Almost savage. "With you, it is always lies."

Xanala laughed and began wielding daggers between her hands.

"I'm such a fool," Bohak said in a low voice.

"Perhaps we all are," I rasped, then leaned forward, claws free to grab his hands, and seized his gifting from his palms. He braced himself. For a moment, I felt a wall between us, a defense tactic I'd never experienced. Then my gifting overcame his, and I showed no mercy as I dragged his Tier 3 Justice to join mine.

Bohak's eyes widened in shock, and when I released him, he collapsed.

I spun to Xanala.

Bellowing, Emeridus charged into me. We rolled together, his boots and my claws scraping against stone. I thrust him away and looked up.

Xanala stood against the wall, gripping a chain, burning eyes on me. She pulled.

The trapdoor beneath us grated open. Emeridus and I began to slide, him crying out and me grabbing the rim of the hole. But the Pirthyian barreled into me, sending both of us plummeting into the darkness below, and I spread my wings–

We crashed onto the stones below. Emeridus groaned, but my resilient form allowed me to get to my feet quickly.

Xanala. I swooped into the air and flew for the exit just as the trapdoor closed again, blocking me from escape and sending me cavorting into darkness.

Below, Emeridus spewed a string of Pirthyian curses. Abandoned to this death hole by his mistress.

My nerves tensed and ears strained for the slightest sound of what else lay among us. Then Emeridus suddenly blasted a cannonball of blue fire in my direction, catching me by surprise.

I threw a shield in front of me and dove. Since when did he have blue fire? Deserts, his borrowed Magnificence was strong, and even with Bohak's fire, my growing Magnificence was just nearing Tier 2 levels. I extinguished my shield and wrapped darkness around me like a cloak.

Emeridus's breath heaved loudly as he stood with fire in his hands, like a beautifully lit target. With a roar, he blasted a volley of shapeless flames toward me.

I scurried away. One attack came close. Too close.

"Foul creature." Emeridus cursed again as he threw another volley.

I tucked and rolled in the opposite direction, avoiding his blazing fire. High walls and closed ceiling hemmed me in. I darted behind large rocks and tripped over bones. Then my sensitive ears heard it. Water sloshing. Something far too large slithered through the blindness. Another wasteful barrage of blue fire blazed toward me.

I gasped a breath and rolled away. Back into the open and Emeridus's line of attack.

He laughed. A strained sound that belied that he knew his end was coming.

I braced myself for another volley, and then I heard the slithering. Dripping.

A mountainous shape unfurled in the dark.

Emeridus heard it, too, and turned.

In the light of his fire, nothingness shimmered in front of us, like a transparent phantom.

I crouched against the wall, heart hammering. Some said knowledge dispelled fear, but not this time. Thanks to the curse of the Terror Lands, I was intimately acquainted with the Killer of Kings.

Emeridus braced himself and flung a volley at the creature. His flames merely glanced across the beast's swaying form, reflecting off its mirror-like scales. The old water dragon's jaws opened to reveal glistening white teeth as long as my arm, the one part of it that didn't shimmer with reflective camouflage. Revealing that it was almost as large as the grotesque statues forming the four corners of the palace.

Emeridus could not so much as choke. This beast, easily three times as large as the curse we had fished from the Terror Lands lake, lunged. Emeridus dove, escaping the attack and tossing an impressive-but-harmless volley of fire that filled the atrium with light. Allowing me to see how far back the chamber extended, how it narrowed into a bottleneck dammed up with stones.

Emeridus scrambled to his feet and ran in my direction, for the boulders. It was a desperate, hopeless attempt. The monster enveloped him in a single bite, and Emeridus vanished with a cry, as if devoured by thin air. Then the almost-invisible beast backed up, scales scratching on the stone floors, to disappear within whatever cavity of water this chasm held.

I gulped a breath. Emeridus was gone, but I'd traded that enemy for one that was far worse. I felt for my fire, growing inside my veins. Mine, Srolo Kapir's, Bor'beti's, and now Bohak's mingling and intertwining with one another. Emeridus's leftover blue flames still sizzled upon the ground.

Water sloshed against walls. Scales crunched against stone. This creature was bigger than the one that had claimed our oasis, but older. Slower. Trapped, as I was. The creature's maw suddenly thrust through Emeridus's flames, and I leapt away. It screeched a low, hollow, throbbing sound that shook the cavern, before whipping its head back and forth and extinguishing the blue inferno that posed no threat to its armor.

I watched from the corner. I couldn't kill the beast with fire. And I couldn't drag it from the water. But . . . I could separate the water from it.

The dragon screeched.

I crept as quietly as I could until I found the bank of inky, stagnant water.

The monster slithered sideways and then back again. Preparing to strike in my direction.

I shot a ball of fire into its face and leapt to the side before opening my hands and releasing an outpouring of flame from my palms across the edge of the lake. Steam began to hiss and rise.

The water dragon tasted the air with a horridly long tongue for my body warmth.

I lurched in the opposite direction just before the creature lunged again. It hit the wall, shaking the foundation of the dungeon. Its long tail swept the ceiling and landed in the water with a crash.

I took refuge behind a massive rock and blasted the water. More hot, hissing steam rose everywhere and filled the cavern. It would burn the monster, but it also burned me. The tail curled around my rock and pinned me behind it. There was another howling screech.

I drove both sets of claws into the animal's tail, sinking them deep through its thick scales and hard flesh, evoking another terrible roar, before I yanked myself free and ducked. Its tail recoiled, and it enveloped the rock with its tremendous jaws. Teeth so close I could touch them, but I skittered away to the opposite side of the cavern and flew through steam and across water until I reached the far pile of rocks.

The monster wailed and surged toward me, closer and closer. I darted up to the ceiling just before the dragon cascaded into the hill of stones, breaking up the dam and sending it crumbling into whatever lay beyond. The monster screeched and writhed, halfway out of water. More of the wall broke apart, and water seeped away.

The creature thrashed back to its pool of water, now a puddle, and uttered a roar. It strove to splash hot water over its exposed gills and slithered deeper into its newly exposed territory. Its long, red, tongue tasted the air for me.

The trap door remained closed. The only way out was forward, before the Killer of Kings beat me to it. I leapt into the air and swooped toward the monster glutting the passage. The water dragon snapped its greedy maw at my fleeing form. Its putrid breath raked over me, and I swerved over the Killer to the back of the cavern, hoping against hope. And I was right. A narrow channel, perhaps how the creature first entered this prison long ago, opened before me.

I landed in the tunnel and skidded against slippery stone. Steam seared my thick skin. The creature beat against the walls, snapping upon my heels.

Cleanse the monster's lair. It could not escape to the sea. Without water, the old dragon was dying, and if it survived, evil would seek to enslave it again. If I could not finish this, how could I fight Xanala?

I pooled fire into my hands and formed a spear. Without hesitating, I hurled it toward the monster's straining gills. Death cries filled the air, and it was finished.

Numb, I vanished into the blindness of the tunnel.

40

THE PASSAGE CURVED SKYWARD into a dark, square chamber, stone columns on either side. I dodged them by sight and sound, cutting through a space that echoed with the beating of my wings, but was once filled with water. The capital's original water reservoir, storage for snowmelt before an emperor or empress demanded the larger, perpetually filled aqueduct now looming behind the palace. I wondered if the Killer of Kings had appeared before or after that architectural decision.

I pumped my wings harder and aimed upward for a rectangular stone shaft, where ancient water once flowed from barrels carried by royal servants. I shot straight up, searching for painful light, and caught the edge of a secondary, horizontal chamber. I pulled myself up to my hands and feet, my wings curving toward my body in the small space.

I crawled through the passage, reached an opening in the ceiling, and struggled with the stone slab sealing the exit. The strength of my Shadow form persevered, and the stone budged. I pressed my shoulder against the rock and shifted it until I could just barely fit through the crevice of space. I stilled. Listening. Faint sounds met my ears. I was certain I was being watched, but no guards roused a cry of alarm.

I slithered my way through the aperture and leapt atop the slab to take in my surroundings.

Cells lined both walls of the room. Lit wall sconces flickered against rough stone and ancient, metal bars. Many hungry faces turned to me, tattered uniforms hanging off their frames. Their surprise and horror weighed upon me. For which was worse, a Shadow slithering through the castle's bowels into their midst, or whatever fate awaited them? They didn't recognize me as I recognized them. Taval, the Rebellion, and the Exiles were here, imprisoned, another promise Xanala had broken.

I stepped off the mouth of the reservoir and landed on the rough stones. Their hands were not bound, but they were drained. It was what I'd done to Bohak, before leaving him at Xanala's mercy. I knew I should experience remorse, but the wall my Shadow form created between me and my human emotions remained high.

One soldier stepped forward, a lanky one, and grasped the bars. "Tol?"

I gasped, my voice scraping. "Roji."

He offered a ghost of his usual lopsided smile. "I knew the counterfeit empress couldn't hold you for long."

I wanted to both laugh and destroy the bars imprisoning him.

"The Reborn Star." In a far cell, kept alone, Samari stood. Memories assaulted me. Seeing him in a different dungeon but in a similar state. This time, after holding my gaze for a long moment, he bowed. Many others watched him before staring at me, reconciling my human self to my Shadow form.

In the cell adjacent to him, darkness shifted. I discerned more Shadows, including Ysterdey and Kean, but not Watch.

"Srolo Samari, this place is unfit for you." I faced the first cell and pressed my palm against the lock. Filling the keyhole and its inner workings with fire, I shaped it until the lock groaned and the door gaped open. Several inhaled sharply. Such a feat surprised me, too, and I moved to the next cell and did the same. So painstakingly slow. I couldn't help but count the moments ticking by. Precious moments given to Xanala to prepare herself and her army–for what? When I approached the cells of Tavalkians, their trepidation matched my own. Whose side were they on? I hesitated before freeing their door and moved to the next. And the next. I waited for the ambush of royal guards, but it never came. Xanala had moved her troops.

After releasing the Shadows, I finally arrived at Roji's cell. He offered me a grim smile and, once out, took his place behind me. Murmuring rose, and many eyes shone bright. Soldiers converged around me, but at a respectful distance. They hailed from all of Vedoa's regions, many with brands seared across their foreheads. Torn uniforms. Fireless. Leaderless. Watching and waiting.

I turned and offered Samari my clawed hands. He raised his brow, remembrance lending a spark to his eyes. He took my hands, accepted my painful rekindling, then wielded a sword worthy of a Tier 2.

Understanding dawned, and the rest instantly clamored into line. One by one, I relit their flames. I barely trembled from the effort. Perhaps it was my four Forms. Maybe it was because I was a Shadow. Their looks of fear as they grasped my claws vanished as they regained their fire and became a wielding army again, one that I knew would follow me unto death.

I moved back through the group, leapt atop the slab covering the dry reservoir, and raised my voice. "The odds are against us. Xanala surely claims the throne room, and the palace will be overrun with her soldiers. Past them, nations surround us to end the judgment. If you seek to keep your life, flee to the desert. Some of you have lost a leader." I forced my breath to steady as I glanced at Taval. "I fight for a new Vedoa. I fight to end the drought, not so we can return to who we were, but so we can become something better. I battle for my fellow Vedoans, to restore honor to her soldiers, for her people twisted in this Shadow form. I seek to tear down the walls between Vedoa and her neighbors." I paused. After being betrayed by their own country, by one they trusted, the whole world had turned against them, but they did not push back against what I said. "If you fight for something else, flee to the desert. Xanala thinks I'm dead, and like a living ghost, I will claim the palace, fight her for the antidote for all Shadows, and seize the Abyss."

Samari stepped forward and bowed again. "We have reached the capital. How could we consider surrendering the fight?"

Following his lead, the Exiles raised their fists into the air. Taval joined them, and then the Rebellion.

A hand gripped my shoulder. I looked back and met Roji's determined gaze. A spark of energy raced through me, and I saw it echoed in his eyes. For Vedoa and the continent.

41

WE NEEDED TO SECURE THE PALACE against Xanala's army and then storm the throne room. Silent as a desert tiger, Samari led our army through the dungeon and into the soldiers' passages. From his youth, he'd marched these pathways as one of Vedoa's many rising soldiers. Before the war with Laijon. Before his country had cast him aside.

Grim-faced Tavalkians, Rebellion members, and Exiles kept me in the middle, like a Shadow queen. The rest of the Shadows created a rear guard.

We approached a closed doorway. Samari waved some of the men ahead, and exultant whispers rippled through the ranks. *Royal armory.* We passed inside. The stone walls were adorned with a scant collection of weaponry. Palace guards had taken almost all of it, but there was enough of what we needed for close combat.

Tavalkians, Exiles, and Shadows outfitted themselves with swords and knives and emptied the walls of hung shields. Samari tested two wicked-looking dueling blades before sliding them inside his belt. Roji settled on a long sword, similar to what he would've carried as a soldier in Laijon. Tavalkians claimed spears. I took nothing. I needed nothing. When Samari raised his hand again, all fell back into loose formation, and we traversed the final passages joining the palace.

A knot of royal soldiers appeared around the bend, walking toward us. They saw us and froze.

The human part of me inside nearly wept at the battle and loss to come. Something even deeper inside me, perhaps not even a part of me, whispered that freedom, justice, and mercy came with a price.

Before Samari could act, I spread my hands and filled the passage with fire. Pressing my palms out, I pushed the enormous shield forward, giving us room to advance and forcing the enemy back. Shouts of warning resounded as they backed away from the passageway into the main thoroughfares of the palace. Turning my hands, I shaped my fire into blazing Tavalkian horses and sent them cantering among the shocked, red-clad guards.

Samari bellowed. Our army roared behind him and ran, weapons glittering and hands filled with fire.

With a shriek, I flew upward and passed their ranks. Srolo Kapir's shield formed in my hand, enabling me to deflect every fiery assault, as more physical weapons clanged below. Ysterdey swooped past me, and then Kean, and then more winged Exiles, to form a barrier between me and an outpouring of Xanala's Shadows.

The world erupted in battle. Roars and shrieks sounded everywhere. Fire soared and died upon metal shields. The cries of the wounded rang in our ears, and the scent of blood and sweat accosted me.

I fought the enemy from on high, untouchable. For every volley of fire thrown my way, I caught the attack, created it in into something new, and threw it back. Just like Srolo Kapir had famously done. And then I guarded the wooden stairwell as tapestries and rugs burned. Smoke filled the air, and for a moment, the palace guards gave way and allowed access to the stairwell. The Rebellion scrambled to seize the opportunity. Tavalkians and the Exiles soon caught up and gained the foot of the stairs.

Royal soldiers filled the floor above.

I abandoned the ground-level battle and crouched at the top of the steps, hands open wide for an oncoming flood of fire. I caught and absorbed storm after storm. They could not burn the stairwell until the time was right.

Inch by inch, our army fought their way up each step.

Now. I filled my hands with fire and drove the army above back.

Giving our men room, until they crested the stairs and could join this new fight. Then I blasted the staircase with fire.

Royal soldiers seeking to climb cried out and tumbled backward. Some Tier 2s gifted in Justice sought to quench my flames, but they failed. Inferno consumed the stairwell. Ancient wood buckled, groaned, and crashed, cutting us off from the lower half of the palace.

Brandishing swords, the Rebellion attacked the upper-level army, and soon, bodies fell from the banister. I tossed fire left and right, trying to save my own.

Shouts. Screams. My Shadow side remained cool as the humanity inside me grieved. Then, as soon as the battle began, it slowed, ending as a Tavalkian defeated the last royal guard.

Gasping for air, I looked around at the living and the dead. Samari remained, also breathing heavily. Ysterdey and Kean. Roji, his sword hilt still gripped tightly, lifted his arm to wipe his face of sweat.

Below, small fires continued to waft smoke. Across from us, Xanala's unscathed red-clad Shadows perched atop statues and in clefts in the palace walls and watched me. Captured by my fire, but unable to aid us.

Now the passage to the throne room loomed, and silence reigned.

I steadied my rasping voice. "Divide in half. One group to guard the stairwell and one to come with me."

Samari repeated the order, and the men split to obey. He appointed Ysterdey as leader of the group to guard access to our upper floor, along with the rest of the Shadows, in case their enemy kind faltered in their new allegiance to my show of power. Samari took his place in front of me, as did Roji.

Once all were in position, we headed down the quiet, carpeted hallway, untouched by our battle. Loyal bootsteps resounded behind me. A pair of golden doors glimmered ahead.

Xanala and I were always meant to fight in the throne room amphitheater. Would Bohak be there, too, if she'd kept him alive?

I quickened my pace, then grasped the doorknobs between my claws and flung them open.

Darkness of falling night filled the tall windows. The glassy floor lay dull without light. Empty.

Xanala was gone.

"Search for her," I commanded.

The army obeyed, and a multitude of hands ransacked the throne room, but found nothing.

I hissed and stormed from the room. Swinging my gaze back and forth. Searching the quiet, adjoining hall for her apartments. Again, Roji was beside me, checking and double-checking after me.

I shoved doors open, looked inside, and continued. Rooms full of royal manuscripts, a secondary meeting chamber for the council, a guardroom, a room fit for royalty–perhaps the executed empress's, it was musty and abandoned, complete with cold-climate fur rugs, its gilded furnishings collecting sand and dust. I flung door after door open until reaching the last one.

Bare walls enclosed a spacious chamber. No rugs. A large, stone platform claimed the center of the floor, serving as a private training arena. Surely, this was Xanala's quarters.

One of Emeridus's young tracking dogs, wearing a golden collar, rose from the ground and bristled.

A Rebellion soldier lifted a handful of unshaped fire.

"Wait," Samari said. "This Pirthyian breed is rare and useful, if it hasn't yet been trained to kill. Leave it for now."

Small statues representing the starpalms lined another wall. Besides the bed, the only other piece of furniture was a tall, stone bookshelf, kept as far from the training arena as possible and stuffed with enough books to fill a lifetime. I hadn't imagined Xanala as a reader, but bypassed the personal library to her bed. The dog backed up against the wall and bared its teeth, but it didn't advance. A worn, wooden toy claimed Xanala's pillow, the likeness of a plump goat. The sight of both the dog and the toy struck a deep, sad chord inside me.

Had she left the antidote here? "Search for a vial," I said.

Everyone looked, an easy feat in this barren room, but nothing turned up. I ground my teeth. Where–

"My Reborn Star?" Samari stepped aside from a recently arrived Tavalkian soldier. "We found something. Please follow me."

We strode from Xanala's quarters back to the throne room, Roji on my right side. Samari led us to the windows and pointed.

Across the balcony, through a lingering veil of dust, I perceived the gaping mouth that was the opening into the volcanoes, to the Abyss, lit by a single smoldering torch, abandoned at the tunnel entrance. But the bridge arched with charred stones, and its middle had fallen below, a gap too long to jump.

"She crossed over, destroyed the bridge, and waits for me," I said.

Samari nodded assent. "Kean scouts to confirm, but Laijon nears, and I believe she sent her army to meet them."

Laijon was already here, with more nations close behind. I studied the bridge again. No human would be able to climb down the palace and up the mountains before war arrived.

Behind, my army filled the throne room, weapons in hand. They waited for my command. To follow me. To fight.

"It's another trap," Roji murmured under his breath.

Samari gave a sharp nod. "Agreed. She wouldn't even the playing field in your favor."

"Or she is desperate. She still holds the antidote." I studied the torch dying on the mountains' doorstep and then turned to him. "Hold the palace against Xanala's troops. When Laijon comes, speak my name, and surrender to them. For Vedoa."

Samari stiffened but inclined his head. "For Vedoa, my Reborn Star."

A memory of when he called me Stable Rat flitted through my mind. I inclined my head in return and faced Roji.

He pursed his lips. "How can I let you go alone again, Tol?"

"How can you follow me without wings?" I said quietly.

A flood of emotions washed over his face, and his gaze fell. "If I could fly . . . but others can . . ."

I studied Ysterdey, Kean, and the other Shadows, and conviction gripped me. "Numbers will not protect me from her. Anything or anyone else will become a weapon in her hand."

"She can't hold a candle to your fire, don't you dare forget." Roji scrubbed a palm down his face then placed his hands on my shoulders and surprised me by pressing his forehead against mine. He closed his eyes, drawing short breaths, his whisper strained. "May light guide your path, until I catch up with you, and after."

He offered me a Laijonese blessing. I accepted it, savored it. "And may light guide yours." Then I created space between us and turned to face the windows again. It was time. I opened the balcony doors, into swirling air, gazing at the mountains and the trap and battle that awaited. I looked back.

Roji regarded me with a steady, determined look. One I'd seen so many times before. He had a plan. May the broken bridge keep him from doing something drastic.

I threw myself off the balcony, spread my wings, and flew over the burned bridge and folded myself into the darkness of the Abyss.

42

THE THIN, SLITTED ENTRANCE in the volcano's flank met me like a snake's unblinking eye.

I was a Shadow, did not feel the pain of returning to this place, and needed no light to see. Plunging into a chasm of ebony stone did not fill me with fear, but shouldering through protrusions of rock proved difficult, as spiced fragrance assaulted my senses.

The passage widened, and monstrously tall metal bars rose on the left. But no hulking shapes swayed or twisted in these dungeons. The seven chained firewyrms were gone.

Past the cages was another slit of crevice in the wall, and my wings scraped as I edged between. The reek of incense grew stronger, and the end of the tunnel glittered with coming firelight. Once through the crevice, I emerged into the atrium of the ancient volcano.

Tapestries covered the walls. Gilt statues, heroes of old, stood everywhere, as they had before, a stone army. Ore and jewel mines pockmarked the ground. Towering carvings of starpalms still stood in the back. Many large, earthen jars lay tipped and cracked on their sides, emptied.

Across the vast chamber, Xanala sat at a circular table covered in dishes, as if she would hold court. She appeared alone, and the cloying sweetness gripping the air made me gag.

I glanced up at the rough volcanic walls, too high for tapestries, to the rock-carved balustrades where I expected her strongest wielders to watch from above. But there was no one. The gloom behind her stood still, and my Shadow eyes discerned that no one stood there. My ears picked up no other sound.

I stepped forward and almost slipped. Smooth, thick, scented oil covered the floor in an extravagant swath, forming a reeking channel between the two of us. She must have had every jar of expensive temple oil–dedicated to the starpalms–brought here and poured out across the ground. A precaution against a firefight. A trap. But she knew I could fly, and she stood on higher, dry ground.

I stepped across the oily surface, allowing the extravagance to smear over my leathery skin.

Xanala waited with her hands folded in her lap. The unnatural sheen of her garments gave the fire-retardant material away, covering her from ankles to wrists, all the way to her chin. On a silver chain, a whistle hung from her neck. I recognized the shape. My old guardian, the dragon trainer, had carried one to summon his animals too. Escape must lurk nearby.

I continued, step by slippery step.

"Seeing you brings me grief. I didn't want to do this to you. I truly wanted us to be friends, perfect halves to Vedoa's destiny. Even now, I refuse to see you as a lost cause, Tol. I know you are wounded from moving home to home. Always on the run. An orphan your whole life, especially now."

I locked my jaw. Why did she say this? She spoke calmly, but I heard the tremor. I sensed her fear.

"You're believed to be the Reborn Star, yet your destiny is chained to the likeness of a Shadow. Do you wish for freedom, Tol of the Desert?"

A question jumped to my lips, and I spoke. "Where's Bohak?"

Xanala lifted her chin. "You'll see him soon enough, if I know you as well as I think I do."

My stomach twisted. What had she done to him?

"But before that fateful reunion, receive your freedom and know that I only hurt you for your good." Xanala raised a closed fist and hurled something small.

A vial.

I dove across the slimy ground to catch the vial before it hit the rock floor and shattered. Spiced oil from the ground covered me and filled all my senses. Heart racing, I quickly regained my feet. It couldn't be. Xanala was a trickster. But I opened my hand and saw the pale liquid sparkling and swirling within the glass.

"Do you wish we were equal now?" I snarled and, upon impulse, tucked the vial into my garments. She was foolish to think I would lose my wings while standing in a pool of oil.

She stiffened at my rasping voice. "Such restraint." Xanala braved a smile. "I hope my offering demonstrates goodwill. You possess four perfected Forms. I will not stand in your way. I only wish–again–to make an agreement with you."

Lies. Like a serpent, she slithered through her falsehoods and never looked away, speaking so carefully, with dripping kindness, as if she spoke to a child or a madwoman. I eyed her. She knew she couldn't fight me and win, so she'd doused this place in oil. Yet she met me alone and surrendered the antidote.

"Do whatever it is the Rebellion has brainwashed you to do. Remove your monstrous form and claim Vedoa. Become the starpalm and end the drought–or don't. All I ask is that you spare my life."

I raised my brow, a gesture she probably couldn't perceive in my Shadow face.

"Promise me my life," she pleaded, but her eyes remained hard.

I watched her and touched the vial through my robes. "I never wanted to take anyone's life. Not even yours."

"Then you swear that my life is safe from fire, weapon, starvation, poison." Her gaze glinted. A jab against my royal parentage.

I felt like I stood on the edge of a cliff, blindfolded. What was I missing? I wouldn't go near her. Not yet. "Keep your life. May the One deal with you." I lifted my left hand with fire.

Her eyes widened.

I hurled my handful of fire into the oil pooling at my feet. Blazing flames leapt across the shimmering surface.

Xanala shrieked as fire engulfed the space between us. Tongues of flame hid her from view and cut her off from the tunnel. Her dragon whistle wouldn't be wasted from her patch of dry ground.

I scrambled into flight and raced the engulfing flames to the Abyss's far cavern. I searched until I saw the far, bottomless hole, so similar to the emptied magma chamber in the Terror Lands, where I'd walked with Seyo. Clinging to that memory, I swooped down into nothingness.

43

A SPIRAL STAIRCASE DESCENDED into the gaping pit.

I dove into the deep, my stomach plummeting with the lengths I descended. Spurred by my own greedy flames tasting the rim of the chasm. Down. Down. Down. Fire licking the stairs. A pool of shimmering, pure water. There was an altar, one where generations of rulers had presented their wartime triumphs and dipped their hands into its sacred pool to strengthen their fire.

I slowed my speed, kicked out my feet, and landed on flat stone, gravel billowing at my landing between the pool and the altar. The sounds of fire crawled closer, filling my ears. But the sight I beheld became a roar in my mind.

Bohak lay gagged and bound to the altar with rope. Rusted metal chains pooled around the altar but lay unused. Bohak gasped seeing me, and winced with suppressed pain from the shimmering, blazing shackles binding his hands. Fire climbed down the walls and spiraling stairs toward us.

Everything screamed *trap*. Intermixed with the numbness pervading my Shadow self, I despised Bohak's weakness and the gaping wound he'd reopened in my inner being. I loathed the apology he'd tried to make, the way his eyes had widened when I'd stolen from him as he'd stolen from me, after promises of friendship, loyalty, and more.

Death crawled down the chamber's walls.

What did Xanala expect from me? To leave him here to die? Yet she hadn't used the chains. Both the dynasty and Rebellion, if they counted Bohak's wrongs, would deem that he deserved death. But I was not the dynasty, though their blood flowed with fire through my veins. And I was not the Rebellion, not in the way that I once thought.

The fire licked so close.

I tasted Bohak's fear before stretching out my clawed hand. He stiffened, but I unraveled the flames binding his hands and effortlessly dispelled it to the air. No hidden tricks yet.

Bohak tore the gag from his mouth and choked. "Tol."

I sliced the rope binding him to the altar and dragged him with me, splashing into the shallow pool as fire engulfed the pit, raging in an inferno all around us. I studied its smoke rising to the crown of the volcano. Breathing would soon become impossible.

Bohak looked at the blaze, the water, then at me. "Why?"

I ignored him, and stepped deeper into the pool, allowing the ancient liquid to come up to my waist.

"Tol, I know I've lost all trust." His voice shook. "Does Xanala still live?"

I continued until I felt a ledge of stone beneath my toes, and I held my arms out and looked into the deepest point of water.

A golden doorway shimmered below, drowning in the depths, just as Roji had described. Perhaps fathoms below, and too far to swim. My wings would slow me down–

"Wait." Bohak splashed toward me. "Tol, this must be a trap."

I growled and folded my wings as tightly as I could against my back.

"The pool is too deep." He brushed my arm.

I yanked away, and he stumbled backward. May the One help me. I drew a breath and slipped under the surface.

Bohak grabbed my wing.

I screeched, pushed off the rocks, and dove–and the world turned upside down.

44

IT WAS AS IF A SWINGING GLASS lid flipped and flung us into another world.

I was flying. Falling. Not drowning in ancient water, but now tumbling down a dune. Stomach swirling. At last, I stilled, face down in soft sand. The memory of jumping off the dragon's back with Roji flickered through my mind, but this sand was fine and white, not charcoal like the desert I knew.

I pushed myself to stand. Nearby, Bohak was doing the same, choking and coughing and covered in sand. I breathed clean, still air, and it suddenly came to me that we were both dry, despite the pool above. An unearthly light filled this place, one that burned my eyes more than the sun, and Bohak glowed as if with stardust, in contrast to his soot-smudged face and hands.

I spread my wings to fly and saw we were on an island. Bohak hesitated before jogging after me. I didn't know if he remained traitorous or not, but I had no reason to fear him in my Shadow form. Trinkets and treasures littered the sandy expanse. A gilded cup encrusted with desert diamonds. All manner of bags of jewels spilled open, fine weaponry, its ore perhaps mined from these mountains. I dove to snatch an iron dagger before reaching the edge of the beach to hover.

Dark water lapped at the beach's edge, vast as an ocean but with no smell of salt, offering relief to my sight. There was no wind. Fear of sea creatures vanished. Somehow, I knew there were none here or, if there were, they were no threat to me. In fact, I felt very little danger at all. The island was small. Surely, we stood in a pocket between worlds.

Bohak caught up and stared dumbfounded at the endless fresh water surrounding us, such a contrast to our parched country. "We're trapped."

"I didn't come here to escape," I said and looked around at the light without source surrounding us. Where did it come from?

Words poured from Bohak's mouth. "I know you can rekindle my fire. Word spread from Samari to the Exiles and then to my men."

Grimacing, I walked away. To find what I came here for.

Bohak followed. "You won't do it. I wouldn't, either, if I were you. But, please, tell me this. Why did you spare me?"

"Because in my darkest moments, someone gave me another chance, if I was willing to take it."

Birdcall shattered the silence.

A multicolored songbird flapped by me, performing a melody I'd never heard, before disappearing again into emptiness. I watched it go before looking up, where water rippled–the water we had just fallen through into this strange, in-between place. Flames flickered around the edges of the pool. Any sound they made did not reach us.

Bohak ran fingers through his hair and looked around, once one of Vedoa's most powerful wielders, now lost as a child. "Why would she allow us to enter this place? What is her plan?" His voice thickened. "Is there any hope left for you or me?"

This wasn't about us. I flew again, leaving him standing by the water. Where was the Abyss? I scanned our little island. On one side, sharp, pale stones pierced a ridge of sand marred by bones. I slowed to a stop, keeping clear of the undug graves, to perch atop the rocks.

Below, in a depression paved by white stone, a glowing aura collected. Though the light seemed gentle, I could only snatch quick looks before needing to cover my eyes again. Was this the source of light? It was different from the spell Xanala had cast to turn me into a Shadow. This atmosphere was calm, quiet, and dangerous.

It was this aura that the empress had been unable to access, and that had killed her. I shielded my gaze. Deep inside the thick glow, the ageless doorway, plundered from Laijon so long ago, lay fallen on the ground, never helped to stand by Vedoa's first conquering emperors. Its carved frame, golden as the sun, pulsed with power, like my Magnificence.

Suddenly, zipping sounds and explosions of sand burst forth. Iron knives, impervious to shields of fire, spiraled from the sky and pounded into the island sand. At Bohak's shout, I looked up.

Above the watery surface, the rippling, revolving lid that held us inside, fire shimmered around a serpentine form. With a low cry, the firewyrm passed through the water into our chasm, wings spread and swooping. Xanala, armed to the teeth, stood atop the dragon's back, lifting hands filled with flames.

45

"GET UNDER COVER!" I LEAPT TO higher ground and flung two massive shields into existence, one in front of me and one as coverage for Bohak. Without fire he was helpless–

Flaming arrows whizzed around us, pinging off rocks and melting into sand.

The dragon thrummed another cry as it swooped closer. Xanala stood free, proud and angry, next to a dragon master wearing thick, fire-resistant leathers and flicking reins across the dragon's jaw. She shouted. "Did I not offer you a way out of this? Did I not give you opportunity to escape from your Shadow hide?"

I raised my voice. "Neither of us has to remain what we've become."

Xanala's face contorted, and she barked a command. The dragon opened its swaying mouth and belched a river of fire.

I dove as the dragon's blaze enveloped the ground and my shield. The attack drove Bohak and me apart, and he rolled to a crouch, hands stretched before him out of instinct. Hands that could no longer take fire like they used to.

I braced myself for another attack, but none came. Instead, Xanala uttered a cry, and I realized there was now a battle raging in the air. She wrestled, arm to arm, with the dragon master, who'd scrambled out of his saddle to attack her. Xanala began to slip. The dragon master pushed, and the false empress of Vedoa plummeted through air toward us and the sand, but not before hurling a ball of fire behind her. She collided with a sand dune and sprawled out of my vision.

The dragon master flung himself away from the dragon, narrowly missing Xanala's attack, and fell into the waves below.

The firewyrm squealed and blew an onslaught of fire that licked across our barren island, cutting me off from the Abyss. I climbed air again, hoping to draw the creature away, but without Xanala, it had no desire to seek me. With a hot breath of wind, the dragon veered across the surrounding waters out of sight, leaving a forest of flames to devour the island.

I tensed and dove. A volley of fire blasted where I once hovered.

Through a curtain of flames, Xanala sliced a path through fire with a white, flaming shield, just like Bohak had once done. Ash smudged her battle leathers, sand sprinkled through her hair, and hatred burned in her eyes. "I cannot believe you let your traitor live. And yet I'm not surprised. Bohak told me what you plan to do. You don't care about Vedoa. You will sacrifice your fire to Laijon's god and offer all of us into the hands of the surrounding nations." She drew closer, her voice filled with contempt. "But it will never happen. Your mercy backstabs you. I told Bohak that, if he lives and helps me overcome you, his place on the council will be fully restored."

Her declarations no longer surprised me, and I regretted nothing. "You can't hold four Forms," I answered, though she wouldn't listen, and quickly flung a second shield in front of myself at Xanala's fresh onslaught, which almost drove me to my knees. She possessed Tier 3 Magnificence, but she wasn't without limit. Time was on my side. Still, I gritted my jaw and held, struggling not to topple backward against the weight of her gifting, as her fire intermingled with mine and small darting flames pierced the shield like knives. I reached with my fingers to siphon her fire, but suddenly her attack ended.

Against a backdrop of flames and smoke, Bohak, great-grandson of an Ai'Biroan, stood in knee-high water, hands outstretched, wielding a gushing torrent of waves. I froze, but he turned his attack upon Xanala. She screamed and coughed for breath as her fire extinguished in her hands.

Joy lent me strength. Bohak fought for Vedoa again, surrounded by enough water to douse the entire island–and his capacity for water was greater than what he'd ever possessed in fire. His shapes were impeccable, with a type of Wisdom I'd never seen before. Waterfalls, watery grasping hands, rivers of Tavalkian horses.

Xanala twisted to the side and tossed another attack. The powerful burst of flame splintered into dozens of swirling orbs.

I leapt in front of Bohak, catching the first orb as it burst into a display of fireworks in front of my face. Then caught another. And another, absorbing Xanala's fire into my own reserves.

Bohak wielded a fresh gush of water that swept half of Xanala's missiles away. The rest sizzled into the sea.

Xanala recoiled to attack again.

But Bohak pushed a wave onto the sand up to her knees, throwing her off balance and dousing her flames. He shouted to me. "Our partner sparring isn't wasted. Now go!"

I spread my wings and flew right over Xanala, cresting the dunes away from her attack. She would follow, and Bohak couldn't leave the water. Where was the dragon master?

Fire exploded behind me.

I tossed shields around me just before the force of Xanala's attack sent me tumbling to the foot of the white rocks paving the depression where the Abyss lay. The aura of strange, glowing light still hovered. Where the previous empress, my older sister by blood, whom I'd never met, had died. And now I approached as a Shadow.

I started down the white rock and scrambled to the bottom. Pebbles sprinkled across my head and shoulders. I ducked and twisted to look but saw no one.

Skeletons, cold and bare, littered the ground. I stepped over them and focused on the Abyss. A heavy, golden door lying on the ground, shimmering as if alive, veiled by the swirling aura.

My breathing came in gasps. Through the calming numbness of being a Shadow, I knew I couldn't survive. Even with my perfected flames, I couldn't pass through the aura that had slain so many others with my guilty blood and tainted form. I could only rectify the latter, but perhaps my fire would still get me just far enough. I reached into my robes, extracted the antidote, and clasped it against my chest. Then I walked for Vedoa. Srolo Kapir. Ami'beti. Bor'beti. The Exiles. Taval. Shadows. Faithful Roji. Even my enemies–

The aura pulsed with otherworldly energy, swirling as if agitated by my nearness. I concentrated on the solid stones beneath my feet and the four Forms pulsing in my veins, my near-divine gift.

I whispered a prayer, voice quivering. "Maker of the Abyss, let my fire and blood repay this ancient debt." Only a length away. I was going to fail. But if I surrendered my life trying, so be it.

Xanala shrieked behind me. My heart pounded. She'd made it past Bohak's defenses. I walked faster. The edges of the aura hovered before me. When its edges touched my skin, it seared, and I recoiled with a hiss. Now, the antidote–

"Tol."

I squeezed my eyes shut to better hear. And then I realized that the still, small voice was inside me, a presence that was not my own. The One. A shimmering beyond my consciousness, in me and around me and through me. I clung to it tightly, as tightly as I pressed the vial to my heart.

"What are you doing, Tol?"

Tears burned my eyes. "I'm surrendering my fire to break the curse."

"Are you worthy?"

I straightened my spine. "I possess the four Forms."

"The four Forms are mine. Are you worthy?"

I knew Xanala stalked right behind me, hands filled with fire, but I didn't feel fear. She would not touch me unless the One allowed her to, and I would not pass through the aura, either, unless he let me. His question seared me. Was I worthy? I set my jaw and lowered my head. "No. The blood of the dynasty who stole the Abyss flows through my veins. I'm–I'm a Shadow." I clenched the antidote in my claws. "Can you help me break my curse and make me worthy?"

"You are right that you cannot do either, but I can. Because my blood is perfect." The air around me glimmered. As if passing from yet another world into this, a human body stepped beside me. His skin and shape belonged to every nation on the continent. He was ageless

and young, with strength and humility that held power. The being I'd once seen in my dreams.

I gazed at his face. He saw me in my Shadow form, and I felt no shame.

The One's gaze filled with compassion and mercy, and he offered his hands to me.

I didn't hesitate. I folded my awful claws into his palms and gave my fire away.

With extreme care, he accepted my gifting. Slowly, without pain. I felt Justice, Wisdom, Srolo Kapir's Temperance, and my endless Magnificence depart. Sadness and joy mixed inside me, a loss accepted and a burden given away. But then I doubted if even the One could take it all . . .

As if he heard my thoughts, he smiled, and drew the last bit of my fire from me, the seed Bohak could not take. I saw it leave me like a flaming ribbon, felt its absence, and then saw that the One held my fire in his hands. A solid orb of fire, swirling and dangerous, but obedient to him.

"Is there more you have to give?" he said.

I nodded and offered the vial of antidote.

As in a far fog, I heard Xanala shout.

The One focused solely on me. "Why didn't you take it?"

Tears somehow filled my Shadow eyes. "It isn't only mine."

"I see your heart, Tol." His gaze flickered. "But there is more."

"I don't have anything left. If I did, it would be yours."

He studied me a moment. I feared I had offended him or failed in a new way. The One balanced my fire in his right hand and pressed his left across my forehead. "All things are mine, and I make my own worthy."

Pain gripped my head and trickled down to my limbs. I stiffened and tried to cry out, but no sound came from my lips. A deep cleaving surged through me, to my claws and the tips of my wings. I felt the pains of transformation, as if the One pulled my wings from my back and tore my skin from my flesh. I moaned as my Shadow form melted away. The moment I couldn't go on, I saw my arms whole, my hands reformed, the incredible strength of the monster dissipating into what felt weak but lithe and light. The palm pressed against my forehead grew larger, stronger, and scratched my softening skin.

I opened my eyes wide and stepped back. But it wasn't the One. An enormous Shadow, larger than any I had ever seen, morphed in and out of darkness. Mighty claws, arched back with a sharp spine, enormous wings extending and hiding the aura. But its eyes were his.

I fell to my knees. Fireless. Vulnerable and human.

The great Shadow loomed over me. I couldn't look away. I couldn't breathe. He spoke, but he did not open his mouth. *"I bear your curse."*

The One growled, startling me, before he moved past on clawed feet and hands, great wings brushing against me, holding my orb of fire to his chest. I looked back.

Xanala stood frozen only three lengths away, hands filled with flames, staring at the abomination coming toward her. It towered over her, wrapped in darkness. Xanala crouched into a defensive position, hands open, eyes hard. Looking ready to snatch my fire from his claws. If he spoke to her, I didn't understand, but I saw her shake her head with a snarl in response to something. Then her form shifted. She undulated between human and Shadow, her wings drawn back behind her, but her face didn't show pain. Xanala gave no sign that her form flickered at all.

After hesitation, the One turned away from her, balancing my fire in both hands. The golden aura in front of him pulled back as if afraid. Wings wide, with a terrible scream, the One passed through the glowing light.

The chasm rocked. Wind blew with a blast that threw me onto my side.

With another cry, the One moved slowly through the aura toward the Abyss, like one passing through a sandstorm. His wings and skin drew back, as if his form was splitting in half. The Shadow part falling behind, and a Being of light, fire, water, and life striding forward, holding my flames. Step by agonizing step, he reached the Abyss and set my orb of fire down as if it weighed the world. He stretched his hands, and the aura shattered.

I fell to my face, covered my head, and after a moment looked up.

Like a tempest, the aura swirled with an unearthly sound, shaking the ground, before exploding into millions of tiny pieces. I cringed as fragments touched me, but they felt like cool drops of rain. One fell in my eye, and I tried to scrub it out. Every time I blinked, the cavern altered. One moment it looked bright and vibrant, another it looked dull and lifeless.

I sat up and searched for Xanala. She sat on her knees, staring at the glittering particles falling around her. With each blink, she looked Shadow or human. Human or Shadow. She stared, grief-stricken. My orb of fire, her hope that would have killed her or slipped through her fingers had she succeeded in seizing it, smoked in a dying heap of ash.

I was only human now. My bare toes gripped rock. I drew a deep breath into human lungs. The light was beautiful. Feeling rough stone beneath sensitive feet was beautiful. The One had healed me and now was gone. The aura had destroyed him.

Tears choked me, and then the Abyss caught my eye. While the rest of the world continued to morph, the doorway remained golden and gleaming. I still gripped the antidote in my hand. The One hadn't taken it.

The chasm shook again, and echoes rebounded from the infinite, surrounding nothingness.

This world between worlds was collapsing.

46

I RACED TOWARD THE ABYSS, gripping the antidote in my hand. My human hand. Strong.

Xanala raised her own palms with fire. She still wavered between Shadow and human forms, but seemed ignorant to her condition. Her fire was severely depleted, but not gone. My veins no longer raced with flames. I couldn't make Srolo Kapir's shield. And the One was gone.

A shout caught our attention. Bohak struggled up the dune, drenched from the lake. But now, on sand, he was severed from his water source and weakened in his second gifting.

Xanala drew a hand back.

I thrust my right hand forward, and my palm burst into light. So, I still had that. Xanala crouched and threw up a shield, eyes wild at my feint. I ran, her scream chasing after me.

Bohak roared, and a wave of water crashed over Xanala.

I chanced a look over my shoulder.

Xanala dodged the brunt of the onslaught and shot a volley of flaming arrows in my direction.

Arms wrapped around my middle and threw me face down against sand, and a body covered me as Xanala's fire raked over us. Bohak? No. Rough, fire-resistant cloth scratched my skin. The dragon master.

"Almost there!" he shouted in the wake of the flames.

I gasped. "Roji?"

My Laijonese friend offered a brief nod. "Don't stop. Go!" He drew me to my feet. I caught my balance and ran.

Xanala shrieked again and threw another attack.

Roji caught up to me and hurtled forward, taking the flaming hit as I continued. I looked back in horror.

Roji lay twisted on his side, fire pooled around him. Then he, too, wavered between human and Shadow, the right side of his torso covered in leathery skin, a wing protruding from his back.

No! Roji's words rang through my mind. *Don't stop.* I fixed my gaze on the Abyss, knowing Xanala filled her hands with fire for one more attack–

I dropped to my knees and slid across stone to grasp the cool, gilded doorframe, lying across rock. Cast panels covered the gate, depicting legendary scenes of the continent's past. Detailing so exquisite, the craftsmanship was beyond mortal ability.

Flames roared overhead. I pressed myself against the fallen door as searing heat surrounded me. Seyo's and Geras's visions appeared in my mind. Seyo and me burning together. My hand, filled with fire, lifted above the opened door. Let it end now.

I reached for the large, filigree latch, fighting to breathe searing air, and pulled the heavy door open to a shaft of blazing light.

Brightness and wind swept from the doorway and over me like a gale. Darkness fled before it. Xanala's fires extinguished with a gasp. I shrank back as light spilled over me, illuminating everything. It did not hurt, but I could barely see. Warmth and desperate courage infused me, and through the bright light, the golden doorway remained visible, shimmering on the ground, surrounded by brilliance. I waited for Xanala's next attack, but it never came, as if somehow the illumination stopped her or time itself. And Bohak. And Roji–

The opened doorway waited, full of mystery and terror, a window to the divine. I had to finish this. Geras had lost his sight looking into an otherworldly gate. What sacrifice would be demanded of me? What of my friends, if they still lived, or would it take them away? Bitter grief consumed me. Although Geras could no longer see, he'd gained something else. Recklessness–no–the part of me that traveled to the 'betis to deliver a message, walked into enemy palaces, rode dragons, joined forces with friends to battle monsters, and now knelt at the threshold of the Immortal Abyss whispered the charge again, *Don't stop.* Finish what began long ago. Shaking, I poured my own light into my right palm, the only substitution I had for fire, and leaned forward to see.

Again, everything turned upside down, as if I were looking skyward instead of down, and I held my breath. Instead of the untouchable, far realm I'd expected, a lush, beautiful world met me. Mountains and rivers. Seas and charcoal sand dunes. Cities and gardens. A firewyrm soared across the portal, and horses Taval would be proud of galloped far below. And people, so many people from nations I recognized and some I didn't, paused to look at me with awe but not surprise.

In their midst, the One stood whole, just like in my dreams.

Tears stung my eyes, and I covered my face to weep. He touched my arm, and I raised my head. Somehow, he'd closed the space between us, less than a length from me, halfway in my world. The One smiled and extended his hand.

It took me a moment to understand, and then I offered him the antidote in one hand and my light in the other.

The One gathered both between his palms, and with them wove a new, glimmering orb the color of sunlight. He handed this back to me.

Gazing at him, I accepted the gift and found it easy to carry.

"Follow me, Tol," the One said.

I bowed my head, and then in response, I lifted the One's orb high.

Chirping song captured my attention. A songbird the color of seeded mangi fruit fluttered and perched on my wrist, head cocked, expecting food or perhaps a palmful of water. Before I could react, it hopped to the One's shoulder and zipped back through the Abyss.

I blinked, and a fresh wave of glowing light spilled over me, spreading across the stones paving the depression I knelt within.

The two worlds, this one and that, melded into one. Neither vibrant nor dull, but another in between. The golden doorframe of the Abyss melted from sight, consumed by glittering illumination.

I longed to tell the One goodbye, but he was gone. And yet he was not. Even now, I knew his presence remained, even as darkness crept into my vision again. Then I remembered Roji.

Balancing the glowing gift between my hands, I looked around, searching. Growing gloom stretched across sand and stone. The chasm continued to rock. Trying to keep my balance, I finally spotted Roji's form lying among ash. Holding the orb close to my chest, I raced over, dropping to kneel beside him. Half his form remained Shadow. Did he breathe? I didn't know what to do and scooped a handful of the radiance of the Abyss and let it fall between my fingers onto his chest. As soon as I did so, the remainder of the orb absorbed into my palms.

Roji shuddered with breath and struggled to stand up. The part of him that was Shadow dissipated, leaving him wholly human. I gasped relief and gripped his hands.

"Tol?" The glow ran like honey from my fingers over his. He stared in wonder. "What is this?"

Squawking sounded nearby. A Shadow was backing away from the growing glow and extending her palms toward me as if to wield fire. But she didn't, out of fear. Xanala, trapped in a Shadow form, screeched and took to the air, flying over us, to disappear into the unknown darkness surrounding the island.

Someone else rose off the ground, broad-shouldered and baby-faced. Bohak, drenched and wild-eyed. He ran toward us.

The chasm rocked.

All three of us gathered together and looked up. Flames continued to rage in the world we'd left behind.

"There has to be a way out," I said, and felt the new gift sweeping through my veins. "We're not meant to stay here."

Bohak glanced at me as if to say something but didn't.

Roji reached around his neck and brandished the whistle. "Allow me." He blew into it, and from the darkness, the royal firewyrm returned and soared into a chasm, landing heavily on a dune.

We struggled to dash across the thick, shifting sand. Roji grabbed the dragon's reins, jumped astride, and leaned to offer a hand. Catching it, I scrambled up the dragon's side. Bohak stood, unsure, before I reached for him–fireless to fireless–and Roji helped haul him onto the dragon's back. I straddled the dragon behind Roji, and Bohak settled behind me, looping his feet through the saddle grips. Roji reached behind to wrap my arms around his waist before flicking the dragon's reins and coaxing it to unfurl its wings.

"How did you learn to–" I began, when the chasm rolled under us.

Hissing, the dragon took to flight toward the watery surface.

I looked back. Everything now rumbled and shook, and I glimpsed the golden doorframe. The island fell below the surface of the rising water, glowing golden, shining brighter and brighter.

Roji hollered, and the dragon growled as it fought the growing wind current to reach the churning waters above us. My mind reeled at the illusion of diving up into water.

The dragon's snout broke the liquid surface, and we did as well, splashing and sputtering. Soon, hot, fire-laden air whipped across our faces, and we broke into the chasm. The golden flow from the Abyss followed us, bubbling and hissing as it extinguished fire.

Roji still held the reins, but I called out the command. "Up!" The dragon ascended higher, climbing the narrowing cone of the volcano, until we burst from the crown and breathed fresh, desert air once again.

In the distance, Nazak's, Ai'biro's, and Laijon's armies encamped around Vedoa's capital walls. Below, the armed inhabitants of the city filled the streets and pointed to us.

The volcano erupted in a blaze of light.

I cried another command, and the dragon veered down into the streets and landed in a square, where a cistern that used to serve the city had long lain dry and abandoned. We dismounted the dragon, and I hurried across cobblestones, deeper into the city, where a crowd gathered, with Bohak and Roji jogging close behind.

Cries of fear and amazement reached my ears. We arrived at the edge of the crowd, and I wove through commoners, soldiers, nobility, old, and young. A youth bracing himself with a cane caught my eye. I offered him my hands. At first he shied back, but then slowly reached out, looking at my face, accepting my grasp, and gasped as he dropped his cane, and his palms opened with the glowing light.

I repeated this over and over. Some accepted the gift immediately, especially when they saw their friends with bent backs standing taller, and those who were sick regaining their strength. Others saw that the glow replaced their fire, shook their heads, and spat. Energy and regret mixed in my heart as I kept moving. Where were the Shadows? I spied one perched upon a rooftop and extended my hands.

The Shadow hesitated before swooping down and landing in front of me. People moved away, and I feared that perhaps this Shadow was too far lost. But it gripped my hands, claws scraping my skin, and transformed into a middle-aged man before my eyes. Shocked, he touched his face. And then he wept with joy.

There was an uproar, and people and Shadows converged upon me. But I was not the only one able to share this gift. Those who had gained this new light joined hands with anyone willing and shared with their neighbors, whether sick, whole, Shadow, or human.

For what felt like hours, a precious time that would become a blurred collage of remembered moments, we worked through the city, until at last we reunited with Samari, the Exiles, Taval, and the Rebellion. Rejoicing, we shared our light with them too. And then the palace gates swung open.

I stilled, gazing at the towering edifice. The place I was meant to rule, and yet also tear down. Roji stood at my side and offered an encouraging smile. Beyond him, Bohak regarded the palace with a pained expression.

I crossed the garden, and my friends and the Rebellion followed.

We passed through the doorway and hesitated at the burned and collapsed stairs. Someone found a ladder, and one by one, we climbed to the second story, where bodies from the battle still lay. Sorrow wove through my heart. There would be much joy, but there would be much sadness too. I pressed through the hallways and burst inside the throne room.

As before, the glassy floor shone empty. The throne, too, sat with no ruler, and we halted before it.

By blood right and the will of the Rebellion, the throne belonged to me. More than anything, I didn't want it. But I thought of the people and the sacrifice of the One. *"Follow me."*

I approached the throne. But I did not sit. Instead, I bowed, and lifted my eyes to the windows.

Dawn brightened behind the mountains and touched the ancient volcano's lingering glow. Pale sky revealed storm clouds rolling in from the ocean. My heart leapt. Sudden thunder cracked, and rain—precious rain—began to fall like life from the sky.

47

AFTER THE ABYSS OPENED and Vedoa's gifting changed, mountains of impossibility rose before us.

When the palace's red-clad army saw that Xanala was gone and that Nazak–the recently unified peoples of the southern lands–the strong islands of Ai'biro, and our old enemy Laijon crouched at the capital's gates, they pledged loyalty to the empty throne and to me standing beside it. In the longest moments of my life, that would later only feel like seconds, an impossible international council made peace between Vedoa and the surrounding nations.

Without Seyo and Geras, Laijon's heroes who'd opened the Eternity Gate, such peace would have likely been impossible. It was another twist of destiny I could only attribute to the One's intervention, reaching back into our childhoods and beyond, when a frightened Vedoan woman carried the emperor's baby across Laijon's border. So, a seemingly impossible continental treaty, fragile as it could be, was made, although it came with an expected price, and many in Vedoa would not approve of the ways our nation would now change. Once agreements were settled, Laijon, Nazak, and Ai'biro returned to their own lands. Roji, at my earnest and pained insistence, returned with Laijon to act as ambassador on Vedoa's behalf. I continued to look into the east, in the direction of his journey, long after he left my side.

I gathered those who'd proven themselves trustworthy and appointed them leaders. After reinstating the Exiles, I elevated

Ysterdey, who retained his Shadow name, to commander of Vedoa's melding forces. This was no easy task, but neither were our journeys back into human form.

I needed to remake the council and set Samari over the people to hear their voice and facilitate communication between village and city leaders. I searched the people of the desert, the capital, and the Rebellion, for all who'd earned an honorable reputation and had not bent their knee to the dynasty, and delegated the power of the throne as well as I could, thus filling out the rest of the council. No more would only those dwelling in the capital hold such seats. Of all the ways to break the dynasty's hold on the people, this division of power seemed best to me, and it honored Srolo Kapir's many lessons on wise leadership.

Rain fell throughout Vedoa, filling cisterns and the reservoir. My council and I worked diligently to change the laws concerning fair division and payment of water, but for a time, it didn't matter. The people filled buckets, bowls, and jars with rainwater, and for a season, they were satisfied from their own supplies.

As one of my first official acts as empress of Vedoa, I banished emperor worship. I knew some persisted in their ancient practices and still called me the Reborn Star, and many fell back into following the starpalm myths. But as for me, I worshiped the One Starpalm, and I hoped many would hear and accept his story.

As for Vedoa's reborn gifting, the intense healing properties ebbed away from many after initial use, but some kept their gift.

Slowly, the walls of the palace began to confine me. I knew I was becoming ill-tempered and was no longer feeling myself. Even the young Pirthyian tracking dog, that I called my own and finally won over, nuzzled my leg, as if sensing my inner turmoil.

I longed to retreat to the Terror Lands. The oasis filled my imagination day and night. When I finally confessed this to Samari at our regular council meeting, after the rest of the members had left, he'd clasped me on the shoulder.

"Go to the villages first. Take your gifting to them," he'd said. "After that, if you still feel restless, go to the Terror Lands. But I think you'll find what you seek well before that."

His words irritated me. There was far too much to do in the capital. More stewardship plans for our abundance of water, and a dangerous Shadow colony growing roots in the mountains–those who refused the Abyss's gift. Perhaps Xanala flew among them. But after a day stewing over his advice, I admitted he was right.

Many villages later, the desert sun climbed the morning sky when my bodyguard and I entered a tiny northern community, a collection of new hovels to a casual observer. I knew more. In even the humblest places, one found deep histories.

When the village spied our approach, they came out to greet us, though subdued and cautious. I imagined how they saw us, a small army in gleaming leathers, travel veils, armored with the scales of monsters slain in the Terror Lands, and the new empress, hailing from their desert, a once powerful Tier 3 likened to a starpalm, who had opened the Abyss.

Little did they know that I feared them as much as they feared me.

Keeping my posture confident, I passed through their midst and accepted their bows. As I did at every village, I asked after their village's sick. And like they had at every village, the people's eyes widened, assessing me and considering all rumors, before the invisible barrier between us broke and they invited me into their tents.

I stepped inside simple, tidy homes, the familiarity paining me with distant homesickness, and removed my veil, before kneeling in the sand beside beds where the sick lay. Always, those present stared at the oractalm circlet, threaded with jewels, woven into my hair as my crown, crafted from Laijon's precious metal that glowed crimson, a goodwill gift from their own young queen. Then I cupped my hands, once filled with Justice, Wisdom, Temperance, and Magnificence, and when my palms filled with golden glow, there were gasps. I pressed my hands against their brows, allowing my gifting to drop across their faces, and illness fled, injuries mended, and sick hearts felt renewed. Families wept as they watched those they loved receive restoration, and often tears trailed down my face as I replaced my veil.

Tent after tent, I offered my gift to my countrymen and saw suspicion and doubt transform into hope. When they bowed to me, I whispered the name of the One and moved on. I didn't know how much longer my gift of healing would last. For most who had accepted the gift the day the Abyss opened, such power endured only a few days before fading. Some despised me for trading their fire for this. Others regained their flame after a time, which I didn't understand. Perhaps it wasn't the fire gifting itself that defied the One, but the act of taking and warping something against his will. I wondered if perhaps my fire would return, or if I would keep the healing glow until I had full understanding of its ultimate purpose. Regardless, at Samari's insistence, I'd begun tucking a staff in my belt again.

When I emerged from the last tent, the village overwhelmed me with joyful celebration. They invited me to stay and partake of several days' worth of feasting. My bodyguard and I were used to this by now, and we respectfully declined before mounting our Tavalkian-bred horses to return to the palace.

I cast a last look at the village and drew a breath, finally seeing it for what it was today. Until now, I remembered only flames charring tents that no longer stood, where I'd suffered at a cruel guardian's hand, survived a raid alone, and where Srolo Kapir had found me.

I closed and opened my eyes again. The village was rebuilt. Those who lived here before were gone, but if I could make the tiniest peace with what had survived, though as an empress and not the orphan girl who had stayed trapped here so many years ago, it was enough. I rubbed my hand over the sleeve of my brightly dyed, goat-wool robes. The smooth, soft cloth reminded me of the 'betis, and remembering them made me smile.

The captain called out, and we headed across the desert back toward the capital.

As the seasons began to shift, and the time of the winter Rain Market neared again with its colorful vendors, I stood on the throne room's balcony, but didn't look for the rainclouds that I trusted would come. Instead, I gazed at the bridge arching into the mountains, the one I'd demanded be rebuilt, though I hadn't crossed over again. Whenever my constant inner turmoil reached its peak, I found myself looking toward the Abyss, now empty. The doorway had been removed to the palace for preservation, and rumors spread that the intricate scenes depicted in its golden panels sometimes shifted as if by magic, forming new stories only remembered in our oldest annals.

I studied my hands that still bore the healing glow. Reports said I was perhaps the last to retain its gifting. It was like a version of endless Magnificence all over again, and the ill and hurting continued to stream into the capital daily. Moments alone like this were rare.

A welcome sound reached my ears. I turned to look in the opposite direction, and a first flock of colorful mangi birds capered across the mountains, returning to Vedoa. My breath caught. Mangi birds had always been a sign, but now they seemed like so much more–

A servant entered the balcony, bowed, and informed me that news from Taval was riding in.

My heart hitched. I hurried from the balcony, down the rebuilt wooden stairwell, and met Samari and the rest of my council at the palace entrance.

A herd of proud Tavalkian horses pounded into the palace courtyard, and the mighty northern village's nobility dismounted.

I watched, chest tightening, as it always did when he returned.

Bohak, dressed in dusty silks and leather, entered the palace with great reverence, as always. What did he feel returning here? I wondered if this place was his equivalent to the remote northern hovels I'd visited recently, a place of brokenness slowly being remade. Like us.

Whispered word spread that Bohak still wielded water, and we, the council, planned to request his assistance as we made decisions regarding Vedoa's rainfall, snowmelt, and oases. He looked well, but I did not know if appearances proved true. With my whole heart, I wished that my glow could repair the damage his betrayal had cost us. That someday healing would triumph over the past, just as good had somehow overcome ill intent. Perhaps aiding us in managing Vedoa's water would help him build his own bridge.

Bohak swept his robes back and offered the council and me an elegant bow, reminding me painfully of when we'd first met. "Taval reports that a retinue from Laijon crosses our border. With our empress's permission, we plan to meet them on the trade route and ensure their safe passage to the capital." Then he met my gaze.

I held eye contact. "Thank you, Srolo Bohak of Taval. We will await your report." That was all that needed to be said, but I spoke again. "May light and peace guide your path through the desert."

Bohak's brow furrowed with lack of understanding at my combination of Vedoan and Laijonese blessings, then a look I couldn't decipher flickered across his face. He bowed once more. "For your good, my lady." Bohak pivoted, marched to his retinue, remounted, and cried the famous desert cry before he and Taval rode from the capital again.

Days later, I paced the palace entrance. Waiting, impatient, until soldiers upon the ramparts sounded the trumpets that Laijon approached.

My council took their places around me. Files of soldiers filled the palace grounds and surrounded the wall, as Laijonese, carrying banners golden as the sun, galloped in on delicate, eastern horses, so different from Taval's steeds.

Riding at the front, Roji leapt off his horse. For several moments, he maintained the appropriate solemnity this visit demanded, before offering a grin.

I smiled back, almost forgetting to incline my head. Surely, my heart would burst.

Formalities commenced. It wasn't every day–or even every century–that anyone from Laijon was welcomed into Vedoa's court. My head rang from the gathering. It occurred to me that we, as Vedoans, were not well versed in entertaining foreign guests, but our desert hospitality managed to show through in a celebratory feast.

As the festivities continued, I caught Roji's eye. When I slipped out onto the throne room balcony, he did, too, and we faced the mountains. Samari or a bodyguard was certainly watching but had the grace to give us a quiet moment. Or really a silent moment. There was so much to be said between us that it seemed impossible to speak. Sunset burned across the sky, a display of heavenly flames only the desert could give, but I knew he studied the new bridge, just as I did. My emotions felt tangled, and he stood so stiff and formal.

At last, I broke the quiet. "I need to ask something."

He nodded, his gaze earnest and serious.

"How did you show up in the Abyss dressed as a dragon master?"

Roji blinked before chuckling. "You taught me the way to the dragon stables. When a whistle miraculously blew from inside the volcano, well, that took care of the rest of my journey." His voice faltered. "I couldn't let you go alone."

I needed you, I thought, but raised a brow in his direction. "Impressive. Almost as much as your sudden capability in flying a dragon."

"Ah, that. After my freshly acquired dragon experience here in your country, I came to the understanding that 'wyrms,' as you call them, are really like large cats–a far more normal animal we have in Laijon, if you remember. If one can agree with cats and dragons on the way they've already decided to go, everyone ends up arriving at the same place with little mishap."

I laughed.

He joined me before sighing, a contented sound, and leaned against the railing. "Also, Seyo and Geras send their greetings."

I sobered. "How are they?"

"Busy. Laijon and Vedoa's new alliance has stirred up the continent."

Oh, how I felt the truth of that. I reached into my robes and pulled out an ancient, leather-bound book. The fateful manuscript holding the Shadow's prophecy. I held it out to Roji. "This is for Seyo. She left it and . . . I've been waiting for an opportunity to return it to her."

Roji studied but didn't take the book. "Word spreads that you still wield healing."

I lowered my hand and focused on the mouth to the Abyss, calling to me over the curved bridge. "I don't know why I still have it."

"The Father of Light has his reason." Roji wielded a ball of light in his hands. It was pale, soft, and floated unlike the healing glow. So, healing had left him, too, and he retained his original gifting.

"Seeking peace is hard," I said.

"Especially in your own heart?"

I glanced his way. Had he seen through me? Or did the restlessness plaguing me haunt him too?

"I feel like there is so much I still need to reconcile within myself," he said, quite seriously for Roji.

"Me too. It's like . . ." I fought to find the words. "It's like I can't accept who I used to be or who I am now. No matter how hard I try or where I go."

Roji played with the light in his hands. It didn't hold shape like the fire I once wielded, but the luminous swirls he created were beautiful. "Maybe you're not traveling far enough," he said.

"I've covered almost every inch of Vedoa."

"What about Laijon?" He juggled light from one hand to the other. "You could be the first Vedoan ruler in—well—ever to visit my country."

Laijon. A burst of joy, then a heavy dose of reality traipsed through me. "Can you imagine Vedoa's resistance?"

"Can you imagine how much good it could accomplish? Or how much I've missed you?" His gaze captured mine.

Surprise threaded through me, and my heart caught.

Roji nodded toward the book in my hand. "If you came to Laijon, you could give that to Seyo yourself."

"Could I . . ." Could I lead my people in such a different course?

Could I pave this new way? It seemed harder than anything else I'd done. I wondered if this was what my healing gift was for. Did this explain the terrible restlessness inside me?

Roji clasped his hands behind his back. "If we leave soon, we can winter in Laijon. Laijonese winters are unlike any other."

I smirked. "I lived in Laijon, remember?"

"Another good reason for you to come. And we could return by summer. After all, an ambassador such as myself should have residence in both countries he serves." His eyes sparkled as he looked at me.

He knew he was winning me over, so why did I feel like crying? I tried to keep my soaring heart grounded. "Anywhere else you'd like to go while we journey across the continent?"

"Why stop at the continent? Surely there are more miraculous giftings across the seas. What if there are other doorways? Can you imagine?" He scooted closer to me, his fingers drumming on the railing.

I placed my hand over his, trying to still his nervous movement, and he wrapped his fingers around mine. I looked up into the eyes of my childhood friend. Roji, who hadn't let me lose myself as a Shadow. Who'd taught me that light was strong and helped me see the One.

Hesitancy crept into his gaze. "Tol?"

I gave him a brilliant smile, surprising him, a reaction that made me smile all the more. "First Laijon. And then finding more doorways sounds like a grand adventure."

THE END

S.D.G.

ACKNOWLEDGEMENTS

With joy and gratefulness, thank you . . .

To my brainstormers, beta readers, critique partners, and fact-checkers: Jessica, Irene, Liam, Marissa, Candace, Meagan, Given, Rachael, Carla Hoch, Steve Rzasa, and DiAnn Mills.

To Given, Meagan, Lizzie, Candace, Karyne, Carli, Kara, Nova, Jamie, Gillian, Sara, Cathy, and Sandra, for sharing the writer life with me.

To Steve, who heard my pitch for *The Eternity Gate* and then helped hone the vision for *The Immortal Abyss*.

To Lisa, Lindsay, Avily, and Sarah, for your editing genius.

To Trissina, for your dedication to every story under your care.

To Jamie Foley, for sketching this new world to life.

To Emilie Haney, for another masterpiece book cover.

To my students, for cheering me on and sharing your wonderful stories.

To my family and friends, for your enthusiasm and support. You are a gift.

To John, for everything. I love you. Thank you for smiling when I grab my laptop and say, "I'm gonna do something crazy."

To the amazing Enclave Publishing and Oasis Family Media team, Steve, Lisa, Trissina, Jamie, Lindsay, Avily, Sarah, Lisa, Steve, Charmagne, and Toni. You are wonderful.

To C.S. Lewis, who transformed Edmund into a dragon and back again, and Kathy Tyers for writing The Firebird Series. You inspire me to create art bravely.

To the Reader. Hold on to what is good.

I love hanging out with readers through my email newsletter. Sign up to receive short stories, writing updates, book recommendations, behind-the-scenes news, and geeky thoughts at my website www.katherinebriggs.com.

ABOUT THE AUTHOR

Katherine Briggs crafted her first monster story at age three. Since graduating from crayons to laptop, she continues to devour and weave fantasy tales while enjoying chai tea. She, her coadventurer husband, and rescue dog reside outside Houston, where she classically educates amazing middle school students, teaches ESL to adults, and enjoys studying other languages.